WIN BY SUBMISSION

ALSO BY MELYNDA PRICE

The Redemption Series

Until Darkness Comes
Shades of Darkness
Courting Darkness
Braving the Darkness

WIN BY SUBMISSION

MELYNDA PRICE

Montlake
Romance

Published by Montlake Romance, Seattle

www.apub.com

Amazon, the Amazon logo, and Montlake Romance are trademarks of Amazon.com, Inc., or its affiliates.

ISBN-13: 9781477828700
ISBN-10: 1477828702

Cover design by Kerrie Robertson

Library of Congress Control Number: 2014955729

Printed in the United States of America

PROLOGUE

W *ham!* Cole slammed his open-gloved fist into De'Grasse's face and smiled in satisfaction when he felt the bastard's nose break upon impact. A crimson geyser shot from his nostrils, splattering the mat. The crowd went wild cheering at the carnage—blood-thirsty vultures, the whole lot of them. But then what did that say about him? He craved their energy, fed off their excitement, consuming their bloodlust like a ravenous sin-eater.

"Oh, man! Did you see that?" Rogan cried into the mic. "De'Grasse's nose is definitely broken, and Easton isn't wasting any time passing his guard."

Rising up over his opponent's waist, Cole hit De'Grasse with a series of quick, hard jabs. Each time his fist connected with the prick's face, the rush of adrenaline surged hotter through his veins. Rarely was it personal; each fighter he faced in the cage was just one more stepping-stone to the title. But with De'Grasse, this shit was for real, and Cole was loving every second of it.

Crazy Dan had lived up to his name when he'd pulled a stunt last month that had nearly tanked Cole's career. The media was still nipping at his ankles like a school of piranha; sponsors threatening to drop him. There were few crimes where one was assumed guilty until proven innocent, and it just so happened that assault and battery while under the influence of steroids and booze was one of them.

He knew De'Grasse had been desperate to hang on to his title. Cole had just underestimated the level that bastard would sink to in order to keep it. *Wham!* Cole nailed him with a right hook that sent De'Grasse's mouth guard bouncing across the mat. His opponent bucked, attempting to displace him, but Cole had his hooks in. He was locked onto De'Grasse's waist so tight, all Crazy Dan could do was roll to protect his face. It was a fatal error many fighters made, giving up their back, but the preservation instinct was strong, and God knew the bastard wouldn't last much longer like this. He was drowning in his blood—a fitting end, since he'd yet to tap.

There was no way in hell this fucker was getting out of this hold. With two minutes left on the clock, time was on Cole's side, and in the next few seconds De'Grasse would realize the inevitable truth as well—he was going to lose his fight, and with it the light-heavyweight title. A reality Cole was more than willing to help him come to grips with as he grabbed De'Grasse's head and yanked it back, slipping his forearm beneath his chin.

"Oh, man! This looks bad for Crazy Dan De'Grasse! Easton's got him in a rear naked choke, and it looks like he's about to finish him! Will De'Grasse tap?"

The crowd roared. Lights from the audience flickered, cameras flashing, as he growled in De'Grasse's ear, "You're finished, you fucking piece of shit." With a swift jerk, he grabbed his wrist and leveraged his forearm tight against De'Grasse's throat, cinching the hold tight and cutting off his breath. The fighter kicked and flailed, but Cole held him with ease, fury fueling his straining muscles. He was starting to wonder if the bastard would rob him of the satisfaction of a tap, opting to pass out instead, when he finally felt that succinct patting on his forearm. He hesitated a moment before acknowledging the surrender, wanting the prick to suffer as long as possible.

"Oh, shit! He tapped!" Rogan yelled in amazement. "For the first time in his career, De'Grasse tapped! If you've ever wondered why they call Easton the Beast of the East, you got a view of it here tonight, folks! There was no way Easton was going to let this fight fall into the judge's hands. He came out swinging and just did not quit! You gotta wonder if this fight was not a bit personal for Easton. There's been a lot of controversy surrounding the fighter these past few weeks. But no matter which side of the debate you fall on, there can be no question of who the new light-heavyweight champion of the world is!"

Cole released De'Grasse and leapt to his feet before the ref could pull him off. He raised his fists in the air and roared with triumph. The crowd went wild. Women screamed, "I love you, Cole!" Several of them raised their tops, shaking their gorgeous tits in salute. Fuck, he loved this job. A few haters booed, but to hell with them. Nothing could overshadow the thrill of having 100 percent pure adrenaline running through his veins.

He turned to acknowledge the other side of the stadium with a *Hell yeah, I did it!* fist pump into the air, when something slammed into the base of his spine. It struck hard and fast, propelling him into the ropes. Cole's body bowed, something in his back snapped, and he legs buckled beneath him. As he collapsed onto the mat, the cheering crowd grew eerily silent. Rogan spat out a nasty curse Spike TV would undoubtedly have to censor. Cole's pulse hammered in his ears as a lash of white-hot pain shot down his legs. He tried to get up, but they wouldn't cooperate. Fire burned through his spine, lighting up every nerve ending all the way to his feet. The pain was excruciating.

A roar of rage tore from his throat as he struggled to ignore the hot poker in his back and focus on the medic suddenly in his face asking questions and yelling commands he couldn't follow: "Lift your legs. Wiggle your toes. Can you feel me touching you here? How about here?"

As Cole lay on the mat, his crew scrambled around him, some shouting demands, others lying their asses off and telling him everything was going to be okay. And then, as if the cage wasn't wild enough, his buddy Kruze hopped the ropes and dove for De'Grasse. Fists were flying, refs were yelling, it was total fucking chaos. The crowd was screaming again, but this time shock and outrage filled their cries.

Turning his head, he fixed his stare at the blinding lights overhead. *This is happening* . . . But the insidious infusion of ice entering his spine told him different. Slowly, burning cold spread down his legs, turning them numb, and in that moment Cole knew deep in his soul that nothing would ever be okay again.

CHAPTER

Six Months Later

F uck. No."

"I'm not asking, Cole. You can't stay here any longer. They've done everything they can. The rest is up to you now."

"If *this* is 'everything they can,' then I want my fucking money back," he growled, slamming his fists against the arms of his wheelchair.

Marcus, his manager, stood a little straighter and defiantly crossed his arms over his barrel chest, refusing to be cowed by Cole's temper. Apparently, the guy was prepared to go the round with him and he intended to come out the victor.

"Just hear me out, Cole. You need to take a step back from all this. Get your head on straight again."

"It's not my head that's the fucking problem, Marcus!"

The man scowled, his disapproving frown hitting Cole below the belt. "Enough with the language, huh, kid? You think I don't know you're pissed off? Hell, *I'm* pissed off. We're all pissed off. But that's not going to get you on your feet again, son. Look, think of this as an opportunity for some R & R, a change of pace, a chance to get out from under the damn media spotlight for a while. In case you haven't noticed, the tabloids haven't exactly been gracious to you lately."

Oh, he'd noticed. Thanks to that bastard De'Grasse, he was a woman-beating drunk under suspicion by the MMA league for roid use. None of it was true, but what the hell did that matter? Those media parasites only reported what sold—sex, drugs, and scandal. No one cared about the hours he spent every month in the Children's Hospital, or the time he donated at the rec center for disadvantaged kids. Hell no, who cared about shit like that when they could be reporting where he went clubbing last night and who he might be fucking.

Now, they speculated whether or not the cripple could ever fight again. According to the tabloids, in the last six months he'd nearly died—twice. He'd faked his injury to avoid getting cut for use of anabolic steroids, faced criminal charges for assault and battery with a deadly weapon—because that was what happened when an MMA fighter punched you in the face—and he might or might not be the illegitimate son of Hugh Hefner. Bullshit—all of it.

Cole tore his gaze from the window where he sat watching the swarm of paparazzi camped outside, circling the front entrance like a flock of vultures, waiting for a glimpse of the crippled CFA light-heavyweight champion. Exhaling a sigh, he fixed his stare on Marcus and dragged his hand through his hair, muttering another foul curse that earned him another disapproving scowl from his manager.

"You need to focus on getting yourself better, Cole. You're like a damn caged lion on display at the zoo here. And your disposition is just about as pleasant."

Cole turned his chair from the window and gave it a hard shove. His four-wheeled prison shot across the room, stopping just short of rolling over Marcus's toes. "Losing one's career tends to do that. You'll have to excuse me if I'm not all rainbows and butterflies these days."

"Dammit, Cole, you haven't lost anything yet! I spoke with Dean, and the Cage Fighting Association has agreed not to challenge your title for at least twelve more months. You've got time."

"What about De'Grasse?" There were days over these last months and many sleepless nights when the agony had been so unbearable that the only thing keeping him sane was the thought of facing that bastard in the cage again. Vengeance was a powerful drug, dulling pain and strengthening will. It was sure as hell better than any of that narcotic bullshit they kept pushing at him. Shit, if he stayed here any longer, he'd become an addict and they'd be sending him to fucking rehab next. Wouldn't the *Enquirer* just love that?

"The CFA is giving him a shot at the interim. His six-month suspension is up next week, and the association agreed, though it was a split decision, they're going to give him the interim title fight."

Cole's grip tightened on the armrests of the chair until it creaked with protest. "Against who?"

Marcus shifted uncomfortably, breaking Cole's stare. "Kyle Cane."

"Fuck me," he snarled. "De'Grasse's going to kill him."

"For what it's worth, Dean is pissed. If it were just up to him, that bastard would never put on a pair of gloves in this organization again. He doesn't agree with the league's decision to put him back in the ring. But De'Grasse is big money now. Everyone wants to see a grudge match between you two. Hell, even *I* want to see you pummel that bastard into the mat."

"You realize if De'Grasse wins interim and if I'm not cage-ready in twelve months, he'll become the undisputed."

"Of course I know that!" Marcus snapped. "You don't have to tell me how this shit works, Cole. I was in the business when you were in fucking diapers!"

Doubtful, but Cole knew when to keep his mouth shut. Marcus was whipping out the effenheimer, which meant he'd been pushed to his limit. But the old man wasn't the only one. "Look at me, Marcus!" Cole slammed his fists on the armrests, rattling the chair. "I can't even walk across this room without a pair of crutches! It'll be a goddamn miracle it I ever fight again!"

"Then it's lucky for you I know an angel."

"What the hell are you talking about?"

"My niece, Katrina Miller. She's a phenomenal physical therapist. If anyone can get you back on your feet again, it's her. She used to work for the Packers, so she knows her way around an athlete's body. I spoke with her a few days ago, and she's agreed to take you on."

Cole tried to think back, but couldn't recall Marcus ever mentioning a niece before. He knew the guy had a younger brother, but just like Cole, the old man didn't talk about his family much. "Where are you sending me?"

Perhaps Marcus was right and it was time to get out of here. His therapy had plateaued, and each day that passed without progress, his hope died a little more. He hated the idea of leaving Vegas. But he hated the idea of staying here like this even more. All in all, he basically hated life in general these days, and if something didn't change soon, he was pretty sure he was going to crack. It wasn't like him to be such a cynical prick. Holy hell, even *he* didn't want to be around himself.

Marcus shifted uncomfortably. At his apologetic grimace, Cole tensed with unease. "Somerset, Wisconsin."

"Wisconsin? Are you fucking kidding me? It's January!"

"I know what month it is, Cole. Katie recently moved back home to help her dad with his PT. I told you my brother had a stroke a couple of months ago."

Shit, that's right. How had he forgotten?

"She's doing his rehab, or I would have brought her out here. Anyway, she has this client who's handicapped. He and his wife go south every winter, and they've agreed to let you use their place. The house is already wheelchair accessible, so it's perfect. Katie will work with you until they get back in April. I'm willing to bet that not only will she get you on your feet again, but she'll have you well on your way to cage-ready."

He wasn't so sure, but what the hell did he have to lose?

"Trust me on this, Cole, it's for the best. We'll leak it to the press that you're in Maui or something. Get them off your back for a little while. Just keep a low profile while you're there, all right? Katie's a very quiet, very private person."

Great . . . She sounded like loads of fun. "What about Under Armour and Tapout?"

"Don't worry about your sponsors—I'll handle them. You just focus on getting better so you can get back in the cage."

Cole wanted to tell Marcus to wake up. He'd be lucky if he ever walked on his own again, let alone set foot into that octagon. He was sick as hell of everyone lying to him, telling him what they thought he wanted to hear because they didn't believe he could handle the truth.

"When do I leave?"

"Now. Your flight from McCarran leaves in three hours."

Three hours? "Dammit, Marcus, a little warning would have been nice." In the fourteen years Marcus had been his manager, Cole knew just how far he could push the man who was more like a father to him than his own piece-of-shit dad had ever been.

"I didn't want to take the risk of you changing your mind. Come on." He stepped into the hall and gestured for Cole to follow. "The aide will pack up your bag and bring it down. There's a private exit in the back. We'll go out that way."

He let Marcus lead the way. They traveled down the elevator and through a back hall that led to an underground parking garage. His manager wasted no time ushering him inside like they were freaking Cloak and Dagger or something. Minutes later, someone was tossing his bag into the backseat and wishing him fare-thee-well. Before he knew it, Cole was in the air and headed toward the land of the Cheese Heads—whatever the fuck that meant.

CHAPTER

2

What in the hell was she thinking? Clearly, she wasn't, and that was the problem. For the thousandth time she kicked herself for telling her uncle yes when he called her, pleading for help. *Please, Katie. He needs you. I need you. No one does this job better than you do. You're a modern-day Christ.* So okay, that had been a little over the top, and that probably should have been her first clue that Uncle Marcus was blowing smoke up her ass. She was a good PT, but she wasn't a damn miracle worker.

In fact, most of her clients probably thought she was the devil for as hard as she worked them. Come to think about it, she'd been called as much a time or two. She wasn't looking to take on any new clients right now. Between working part-time in the physical therapy department at the hospital, and devoting the rest of her time to her father, who was just now regaining adequate use of his right side, Katie had no interest in taking on another patient—especially one called the Beast of the East.

She'd tried to tell Uncle Marcus no. Now just wasn't a good time, blah, blah, blah . . . but when had the guy ever taken no for an answer? It was what she loved and hated the most about him. She supposed she should just count herself lucky he hadn't tried to force her to come down there. In all fairness, she did owe him— big. It was just that when the phone rang last week Katie never expected he'd be calling to collect. So, in a regretful moment of weakness, and temporary insanity, she'd agreed to help this Beast of the East, and in doing so, broke the number one rule she now lived by: no athletes—never again.

Katie parked her RAV in the MSP parking lot and stepped out, burying her booted foot in six inches of snowy slush. "Dammit," she grouched, setting her other one into the muck now that she was already committed. Hiking the strap of her purse over her shoulder, she slammed the door shut and tromped across the parking lot to the Delta 1 terminal.

The bitter wind gusted, cutting right through her plaid pea coat. Reaching up, she pinched the collar closed with her fur-lined glove and quickened her pace. She'd just stepped through the roundabout doors and into the pick-up/baggage claim, when she spotted said Beast, riding down the escalator—in a freaking wheel-chair! What in the hell was this guy doing? It was bad enough his back was broken, was he trying to break his neck next?

Katie raced toward the moving stairs, her calf-high boots with the horribly impractical three-inch spiked heels clapping loudly across the atrium, drawing almost as much attention as the daredevil in the wheelchair. She wasn't sure what she could possibly do if he fell—get run over, most likely—but for some crazy reason, she planted herself between the man and the bottom of the stairs. It wasn't the smartest thing she'd ever done, but the only thing she could imagine right now was the horror of calling her uncle and telling him his prizefighter gacked in the MSP terminal from a cervical fracture.

The man seemed to register there was a problem before she did. And as he approached the end of his ride, a dumbfounded expres-sion flashed crossed his face. He was probably thinking the same thing she was: *Why in the hell isn't she getting out of the way?*

"Lady, you need to move!" he called down to her, his deep, rich voice holding a distinct tone of warning and alarm.

Yes. Yes, she did, she suddenly realized, because the Beast of the East was headed right for her. The only problem was, her icepick heel happened to be stuck in the grate at the bottom of the stairs. Katie tried to lift her foot again, but it wouldn't budge. Again, the man warned her to move, this time with a bit of profanity. Damn, he was approaching fast.

The fighter shot a quick glance behind him, probably checking to see if the area was clear and looking as if he had every intention of forcing that chair back up those stairs. But he couldn't move. People were actually crowding in behind him, openly staring. Some began to whisper among themselves, and she was pretty sure she heard someone say, "Oh, my God, that's Cole Easton! Why won't that stupid woman get out of his way?"

Another replied, "She must be a crazy fan or something."

Like watching a train wreck about to happen, but unable to look away, the escalator gawkers seemed to take a collective gasp as they waited for impact. Cole cursed. Katie squeezed her eyes shut, bracing for impact as she gave her heel one final yank.

It popped free just as Cole collided with her. She let out a startled yelp as an arm wrapped around her waist and lifted her off the ground. The momentum sent Katie falling forward, and her hands shot out to keep her from catapulting over the man's head. She grabbed his shoulders, which felt like she was clutching rock, and braced herself, but not before planting her stomach into his face. She felt like one of those Olympic ice skaters, suspended in the air—only a lot less graceful. With his chair now one hand short, they coasted to a slow, gliding stop, and the terminal erupted into a chorus of clapping cheers and wolf whistles.

Cole cursed again—a muffled expletive she couldn't exactly hear through her coat—and she wondered if it was possible to die of embarrassment. She prayed the answer was *Yes, it is*, and that Jesus would just take her now, because this, without a doubt, was the most humiliating experience of her life.

No such luck. The heavens did not open, and there was no beam of light to suck her up into glory. *Shit . . .*

Cole leaned forward and set her on the ground, none-too-gently, and then leaned back, pinning her with a *what the fuck was that?* scowl.

She had to admit, this probably wasn't the best time to admire how blue and unnaturally bright his eyes were. The words that came to mind as she stared at him were *fire* and *ice*, leaving her feeling like she'd been touched by both. She'd watched his last fight and thoroughly Google-stalked him, but good Lord, the camera didn't do him justice, that was for sure. The lens failed to capture the proper angle of his chiseled jaw, or the regal line of his impossibly straight nose. Fighters just didn't look like this . . .

But then she noticed the thin scar over his right cheekbone and the white vertical line through the vermillion border of his bottom lip—now *those* fit. Unfortunately, they only seemed to add to his looks, giving him a raw, dangerous edge. Were it not for the masculine fullness of his mouth, his face would have been too fierce, too severe, to call handsome. But as it happened, Cole Easton, aka the Beast of the East, was positively the most gorgeous man she'd ever laid eyes on.

"What in the hell were you thinking?" he demanded, snapping her back into reality and looking wholly pissed off as bystanders' cell-phone cameras flashed all around them.

Katie took a respective step back, and the heel of her boot wobbled precariously. Losing her balance, she rolled her ankle and winced against the burst of pain shooting into her foot. How utterly mortifying. "My heel was stuck in the grate," she tried to explain, but yeah . . . it didn't sound any better out loud than it had in her head.

He gave her a skeptical scowl as if trying to decide whether she was telling him the truth or what?—trying to assault him by planting her gut in his face? Jeez, that he even had to wonder said volumes about what it must be like to be Cole Easton on any given day. Maybe he had women feigning accidents and throwing themselves at him all the time, but this was definitely a first for her. Perhaps an introduction would help. At this point, she doubted it could hurt.

"Cole Easton . . . ?" She asked his name, just to make sure she'd assaulted the right man, and got her answer when he gave her an arched look that said, *Seriously? Cut the crap, lady*, and crossed his arms over his broad, muscular chest.

Having no clue what else to do or say, she thrust out her hand and, with more confidence than she was feeling, stepped forward and said, "It's nice to meet you. I'm Katie Miller, your physical therapist."

Surprise briefly registered in those icebergs called eyes before he quickly shuttered his expression. Slowly, as if he still didn't trust her not to jump him, he unfolded his arms and took her hand in a firm grip, shaking it. The moment their palms connected, a jolt of awareness raced up her arm, zinged into her breasts and headed south like she was a freaking pinball machine. The unexpected spark of pure, unadulterated lust startled her, and she pulled her hand back.

At her tugging, he released his grasp on her hand. His keen gaze narrowed with disapproval and she could all but hear him thinking, *Strike two*. "I assure you, Ms. Miller, I don't bite—at least not unless you ask nicely."

Her cheeks flamed with embarrassment and she dropped her eyes, unable to hold his eerie azure stare another second. Wow, she pitied Cole's opponents. She hadn't been the recipient of that glower for sixty seconds and already she wanted to tap.

This was a bad idea. And to make an awkward situation worse, she couldn't tell if he was flirting with her, because that usually involved smiling, and so far Cole hadn't cracked so much as a grin.

Opting to ignore his comment and possibly inappropriate offer, because she'd already made a big enough ass of herself today, Katie cleared her throat and forced herself to meet his bold stare. "The umm . . . baggage claim is down the hall. We should probably head over there. It's about an hour's drive to Somerset from here." She swept her gaze over him and added, "Is that all you're wearing?—because if it is, we need to stop somewhere and get you a coat. It's negative five out there right now and expected to hit twenty by tonight."

"Below zero?" He looked as if she'd just told him the moon had turned to blood and it was the dawn of the apocalypse or something.

"Yes. Twenty—below zero."

"Shit . . ." he grumbled under his breath, looking as if he was contemplating turning that chair of his around and hauling his ass back up the escalator. Katie had no doubt if he had a mind to do it, there'd be no stopping him. Despite his current disabled state, there was something about Cole Easton that seemed larger than life. Even in a chair, the man was intimidating as hell. His broad shoulders and definably muscled chest stretched the limits of his worn-out Dr. Pepper T-shirt. His long tree-trunk legs didn't fit the confines of the chair very well at all, and his combat boots well overshot the foot rests.

As she stood there staring at him, a single thought kept playing over and over in her mind—*You don't belong in there.* Something inside her chest stirred at the injustice wrought upon this man, and Katie inexplicably found herself wanting to fight for him, to champion his cause, but Cole didn't exactly strike her as a man who would ever let anyone fight his battles.

Her gaze strayed to his scarred hands, and she noticed his knuckles were blanched white. He gripped the wheels of his chair so tightly, the ropes of muscles tracking up his forearms flexed in an impressive display of masculine power.

Katie's pulse quickened with feminine awareness, and it suddenly felt much too hot in here—until she met Cole's stare again and got hit with an arctic blast of *what the fuck are you staring at?*

"Perhaps you guys do things differently here in the Midwest, but where I come from, it's rude to stare. I didn't fly halfway across the United States for your pity, Ms. Miller. So let's get something straight right now. I don't want to be here. I'm doing this for Marcus because he refuses to accept what countless doctors have already told him. I'm not going to fight again. Hell, I'll probably never walk again, so between you and me, you're wasting your time."

Spoken just like a typical headstrong, arrogant athlete. If she'd needed a reminder why she hated working with these cocksure jocks, well, here it was. Schooling her features to match his bullheaded attitude, she replied, "Well then, I guess that makes two of us."

His brow arched in surprise as if he'd expected her to try to convince him otherwise, and she nearly laughed. Cole wasn't the only one who could be blunt, so if that was the way he wanted to play it, that was the way he was gonna get it. "As long as you have that pissy, dogmatic attitude, I am wasting my time. I've reviewed your medical records and I happen to agree with my uncle. Between you and me"—she paused dramatically, throwing his words right back at him—"the only reason I agreed to take your case was because, as I'm sure you well know, my uncle Marcus is nearly impossible to say no to. He thinks the world of you. Though as of yet, I can't see why."

Turning away, she headed toward the baggage claim and tried like hell not to roll her ankle as the heel of her boot wobbled. The brisk staccato of her boots—*clip, clomp, clip, clomp*—proudly proclaimed her ire.

A moment later, Cole went whisking by her, maneuvering that chair as if he'd been in it all his life. Then again, as far as first impressions went, she couldn't imagine Cole ever letting anything dominate him. Well, this was certainly going to be fun. Katie made a mental note to tell her uncle Marcus, *Fuck you very much.*

By the time she reached the baggage claim, Cole had his duffel on the ground and was yanking a charcoal-gray hoodie over his head. After poking his arms through the sleeves, he pulled the waist down and dragged the hood off, leaving his dark hair a sexy, disheveled mess. Zipping the bag shut, he propped the single piece of luggage on his lap, and spun his chair around to face her. CFA was emblazoned across the front of his duffel, and for some reason, seeing that logo hit her with a wallop of reality.

This was Cole's life—his career—and the only thing standing between him and ruination was her. In that moment, she felt a renewed sense of purpose and a deep desire to help this man, but she was quick to avert her gaze lest he confuse it with pity.

CHAPTER

3

ole led the way as if he knew where he was going. The heel on Katie's boot continued to loosen until she wobbled precariously with each step, forcing her to slow down before she twisted her ankle again. When they neared the exit, Cole turned down the hall and stopped at a bench outside the bathrooms.

"Sit down," he told her as she approached.

Katie bristled at his command and stopped short of the bench, everything inside her immediately revolting at his overbearing briskness. Most of the time when her panic attacks hit, she could get someplace quiet and ride them out, talking herself down from the sudden rise of adrenaline surging in her veins. The triggers were never the same, but they were always instantaneous—the familiar scent of cologne, the tone of a man's voice . . .

The noose of dread squeezed her throat, trapping the air in her lungs. She couldn't breathe! The instinct to flee was riding her hard, and if she thought she could outrun him, she might have done just that. Cole reminded her too much of *him*. Not in looks, but in that masculine, domineering arrogance . . . Lord, what was she thinking? This was such a mistake! How had she ever thought she could help this man? She couldn't even help herself, for crissake!

Katie stumbled another step back and her ankle buckled. Cole's hand shot out to steady her. His grip on her arm was firm, but gentle—nothing like *his*, she reminded herself. She took several deep breaths and focused on Cole's touch as an anchor to reality before her mind took her someplace it didn't want to go. There was no pain, only steadying strength—no malice or suspicion in his eyes, just a mixture of surprise and concern.

Stop it! You're all right, she scolded herself, repeating the mantra over and over inside her head. Dammit, it'd been almost a month since she'd had one of these panic attacks. She was so certain she'd finally made a breakthrough in putting the past behind her. How could she let a bossy stranger get to her like this?

"Hey, you okay?" Cole asked, guiding her to the bench.

Numbly, she nodded and plopped down across from him.

"Well, you don't look all right," he added unhelpfully. Letting go of her arm, he sat his bag on the ground and unzipped the side pouch. Pulling out a roll of fighter's tape, he learned forward and caught hold of her thigh, lifting her foot onto his lap. "You're going to break your ankle in these boots," he grumbled, pulling off a long strip of the white tape and ripping it free of the roll with his teeth. Grasping her ankle, he lifted her leg and wrapped the tape around the heel of her boot, crossing over the top of her foot, and weaving it around her heel a few more times.

"Believe it or not, these boots have great traction," she replied. Thankfully, the surge of panic began to recede as quickly as it'd come. "This heel is like an icepick sticking into the ground."

His dark brow arched as he glanced up from his tape job. His top lip twitched, not quite breaking into a smile. "So I've noticed."

Was this his attempt at making a joke? He sealed the end of the tape across her boot and wiggled the heel to test his wrap job. "There," he said, setting her foot on the ground. "Only one of us gets to be the cripple, and that's me. Sorry." He dropped the tape back into his bag and zipped it shut before hefting it onto his lap and putting his chair into motion.

"Thanks," she mumbled, unsure what else to say. Either Cole Easton had a very dry sense of humor, or he was just about the snarkiest man she'd ever met.

By the time Katie caught up with him, Cole was at the edge of the sidewalk. It had just quit snowing, and the plows hadn't been by yet to clear the roads. The slush was thick. It wouldn't be easy for him to navigate his chair through this muck. Without thinking, she stepped behind him and grasped the chair's handles, setting them in motion. Cole immediately grabbed the wheels, stopping them more effectively than the brakes, and whipped his head around to glower at her.

"What are you doing?"

Startled, Katie froze. "I . . . I'm helping you," she babbled lamely. "Through the snow."

"Well, I don't need your help!"

But wasn't that why he was here in the first place? Though judging by the scowl on his face, she didn't particularly think now was the best time to point that out. She didn't want to do anything to further incite his ire. When he continued to stare pointedly at her hands, she realized she'd yet to let go of the handles and jerked her hands back as if they'd burned her.

He gave the wheels a hard shove, shooting out into the street. The chair cut through the slush like a knife through hot butter, and Katie stood there dumbly, in awe of the upper body strength he possessed to be able to move like that.

Cole must have realized she wasn't following him, because he suddenly stopped in the middle of the street and looked back at her. His scowl darkened, and she fought the involuntary shudder rising up inside her.

"Are you coming?" he asked curtly. "I have no idea where you're parked. Unfortunately, I lost my psychic abilities along with the use of my legs." He gave a negligent shrug. "Who knew?"

Yeah, Cole was definitely bitter, and she could add *sarcastic smartass* to the fighter's character analysis as well. His exhaled breath billowed in the frigid air, which no doubt did zero to sweeten his disposition. The wind must have been cutting right through that hoodie.

"It's the silver RAV across the street," she called, stepping into the slushy road. As she entered the parking lot, she dug into her purse, fishing for her keys. Finding the hot pink cylinder in the bottom of her bag, she pulled out the pepper spray key chain and started her car with the remote.

The lights flashed and the car fired up, leaving no doubt which SUV was hers. As she popped the hatch, she was pretty sure she heard him grumbling something about, "colder than a well-digger's ass" and finally having proof that hell has indeed frozen over.

On that assessment, she couldn't agree more, though for probably a slew of different reasons than Cole thought. In fact, she specifically remembered swearing hell would freeze over before she ever moved back home to Somerset, or before she'd ever treat an athlete again, or before she ever allowed herself to feel those stirrings of feminine awareness the fighter had sparked to life in just the brief time she'd known him . . . Yeah, Cole was right. Hell had definitely frozen over.

The last thing Cole expected when he rolled off that plane and into this frozen wasteland was to discover his physical therapist was smoking hot. Holy hell . . . How it was possible that craggy old geeze, Marcus, was related to this Scandinavian beauty sitting beside him, Cole would never know. Ms. Katrina Miller was easily the most beautiful woman he had ever seen. With hair the color of corn silk that looked just as soft, too, and he'd be willing to bet those shoulder-length tresses were all natural. *Only one way to find out . . .*

The thought came unbidden and was most unwelcome. He was not here to fraternize with Marcus's niece. But damn . . . she possessed a wholesome beauty Cole rarely saw in the circles he ran. Most of the women he encountered were more plastic than flesh.

He found himself wondering what she looked like beneath that thigh-length coat and then promptly stopped that train of thought. First of all, she was his manager's niece—so off-limits. Second of all, she was his PT, and it was a bad idea to mix business with pleasure. And third of all, Katie Miller was so out of his league, it was fucking ridiculous. Women like her wanted the American dream. Women like her got wet for white-collar men who were stable— guys who lived in a house with a white picket fence and would give them those three kids and a yellow Lab, and drove a fucking mini-van. That shit just wasn't him. It never had been and it never would be, so if he could just cool his cock right now, that'd be real great.

The flavor of women Cole tended to attract wanted a man who could fight hard and fuck harder. They weren't interested in the long-term bullshit and that was okay, neither was he. So yeah, Ms. Miller was definitely Do Not Touch material—on so many levels it wasn't even funny. But most important, he wouldn't disrespect the only man who ever gave a shit about him by messing around with his niece.

Cole watched the young woman sitting beside him as she navigated rush hour traffic. Her white-knuckled grip on the steering wheel could mean only one of two things—either she was uncomfortable driving in the cities, or he made her nervous. And if the latter was the case, then he was glad he wasn't the only one.

Katie's fine-bone features accented vibrant green eyes that he'd swear could see right into his soul. Something about the way she looked at him made him feel raw and exposed—and that vulnerability put him on edge. He wasn't used to seeing pity in a woman's eyes when she looked at him, and it only soured his already surly mood. He'd be damned if he'd become this woman's charity case. Yet here he was, so wasn't he just that?

Not even when he'd been a homeless teen and fighting for his life in the streets of Reno had he considered himself as helpless as he felt now. His life had always been his own—shitty as it had been at times. He had depended on no one, needed no one, but for the first time in his adult life, Cole's future was solely dependent on someone else. That knowledge seeded a bone-deep resentment rotting in the very fiber of his being.

He didn't realize he was staring until Katie cast him a nervous glance and tucked a lock of hair behind her ear. A twinge of guilt knifed in his chest. Fuck, what in the hell was the matter with him? Katie wasn't the enemy here. It wasn't this woman's fault he was injured, and it wasn't her fault he was attracted to her. Acting like a sulking prick sure as hell wasn't going to get him walking any sooner. So if he had any last remnants of self-respect he'd check his asshole attitude right now.

"Where are we going?" he asked, for lack of better conversation.

"I was thinking I'd take you to the Mall of America. It isn't very far from here, and they'll have everything you'll need to get winterized. January in Wisconsin can be pretty brutal. You'd be surprised."

He was surprised all right. Surprised how his blood heated when the tip of Katie's tongue slipped out to moisten her bottom lip before she caught the corner of it between her teeth. She worried at the plump flesh as she waited for him to say something instead of staring at her like an utter dumbass.

"Anywhere is fine, as long as they sell Under Armour or Tapout."

Katie glanced at him in question before turning her attention back to the road. "I'm sure they do. They have everything there."

She seemed on edge. Not that he blamed her. He'd been throwing her a lot of attitude, and then there was that incident in the hall with her boot. He hadn't expected her to be so jumpy. She'd swung from self-assured and sassy to anxious and fearful in the span of a second. A part of him wondered what that had been all about, but not enough to ask, or make the effort to put her at ease. His unwanted attraction to the woman only fueled his feelings of frustration, driving home the need to keep her at a distance. Not that it would be a difficult feat. He was a master at shutting people out—he'd been doing it for years.

In Cole's experience, people wanted him around for what they thought he could do for them. Whether he was getting them rich in the cage, or making women feel important as they hung on his arm and got into the VIP clubs. Hell, even Marcus was probably shitting himself at the thought of all that green he'd lose if Cole never fought again. He'd practically forced Cole onto this poor woman, and per her own admission, she wasn't any happier about this arrangement than he was.

"That's fine," he said when he realized he still hadn't answered her. Exhaling a pent-up sigh, he dragged his hand through his overgrown hair. He kept it short when he was training. It was too hot otherwise, and he hated the sting of the sweat-drenched ends poking in his eyes. But since he hadn't seen the inside of a gym in six months, he'd had no reason to visit the barber. What he wouldn't give to feel that burn right now or the fire in his calves as he hit that ten-mile mark on the elliptical, or the thunder of his heart crashing inside his chest as he pushed his body to its limit.

Settling into the seat, he braced his elbow against the door and turned his attention out the passenger window. He ignored the stretching silence growing between them. The day was quickly losing the battle with night, as the last vestiges of pink and purple streaked across the skyline. Cole couldn't remember the last time he'd seen a sunset. In Vegas, there were so many towering buildings and city lights it always seemed like daytime there.

"It's quiet here," he mumbled the observation, not expecting a reply, so he was surprised when he got one.

"This is quiet to you?"

Despite himself, he felt his top lip tugging up at the faintest hint of her accent. The way she pronounced her *o*'s showed her true Scandinavian roots, and was . . . well, charming and innocent sounding. It wasn't a very strong accent, which made him wonder if she'd lived somewhere other than Wisconsin recently.

"Where do you live?" she asked, when he said nothing more.

"Vegas."

"Why Vegas?"

He turned to look at her. "Why Somerset?"

She bristled at the question, and he could practically see her walls slamming up. *Interesting . . .* It was an innocent enough question, yet not one she seemed particularly inclined to answer. Perhaps there was more to Katie Miller than what met the eye. It appeared he wasn't the only one who didn't like talking about himself. Curious now, and in a show of good faith, he said, "My camp is in Vegas. That's where I primarily train. I've occasionally visited other camps when I need to tighten up a hole in my game, but in general, I don't like to travel. I fight out of the MGM, so it makes sense to live there."

"I suppose it does. Do you like living in Vegas?"

He shrugged. "Not particularly."

"What other camps have you been to?"

"The last one was called the Pit—"

"That sounds . . . charming." She gave him the faintest hint of a teasing grin that did funny things to his insides he didn't particularly like. He was around women all the time, and he wasn't used to having such a strong reaction to one. "Where was this *Pit*?"

Boy, she was good—and smart—guiding the conversation like a pro, careful to keep the topic off herself. He didn't miss how she kept the subject light and neutral, pulling out just enough bits and pieces to keep it flowing in his direction without making Cole feel like he was talking about himself—something he hated to do.

"Arroyo Grande, California."

"Why did you pick that camp?"

"I was training for the light-heavyweight title fight with Crazy Dan De'Grasse. He's primarily a striker, and I'm more of a ground-and-pound guy. My jujitsu was solid and I wanted to perfect my stand-up. This camp mainly focuses on striking. So . . ."

"Did it help?"

"I won, didn't I?" Now she was moving onto a touchy subject. His tone warned her to tread lightly.

"Yes, you did."

If he didn't know better, he'd have sworn he heard the distinct inflection of emotion lilting in her voice, but he didn't know her well enough to name it. His jaw tightened in response, molars grinding. "Did you see the fight?" Why did the idea of this woman witnessing the collapse of his career piss him off so much?

Her gaze flicked to him hesitantly, as if she were debating answering the question, or at least honestly. She'd better not lie to him. He'd already seen the truth in her eyes, and if she hoped to have any sort of trust between them, now was the time she'd either make it or break it. His gut tightened. Every time he thought of that night, his stomach threatened to puke.

"I saw it . . ." she confessed softly.

Fuck. That *was* pity he saw in her peripherals. Rage tore through him like a hot lance. His hands clenched involuntarily, and it took every last bit of self-control not to slam his fist into her dash. He turned his head and faced the window, unwilling to let her see the battle waging inside him—the pain, the anger . . .

"—after Uncle Marcus called and asked me to be your PT . . . I watched the fight. I watched them all. I'd never seen MMA before and I wanted to know what I was up against—what kind of condition my uncle expects me to get you back to. You're an amazing fighter, Cole."

She placed her hand on his forearm. He tensed at the current of awareness that shot up his arm and flinched at the unexpected contact. He didn't want to be touched, to be placated like some child whose favorite toy had been broken. "*Was* a great fighter," he corrected with a frustrated growl. "Now, let it go."

As quickly as it came, her hand left his arm, but the break in contact bothered him more than her touch had. The wary look in her verdant eyes and nearly inaudible catch in her breath suggested he'd offended or perhaps scared her. Why was this woman so touchy? Except for this subtle chink in her armor, Katie Miller appeared to be a very self-confident, well-put-together woman. The way she dressed, the way she carried herself . . . classy and smart.

Her beauty would easily intimidate a lesser man. But something told him Marcus's niece wasn't exactly what she appeared to be, and that sparked Cole's curiosity, if not his interest. Perhaps they should pick *her* scabs a while and see how much *she* liked it. He'd be damned if he was going to be the only one bleeding by the time they got out of this car.

CHAPTER

 4

Cole made no attempt to hide his stare, his expression completely locked down and unreadable. Sitting across the table from the famous MMA fighter as they ate supper at the Hard Rock Cafe, Katie could easily see how he'd earned the nickname "the Beast of the East." Cole was a formidable man, exuding a certain dominance that put her on edge. After meeting him in person, she quickly realized there was a tumultuous undercurrent of energy radiating from him that the camera just did not capture. She'd done a lot of research beforehand, watching Cole's interviews, his weigh-ins, trying to get a feel for the man behind the fighter. And this was not him.

The public Cole Easton was phlegmatic. His fans went wild for him. He didn't stoop to trash-talking his opponents, which had earned him her grudging respect, and he'd always had a smile for the camera. Oh, and the women loved him. This woman?—not so much.

Perhaps his on-camera persona had been just that, a fictional character putting on an act to draw fans, because this Cole Easton she'd had the distinct displeasure of meeting was a decidedly reclusive and bitter man. It seemed that the camera had lied on all accounts, because he was more gorgeous in person, which only heightened her distrust of him. In Katie's admittedly limited experience, men who looked like Cole were complete and utter douchebags. They went through life with an attitude of entitlement; the world owed them because they were beautiful. They sucked at relationships because they never had to work at one. Women just fell at their feet, and were possessions to be used, abused, and discarded at their whim.

Katie returned Cole's stare, taking his measure just as blatantly as he did hers. The music was playing loud enough to drown out any conversation they might have had, which was fine with her, because at this point she didn't know what to say. The more time she spent with him, the more glaringly obvious it became that he was just as broken on the inside as he was on the outside. She got the feeling his legs were going to be the easier of the two to fix.

Cole had just finished his beer, and Katie was about to suggest they head out when two women stepped, or rather stumbled, into her peripherals. They were whispering to each other and pointing at Cole. If he saw them, he paid the very busty Barbie-doll beauties no mind. Then again, this sort of thing probably happened to him all the time. One would think she would have grown used to this after dating Carter Owens for nearly two years, but she never had. The quarterback for the Packers couldn't get enough of the T & A women constantly threw at him. It was just one of the many reasons she didn't get involved with athletes anymore.

Katie's hope that the women would just stumble on by was dashed when she heard one of them announce, "Who cares if he's with someone? I'm going to go talk to him."

Great . . . It was always so humiliating and awkward, sitting there like the Plain Jane wallflower, while these gorgeous women with their fake hair extensions batted their fake eyelashes and flaunted their fake boobs in these guys' faces. And they always ate it up. Men were so predictable, it was disgusting.

"Don't look now, but I think you've got some fans." Settling back in her chair to "enjoy" the show, Katie picked up her mint mojito and slipped the straw between her lips. As she sucked her drink down with more vigor than necessary, something darkened in Cole's azure stare as his eyes locked on her mouth. She bared her teeth in a snarky grin as she bit down on the bendy plastic.

At first, she wasn't sure if he'd heard her past the thrumming music. But at the last possible second, Cole turned to look at the woman wobbling toward him in her red fuck-me pumps and skin-tight skinny jeans. Katie wondered if the woman realized her maroon lace top was actually an undershirt—and her black bra was showing through.

Please don't tell me he actually believes those tits are real. Seriously . . . no one can defy gravity like that.

"Cole Easton?" the woman asked, bending down to *speak over the music* and flashing him a nipple-bearing shot of cleavage. Before he could confirm or deny, the woman glanced over her shoulder to her friend who was still standing a couple feet back, and yelled, "Oh, my God, Rachel, you're right! It is him! I can't believe it!" She waved her friend over and then turned back to Cole.

When he gave her one of those camera-glam grins, Katie nearly kicked him in the shin under the table. *Are you kidding me?* she thought. He hadn't so much as flashed a glimpse of those pearly whites at her, and here he was, smiling at these two trollers like the damn Cheshire cat. *Unbelievable!*

"Oh, Cole, it's such an honor to meet you!" the woman gushed. *Oh barf . . .*

Katie took another sucking chug of her mojito, not even attempting to hide her *puleeze* eye roll. It wasn't like he was going to notice her over here anyw—

Aaaand Cole noticed. That vibrant blue gaze locked on Katie with an intensity that made her acutely aware that the warmth flooding through her veins might not be the alcohol. Well . . . shit.

Now she just looked like a petty, jealous chit. And the flirtatious grin he gave her for it . . . Oh, Lord, it sent a dart of heat firing right into her core. It wasn't one of those practiced, smile-for-the-camera glam shots that no doubt had women all over the country Facebooking, screenshotting, and Pinteresting. It was a genuine smile, meant only for her. In that moment, Katie became acutely aware of two very important things. One: Cole Easton was far more handsome than she'd originally given him credit for. And two: that made him a very dangerous man.

Cole suffered through the women's attention, but what made it slightly more bearable was watching Katie's response to it all. She looked about as prickly as a porcupine, sitting over there, sucking down her mojito with a vigor that had him wishing he were a straw. He wasn't even sure the women noticed her. More than likely not, as sauced as these two were. But this was par for the course of a typical night out for Cole, and he'd learned a long time ago to roll with it. They were fans, they meant no harm, and he certainly didn't want to give them the impression he was an asshole. Those kinds of rumors could kill a guy's career, cost him sponsors, and he already had a hard enough time combating the media's lies. He didn't need to add any more fuel to their fire.

As soon as he and Katie had gotten to their table, he'd ditched his wheels for an actual chair. It was sitting in the corner behind her, buried under bags of "winter essentials." Man, that girl could shop.

As the two women chatted him up, he politely answered their questions, only half-paying attention as they flashed him wanton grins and cleavage shots. Try as he might, his focus kept straying to the woman sitting across from him. Did she have any idea how beautiful she was? Or what she did to him every time she slipped that straw between those luscious lips of hers? Fuck, Katie put these women to shame, and he'd be willing to bet his last fight's winnings that she didn't even know it, which only made her all the hotter. Damn, keeping his hands off her for the next four months was going to be one hell of a fight that he wasn't sure he was up to.

He'd been wondering for hours what she looked like beneath that coat, and when she finally slipped it off and draped it behind her chair . . . it'd been like watching her unwrap a beautiful present. Unlike the disproportionate women hanging on him right now, her curves were subtle, but definably and deliciously feminine. She wore a modest gray cashmere sweater that hugged what looked like a full C cup. The wide black belt that accented her narrow waist and the gentle flare of her hips matched her form-fitting dress pants. The new boots he'd insisted she get—there was no damn way his fighter's tape was going to hold that heel through their power shopping—were mid-calf silver-buckled heather-gray flats. It wasn't until she'd put them on that he'd realized just how petite she really was. Those icepicks she called boots had given her a deceptive three-inch advantage. If he had to guess, he'd say this woman wasn't a centimeter past five-four.

God help him, as he sat across the table—staring—wondering what it'd be like to have such a small, naturally soft woman like her naked and writhing beneath him. Katie was the kind of woman a man would want to take his time with—to learn every dip and curve, to savor every little gasp and sigh.

Katie was nothing like the woman who was currently bent over him, reeking of stale cigarette smoke and the cheap perfume she coated herself in to try to hide the nasty habit. Her beer-soured breath brushed hot against his ear as she leaned closer, her hairsprayed curls snagging in the stubble of his jaw as she invited him to come home with her and her friend for a three-way. She attempted to seal the deal by flicking her tongue against the lobe of his ear and catching it between her teeth.

There would have been a time when he'd have been all *fuck yeah, let's do this*, but for some reason, this woman's indecent proposal offended the shit out of him. He wasn't sure if it was the blatant disrespect she showed to Katie, who'd clearly overheard this woman's drunken *whisper*, or the fact that that these woman wanted to fuck him simply because he was Cole Easton. They didn't give a shit about him. They only wanted a famous cock to rock on and a story to tell their girlfriends in the morning. He was nothing more than a good ride, and for the first time in his life, for some godforsaken reason, that mattered to him.

Cole tipped his head to the side, pulling his earlobe free of the woman's teeth, and braced his hands on her hips, moving her a full step back. "That's a flattering offer, Shayla, but I don't think my girlfriend would appreciate that very much, nor do I think you'd appreciate being the one sitting in that chair having to watch this."

The woman looked at him as if he'd slapped her, but the reaction that surprised him more was Katie's. She appeared utterly shocked, which kinda pissed him off because what the hell did she think, that he was going to take off with these two and leave her here? Wow, she must think little of him to look this fucking surprised.

If she'd thought Cole's mood was foul before, she hadn't seen anything yet. When he shot those two women down and called her his girlfriend, her jaw had nearly hit the floor. She'd been so sure he would leave with them and just hire a taxi to take him to Somerset. It was what her ex would have done. Hell, it was what he *had* done.

Her ice had been in a full-on thaw at that point, and for a moment, she'd entertained the glimmer of hope that maybe Cole was different, after all. But then those women left, and that frosty glower turned on her. He was angry—at her! For what? Ruining his good time? Probably. Asshole.

Hey, if he wanted to get laid that damn bad, she wasn't stopping him. Katie was just about to tell him so when he growled, "Let's go."

His speed and agility surprised her. To see how fluidly he moved from one chair to the other was like watching an Olympian on a pommel horse. And then it suddenly dawned on her, the reason he hadn't taken those women up on their indecent proposal. It had nothing to do with her. That whole girlfriend thing had been to save face, and damn if that didn't sting more than she wanted to admit. Cole hadn't left with those two women because he *couldn't* leave with them. They obviously didn't know about his accident. If they had, they would've asked him about it. His medical records made no comment about sexual function, or perhaps lack thereof. What if he . . . ?

"Now, Katie," Cole barked, slapping a hundred-dollar bill on the table, leaving a more than generous tip before turning away. He didn't wait to see if she followed. The bags looped over the back handles of his chair made a whirring sound against the accelerating wheels.

As she watched him leave, she couldn't decide who she was more upset with: him for proving her right, or herself for daring to hope he was different.

CHAPTER

Dead. Silence.

Neither of them spoke the entire ride back to Somerset. By the time Katie pulled up to the Murphys' house, the tension had grown so thick between them she could cut it with a knife. If she'd thought it would help, she would gladly Norman Bates that shit right here and now because there was no way she could share a house with this man for four months if they were constantly going to be stonewalling each other every chance they got. Clearly, they'd gotten off on the wrong foot here.

So in the effort to clear the air before they entered the house and brought their bad blood inside it, Katie came to a stop in the garage, cut the engine, and turned to face Cole. The overhead light from the garage door opener lit the inside of the RAV with a soft, warming glow—too bad it failed to soften the hard lines of his stony, irritatingly handsome face. It was such a shame a man this gorgeous had to be such an incredible ass.

Clearing her throat, she extended the proverbial olive branch. "Listen, Cole, I'm not sure why you did what you did back there, but I want you to know that you don't owe me anything. You're an adult, and who you choose to spend your time with is none of my business. I'm not here to judge you. I'm only here to help you."

He defiantly crossed his arms over his broad chest and leveled her with a *you have got to be shitting me* glower. "You're not judging me? I don't know who you're trying to kid, but that's all you've done since the minute I got off that plane. You judged that I couldn't make it down the fucking escalator by myself and nearly got us both into a wreck. You judged that I was going to hurt you when I only wanted to fix your busted heel before you broke your ankle. And you judged that I wanted to go home with those women when I haven't been able to take my eyes off you all night long. Your judgments of me are exactly the problem here. So if you don't mind, I'll thank you to take yourself and your opinionated judgments home. I've had a long day."

Katie was pretty sure she couldn't remember when she'd felt like a bigger ass. So it was with mounting dread that she politely informed him, "I am home. This is where I live."

Un. Fucking. Believable. This day just kept getting better and better. "You're what?" Cole snapped.

She flinched at his anger, which only served to piss him off more. What in the hell was her problem? "This is the second time you've done that today," he accused.

"Done what?"

"Acted like you're afraid of me. Is this another one of your judgments, Katie? You think that just because I earn a living with my fists that I'm going to hit you? Or maybe you've been reading too much of the *Enquirer*. Is that it? Well, it might surprise you, love, but you can't believe everything you read."

Perhaps that statement was only half correct, because if he didn't get out of the car right now, he was going to hit something.

It wouldn't be her, but she had a glove box that was about to get a facelift. He wasn't sure why it mattered what Katie thought of him. He was used to people casting judgments and stereotyping him. Hell, if he was honest with himself, he'd probably deserved some of it. He just never let it bother him—before now.

"You're right, Cole. I don't know you. And maybe I have judged you unfairly. I guess only time will tell. I realize your life has been turned upside down, and that this can't be easy for you. In the future, I will try to give you the benefit of the doubt."

"I'd appreciate that," he grumbled, her concession nailing him like a punch to the solar plexus, right along with the realization that not only was he going to be rehabbing with this beautiful, intriguing woman, apparently he was living with her. When Marcus told him he'd be staying in a wheelchair-accessible home, he'd failed to mention anything about a roommate.

"Just so you know, I'm not much of a morning person. And I've never lived with anyone before."

She surprised the shit out of him when she replied, "Well I have. It's not all it's cracked up to be," and then climbed out of the car.

The house couldn't be better designed if Cole had laid it out himself. His only complaint—there was one bathroom to share, albeit it was one of the largest bathrooms he'd ever been in. Everything was handicap accessible, including the shower and the whirlpool. The house was even equipped with a gym, which he immediately fell in love with. There weren't a lot of rooms in the two-bed, one-bath rambler, but the floor plan was open and accommodating.

"This is your room," Katie said, finishing the brief tour. As she reached inside the bedroom and hit the light, a cat darted into the hallway with a complaining *meow*. "Oh, that's Scarlet. Just ignore her. She can be a bit bitchy."

"You have a cat?"

"Well, no . . . not really. Technically she's the Murphys' cat. She comes with the house. I'm house-sitting for them while they're in Florida this winter. Hopefully, by the time they get back my dad will be doing better. I hope you're all right with the cat. I didn't think to mention it to Uncle Marcus."

"Cats are fine. It's no problem."

"Great. Well, then, I guess I'll just let you get settled. If you need anything . . ."

"I'll be fine. Thanks."

It didn't take Cole long to unpack. As soon as he finished, he headed to the weight room and immediately felt at home—except for the wall of mirrors and the ballet bar. That just made him feel like he was in dance class again, something he'd had the distinct displeasure of partaking in early in his career to gain flexibility and balance. Though it had been instrumental in his training, he wouldn't be caught dead doing it now.

It had been too long since he'd had a good, hard workout. Training and fucking had always been his stress outlets. He'd been doing neither of late, so it was no wonder he was feeling pent up and irritable. Perhaps after he shed a pound or two of sweat, he'd feel more amiable about this whole damn situation. The challenge was going to be tailoring a program to effectively work his cardio, given his current limitations, but with the modifications made to the equipment, it might be doable.

Sticking to his old routine as much as possible, Cole moved to the mat to warm up with some stretches. Wrapping the pant leg of his sweats in his fist, he pulled his left leg to the side, and then did the same with his right. With his legs parted wide, he bent forward, stretching his arms above his head. The strain on his lats felt good, the pull in his groin a familiar and welcome pain. He leaned over his left leg and grabbed his heel, pulling his chest to his knee. After holding it to the count of twenty, he began doing the same with the right. His back was tight, the muscles protesting the stretch, but his surgeon assured him his vertebra was completely healed, so his back was just going to have to quit bitching and get with the program.

"You could pull a hamstring like that and you'd never know it. You should take it easy."

Cole glanced at the mirrored wall and locked eyes with Katie standing in the doorway behind him, a motherly scowl on her face. She'd already gotten ready for bed, wearing one of those pants-and-tank-top pajama combos that hugged her trim waist and revealed the ripe teardrop flare of her breasts. Her hair was piled high into a messy bun, and she was rubbing some kind of night cream on her cheeks. She'd accidently smeared some across the tip of her nose—how adorable and utterly charming.

It was such a natural thing to do—a woman's nighttime rituals—yet they were completely foreign to him. The women he'd hung out with would never have allowed him to see them with even a hair out of place, let alone an entire head in disarray. And without makeup?—God forbid. But Katie looked so damn irresistible standing there in her moon-and-stars pajamas, he could hardly breathe. He stared at her, his pulse hammering inside his chest as he struggled to put two intelligible words together, because the only ones knocking around inside his head were *Holy. Fuck.* And he couldn't very well say that, now could he?

"You did it, didn't you?" Her frown deepened as she walked into the gym and weaved around the equipment to stand in front of him. Cripes, even her bare feet were adorable with her French-tipped toenails and hot-pink flower design painted onto each big toe. "You pulled a hamstring."

He pulled something all right, but it sure as hell wasn't a hami. Thank God he'd decided to put a T-shirt on. He usually worked out without one, and would have had a pisser of a time covering the bulge in his sweats.

She knelt between his legs and pulled each calf closer to her. It was surreal, watching her touch his flesh and yet not really feeling it. Little by little, his sensation was coming back. For the most part, his legs were numb from the knee down. The left was worse than the right. It was hell on his balance, making walking damn near impossible without crutches and severely limiting his distance. For a guy who was used to running ten miles a day it was fucking hell.

Katie's delicate hands were clutching his calves. There was such a disconnect to the lower third of his body, it was like watching her touch another man, which was decidedly unsettling for a number of reasons he'd rather not explore.

"You have to be careful," she scolded, completely oblivious to the tension coiling in his groin. "You can't push yourself like this or you could do damage that will set us back even further."

He didn't say anything as she carried on. Rather, he watched her, waiting for her to finish her speech as he debated whether or not to tell her she had face cream smeared across her nose. She glanced up at him, and she must have noticed the amused smirk he was trying to hold back, because she suddenly stopped lecturing him and braced her hands on her hips. "What? Do you think straining a hamstring is funny?"

Cole liked her like this—in her element, all fired up and sassy. What he'd seen before, those frightened, timid reactions, he'd be willing to bet were a result of something that had happened to her—from childhood, or perhaps a bad relationship? He couldn't know, but it surprised him to discover he wanted to find out. Who had hurt her so badly?

Unable to help himself, he reached up and brushed his thumb across the tip of her pixie nose. She instantly jerked back, her beautiful emerald eyes wide with alarm. "You have face cream on your nose," he explained, holding up his thumb as proof and then rubbing it between his fingers.

"Oh," she murmured, swiping her palm across her nose, making sure it was gone.

"You don't have to worry," he said, purposefully ignoring her startled reaction. "I didn't pull any muscles. I could stretch further than this if my back wasn't so tight. I know my body's limits."

She looked surprised and not entirely certain of his claim. "Well," she said, rising to her feet, "if it's all the same to you, I'd appreciated it if you'd take it easy tonight. Tomorrow I'll do a thorough assessment of your baseline and I'll test your range of motion. We'll set up a therapy plan from there."

"Fair enough." Cole had no intention of copping out on his training routine, if that was what she was asking, but she didn't need to know that. "Was there anything else?" he asked when she made no attempt to leave and just stood there, standing between his legs, staring at him.

"What? Oh, no. I uhh . . . I'm going to bed."

So then why was she still standing there? *Awkward . . .*

"All right, then. Good night, Katie."

"Good night, Cole." She turned and started to walk away, then stopped halfway to the door. "We'll get started early in the morning—before I leave for work."

"Sounds good, but fair warning: I told you I'm not a morning person."

Not a morning person was an understatement. Despite several summons, seven o'clock came and went with no sign of Cole. When he still wasn't up by the time Katie finished her coffee, she went to his bedroom and rapped her knuckles against the door. "Cole, it's seven thirty. Time to get up."

When she got no answer, she waited another five minutes. By then, the limit of her patience was exhausted, and when she knocked for a third time, she was royally pissed off. How rude! She told him she only had a specific window of time this morning. If he thought he was going to dictate her schedule and be so flippant with her precious little free time, then this guy had another thing coming. Maybe in Vegas he was the Golden Boy, catered to and coddled by her uncle, but she had news for him. He was in Wisconsin now, and some people actually had to punch a clock for a living.

Without further consideration for what a horrible idea it might be, Katie threw open his bedroom door and her breath immediately stalled in her lungs. Cole was sprawled across the bed—prone, thank God—without a single stitch of clothing on. The covers were tangled around his legs, his bronze flesh starkly contrasting the white sheets. It was as if the heavens had opened up and dropped this Greek god into her bed—*his* bed, she corrected herself. Katie was no stranger to seeing muscular, well-formed men, but the sight of Cole's body sent a rush of tingling heat coursing through her, stirring an awareness deep inside her she'd been certain was long dead and buried.

Her pulse kicked into her throat as she stood there, taking in the view. Cole's arms were stretched up over his head, hugging the pillow he slept on. The position flared his lats. His broad shoulders were definably muscled, his sculpted back tapered to a narrowed waist and trim hips. His ass was nothing short of perfection—rounded muscle that dimpled in the cheek, proving there wasn't a spare ounce of fat on this fighter's body.

His legs were thick and long. She'd known Cole was tall, but in the queen-size bed, he looked huge. His feet hung off the end, as did most of his blankets. Sweeping her gaze back up his body—and by body, she meant his ass—Katie noticed a dark pink scar three, maybe four, inches long at the base of his spine.

Seeing the evidence of why this man was here helped yank her back to reality and the impropriety of her standing in his doorway gawking at his naked body like some desperate groupie. Because, yeah, if she was honest with herself, she'd been secretly wishing Cole was a back sleeper. Hell . . . she was no better than those women last night, except she would never have shared him with a friend.

Faced with the discomforting truth that she was a hypocritical voyeur, Katie marched over to the bed and yanked his blankets off the floor. It took sheer willpower to cover his deliciously tempting body. She'd thought herself immune to men, and that this one was getting under her skin, waking places she'd rather keep dormant, pissed her off all over again.

"Cole! It's almost eight o'clock. Wake up!"

When she got no response, she grabbed the pillow his arms weren't wrapped around—annoyed to admit she'd never been more envious of down, but that was okay, because it gave her even more fuel for the windup as she smacked Cole in the back of the head with it. "I said get up!"

He flinched and uttered a groan into the downy fluff that sounded more like a growl, but she didn't heed the warning and wound up to smack him again. Only this time, his arm shot out at the last second and he ripped the pillow out of her hands, pulling it down on top of his head as he sandwiched himself between the two cushions.

Unbelievable . . . He moved so fast, she didn't even have a chance to react. "How did you do that?" she demanded.

"Do what?" came the muffled reply from between the pillows.

His sleep-roughened voice was so damn sexy, she swore she could feel it vibrating into her toes. *Focus, Katie!*

"Catch that pillow without even looking. It's like you knew it was coming."

"Yeah, well, you get punched in the skull enough times, and after a while you start to grow eyes on the back your head."

She wasn't sure what to say to that. But now that he was awake, it was about time they got down to business. "It's almost eight o'clock, so if you want me to do your assessment, you're going to have to come to work with me. I can fit you in between the appointments I have this afternoon, and you can use the gym while you wait. Otherwise, you'll be stuck here until I get back tonight. I still need to stop at my dad's this morning before my nine-thirty appointment, so if you're coming, be ready to leave in the next thirty minutes."

Cole lifted the top pillow from his head, rolled onto his back, and stretched. It was a lazy catlike sprawl that showed off every cut of muscle, every dip of flesh. Katie's mouth went ash dry. Cole had a body made for two things—fighting and sex—and she had no doubt he was a champion of both.

"What's the matter with your dad?" he asked, lacing his hands behind his head as if he had all the time in the world to lie there, half naked, and shoot the shit with her. Obviously, he was completely comfortably in his bare skin. Then again, with a body like this, who wouldn't be?

If she hadn't dragged those covers past his hips before waking him, would he still have turned over? He certainly made no effort to pull them any higher now. The white sheet was draped so low on his waist, she could see the bands of corded muscle, cutting divots at his hips, guiding—tempting—her gaze to travel lower and totally debunking her theory about why he'd refused that woman's sex-fest offer last night.

Holy hell, there was nothing wrong with this man's phallus. Clearly, it was in well-working order. The thin white sheet was nearly sheer against his tanned skin. The shadows in the room were the only things obscuring her view of his impressive display of morning wood. Her cheeks heated with embarrassment, her jaw dropping in shock. She tried to speak, but nothing came out.

Her gaze shot up to his. Perhaps he hadn't noticed her staring. Sleep darkened his eyes to shiny sapphires, or maybe it was something else—something more carnal. The faintest hint of scruff shadowed his jaw. For crissake, the guy even woke up sexy as hell and ready to go. How was that even possible? His brain clearly failed to recognize he had a disability—which was good for him, because she couldn't imagine a man like Cole being stripped of his sexuality.

Not that she wanted to partake in it, she reminded herself. She was here to help him, not fall victim to his charms. To give a man like this access to her body would be to hand over all her control. Never again would she be helpless or allow herself to become another man's property—his prey. Appreciating masculine beauty was not the same as wanting it to touch you. She'd learned the hard way that men like Cole were a ball of fire, and the old adage was true, if you played with fire, eventually you'd get burned—and she had the scars to prove it.

"He had a stroke a few months ago," Katie finally replied once her brain and mouth finally reconnected.

"I'm sorry to hear that."

"Can we . . . umm"—she cleared her throat—"not do this in here? I think if you and I are going to be living together for the next couple of months, we need to set some ground rules and establish a few . . . boundaries."

At her suggestion, his dark brow arched in question, his top lip tugging into a smug grin that did funny things to her stomach. "Why are you looking at me like that?" she snapped.

He broke into a full-on smile and damn if that wasn't a panty dropper. Was that . . . a dimple in his right cheek? Seriously, this wasn't even fair.

"You're standing in *my* bedroom—uninvited—lecturing *me* about how we should be respecting one another's privacy? Kind of ironic, don't you think?"

If her cheeks burned any hotter, her face was going to melt right off.

"I should probably warn you, if you're going to insist on invading my privacy like this, I sleep naked."

Katie opened her mouth to respond, but nothing came out. Dammit . . . Cole's ability to render her speechless was infuriating. Exhaling an exasperated huff, she spun around and marched toward the door, never feeling more humiliated than when his gloating chuckle followed her out.

"Hey, Katie . . ." he called after her.

The sound of her name on his low, husky voice sent an unwelcome shiver of desire rippling through her body with the finesse of a tsunami. Her feet halted at his call before she was aware they'd stopped. "What?" she snapped, refusing to allow herself to turn around and indulge in that visual feast for one more second.

"Will you close the door behind you?"

CHAPTER

 6

Holy shit, that woman was gorgeous when she was mad—well, she was gorgeous anyway, but when the fire of ire burned in her verdant eyes . . . she heated his blood like nobody's business. Cole would be willing to bet that rendering her speechless was a coup not many men had counted, and she was damn lucky those covers hadn't fallen any lower than they had or she'd have gotten one hell of a surprise when she'd busted in and so rudely awoken him.

He chuckled at the thought—would have served her right, presumptuous little thing, standing there, lecturing *him* about boundaries. He normally didn't sleep late, but he hadn't slept for shit and he was still on Vegas time. Did she realize it was only quarter to six by his internal clock? Probably not. Damn, it felt like he'd just closed his eyes and a moment later, Katie was smacking him with the pillow. Last night's workout had felt amazing, but it hadn't run him into total exhaustion like he'd hoped. Every time he closed his eyes, a certain fair-haired, green-eyed female had been there to haunt him. This was crazy. He hadn't known Katie for more than a day and already she was getting under his skin.

"Twenty-five minutes, Easton!"

Gol-damn, she reminded him of Marcus when she talked like that, which effectively killed his cock. Too bad she'd didn't look more like the old bastard.

"I'm up," he growled, forcing himself vertical and snagging the clothes he'd piled on the night chair before. He quickly dressed, making a note-to-self to have her hook him up with some crutches today. Being confined to this chair all the time was annoying as hell.

Twenty minutes later and with five to spare, he entered the kitchen to find the dower woman scowling into her cup of coffee. She looked as if the weight of the world rested on her shoulders, and he couldn't help but wonder what burdens she carried that made her appear so bleak at times. Something inside him stirred at the sight of her, but he quickly dismissed the concern as misplaced gratitude.

He was generously compensating Ms. Miller for any inconvenience or disruption his presence caused her. He'd be damned if he was going to feel bad about making her a minute or two late. "Ready?" he asked, grabbing a PR Bar off the counter and shoving it into his coat pocket. He poured a cup of coffee into a to-go cup and turned around to find her watching him.

The expression on her stoic face was unreadable, and maybe that was a good thing, because she was probably still pissed about that whole bedroom thing. He grabbed a banana from the fruit bowl in the center of the table as he made his way to the door. "If you don't hurry up, you're going to be late," he called over his shoulder as his wheels hit the ramp. By the time Katie got to the car, he was already inside, ready to go, and waiting for her.

"How long have you lived in Somerset?" Cole asked as they drove through the middle of town. He was pretty sure if he blinked, he'd miss the entire thing. It wasn't too difficult to orient himself, except everything basically looked the same under this blanket of snow.

"I don't live here."

The briskness in her voice caught his attention.

"Well, not anymore, anyway. I grew up in Somerset."

"Where do you live?" He glanced at her before turning his attention back out the passenger window. Was that actually a full-service gas station? He wasn't aware they still had those. Hell of an idea, though, considering it was negative ten right now and there probably weren't a lot of people excited about standing outside to pump their gas.

"Nowhere right now. I guess you could say I'm in between places. When I left Somerset, I swore I'd never move back." Her bark of half-hearted laughter held no humor. "But then, never say never, right? I hadn't counted on my dad having a stroke, so I guess you could say I'm in the middle of an extended visit right now."

"I see . . ." But he really didn't. Cole had the feeling there was more to Katie's situation than she was telling him. Curiosity and boredom made him prompt, "Where were you living before you came home to"—air quotes—"visit?"

"Baltimore."

"Maryland? That's far from home. What's in Baltimore?"

"The John Hopkins Spine Center."

"Your uncle said you work for the Packers."

The slight stiffening in her spine was nearly imperceptible, but the tension in her voice was not. "Worked," she clarified.

"What happened?"

"It's a long story. I'd rather not discuss it."

"Must be an interesting one to make you want to walk away from a job like that. They're not easy to come by."

"There's more to life than money, Cole. It doesn't buy happiness."

He swung his head around to look at her just as she pulled into the driveway of a modified two-story home. "No, you're right, it doesn't. But it sure as hell makes life easier. Take it from someone who's lived on both sides of that coin. And don't tell me you'd still be doing this for me if I wasn't paying you a shit-ton of money."

Katie looked at him, her frown pulling her arched brows tight, making her look more quizzical than irritated. "What money? I never asked for any money from you."

Then where in the hell did that thirty grand go? "Marcus didn't wire you thirty thousand dollars?"

"No, and I wouldn't take it even if he tried. That's a lot of money, Cole, and that's not why I'm helping you."

She put the SUV into park and cut the engine. When she turned to open the door, he caught her arm, stopping her. She instantly froze, turning to stone beneath his grasp. "Then why *are* you doing this, Katie?"

Her full lips thinned as she pressed them together, lines of displeasure bracketing her mouth as her frown deepened. He didn't understand why she'd look offended. It was a reasonable question. If life had taught him anything, it was that no one did something for nothing—everything had a price tag. It might not be paid in green, but there was always a cost. And if Katie's fee wasn't monetary, then what in the hell did she want from him?

"I'm doing this for you because you need my help, Cole. Because you didn't deserve what happened to you, and my uncle believes I can get you back in that cage again."

It sounded good—too good, actually—which naturally made him suspicious. How altruistic and genuine, but Cole knew there was more to it than that, and he'd be damned if he was going to be indebted to someone. "That still doesn't explain why you didn't take the thirty grand Marcus was supposed to pay you."

Katie glanced at the clock on the dash and then up to the house before exhaling a frustrated sigh. He knew she was in a hurry and was banking on that to aid him in breaking down her resistance.

"I owe Uncle Marcus a lot. If it wasn't for him . . ." Her voice trailed off, and she grimaced as if assaulted by a barrage of bad memories. "Listen, my reasons for helping you are my own, okay? I don't want to discuss them, nor do I owe you any explanations. Just be glad I'm helping you and leave it at that, all right? And I'll make you a deal. You don't ask me about my past, and I won't ask you about yours, all right?"

It was a deal he knew he should take, because if there was anyone who didn't want someone digging into his past, it was him. But there was something about Katie Miller that sparked Cole's interest in a way no other woman ever had. She had depth and complexity—a paradox of contradictions. It seemed as if her nature was continually at odds with her nurture.

One moment she appeared pensive and untrusting of him, and the next she was this self-assured, confident woman whose eyes sparkled with attraction and desire. For fuck's sake, every place her gaze had touched him as he had lain in bed this morning had felt like a caress, heating his flesh until his skin felt too tight for his body. And when that curiously aroused gaze fell to the covers draped across his waist, lighting on the tented sheet as his erection strained to breach the cover's edge . . . he'd just about lost it, necessitating the cold shower he'd taken this morning to clear his head.

Obviously, he and Katie shared an attraction he could not, would not, act on, but that wasn't the point. Every time he touched her, she recoiled as if she thought he was going to jump her or something. A reaction like that was reflexive, born from painful experience and the need for self-preservation. He'd be lying if he said that didn't bother him—the thought of someone abusing women, especially this woman, stirred his protective instincts. She might not admit it, but with her odd behavior coupled with the refusal to discuss her past, he'd be willing to bet someone had hurt this woman—badly.

When she pulled her arm from his grasp, he let her go. She wasted no time fleeing the SUV. Once outside, she hesitated a moment, looking as if she were debating whether or not to offer him help. Before she could emasculate him more than the chair already did, he snapped briskly, "I've got it." He didn't mean to sound harsh, but this was a sore subject, and he'd be damned if he'd have this woman waiting on him. It took some effort, but using the RAV for leverage, he managed to make his way to the back of the vehicle and unload the chair.

The ramp in her parents' garage made it easy to get into the house. Katie stood at the entrance and held the door open for him, calling, "Hi, I'm here! Sorry I'm late!"

Cole gestured her to step inside and he followed her in. He nearly ran into her when she stepped into the kitchen and abruptly stopped, muttering "shit" under her breath. Her attention was fixed on the table—more specifically, the dozen red roses sitting in the middle of it, with a yellow card from Studio Fleurette poking out of the bouquet that read, *I love you, Katie. Please forgive me.*

Tossing her purse and keys on the counter, she marched over to the table and plucked the flowers from the long-necked vase—card and all. "Ouch!" She cursed, shifting her hold on the roses as she carried them over to the sink and flipped the switch on the wall. The garbage disposal roared to life, gurgling and grinding. It surprised the shit out of him when Katie began shoving the bloodred flowers into the sink, head first. The disposal greedily chewed up the roses, consuming the bunch until there were only spiky stems left.

"Katie!" A woman, presumably Katie's mother, shouted her name as she rushed over to the sink, sounding appalled and looking utterly horrified. "What are you doing? Stop that!" The woman—a dead ringer for Katie, only about twenty years older—reached over her and flicked the switch. As the gurgling came to a growling halt, Cole made a mental note never to buy this woman flowers. When she let go of the stems, they were sticking out of the sink like little green pikes. Her hand was bloody from where the thorns had bitten her.

"What is the matter with you?" the woman scolded, ripping a towel free from the handle on the refrigerator door and then grabbing Katie's wrist to wrap it around her bloody palm.

He could see Katie was trying to hold it together, fighting back tears she refused to let fall, reminding him once again of the contradictions that were Katrina Miller. On one hand she was bold and aggressive, taking her anger out on those poor little flowers, which had surprised the hell out of him. And on the other hand, she reminded him of a desperate, frightened young woman, whose ghosts refused to stop haunting her. She looked so fragile standing there, struggling to keep it together while her mother unwrapped the towel and held her hand over the empty side of the sink while she stared numbly at the crimson drops escaping her fingers.

The impulse to go to her, to pull her into his arms and tell her it was going to be all right, was nearly too strong to resist. If her mother had not been there, it would have been a battle he'd have lost. Cole held himself in check, reminding himself that Katie's problems were just that—her problems. He shouldn't get involved. He couldn't fight her demons for her, not that she'd even let him if he'd wanted to.

"What in the world has gotten into you?" her mother scolded. "How long are you going to let this go on? Maybe if you would just talk to him—"

"No. Mom, I told you before. I'm not talking to him. Stay out of this. Please." A silent pause, then she gasped, "You told him I was here, didn't you?" The note of fear in her voice licked up his spine, setting his protective instincts on edge.

"Of course I didn't tell him. He heard about your father's stroke from Aunt Valerie on Facebook. He was just calling to express his sympathy—"

"No, he wasn't, Mom. He's using you to get to me. He's fishing to find out if I'm here. Don't you find it a bit odd that he's friends with Aunt Valerie on Facebook?"

"Katrina, be reasonable. Maybe if you'd just—"

"Please. Stop. I can't have this conversation again. You don't understand—"

Her mother clutched Katie's hand. "You're right, honey, I don't understand, because you won't talk to me! What could he have possibly done to make you hate him so much? He clearly loves you."

Katie let out a harsh bark of sarcastic laughter. "If that's love, then I'm joining a convent."

Cole was pretty sure Katie had forgotten he was there. Her gaze didn't stray his direction even once—until he began backing out of the kitchen to give her and her mother some privacy. His movement must have caught her attention, and when she looked at him, he felt like he'd been sucker punched in the gut. That this woman had the ability to affect him so strongly sent alarms sounding off in his head so loudly, he barely heard her say, "Oh shit, I'm sorry. Please, Cole, don't leave. I didn't mean for you to see that."

After some insistent tugging and reassurance that she was fine, her mother finally let go of her hand and left to go retrieve a first aid kit.

"You're looking pretty pale. Maybe you should sit down." He wasn't sure what else to say. She nodded numbly and moved toward a chair at the kitchen table, eyeing the vase as if it were the enemy. He approached as she took a seat and reached for her wrist. "Let me see your hand."

She gave him a wary frown and didn't move.

"Come on, let me see it."

Slowly, as if she were reaching out to touch a wild animal, she hesitantly laid the back of her hand in his waiting palm. Damn, he knew she was small, but he didn't realize just how small and delicate until her hand was resting in his. Her fine bones were so fragile and gracefully designed, her skin so soft, it was like holding a porcelain doll in his large calloused mitts.

He swept his thumb over her fingers, opening her hand to get a better look at her palm. Three wounds marred her pale flesh. Two were superficial cuts, but the third was a deeper puncture wound. As gently as possible, he pressed around that spot with his thumbs. "Does it feel like there's anything in it?"

When she didn't answer, he glanced up, searching her blank stare. She wasn't here. Her mind had taken her somewhere else—someplace dark. "Katie, answer me. Is the thorn still in there?"

Her gaze came into focus, connecting with his, and something tightened in his chest. She looked so forlorn, so broken, his grip on her hand instinctively tightened. Absently, his thumb brushed over her wrist, back and forth—gently, comfortingly. Her pulse fluttered beneath his touch. Holy shit, what in the hell had happened to her?

She shook her head and mumbled, "Nothing's in there."

It relieved him to see her color returning, that she was no longer starkly pale. For a moment there, he worried she might pass out. Now her cheeks bore a flushed rosy hue—almost feverish. Lord, she was pretty. The pink glow brightened her lips, and the thought briefly crossed his mind of what that mouth would taste like, feel like, moving against his—against his cock . . .

Whoa, where did that come from? Too far . . . he scolded his inner male, the one controlled by his other head. And he'd be damned if that little buddy didn't begin to rise to the notion. The effect Katie had on him was swift and powerful. He'd never felt anything like it. For crissake, if simply touching her hand could evoke such a reaction from him, he'd hate to see what kissing her would do. The woman had his body responding like some pimple-faced adolescent. It was fucking embarrassing.

He shut down that train of thought with a sound *What the hell are you thinking? Get your mind out of the gutter, asshole!* He turned his focus back to Katie's hand. And that was when Cole realized he was still caressing her wrist. He could feel her pulse hammering a rapid staccato against his thumb. Once again, the sudden urge to pull her into his arms nearly overpowered him—as did the need to find whoever sent her the flowers and break the bastard's neck, just as he'd obviously broken this woman's spirit.

The primal knee-jerk reaction surprised him, as did the protective instinct rising up to take root in his gut. He wasn't the kind of guy that got involved in other people's shit. If he'd learned anything living on the streets of Reno, it was that life was cruel, and people hurt other people. That was just the way it was. So why would he expect things to be any different in this little frozen patch of the world?

"I finally found the first aid kit. Your father had it shoved behind the—" Katie's mother came to an abrupt halt when she blew into the kitchen and found Cole holding Katie's hand. The arched-brow look she shot him was one a mother might give a child who'd just gotten caught with his hand in the cookie jar. Afraid the overly perceptive woman might get the wrong idea, he quickly released Katie's hand and moved back to make room for the woman to sit down.

A polite, somewhat reserved smile graced her lips as she walked over to the table and set the box down. "Hello. I don't believe we've met."

Before he could respond, Katie said, "This is the fighter I told you about, Mom. The one Uncle Marcus asked me to see."

"Cole Easton," he introduced himself, moving forward and extending his hand. "It's nice to meet you, ma'am. You must be Marcus's sister in-law?"

"Carol—and yes, I am." She took his hand and shook it before turning back to Katie and opening the medical kit. "And you must be his . . . ?" She glanced over, as if expecting him to fill in the blank as she pulled supplies out of the kit and set them on the table.

"Marcus is my manager—among other things, I guess."

Katie shot him a curious glance, probably wondering what "other things" could mean. She refrained from asking, no doubt remembering the deal she'd struck with him in the car.

"How long have you been fighting?" Carol asked, popping the lid on a bottle of peroxide and pouring it onto a cotton ball.

"Professionally? Fourteen years."

"How many years total?" Katie asked, glancing between him and her mother.

Carol dabbed the cotton ball on Katie's hand and he winced when she sucked in a sharp breath through clenched teeth. For crissake, this must run in the family, because he'd lost count of how many times Marcus had doused him in that shit when he'd come home with broken, bloody knuckles, or a busted-up face. He wanted to distract her from the burn he was all too familiar with. Problem was, he found himself telling her more about himself than he'd intended.

"Total?—sixteen. I left home when I was fifteen. Back then, I fought to survive." When pity shadowed her beautiful face, he shrugged to say it was no big deal. "I did some unsanctioned fighting for a few years."

"Unsanctioned?" Her brow arched in question. "Ouch!"

Like Cole had done, her mom was making sure there wasn't a thorn buried in that puncture wound.

"Underground fighting," he explained, drawing her attention back to him. "Like fight club stuff."

"Are you serious? That's actually a thing?"

Oh, it was a thing, all right. But that was about all he was going to tell her about it. "You know what the first rule about fight club is, right?" he asked, lowering his voice as if he were about to tell her a carefully guarded secret.

"No. What?" she whispered back, her attention completely fixed on him.

Damn, he loved the way her eyes seemed to swallow him whole. Keeping a straight face, he leaned forward and whispered back, "The first rule of fight club is you do not talk about fight club."

It took her a moment to realize he was teasing her. When she made the connection to the movie the smile that broke across her lovely face sucked all the air from his lungs. Good Lord, she wasn't just beautiful. Katrina Miller was stunning.

"You're teasing me," she accused with mock anger as she tried not to laugh. Carol chuckled as she finished applying the ointment to Katie's hand.

"I am about fight club. I was trying to distract you. Did it work?"

She glanced down at her hand as Carol was putting the first bandage across her palm. "I guess it did. She's nearly finished."

"That's good." He smiled with satisfaction, glad he wasn't baring a part of his painful past for nothing. "But I really did spend two years fighting unsanctioned. That's how I met your uncle. A scout told him about me, and he came to see me fight."

"Unsanctioned? Isn't that illegal?"

"Very. It's MMA at its rawest—no gloves, no holds barred. But when you're starving and need a roof over your head, legal is the least of your concerns. Making it out of the cage alive . . . ? Now, that one ranked up there pretty high. Believe me, the irony isn't lost that after all these years, *now* I'm injured. Then again, if you let your guard down in the pits I was fighting in, you were likely to get shanked, not just kicked in the spine."

"I still can't believe this happened to you," she murmured as her mother finished putting on the last bandage.

"Yeah, well, join the club." He was glad Carol was finished, because this conversation had moved from sore and sensitive to downright painful. He didn't talk about his past—not with any-one—and he sure as hell didn't discuss his injury, not even with Marcus. So why in the hell was he spilling his guts to this woman he barely knew?—besides the desire to distract her, that was? Maybe it was because he suspected her past was just as fucked up as his own, and misery loves company. Perhaps if she knew a little about him, she'd let her guard down enough for him to discover who in the hell was scaring her, and what he had done to evoke such a vio-lent reaction from her.

"There," Carol told her, packing her medical supplies back in the box. "You're all done. Why don't you go see to your father? He's waiting for you in the living room. I'll keep Mr. Easton company while you're busy."

Katie scowled at her mother, who seemed impervious to the emerald-eyed glare. How was it possible to look so damn adorable and yet utterly pissed off at the same time? "That's what I'm afraid of," she grumbled, pushing her chair back.

CHAPTER

Longest damn hour of her life . . .

She should have warned Cole her mother could be a bit . . . blunt . . . and bull-headed . . . and outspoken sometimes. But before she'd thought to mention it, they'd been entering the house and she'd seen those roses—aaaand promptly lost it, behaving like a fricking head case. No doubt, right about now, Cole was wondering what the hell he'd gotten himself into. If he wasn't scared off by her flower massacre, he sure as hell would be after spending an hour with her mother. Clearly, she hadn't thought this one through when she'd suggested he come with her today.

Then again, she'd hardly been able to think, let alone do it rationally, after walking in on him this morning. And it *was* his fault she was running late. If he'd have gotten his naked ass out of bed in the first place, she'd have had plenty of time to do him before leaving. *Do him* . . . She nearly choked on the mental picture her slip-up conjured. What the hell was the matter with her? *His evaluation* . . . Do his evaluation.

After finishing her father's PT a few minutes early, Katie crept down the hall toward the kitchen, taking care to avoid the squeaky floorboard that would alert them she was on the other side of the wall. It was a path she'd taken many a times as a teen, sneaking out of or into the house after breaking curfew. Being an adult and still sneaking about in her childhood home certainly wasn't one of her proudest moments. Then again, since she'd met Cole, she seemed to be having a whole slew of those. What was one more? She knew she shouldn't be eavesdropping on Cole and her mother, but curiosity overruled propriety, and she really wanted to know what they were talking about. By the sound of things, she couldn't have come at a better time.

"Are you married, Mr. Easton?"

"Cole. And no, ma'am, I'm not married."

"Ever been?"

Oh, jeez . . .

He chuckled. "No. I've never married."

"Do you have a girlfriend back home?"

Katie cringed. What was with the third degree? For crying out loud! But even as she stood there in the hall, mentally berating her mother, she found herself holding her breath while she waited rather anxiously to hear his answer.

"No. No girlfriend."

An unexpected surge of joy bloomed inside her—

"My career isn't exactly conducive to healthy relationships."

—followed by a crashing wave of disappointment. Why did she care? She didn't, she decided. Katie wasn't looking for another relationship. The last one nearly killed her, and she vowed she'd never put herself in that kind of a position ever again.

It was just as well, but it stung no less when her mother bluntly said, "So then you *aren't* interested in Katie?"

Cole replied without a second's hesitation. "No, I'm not. That's not why I'm here."

Ouch . . . Hearing more than enough and ready to nip that convo in the bud, Katie took two steps back and planted her foot on the squeaky board. On cue, it protested under her weight with a loud *creeeeak*, and big surprise, their little coffee talk abruptly ended. Pasting on a smile, she stepped into the kitchen to find her mother and Cole sitting at the table. Each had a coffee mug in hand, and he was just finishing an egg sandwich she must have cooked for him. Typical Carol Miller, born and raised one state over, her "Minnesota Nice" style of feed 'em then grill 'em never changed. Not that Cole seemed to mind, with his mouth full of fried egg and toast.

"Ready?" she asked, with falsetto cheer as she walked over to the closet in the mudroom and snagged her coat.

"You're done early," her mother commented innocently, pushing back her chair to rise.

She could feel Cole's gaze tracking her across the room. That she was so blasted aware of him ground salt into her wounded pride. Would it kill him to want her a little bit? Not that she'd ever let things go down that road, but her ego could use the stroking after the battering it'd just taken. He could have at least thought about it for a second—asshole.

"Yeah, well, I have a ten-o'clock appointment and unfortunately we kinda got a late start. So . . ." As she wrestled with her boot, she shot him a *thanks to you* glower and then focused her attention on tucking in her pant leg. She tossed Cole his coat before stepping into the other boot. She lost her balance, hopping around as she tried to zip the leg closed, feeling the heat of his amused gaze on her the whole time. Graceful, she was not, but what-the-hell-ever. It wasn't like she was trying to impress him.

Cole thanked her mother for the breakfast and the conversation, sounding genuinely sincere. Well, wasn't he the polite one. She mumbled a hasty good-bye, promising she'd be back in the morning—on time—and then rushed out the door.

Katie was upset, and it didn't take a rocket scientist to figure out why. As she drove to the hospital in absolute silence, the tension between them seemed to take on a life of its own. "I know why you're upset."

She gave him no response.

"You have no right to be mad if you can't be honest about your feelings."

Katie whipped her head around and daggered him with her emerald glare. "My feelings? I've known you for a whole day, Cole. That's pretty presumptive of you to assume I care either way."

She was right. It had only been a day, yet he'd spent more consecutive hours with her than he had with any other woman in the last year. So yeah, to him it felt like they'd known each other a whole hell of a lot longer than just a day. Then add the Marcus factor to their unique living situation, and they might as well be BFFs. Retrospectively, maybe it wasn't his place to say anything, but he could hardly not when she was so clearly troubled.

"Why don't you just tell your parents the truth?"

Her face scrunched into a confused scowl as if she wasn't quite following the conversation. "What truth?"

So now she was going to be obtuse. He exhaled a frustrated sigh. "That the guy who's sending you those flowers is scaring the shit out of you."

"Oh, that." She turned her attention back to the road and it was a damn good thing, too, because she just about clipped a black cat that had darted out in front to them. Katie hit the brakes and the SUV began fishtailing. A grinding sound echoed from beneath the car, and they began to pull out of the slide as a high-pitched beeping sounded inside the cab.

"What the hell is that?" he asked, grabbing the oh-shit bar beside his head. Katie steered out of the slide and then kept on going as if it hadn't happened. If he could somehow manage to dislodge his heart from his throat, that would be real fucking swell.

"It's my traction control. I suppose you don't have much use for that in Vegas. No snow, huh?"

"No. This is a first for me. Can't say I'm a big fan of it yet. And what's 'Oh, that' supposed to mean?" He wasn't letting her off the hook that easily.

"Who said I was scared?"

"Please . . . I've seen that look in the cage a hundred times, Katie."

"What look?"

She was going to hold on to to this façade right up until the bitter end, wasn't she? "Like you just got punched in the gut and you're about to puke. *That* look," he bluntly said, calling her out. "Your parents have no idea—"

"—and I don't want them to, either," she cut in, stalemating him with a *don't you even think about talking to my mother* glare. "They have enough on their plate right now without worrying about me."

"Should they be?"

"Should they be *what*?" she snapped.

"Worried about you?"

"I'm done talking about this. Now let it go," she said, throwing his words from yesterday right back at him. "I have some time between one and two to start your therapy." She didn't even try to be subtle about changing the subject. "You might want to take something an hour before we start. It's probably going to be painful."

"Like what? I'm not on anything."

She shot him a surprised glance, and considering they just about creamed a cat the last time, he wished she'd keep her eyes on the road. It had snowed overnight. Only an inch, but apparently that was enough to make the roads plenty slick.

"Really? You're not taking anything at all?"

"Katie, I'm a fighter. If I popped a pill every time I was in pain, I'd be a drug addict." As they reached Main Street, Cole turned his attention out the side window, making note of the stores they passed and looking for one in particular.

"Well, you should at least be on Relafen or something. The NSAID will help with the swelling in your spine and you'll regain sensation faster. It'll also help take the edge off the pain. It's not addictive, but it can be a little hard on your kidneys with long-term use, so drink plenty of water when you're on it. When we get to the hospital, I'll see if Dr. Wilcox can work you in and get you a prescription."

There it was, Studio Fleurette. The same place whose name had been stamped on that flower card. They turned onto Church Hill Road and headed south. "I'll see him if you want me to, but I really don't think it's necessary. I'm used to pain."

"You say that now. But just wait until I get my hands on you." If she'd meant that to sound intimidating, it was an epic fail. There was a particular part of his body he wouldn't mind her getting ahold of. And her threat had the damn thing rising up to volunteer as tribute. He shot her an arched-brow glance, wondering if she realized how bad that sounded. She must have, because a blush stained her cheeks.

"I mean, for PT," she clarified with an exaggerated eye roll. "It's painful and I'm going to work you hard."

Oh, for crissake, she was killing him. He bit his tongue to hold back the slew of inappropriate comments running through his mind.

"I mean, the physical therapy is strenuous."

"You can stop now," he said, holding up his hand. His poor cock was thoroughly hard and aching. "I get the gist. You're only making it worse." Damn, he couldn't remember the last time he actually looked forward to a PT session.

Fuck! This hurt!

"You doing okay?"

"Uh-huh . . ." His back was on holy fire, and the pain shooting down his legs was nothing short of excruciating.

"You were right. You do have amazing flexibility. I was wondering if you'd be getting contracted in the months since your surgery, but I'm not feeling any of that. Your hips are nice and loose." Katie bent his knee and brought it toward his chest, using her weight to lean into his stretch. "The first time is always the worst. I need to find your limits so I know how hard to push you. After we finish your range of motion, you can rest while I test sensation and motor, then we'll finish with strength. I'll tailor a therapy plan for you after that. I'm thinking twice-a-day sessions. I know it's intense, but I want to maximize your gain. The first nine months after a serious injury are critical. You think you can handle it?"

"I can handle it," he gritted out between clenched teeth, wondering if that wasn't a big fucking lie. But he'd do whatever it took to get back in that cage again—the sooner the better. So if that meant he'd have to gut out some painful sessions with the world's hottest slave driver, then so be it. He was thankful the pain was so intense, because that was the only thing keeping a leash on his cock right now. Having Katie this close to him, touching him, was pure torture. Her lavender scent infused his senses, a blessed distraction from the torturous grind she was putting him through.

Seeing Katie in her element—strong, confident, and in control—was hot as hell. She stoked the alpha in him that wanted more than anything to pull some serious jujitsu on her and take this woman to the mat. Just the thought of trapping her petite five-four, hundred-twenty-pound body beneath his six-four, two-hundred-pound frame heated the blood in his veins until his body was coated in a light sheen of sweat. A tortured groan escaped his throat.

"We're almost done," she encouraged, mistaking his source of pain and coaxing him to hold on a minute longer. Hell, if he caught another whiff of the light floral scent, or if her breasts brushed his thigh one more time, they'd both be done. He swore to the Almighty he'd be pulling full guard on her so damn fast . . .

Cole fixed his gaze on the water-stained ceiling tiles, counting each of them to the cadence of Katie's soft, melodic voice—anything to get his mind off the feeling of her hands on his thigh and the fire in his spine.

"How did your appointment with Dr. Wilcox go?"

She straightened out his leg and tucked his knee against her ribs. The side of her breast fit perfectly against the indent near his patella as she wrapped her arm around his thigh and leaned back, stretching another set of muscles.

"Fine," he ground out between gritted teeth.

"Did you take the Relafen?"

"Not yet. I couldn't get the script filled. The pharmacy wasn't open."

Her face pinched into a concerned scowl and she took the pressure off the stretch. "Cole, you should have said something. This has got to be killing you."

She was killing him. Being this close to her, cocooned in her scent while her hands were all over his body . . . Holy hell, he couldn't remember the last time he'd wanted a woman more. And the fact that Katie was hands-off certainly didn't make him want her any less. Human nature sure was a pisser sometimes—always making us want what we can't have the most.

"I'm good," he grunted, turning his attention back to the ceiling tiles as she folded his left leg into a butterfly stretch. They were in the lower level of the hospital, down the hall from radiology. PT shared a gym with cardiac rehab. It was a large, well-equipped space, but not very private. Fortunately, there hadn't been any afternoon rehabs scheduled, so they had the place to themselves. He didn't relish the idea of doing this with an audience.

Twenty-seven, twenty-eight, twenty-nine . . . Fuck. "Katie, stop." He pulled her hand off his upper thigh, but damn if he couldn't seem to make himself let her go. Her wrist was so small, so fragile in his strong grip. Instead of pushing her a step back, like he'd intended, he pulled her closer. God would surely damn him a liar, because not even four hours ago he'd sat across the table from this woman's mother and told her he wasn't interested in her daughter.

With his other hand, he tugged his T-shirt over his crotch. It was so not cool, getting hard over your PT during therapy. He had to be violating some code of ethics here.

"What's the matter, Cole? Is it too hard?"

Oh, it was hard, all right. Thank God she was too worried about hurting him to notice. "Can we take five?" *And a cold shower?*

"Of course."

She moved to step back, but didn't get very far with him holding onto her. Katie's gaze flickered to his hand and then back to meet his unwavering stare. Uncertainty hedged in her beautiful face; her skittishness reminded him of a cornered hare—frozen in fear and tensed to bolt at any moment. She caught her bottom lip between her teeth, a nervous habit that, no lie, was sexy as hell.

He wanted to kiss her—to pull her into his arms and trap that lush bottom lip between his teeth. He wanted to feel her hammering pulse beating against his tongue as he tasted that spot below her ear, drowning himself in lavender. He wanted to fist his hands into that pale, silky hair and never let go. He wanted *her*—which was a hell of problem, since she wasn't his to have.

But he wasn't going to let that stop him. Despite all the reasons he kept telling himself to keep his hands off her, Cole tugged Katie another step closer and reached up to brush his thumb across that plump bottom lip he thirsted for like a man who'd been lost in the desert. Somehow, overnight, this slip of a woman had become his oasis. His career—his future—hinged on this woman's ability to heal him. But looking into Katie's eyes made him forget his problems. She gave him hope he hadn't felt in months, and damn if that didn't endear her to him.

He brushed his hand over her cheek and slipped his fingers into her hair, cupping the back of her head and drawing her closer. Her lips parted on a surprised gasp, as if she'd just now realized what he was going to do. A moment before their lips connected, Katie pulled her head back and planted her palm in the center of his chest for leverage.

"This isn't a good idea, Cole."

No shit. It was a fucking horrible idea. But he wasn't about to let that stop him. "Don't pretend you don't want this, Kat. I saw the way you were looking at me this morning." The pet name slipped off his tongue like a velvety caress—husky and intimate.

Her brows tightened to a scowl. "And I heard what you said about me this morning," she challenged back.

Now she pulled back in earnest, wresting from his grip. He had no choice but to relent or risk hurting her. Muttering a curse, he dragged his hand through his sweat-dampened hair, leaving it to stand on end. "You heard that?"

"Yeah, I heard that."

So the little minx had been eavesdropping on him. "What the hell was I supposed to say? That you make me so fucking hard I could split granite? I'm sure that would do wonders endearing your mother to me."

Surprise briefly registered on her lovely face, and he could practically hear her unspoken question: *Do I really?* To which he was sorely tempted to answer her by grabbing her wrist and sliding her hand down to his crotch. But before he could act on the impulse, she swiftly shut down all emotion, freezing him out.

Squaring her shoulders, she tartly replied, "There's no need to be vulgar, Cole. And you said it yourself—your lifestyle leaves no room for a relationship. And I certainly don't need mine any more complicated than it already is. You, uhh . . . caught me off guard this morning, that's all, and if I gave you the wrong idea when I was in your bedroom, then I sincerely apologize."

Before he could respond, she turned and headed toward her office. "Why don't you rest a few minutes, shake it off, and I'll grab you some ibuprofen."

Shake it off? What the fuck? That was exactly what Marcus had said to him when he'd taken a misplaced side kick to the nads—and the ache in his balls wasn't any more pleasant this time around.

CHAPTER

8

Katie's hands shook as she struggled to pop the lid off the ibuprofen bottle. This was so not what she'd signed up for when she agreed to help Uncle Marcus get his fighter back on his feet. Despite his disability, Cole radiated vitality and masculine prowess of the likes she'd never seen before—and it was hell on her defenses.

It embarrassed her to discover she'd been so transparent this morning, letting him see the depth of her need, the arousal that had swept upon her with the force of a hurricane, catching her totally off guard when she'd found him naked in that bed. There was absolutely no denying it—Cole was without a doubt the most handsome, well-formed man she'd ever crossed paths with, but being gorgeous didn't change the facts: (a) he was an athlete, (b) she was finished with men, which equaled (c) this was so not happening.

If she didn't draw the line now, it was only going to get worse. Already the sexual tension brewing between them hovered in the air like an impending storm. For the briefest moment in that gym, when Cole had slipped his hand into her hair and pulled her toward him, she'd been oh-so-tempted to just go with it. Her pulse had spiked, anxiety warring with desire and a healthy dose of curiosity to discover what it felt like to be kissed by Cole Easton. No doubt it'd be a heady experience. To be had by a man like this would be an all-consuming, overwhelming possession—a thought that both thrilled and terrified her, especially after everything she'd endured at Carter's cruel hands. She might as well face it—there was a part of her that would forever be broken, and not even this sexy Vegas fighter could make her whole again.

She kept wrestling with the cap until it finally popped loose. She shook her head in frustration. Cole was so out of her league it was ridiculous. As Katie had worked him through the stretching routine, she'd sensed a restlessness churning deep inside him, an undercurrent of power reverberating just beneath his surface. He'd been fighting to contain it—to hold it back, but little by little his resolve was slipping. She didn't have to ask him about his recovery of sensation. It was obvious in his reaction. By the twitching of taut muscles, and the lines of tension bracketing his mouth, she knew exactly where he felt her touching him.

At the time, she'd thought it was a response to pain, because there was no way that it wasn't hurting like hell. But then she'd met his eyes and the cerulean began darkening to slate, reminding her of a late-summer storm rolling in, causing an uncomfortable awareness to stir deep inside her. Her skin had grown flushed and tingly, her nipples hardening to taut peaks as she'd suddenly become aware that her breast was pressed against the crook of his knee and her hands had migrated up his thigh, scant inches from his crotch. Accidentally or subconsciously—she wasn't sure, because there was a part of her that wanted to touch Cole badly—and under the guise of therapy, they were on a different playing field, one that operated by her rules.

"You got that Motrin?"

A startled yelp escaped her throat and she jumped, sending the ibuprofen pills flying into the air. They pattered onto her desk, scattering across her stacks of charts and rolling onto the floor. Her gaze darted up to find Cole hovering in the doorway—on crutches! "You can walk?"

"I'd hardly call it that," he scoffed, leaning heavily on the aluminum braces propped beneath his arms.

"What do you mean? It's a great start," she chided, shaking a few remaining pills into her palm. "Why didn't you tell me you were walking?"

He shrugged. "You didn't ask. I thought you knew."

Realizing her mistake, Katie's cheeks heated with embarrassment. She hadn't asked, had she? She'd just assumed, since he'd been in the chair, that he couldn't walk. Of course he'd need the chair to travel. It was a stupid mistake, and one that as a professional PT she should never have made. Then again, Marcus hadn't told her Cole could walk, either. An important piece of information he'd left out. But why? He'd led her to believe Cole was much less advanced in his recovery than he obviously was. Had he done it to play on her sympathy? Had he known she would have refused him otherwise? No doubt, the bugger!

Uncle Marcus was the only person who had any idea what she'd been through, hence her subsequent aversion to men. She'd done her damn best to tell him as little as possible. But he was a smart man, and he had put it together easily enough when she'd called him from a bus stop in Michigan with nothing more than the clothes on her back, asking him to wire her money. Carter had taken control of all their accounts; her income had been tied up with his—another mistake she berated herself for making. Along with her dignity, he'd stripped her of her financial independence, making it that much harder to get away.

She and Uncle Marcus had always been close growing up. It'd broken her heart when the man who'd taught her to swim, ice fish, and hunt had moved to Vegas when she was twelve. Hell, he'd even given her her first beer (which her parents still didn't know about). At discovering she was in trouble, he'd wired her fifty grand—way more money than she'd asked for—with no questions. And in doing so, Uncle Marcus had saved her life.

It'd taken months before she could sleep through the night. The nightmares still came, but not as often as they used to. She still couldn't go out in public without constantly looking over her shoulder. She'd cut herself out of the social network, severed all contact with friends and family—except her parents and uncle. She'd finally achieved a glimmer of hope that she could have a fresh start and put the past behind her, when disaster struck.

Her father had suffered a massive stroke, and the doctors couldn't be certain he'd survive. By the grace of God he lived, but with a profound right-side deficit that would take months of intense rehab to correct, if at all. She'd had no choice but to return home. When Marcus had discovered she was coming back to Wisconsin to help her dad, he'd expressed concern about Carter finding her again. A fear she silently shared, but it was a risk she had to take. Her dad needed her.

But now, standing here, staring up at the champion MMA fighter filling her doorway, something clicked into place, and Katie couldn't help but wonder if there wasn't another reason her Uncle Marcus hadn't called in his favor and sent this imposing man to live with her. She wouldn't put it past him. Katie wasn't entirely sure how she felt about her uncle's meddling. Did Cole know more about her past than he was letting on? What had Uncle Marcus told him about her?

"You okay? I didn't mean to frighten you."

"I'm fine. I just . . . wasn't expecting to see you—upright, that's all. Where did you get those?" She crossed the room to the water dispenser, pulled a cone cup out of the holder, and filled it for him. "Here," she said, walking over. Cole leaned more heavily on the right crutch and held out his left hand. She dropped the pills into it and he popped the tablets into his mouth before washing them down with the cup of water.

"Thanks." He handed the cup back to her. "The crutches were leaning next to the supply closet. I left mine back home. Figured they'd be a pain in the ass to travel with, especially on the plane."

They would have been. It made sense he'd leave them behind. "Well, these are definitely not the right size for you." She gave him a quick head-to-toe. Even hunched with these ill-fitting crutches, Cole was an impressively large man. "How tall are you?"

"Six-four."

A whole foot taller than she was. At five-four Katie was used to guys towering over her, but Cole was huge. Carter hadn't even been this big. "I'm not sure I have a pair that tall. I might have to order them in. Let's go check." He stepped aside to let her pass, and she gestured him forward. "You go ahead. It'll give me a chance to assess your gait."

He cocked his brow and gave her a crooked grin that made her pulse quicken. "I don't know," he said, skeptically crutching into the hall. "I think you're just looking for an excuse to check out my ass."

An unexpected bubble of laughter burst from her throat and she quickly slapped her hand over her mouth to cut it off. When his own deep, throaty chuckle filled the hall, she couldn't resist joining in. How long had it been since she'd truly laughed? So long she couldn't remember. How sad was that? "You caught me," she confessed, rolling her eyes. What he didn't know is that she'd already checked out that ass—bare—this morning, and since then she'd had a difficult time thinking of much else.

As she followed him into the gym, she tried to keep her mind work-focused—watching the steadiness of his gait, the fluidity of his movements, and the weight distribution of his steps. But time and again her gaze kept straying to the white CFA lettering printed across the ass of his red nylon gym shorts.

He moved surprisingly well, especially for having poorly sized crutches. His steps were a bit slower, more purposeful, but that was to be expected. "How long have you been walking?"

"A month."

"Are you having any numbness?"

"Some. It's hell on my balance."

She could see it. He was having more trouble lifting his left leg than his right. But still, he compensated well enough. His progress truly was amazing. With the right therapy plan and diligent rehab, Katie was sure she could get him back into fighting condition.

"That may still pass with time," she encouraged. "We'll get your prescription filled on the way home. I really think the Relafen will help. I don't want you doing therapy anymore without having taken something for pain."

Cole chuckled and cast her a backward glance as they entered the gym. "You know what your uncle would tell me if he heard you say that?"

Katie rolled her eyes, but couldn't help smiling. "I can only imagine." Then, unable to resist, she asked, "What *would* my uncle say?"

"He'd tell me to leave my vagina at the door and get my ass in there and train."

Another burst of laughter bubbled up inside her. Wow, who would have guessed the grumpy, hard-as-nails fighter had a sense of humor? It felt good to laugh, and despite the undercurrent of sexual tension passing between them, she was finding she rather enjoyed Cole's company. Perhaps it was his connection to Uncle Marcus, but she felt surprisingly comfortable with him considering the short amount of time they'd known each other. Sure, she had her anxious moments, but that was nothing new. "What an inappropriate and totally Uncle Marcus thing to say."

"Oh, believe me, he's said worse."

"I'm sure he has," she said, still laughing at the imagery of her uncle busting Cole's balls.

She followed him into the gym, and they weaved around equipment as they made their way toward the ortho closet in the back.

"What's that?" he asked, nodding toward the elliptical and harness as they passed by.

"It's for walking therapy. We'll use it to strengthen and retrain the muscles in your legs. The sooner we can get started, the greater your chance of regaining full function again."

When he stopped abruptly and pivoted, she almost ran into him. "Then what are we waiting for? Let me on this thing."

Katie laughed. "Well, one day isn't going to make a difference. As much as I can appreciate your enthusiasm, I need to finish your testing first." Getting him away from that elliptical was like trying to pry a new toy away from a little kid, and he looked just about as pleased, too. "Okay, Cole, I tell you what. Give me another half hour to finish with you, and then after my four o'clock is done, we'll let you on it and see what you can do."

Her acquiescence earned her a smile that warmed Katie to her core and woke the long-dormant butterflies in her stomach. She turned away and headed for the closet before she melted into a puddle on the floor, grumbling, "Do women ever deny you anything?"

She wasn't sure he'd heard her, but then he replied, "That depends on if you've changed your mind about that kiss."

CHAPTER 9

"It's beyond me how Margaret ever found anything in this closet."

"Who's Margaret?"

"The woman who retired just as I was getting hired."

Cole stood in the closet entrance, leaning against the jamb, silently thanking Margaret for her disorganization. Katie had spent the last five minutes bent over a pile of ortho equipment, searching for a pair of crutches that would fit him. The lacy imprint on her cheeky panties showed through her thin cotton scrub pants. He bit back his amused grin as he unabashedly enjoyed the view. He'd never thought himself an ass man, but Katie was making him a convert. Holy hell . . .

"I keep meaning to get this closet cleaned out and reorganized, but I haven't found the time," she continued to grouch, clearly irritated at not finding what she was looking for.

"There's a pair over there." He pointed to the crutches in the corner, half buried beneath a stack of knee braces. The path to them was blocked; she'd have to reach for them. *Oh, darn . . .*

Katie braced her knee on a box and kept one foot planted on the floor as she stretched her arm forward. The hem of her scrub top rode up, flashing him a glimpse of her lower back. A sculptor couldn't have shaped a more beautiful woman. The way her narrow waist curved to the gentle flare of her hips . . . His pulse spiked with a familiar stirring of lust. The beat of his heart seemed to be centered in his groin.

He felt like a bit of a lecher, standing there, gawking at this woman's ass and getting hard as granite over the view. But the twinge of guilt wasn't enough to spur his conscience into looking away. "Is that a tattoo?" he asked, catching a glimpse of ink on her low back peeking out from the waistband of her scrubs.

Katie gasped in surprise and immediately slapped her hand over her back, fingers splayed over the rounded curve of her ass. The sharp crack of palm against flesh reverberated straight into the base of his cock, sending a deep groan of masculine appreciation rumbling in his throat.

"Cole Easton! Are you standing there staring at my ass?"

The corner of his top lip tugged up in a guilty boyish grin.

She tugged the hem of her shirt down and removed her hand long enough to snag the crutches. Scrambling back over the boxes, she turned around to face him. He chuckled at her mock affront, not believing for a second she was actually mad at him. She didn't strike him as that touchy. Unable to resist teasing her, he arched a brow. "Let me see it."

"What? No. I'm not showing you my ass."

"Not that." Though he certainly wouldn't have any objection if she was so inclined. "The tramp stamp. Let me see it."

"No." Pretending to ignore him, she focused her attention on the crutches in her hand, located the height range, and then began ripping the cellophane off the pair.

"Come on," he goaded, watching her as she leaned a crutch against a stack of boxes and turned the other upside down. "Now I'm curious."

"Well, don't be," she grumbled, pushing in two buttons and extending the crutch length as far as it would go. "I did it a long time ago, when I was young and dumb."

He chuckled and took the crutch she handed to him, propping it under his arm to test the height—much better. "So what, now you're old and wise?"

"Yes, I am," she answered matter-of-factly. "Wise enough to see through your charming tricks."

"Ouch!" he laughed, splaying his hand over his heart. "Cynicism doesn't become you. Come on, Katie, let me see your tat, you wild rebel." Taking the other crutch, he adjusted his stance, filling the doorway.

He knew he had her when she cracked a grin as she took the other pair of crutches from him and turned away before he could totally see her full-on smile that did funny things to his chest and other more lurid places. She hung the crutches on an empty hook, probably the only thing in this storage closet properly in its place.

"You really want to see it?"

"Yes, I do. I'll make you a deal. You show me yours, and I'll show you mine."

Her delicately arched brow rose in question at his flirtatious remark. "Ha, you're a dirty liar," she teased back with mock offense. "You don't have any tattoos."

The moment the words left her tongue, her mouth snapped shut, and a guilty crimson blush stole across crossing her face. Folding his arms over his chest, he cocked his brow and smirked triumphantly. "Oh, really? You seem awfully sure of that fact. I'm curious to discover how you'd know." He really shouldn't give her such a hard time, but damn, teasing her was fun.

Rather than answer him with what he suspected was the truth—she'd seen a hell of a lot more of him this morning than he'd realized—Katie exhaled an exasperated sigh, muttering "Fine . . ." as she spun around. Presenting him with her back, she hiked up her scrub top, bent forward, and hooked the drawstring waistband with her thumb, tugging her pants down to reveal not only her tattoo, but the top of her delectable ass crack.

The air froze in Cole's lungs at the sight of her creamy flesh, starkly off-setting the black ink centered low on her back. He hadn't been expecting her to flash him that much skin, but in her haste, she'd overshot the bare necessitates, displaying the top curves of a bottom he would very much have liked to see more of. With a great deal of effort, he dragged his gaze back to her tattoo. The design looked tribal, with symmetrical curves and flourishes intersecting and twisting. As he looked at it, a picture began to take shape in the design. It was a pair of wings, he realized, with the words *Alis volat propriis* written above it.

"What does it say?"

"'She flies with her own wings.' I got it after graduation, right before I started college. Like I said, I was young and dumb."

"Why do you say that? I think it's an inspiring and courageous message."

Katie laughed, but the sound held no humor, only bitterness and resentment, though he sensed her scorn was not directed at him. She straightened and tugged her scrubs back into place. "Perhaps. If it were true. But then what did I know about the harsh realities of life? When you're eighteen you think you can tackle the world."

She clicked off the closet light and moved to slip past him, but he caught hold of her arm, stopping her. "Being courageous doesn't mean you win every battle, Katie. It just means you never give up." Whether she was more surprised by his words or his touch, he couldn't be certain. She looked comfortable with neither. "You're still here. That's what matters, right?"

Yeah, he should probably let her go now, but damn if he couldn't seem to make his fingers uncurl from her bicep. He liked Katie—more than he ought to, probably. It wasn't just her beauty that attracted him. She had depth, and substance. And she was the first woman he'd been around in . . . who in the hell knew how long, who wasn't throwing herself at him.

"Spoken like a true fighter," she conceded.

He released her and reached up to cup her cheek. Damn, her skin was soft . . . like the delicate petals of a flower. She tensed but, to his surprise, did not pull back, though he sensed a part of her was telling her to do just that. "Not just a fighter. A survivor," he corrected. "Just like you, I suspect. We all have our battle scars, Katie. Some are just more visible than others."

She nodded, his words seeming to resonate with her. Katie broke his gaze to seek the safety of the floor. God help him, he wanted to kiss her. There was something about Katrina Miller that provoked his protective instincts. She just looked so damn fragile, so utterly beautiful . . . His thumb brushed across her cheek, dangerously close to that bottom lip he desperately wanted to taste. The urge to pull her into his arms was a wicked temptation nearly too strong to deny—and he might have caved to the desire had a deep male voice not filled the gym.

"Hey, Katie . . ."

She startled, her eyes briefly locking on his, her cheeks flushing hotly. Had she been hoping he'd kiss her? Despite her earlier refusal, the look in her eyes told him she might have been contemplating changing her mind—until they'd been so rudely interrupted, that is. Cole made no attempt to let her pass. If she wanted out of this closet, she'd have to squeeze past him to do it.

"Hey, Katie Bug, you in here?"

Cole's brow arched in question. *Katie Bug?* Who in hell was this guy? The unexpected spark of jealousy caught him off guard. Tamping down the unwelcomed reaction, he donned a shit-eating grin. Before he could give her a hard time about the nickname that conjured mental images of red beetles with little black spots, she hissed under her breath, "Don't you dare start, Cole Easton."

"Hey, I didn't say anything," he smirked, holding up his hands defensively.

"Yeah, well you're thinking it." Then louder, she called out, "Hey, Tom, I'll be there in a minute."

When he didn't move out of her way, she crossed her arms over her chest, drawing his gaze to the wealth of cleavage visible from the V-neck of her scrubs. "Are you going to let me out?" She stared up at him expectantly.

"Do I have a choice?" What would she do if he slipped his hand around her waist right now and kissed her? Would the guy in the next room see them? At the thought, he found himself hoping the answer would be yes, which was ridiculous, because he had no claim on this woman. So why in the hell was he getting all territorial?

"No. You don't. That's my four o'clock. Your time's up."

"Already? Aww . . . Katie Bug, I thought we were just getting started." He flashed her a flirtatious grin that had gotten him laid too many times to count.

Despite her effort to appear otherwise, her blush confirmed she wasn't immune to his charms, after all. "Sorry. You thought wrong. As you can see, I'm in high demand," she quipped glibly, moving forward to squeeze between him and the door frame.

As she slipped by him, his hand shot to her waist, stopping her. She tensed, her gorgeous green eyes widening in surprise as he reached for the hemline of her scrub top that was still flipped up and showing a sliver of bare stomach. He'd be damned if he'd have her walking out there looking like this. When he unfolded the hem and put her top back to rights, his fingers accidently grazed the flesh stretching over her hip, sending a jolt of lust flooding his veins. Raw need gripped him hard. Holy fuck, never in his life had he felt this kind of a reaction to touching a woman—accidentally or deliberately.

Time momentarily stopped, as did the air in his lungs. He froze, unable to pull his hand away, the heat of her flesh scorching his fingertips. Cole's gaze shot to hers. Did she feel it too?—the shift of energy in the air?—the headiness of desire that seemed to suck all the oxygen from this room?

Cole was painfully aware of just how fast his pulse was racing. With every hammering beat, he seemed to grow painfully harder, the pressure in the base of his spine coiling tighter. Lust never felt so good, nor did it hurt this damn bad. He was paying the price of his cock's repeat performance—without a grand finale. If he didn't figure out a way to bring the rebel to heel, he'd be sporting a severe case of blue balls before he knew it.

A startled gasp broke the silence stretching between them. Hell if he knew who it came from—her, him, or the guy that just stepped into his periphery.

"You okay, Katie?"

The protective note in the approaching guy's voice lit the spark of Cole's testosterone-fueled temper. It also effectively shattered the connection between him and Katie. She startled, pulling away from his touch, and damn if letting her go wasn't one of the hardest things he'd ever done. There was no denying it—something was brewing between them, something visceral, and it was about all Cole could do to stand there and watch it slip through his fingers.

She mumbled a hasty "Thank you" for his poorly executed attempt to straighten her clothes, and finished slipping past him. At least she realized what he'd been trying to do. It wasn't until her own hands lifted to check her hem and verify everything was in place that he realized they were shaking.

Was she nervous? Had he scared her? Or was she as over-whelmed by this startling attraction as he was? He would have liked to explore the question more, but with her four o'clock glaring daggers at his back, that obviously wasn't happening.

"I'm fine, Tom. Thanks for your concern. I was just looking for something in the closet. A person could get lost in there if she wasn't careful."

"Good thing you had someone to stand point."

Cole couldn't decide if that sarcasm was for his benefit or hers, but either way, it was not appreciated. He stepped back and turned to face Katie's patient, not even attempting to disguise his irritation.

"Oh, cut it out, Tommy," she scolded, walking up to the guy and playfully cuffing him on the shoulder. "If I needed a guard dog, I'd buy a German shepherd."

Cole sized up the man who smiled down at her, looking a bit sheepish. He stood maybe six-one, was about Cole's weight, but with more bulk than real muscle. As the guy's gaze cut to him, it took about all of two seconds for his overprotective scowl to morph into surprise. "Holy shit! You're Cole Easton!"

"Yeah." He didn't return the guy's smile. Not that he seemed to notice.

"Oh, man, I'm a big fan—big fan! Katie Bug, why didn't you tell me you knew Cole Easton?"

"Oh, I don't know. Maybe a little thing called HIPAA."

He rolled his eyes as if the idea of confidentiality were prepos-terous. Ignoring Katie's playful elbow to his ribs, Tom limped for-ward and stretched out his hand. Obviously, this guy wasn't romantically involved with her or he wouldn't be beaming at him with a starstruck, ear-to-ear grin right now. But they were obviously friends, which meant Cole needed to stuff his inner Neanderthal and mind his manners.

"I've seen all your fights. And whoa, that last one . . . You were amazing!"

Defiantly *not* the words Cole would have used to describe that last fight.

"Man, I hope they kick that fucker De'Grasse out of the league for what he did."

"Hate to break it to you, but that's not going to happen."

"Aww, seriously? That sucks. So what are you doin' here?"

"Same thing as you, I suspect."

"No shit? Our little Katie Bug is going to PT Cole Easton?"

"It's not that big of a deal, Tom. I've rehabbed athletes before. You know that."

"Yeah, but this is Cole freaking Easton! The Beast of the East. He's not just an athlete, he's *the* athlete of MMA."

Damn, he was used to people making a big deal out of him, but this was getting downright embarrassing. Too bad his physical therapist wasn't half as enamored with him as her client.

"Man, you gotta let me buy you a beer. How long you gonna be in town?"

Perhaps a bit delayed, Cole smiled, putting on his media face, the one his sponsors paid him very well to wear. "I guess that depends on how fast Katie Bug here can fix me up." He winked at her. "I gotta tell you, that's an interesting nickname."

"Katie Bug? Aww hell . . . we've called her that since kindergarten, right, kiddo?" Tom slung his beefy arm around her neck and pulled her into a sideways brotherly hug. He half-expected the guy to rub his knuckles on top of her head.

"Let go of me, you big oaf."

She tried to shove him away and Tom laughed. Cole couldn't help chuckling as Katie's face squished into an embarrassed grimace. It was obvious they were old friends, which helped him warm to the guy. "So, you're an MMA fan. Do you fight?"

Tom released his hold on Katie—whose hands immediately began fixing her messed-up ponytail—and shrugged. "I wrestled in high school and dabbled in MMA for the last few years, but nothing competitive. There aren't any good gyms around here that cater to the art, or are interested in turning out a well-rounded fighter."

"I tell you what, you get that knee fixed up, and I'll ditch these gimp sticks, and we'll throw around in the ring a little bit and you can show me what you got before I head back."

"Seriously? Oh, man, that'd be awesome!"

"So you know what that means?" Katie said, giving Tom a motherly scowl. "It means you gotta listen to me and quit stressing that knee."

Tom blushed like a kid whose mom just called him out in front of the cool kid.

Cole chuckled, "Don't worry about it, man. She does the same thing to me."

Katie gasped, propping her fists on her hips and looking wholly offended were it not for that grin she was fighting back.

"I'll let you two get started. She can torture you for a while."

Tom laughed. Katie huffed. Cole winked at her as he turned to leave, pleased to see a rush of color brighten her cheeks.

CHAPTER

10

"So this is the best restaurant in town?" Cole surveyed the bar lining the front right side of the pub, his gaze catching and briefly meeting the eyes of a man sitting at the corner. The guy quickly broke contact and elbowed a man sitting beside him. He leaned over and said something to his buddy. At first, it didn't strike Cole as odd. It wasn't uncommon for someone to recognize him when he was out in public. What did catch his notice though was the guy's friend, whose head snapped around like he'd been fish-hooked and boldly stared—at Katie.

She didn't see him. His sexy little PT was leading the way to a table that had just emptied, which was taking a hell of a lot longer than it should have, because every few steps someone she knew stopped her to say hi and ask her how her father was doing. Growing up in Reno, Cole had zero experience living in a small town, which he suspected was much like living under a microscope. Everyone seemed to know everyone here, and he had no doubt that guy watching her from the bar knew exactly who she was, too—and he wasn't happy to see Cole with her.

He locked gazes with the guy over the top of Katie's head. She was leaning down, her attention focused on the woman she was talking to. Holding his stare, it felt more like a CFA weigh-in, and

Cole gave the guy no quarter, donning the same malicious glare he used to strike fear into the hearts of countless opponents.

It took longer for the guy to look away than he'd expected, and all the while Cole's instincts were clamoring. His pulse quickened to the rush of adrenaline hitting his veins, his muscles growing tight, senses heightening as his body grew restless, hungry for a long-overdue fight. He craved it like the very air he breathed. Cole thought the lack of action must be getting to him, because he would have sworn this guy at the bar wanted to throw down. He saw no recognition in the man's eyes that he knew who Cole was, or the ass whupping he was courting if he kept looking at Katie like that.

It wasn't uncommon for some liquored-up prick who recognized him from TV to act like a big shot in front of his buddies and pick a fight. Somewhere in their alcohol-sodden minds, those assholes thought if they could best a professional fighter, it would prove their badass status with their friends or something. But this was not the case with the man at the corner of the bar. This was personal.

Cole was about two seconds from heading over there with a whole lot of *what the fuck is your problem?* when the guy suddenly broke his stare and turned his attention back to his beer. The woman talking to Katie said, "Give your father our best, dear. Tell him we're praying for him."

"I will. Thank you, Charlotte." Katie shot him an apologetic smile, and they proceeded forward. People were packed into the quaint little bar, and it took some maneuvering to reach their table. Cole decided not to mention the guy at the bar. There was no reason to risk upsetting her. He pulled out a chair for Katie to sit, positioning her with her back to the bar. He took the seat that gave him the clearest view of the guy throwing off all the hostility.

"Thank you," she said, taking her seat and scooting her chair closer to the table.

"No problem. Is it always this busy in here?" The tables lining the right side of the long, narrow building were completely full, as was the bar. There was no way this place wasn't exceeding the fire code limit.

"Uh-huh. That's because it's the best and the oldest place around. See that ceiling?" She pointed up. "That's the original tin. This building is a historic icon." She leaned across the table and gave him a conspiratorial grin that kicked his pulse up a notch. "Some even say it's haunted. People come from all around to eat here."

Cole couldn't resist partaking in her infectious smile. Leaning across the table to meet her halfway, his mouth a few tempting inches from hers, he whispered back, "I don't believe in ghosts."

Her smile grew bigger, amusement dancing in her emerald eyes that sparkled like jewels. "Really? That's interesting. You know it's an interesting fact that 45 percent of the population believes in ghosts. You believe in miracles, don't you?"

Unmindful that he probably shouldn't be touching her in public—or in any other place for that matter—Cole reached up and brushed the back of his knuckles across her cheek. Lord, her skin was soft . . . "I must. I'm believing in you."

At his confession, her lips parted with a surprised gasp. But damn, if it wasn't the God's-honest truth. This beautiful woman sitting across from him was the only thing standing between him and ruin. If she couldn't get him back into fighting condition . . .

"Good evening. Oh, hey, Katie."

The waitress seemed to appear out of nowhere and set two waters down in front of them. Cole dropped his hand, and they settled back in their seats as the waitress handed them each a menu before rattling off the specials and then quickly moving on, promising to be back shortly.

As Cole opened the menu and began to read through the choices, the fine hairs on the back of his neck began to prickle with unease. Casting a quick glance over Katie's shoulder, he locked eyes with the man who seemed to be having a hell of a time keeping his eyes to himself. Cole glanced at Katie, checking to see if she'd noticed the stranger watching her, but she appeared none the wiser. Her face was hidden behind the menu as she chatted away, making recommendations for some of her favorites. She seemed completely at ease, causing him wonder if she wasn't used to being stared at. With a face and a body like that, one would probably grow accustomed to the attention. It made sense she'd learned to tune it out. Which begged the more interesting question: Why the hell did it bother him so much, then?

Cole promptly pushed that conundrum aside, because he was pretty damn sure he wasn't going to like the answer he came up with. Cole read through the menu. When he flipped it over to the back page, he gave Katie an arched-brow look over his laminated list of meal options and asked, "So . . . what exactly is Redneck Juice?"

She busted out laughing—a throaty belly laugh that made something in his chest tighten, his pulse quicken. Her uninhibited amusement rang out like a siren's call, drawing the attention of more than one set of eyes from the bar. If she noticed the men staring at her, she gave no indication. But Cole sure as hell noticed, and the spark of possessiveness lighting up his veins was a wholly unwelcome experience.

"It's a Bloody Mary mix," she explained. "The Sportsman Bar is famous for it. You should try it."

"No thanks. I'm kind of a beer guy."

"You don't like tomato juice?"

"No, I like it just fine. I don't drink hard liquor." *Not in public, anyway.* Been there, done that, and he had the mug shot to prove it. After spending a night in the drunk tank, he vowed he'd never drink to the point of losing control again. Perhaps if he'd learned that valuable lesson a few months earlier, he wouldn't have been arrested for assault and battery.

She nodded, seeming to approve of his self-imposed limits. If she only knew what it'd taken to get him to this point, she wouldn't be looking so proud of him, that was for damn sure.

"Are you ready to order?"

The waitress swept over, pen and paper in hand. She looked a bit frazzled, not that he blamed her. Wanting to keep it simple, he ordered the house special and a dark beer on tap. Katie ordered the same but with a lemon iced tea. The waitress hurried away. Cole watched her approach the bar where he checked the status on the guy in the corner. He wasn't there. Cole tipped his head to the side, trying to see around the woman.

"She's pretty, isn't she."

Oh hell . . . Katie thought he was checking out their waitress. His gaze shot to her, but her expression was completely guarded. "Is she?" he asked blithely. "I didn't notice." And he really hadn't. Katie had him so cranked up, he couldn't even tell her what their waitress looked like if she asked.

She rolled her eyes like she didn't believe him, but before he could press her on it, she jumped subjects. "Listen, I want to thank you for today."

"What for?"

"What you did for Tom. You can't imagine how hard this rehab has been on him."

Cole arched his brow as if to say, *Oh really?*

She promptly realized her error because in the next breath, she rushed to say, "Wow, I'm sorry. That was pretty insensitive. I guess you do, don't you?"

He knew, all right. He knew all too well the physical and emotional torture that went hand in hand with rehab. It was a lot of pain for little gain, and it took steely determination not to let that shit break you. How many times in the last six months had he been tempted to give up? Too fucking many to count, that was how many.

"What happened to his leg?"

Katie smiled and something in his chest tightened. Damn, it should be a crime for a woman to be so beautiful.

"What, now *you're* trying to get me to violate patient confidentiality. I tell you . . ." she tsked, shaking her head as if he should be ashamed of himself.

He smiled at her playfulness, realizing it'd been a long damn time since he'd cracked a genuine grin, and too damn often since meeting her. "Come on, you rebel. You know you want to tell me," he goaded.

She thought about it for a moment. "I'm trusting you to keep it a secret. And I'm only telling you because I know Tom so well and I know without a doubt he wouldn't mind."

Cole lifted his pinched fingers to his mouth, dragged them across his lips, and turned his wrist—a silent vow they were sealed. "Okay."

As she began to tell him what happened to Tom, she leaned forward so as not to be overheard, giving him a gorgeous view of the most perfect, creamy breasts he'd ever seen. The ripe mounds of flesh were barely contained by the demi cut of her pink lace-trimmed bra. That familiar stirring in his groin warned him to drag that stare back up to her eyes before he embarrassed himself in public.

". . . snowmobile rolled, pinning his leg under the machine. He was the last in line, so it was a while before his group realized he wasn't behind them anymore. It took over an hour for EMS to rescue him, and he spent a week in the trauma center at Regions having multiple surgeries to rebuild his shattered leg. Tom's been coming to me twice a week for the last two months. He's healing, but of course not as fast as he wants to, or thinks he should be. I think seeing you today, knowing what happened to you, gave him hope. You encouraged him more than you realize. Just giving him the goal of sparring with you seems to have renewed his drive to keep pushing forward. I just can't thank you enough for helping him."

That look of gratitude on her beautiful face was all the thanks he needed. In all honesty, he hadn't really done anything. He sparred with lots of trainees in the youth center. It wasn't a big deal, but listening to Katie, you'd think he was a hero or something, which made him more than a little uncomfortable, because he wasn't a damn hero. He was a crippled MMA fighter who was scared as hell he was going to lose his career.

Cole cleared his throat uncomfortably and mumbled, "Well, I'm glad you think it helped." And he was. Hell, he knew better than anyone the endurance, the fortitude, the frustration, and the pain one had to go through to get back on his feet after a devastating injury.

The smile she beamed at him could have lit the restaurant. "I know it did. So tell me . . . does it ever get old?"

"Does what ever get old?"

"The fans, having people recognize you wherever you go?"

"I enjoy the fans, for the most part. If it weren't for them, I wouldn't have a job. Then I'd actually have to work for a living." He gave her a teasing wink and she laughed.

"Oh, something tells me you work plenty hard."

"Is it work when you love what you do?"

"As long as you're getting paid for it, it is. I love what I do, too. I guess we're just lucky that way."

She shot him a grin over her glass as she lifted it to her parted lips and took a sip of her ice water. Good God, he'd never wanted to be an inanimate object more than he did at this moment. Thinking of all the places he'd love to feel those luscious lips of hers was absolutely counterproductive to his hope of getting through this dinner without having the imprint of his zipper imbedded into his cock.

Tearing his gaze from hers, Cole did another sweep of the bar.

"What are you staring at?" Katie turned to look behind her. "You're all glary and it's making me nervous," she teased, but as she searched the crowd, her gaze strayed to the group of men standing near the bathroom. Her smile immediately fell, and that becoming pink blush she'd worn so often today blanched.

Cole followed her gaze and promptly found the guy he'd been looking for exiting the bathroom, weaving his way through the crowd. Dammit, he knew he hadn't been imagining that shit. "Katie . . . ?" He reached across the table and grabbed her hand. The moment his fingers closed around hers, she whipped her head back around to face him and slinked down in her chair. He didn't have the heart to tell her the guy already knew she was there. He'd been watching them since they'd walked in. Her fingers slipped between his, curling tight until her blunt little nails bit into the back of his hand.

"Hey, Katie," he rubbed his thumb over the top of her hand to get her attention. Her palm was clammy against his, her wide, verdant eyes staring unfocused. He could see her pulse hammering in the little divot at the base of her throat. His arms ached to pull her into them, to shelter her from the terror that so clearly had overtaken her.

"Oh, my God," she whispered breathlessly. "OhmyGodOhmy-GodOhmyGod!"

"Do you want to go?" He squeezed her hand to get her attention, when what he really wanted was to drag that asshole out back and beat him senseless for whatever he'd done to put that look of fear in her eyes. It didn't matter he could hardly walk. He was a well-enough-rounded fighter he could still kick this guy's ass.

Despite the burning desire to confront Katie's demons for her, the need to take care of her proved greater. Katie nodded numbly, moisture rimming her eyes. He could tell she was fighting like hell to hold it together, and he was fighting like hell not to pull her into his arms. Bracing his hands on the table, he stood, slipped his crutches beneath his arms, and stepped between her and the bar, using his body to shield her as she slipped from the chair.

"Is there another exit? Maybe in the back?" He didn't want her passing by the bar if it could be helped.

"Straight back."

"I'll follow you." Cole grabbed his wallet and tossed a hundred-dollar bill on the table to cover their tab. Keeping himself positioned between Katie and the bar, they weaved past the tables and made their way through the crowd to the back exit. He reached forward and held the door open as she slipped outside. Before leaving, Cole shot one final withering glare at the man whose gaze had never left them.

CHAPTER

"What the hell just happened in there?"

Katie's hand shook so violently, the keys rattled as she struggled to put one into the ignition. *Shit. Shit . . . shit . . . shit . . .* If she hadn't seen him with her very own eyes, she never would have believed it. How had he found her? She'd been so careful.

Cole reached over and steadied her hand. "Katie, talk to me." He helped her guide the key home, and she turned her wrist, firing up the RAV. She let go of the keys, but he didn't let go of her hand, slipping his fingers around hers just like he'd done in the bar. This time she pulled back. If she let him comfort her now, there was a good chance she'd lose it, dissolving into a puddle of tears. It'd taken every last ounce of her courage to keep it together in there— courage she must have drawn from him, because there was no way in hell she could have stood on her own two feet and walked out of there like she had without him.

Lord help her, that was close. What if he'd seen them? The thought struck her with paralyzing fear. Surely he hadn't. If Carter had seen her out with another guy, he would have lost his mind. Then again, this was Cole Easton she was with, and crutches or not, he was one hell of an impressive male—not exactly the kind of guy you'd tangle with and live to tell about it.

Cold air blasted out of the vents, adding another layer of goose bumps to her already prickly flesh. She reached forward and switched off the fan blowing cold air at them. Her rapid breaths steamed the cab, bearing witness to her panic. The dash lights illuminated the sharp angles of Cole's face, concern cutting his features into an apprehensive scowl.

"Katie, tell me what's going on."

She didn't want to do this. Not here. Not now—with the bitter cold biting through her clothes to take root in her bones, or maybe that was the fear. Besides Uncle Marcus, no one knew about the hell she'd endured at Carter's hands. She wasn't about to take that trip down memory lane any time soon, and she sure as hell wasn't doing it with Cole.

But he had the pit-bull tenacity of a born fighter, and wearing his opponent down with well-timed jabs was his MO. That iron-clad will of his reared its ugly head once again as Cole hit her with a one-two punch that threatened to obliterate her resolve. "I want to help you, Katie. But I can't if you won't tell me what's going on."

If she actually thought he could, she might have given in. Problem was, he couldn't help her—no one could.

"Who's the guy in the bar, Katie?"

She held his unwavering stare—so strong, so fiercely protective. What she wouldn't give to have a tenth of the courage and strength that flowed through this fighter's veins.

"Either you tell me, or I'll go back in there and get the answers myself."

She had no doubt he would do just that. It didn't matter that his legs weren't currently with the program. Something she'd learned about Cole in the short time she'd known him was that he was headstrong and determined, and when he said he was going to do something, he was damn well going to do it.

When she didn't speak, he made a grab for the door handle, and Katie lunged to stop him. She grabbed his arm and was surprised to feel his muscles tense beneath her touch. "Please. Just let it go. He might not have even seen us."

Cole canted his head, leveling her with one of those heated stares that should not have woken the butterflies in her stomach or stirred that ache between her thighs, a painful reminder of how long it'd been since she'd let a man touch her—but then his next words stole every last bit of heat from her body.

"Oh, he saw you. He couldn't take his fucking eyes off you."

Katie didn't miss the deep inflection in Cole's voice, or the growl that sounded a lot like possessiveness. The look on her face must have mirrored the terror ripping through her chest at this remark because Cole immediately swore. He started to reach for her, and then seemed to think better of it, scrubbing the back of his neck as if trying to ease the ache of sore, stiff muscles. "Shit, Katie, I'm sorry. I shouldn't have said that."

"It's okay," she mumbled numbly.

"No, it's not. Just tell me this, is that the guy who sent you those flowers?"

She hesitated to answer, but her lack of response told him more than she wanted to.

"Dammit, Katie, how can I help you if you won't even talk to me?"

She could hear the impatience in his voice, sense his frustration, but he wasn't the only one feeling it. "That's just it, Cole. I don't want you involved in this, so I'd really appreciate it if you'd just drop it." It was bad enough he'd witnessed her floral meltdown and freak-out in the bar. She felt like a pathetic loser. This man was here to heal, to get back into fighting condition so he could hold on to his title—and his career. He most definitely wasn't here to fight her battles for her. But what she didn't understand was why he would even want to.

Before Cole could do something crazy like get out of the car and go back in there to confront the man who'd made her life a living hell, Katie put the RAV in gear and pulled out into traffic. She chanced a glance at Cole after checking over her shoulder to make sure they weren't being followed. He looked pissed. Why? Why would he care? He had enough on his plate without getting caught up in her drama.

Neither of them spoke the rest of the drive home. The minute they entered the house, each went their separate ways—Cole to the shower, and Katie to the kitchen. It wasn't that she was some super domestic Martha Stewart type. In fact, her culinary skills were rather limited to microwaves and rice boiling. But considering it was her fault they hadn't eaten yet, the least she could do was scrounge up something—scrounge being the key word, because it didn't take a lot of effort to pull together a couple of BLTs.

She'd hoped the aromatic bacon permeating the air would be enough to bring Cole around, but as she set the plates and sandwiches on the table, and poured two glasses of milk, there was still no sign of the cranky fighter. A part of her wanted to slip into the chair and eat her meager supper before going to get him. She wasn't sure she could stomach much more of his prying questions or judgmental looks.

It was obvious Cole confronted life like he did his opponents—fearless, bold, and in your face. And that was great, if you were the light-heavyweight champion of the world, but he didn't understand she was out of her weight class. How do you begin to explain to a shark what it's like to be a minnow? She didn't want Cole's pity any more than he wanted hers. He should understand that.

"Cole, supper's ready!" Katie called from the kitchen as she drained the still-sizzling bacon grease into an empty coffee can she kept under the sink. Turning the faucet to high, she ran cold water into the pan and added a squirt of Dawn. It sizzled and popped, steam billowing from the sink as she used the spatula to scrub off the burned bacon bits. When the pan was so shiny she could see her reflection—oh wow, she looked like hell—Katie used her shoulder to shove back a rogue lock of hair that had fallen loose from her ponytail, and then rinsed the pan before setting it in the strainer to dry.

She craned her neck to look down the hall and scowled when she saw no sign of Cole. "Come on, Cole! Get your ass moving! Before supper gets co—oh . . ."

He emerged from the bathroom—clean shaven, his dark hair a sexy, towel-dampened mess. Her fingers itched to touch his shaggy locks, but instead, she nervously dried her hands on her thighs. His eyes were so electric blue they looked almost otherworldly. As they connected with hers, Katie's heart stuttered in her chest. The little muscle in Cole's jaw ticked as if he were grinding his molars. Obviously someone was still pissy.

She turned away, breaking his stare, and busied herself with the few remaining dishes.

"You may not look like your uncle, but you sure as hell sound like him," Cole grumbled. "For a minute there, I thought I was back in camp."

Katie wasn't sure if he was insulting her or joking. She chose to assume the latter, hoping it would break some of the tension growing between them since they left the Sportsman. She wanted the comfortable camaraderie they'd shared BF—Before Freak-out. She shrugged and turned toward the table, taking her seat across from him. "What can I say? Motivational speaking is a gift that runs in the family. I considered being a drill instructor, but I decided on PT instead."

He choked on a surprised laugh, looked at the BLT with wilted lettuce peeking out from the corner of his toast, and said, "I can see your culinary skills run in the family, as well."

That teasing smile he shot her was a panty dropper if she'd ever seen one. "Hey," she fired back, feigning offense. "I'll have you know I can also boil rice!"

Now he laughed—a deep, rich cadence she felt all the way to her bones—and in other places she didn't want to think about. Picking up the sandwich, she took a bite, feigning orgasmic deliciousness. "Mmm . . ." she moaned, "this is sooo good!"

Okay, too far?

Cole's laugh abruptly cut off with a strangled cough that sounded more like a pained groan. His cerulean eyes locked on her mouth, and the hunger banked in them stalled the breath in her lungs. She swallowed the bite, forcing it down her ash-dry throat, all the while praying she wouldn't choke. Of course, then he'd have to give her mouth to mouth . . .

Yeah . . . so now would probably be a good time for a subject change. Clearing her throat awkwardly, she fixed her gaze on her plate and pretended to be really interested in a piece of limp lettuce, while definitely *not* noticing how in a spilt second, Cole had gone from teasing and smiling to looking like he wanted to leap across the table and have *her* for supper instead of this poor excuse for a BLT.

She waited for that familiar panic to grip her, the whitewash of fear that sent her heart racing and her vision tunneling whenever she so much as thought about being touched by a man. The tachycardia hit with record speed and she tensed, waiting for the inevitable terror to come. Her breaths quickened, the blood thundering through her veins sent a rush of heat into her chest—her nipples hardened. Wait. What? That wasn't supposed to happen. But as that alluring heat continued to travel south, it melted her icy core. Moisture pooled between her legs, dampening the slip of cotton against her sensitive flesh, and confirming what she'd been trying to deny since the moment she first saw Cole at the airport—she wanted him. Well, *she* didn't want him. Katie didn't want any man. But her body was clearly having other ideas.

Oh, please . . . she scolded her inner goddess. *You wouldn't know what to do with a man like Cole Easton if he swept this table clean and tossed you on top of it. You'd probably panic the moment his mouth touched yours. Just like you nearly did in the gym today.*

"Katie, are you all right?"

Why was he always asking her that? *Because you're fucking nuts. That's why.*

Shut up, Goddess! Who asked you anyway? "I'm fine," she answered Cole. "Why?"

He shrugged. "You just looked like you went somewhere else for a minute." Picking up his BLT, he took a bite and groaned—a rumble of pure masculine satisfaction that made her core contract with long-denied feminine need. "You're right. This BLT is amazing!"

Katie's own sandwich froze midway to her mouth as she stared at Cole, slack-jawed. *Holy. Hell.* She couldn't tell if he was serious or just giving her shit. But he was damn convincing, either way. "Are you for real?" He stopped chewing and stared at her across the table. She was pretty sure he'd say *What?* if his mouth wasn't full. "You actually think this is good?"

He finished chewing and swallowed. The bob of his Adam's apple drew her gaze to his thick neck and the ropes of trapezius muscle stretching to his shoulders. The outline of his chest was visible through his threadbare black T-shirt that had *CFA* emblazoned over the chest. For probably the one hundredth time, she found herself admiring the impressive cut of his biceps, the carved lines of his triceps. If God himself hand-sculpted a man, he'd be hard-pressed to outdo the male sitting across from her right now.

"Well, to be fair, I probably burned a thousand calories this afternoon and I am starving, so a frozen turd would probably be appealing right now. And BLTs are on my list of five faves. Bacon's not one of my diet foods. I honestly can't remember the last time I ate a greasy piece of pork. This lettuce, on the other hand, leaves a bit to be desired."

Wow, gorgeous and funny—who knew? "I didn't realize you were dieting." Which sounded like a really odd thing to say to a guy who must be tipping the scale at two hundred pounds. But there wasn't an ounce of spare flesh on that amazing body, so whatever he was doing, it was obviously working. "We can go to the store tomorrow and you can pick up some food you'd like."

"I'm not dieting anymore. I had to cut weight for the De'Grasse fight. As a general rule I try to eat healthy, but I'm not a freak about it."

Good to know. "Why cut when you could just fight heavyweight?"

Cole shrugged. "I feel better at two hundred. And right now I think the best fighters happen to be in the light-heavyweight division."

"Would you ever jump classes?"

He took another bite of his BLT before answering, seeming to take the time to chew in contemplative silence. "I don't know. Don't you kind of think that's getting the cart before the horse, considering my career might be over?"

"You can't think like that, Cole. You're going to fight again."

He didn't look wholly convinced. "Are you always so optimistic?"

"Are you always so pessimistic?" she countered with a teasing grin.

"I wouldn't say pessimistic as much as realistic. There's a difference."

"I guess that's true. We should stretch you out after supper, so your muscles don't tighten up. You worked them hard today." She paused a moment, working up the courage to speak her mind. "Listen, Cole, I just want you to know—" Her phone rang, cutting her off. "Excuse me." Her chair grated against the tile floor as she pushed it back and got up. The heat of his eyes followed her as she crossed the kitchen and grabbed her iPhone off the counter. The caller ID came up "unavailable."

For a moment she considered not answering. It was rude to leave a guest and take calls during supper, then again, this was hardly supper and Cole was hardly a guest. Her parents were probably calling. More than likely her mom was calling to ask her to bring more orange juice in the morning. Her dad swore by that stuff and couldn't get enough of it.

OJ was her father's cure-all for any ailment. Whenever she'd ask "How ya feeling, Dad?" he'd always respond, "I'll be fine. Just give me some orange juice." It'd become a joke in their family. Her dad was a rock—never sick a day in his life. So it had come as a horrible blow when she'd gotten that dreaded call. At the time, no one had known how bad it was, or if he'd even survive. Now, every time the phone rang and the caller ID showed "unavailable," her pulse quickened with dread.

"Hello?"

"Katrina?"

Katie's stomach lurched into her throat. She'd know that deep baritone anywhere. It was the voice that echoed in her nightmares. "How did you get this number?" her voice broke, barely above a whisper.

"It doesn't matter. Baby, we need to talk."

Oh, it mattered. It mattered a whole hell of a lot. For all she knew, he could be standing outside her door right now. The blood in her veins turned to ice as dread slowly licked up her spine. Her legs trembled with the urge to bolt, knees weakened by panic. If she didn't sit down, there was a good chance she was going to fall on her ass.

Katie cast a quick glance at Cole, subconsciously seeking out his strength. He watched her intently, his dark brow raised in concern. He knew something was wrong. Then again, how could he not with the way her voice broke, her knees quaked with terror. She hated that he saw her like this—hated being weak—but most of all, she hated that no matter what she did or where she went, she couldn't seem to escape this monster.

"There's nothing to talk about," she said under her breath as she left the kitchen to sit on the couch. "Please, just leave me alone."

"I can't. Baby, I love you. I've been a wreck since you left. And after seeing you tonight . . . I need you back, Katrina."

The last sentence held the unmistakable note of warning. Exhaling a shaky breath, she said, "Carter, you were a wreck before I left. You can't blame this on me."

"Goddammit, Katrina! Can't you see I'm trying here?" And just like that his switch had flipped. She held the phone away from her ear and winced, feeling that familiar rise of panic squeezing her throat like an invisible hand—Carter's hand gripping her neck. She could still feel the bite of his fingers clamping onto her throat. She couldn't breathe! "If you weren't such a fucking bitch—"

The phone was yanked from her hand, and Katie whipped her head around as Cole disconnected the call. He looked positively livid. His jaw was clenched tight. The hard lines bracketing his mouth accented the dark scowl. His sapphire eyes that burned with something akin to possessive rage.

A part of her was furious he dared to intervene by doing something so high-handed. But another part of her wanted to throw her arms around his neck and pepper his face with kisses. She should thank him for stepping in and doing something she should have done herself, but just the sound of that bastard's voice had ripped Katie back into that paralyzing fear, rendering her powerless to act or defend herself.

"You don't need to listen to that." Before he could give her phone back, it began to ring in his hand and Cole didn't hesitate to pick up the call. "Hello?" It was more a demand than a greeting—brisk, commanding. Oh God, what was he doing? If Carter knew Cole was here with her, he'd absolutely lose it.

"She's right here. Okay. I'll tell her."

Cole hung up the phone and handed it back to Katie. Her heart was hammering so loudly, she barely heard him say, "Your mom wants you to bring them some orange juice in the morning."

CHAPTER

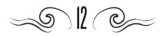

Who in the hell had Katie gotten herself tangled up with? By the sounds of it, and the look of terror that crossed her face when she picked up that call, Cole would guess a persistent ex. Was it the guy who'd been at the bar tonight? Considering she was sporting the same look of terror, it wasn't too damn hard to wager a guess.

He hadn't been eavesdropping—oh hell, who was he kidding? If he'd strained any harder to hear her conversation, he'd probably have popped an eardrum. If he had any doubts a jaded lover was on the line, there certainly wasn't any question after that assclown professed his love and then promptly called her a fucking bitch. *Real smooth . . . Keith Stone smooth. That oughtta soften her up, Romeo.*

It hadn't been difficult to follow her conversation; the bastard's voice had echoed from her phone like a bullhorn. Apparently, he was "trying." If that was trying, Cole hated to see what the antithesis of that would be. But then the yelling had begun, and that was where Cole had drawn the line. Katie might not be his responsibility, but for reasons he had no interest in exploring, she lit up his protective instincts like the freaking Fourth of July, and he'd be damned if he was going to sit here and let some dickwad talk to her like that.

"That the guy from the bar?" he asked, already suspecting as much and not expecting her to answer, so it surprised him when she nodded. "Same guy who sent you the flowers?"

She nodded again, her stare fixed on her hands clenched tightly in her lap. Then she surprised him when her gaze snapped up, locking on his. "Why did you do that?" she demanded.

"Do what?"

"Take the phone from me. When you answered, you didn't know my mother was going to be on the other end—and we're both lucky she was, because believe me, my life is one hornet's nest you do not want to stick your hand into."

"Are you trying to scare me? Because if you are, it's going to take a hell of a lot more than a pissed-off stalker boyfriend to do it. Although I gotta say, you don't seem to have the best luck with guys, do ya?"

She let out a bark of unamused laughter that sounded a bit on the hysterical side, but at least it was something, which was what he'd been going for. Adding to the gravity of Katie's situation by going all commando on her was not going to be helpful. He'd gotten that message loud and clear in the car tonight. She wasn't going to help him help her, but if he could keep it light, tease her a little bit, maybe she'd let her guard down long enough for him to learn a thing or two about just how serious this situation with her ex might be. His instincts were telling him it was pretty damn bad.

"Is it that obvious?" she asked, tucking her bottom lip between her teeth.

"Sorry. It is. You're kinda like a shit magnet for crazy, huh?"

She laughed again, a little more genuine this time, and damn if that light, feminine giggle didn't do funny things inside his chest and farther south. The urge to reach out and tuck that fallen lock of pale blonde hair behind her ear was nearly too much to resist.

"I guess so. I'm not sure what that says about you, though."

Her wit was so damn sexy. It wasn't hard to see how this woman could drive a man crazy. After only two days with her, he was already falling under her spell. Katie stirred something inside him Cole never knew existed, and he wasn't entirely pleased about it, either.

"Are you kidding me?" Cole sat down beside her and teasingly bumped her arm with his shoulder. "Sweetheart, no one's crazier than me. It just depends on what kind of loco we're talking about."

Katie watched him a moment, curiosity brimming in those emerald eyes. "Have you ever been in love, Cole?"

Wait, what? Well, that certainly escalated quickly. Cole wasn't in the habit of talking about himself, but he also knew there wasn't a snowball's chance in hell of her opening up to him if he didn't at least make some sort of an effort first. "I thought I was—once. But then it ended up being the stomach flu."

Katie laughed, a sweet belly laugh, and the sound of her melodic voice was like audible foreplay that shot straight into his cock. Damn, he wanted her. Everything about this woman intrigued him to the point of madness—her intelligence, her beauty, her vulnerability. Hell, even the mystery surrounding her called to the competitor inside him. But something told Cole if he accepted this challenge, the stakes were going to be a lot higher than a title match. He'd be fighting for his heart, because without even trying, in a matter of days, Katie had managed to pass his guard and was laying some serious ground and pound against his defenses.

"Come on, now. I'm serious. Tell me what kind of a woman manages to steal Cole Easton's heart."

Look in the mirror, sweetheart . . .

Katie sat back on the couch and tucked her feet beneath her, settling in for what she probably expected would be a juicy, torrid love story. The look of rapt fascination on her beautiful face almost made him want to make something up. This was a hell of a lot better than the fear she'd worn a few minutes ago. "Tell me," she pleaded.

He shrugged. "There isn't anything to tell. I was just joking around. I've never been in love."

She looked at him like he was some sort of a freak or something. "Seriously? Not ever? How old are you?"

"Thirty-two."

"And you've never been in love?"

"Nope."

"Not ever?"

"Never."

"Jeez, what's wrong with you?" Her top lip curled up into a teasing grin.

"Nothing. I thought. But now you're starting to make me wonder. You gotta understand, my line of work doesn't exactly attract the long-term type of girl, and if a guy is lucky enough to find one in Sin City, it isn't very long before the cage bangers run her off."

Damn, she had a beautiful smile—full shell-pink lips and straight, white teeth . . . This woman had a mouth that could bring a man to his knees.

Her delicately arched brow hiked even higher. "Okay, what's a cage banger?"

"It's what we call the MMA groupies."

"That's . . . lovely."

He shrugged again. "It's life in the fast lane. Most of the time my training keeps me too busy to think about what I might be missing out on. What about you?" He lifted his brow in challenge. "Quid pro quo?"

A shadow of sadness crossed her face, and he felt like a dick for putting it there, but he wanted to know about her past, what secrets was she hiding.

"I thought I was in love—once. I was wrong. End of story."

Yeah, he seriously doubted that. "Hey, I just confessed to being a man-whore. The least you can do is tell me about it."

Her smile chased away those shadows, and the knot of guilt fisting his gut loosened just a touch.

She shrugged. "I already knew that though. I mean, according to the *Enquirer*, you *are* Hugh Hefner's illegitimate son, so . . ."

Cole laughed. It was so not funny, but he couldn't seem to stop. Those damn tabloids had caused him so much grief over the last several months. He certainly wasn't missing the paparazzi, that was for sure.

Katie's sense of humor was surprisingly sarcastic and witty—much like her uncle's. In fact, the more time he spent with her, the more it was like hanging out with a very hot version of Marcus. It was comfortable—familiar. Perhaps that was why he felt so at ease with her, like he'd known her for years rather than just days.

Katie reached over and laid her hand on his thigh, giving him a friendly pat that effectively derailed his train of thought. The cat must have thought she was calling it over, because Scarlet came bounding into the living room and leapt onto his lap. The cat immediately began purring and kneading his legs with her declawed paws. Katie smiled as she scratched the cat's ears. "Well, Scarlet certainly likes you. And that's saying something. Siamese tend to be one-owner cats and very possessive. She seems to have claimed you for her own."

"Competition getting too tough for you?" he teased.

She laughed. "How did you know? I give up. There's no use even trying to compete with that." She nodded to the cat that was now rolled over in his lap, feet up in the air, rubbing her head against his thigh, dangerously close to his groin.

"Oh, come on now. You could at least try," he said, trying to keep a straight face and failing miserably.

Katie busted out laughing. "You *are* a man-whore. Propositioning me right in front of poor Scarlet."

He laughed, thoroughly enjoying her quirky sense of humor. It was just one more glaringly obvious difference between Katie and the other women he was used to being around. She was genuine—authentic—having no agenda other than to help him fight again, and damn if that wasn't hell on his defenses.

"But seriously, I want you to know that I'm glad you're here, Cole. I think you're doing amazingly well, considering your injuries. I'm really pleased with your eval today, and I'm confident I can get you back into fighting condition."

She brushed her hand over the cat, leaving it to rest on his leg. The heat of her touch seared up his thigh. His flesh swelled, straining against his gym shorts. Before she could think better of it and move her hand, he laid his over hers and laced their fingers. "I hope you're right." His thumb brushed over her knuckles, drawing her anxious gaze to his thigh. She moistened her bottom lip before catching it between her teeth. A surprising amount of anxiety radiated from her. What was that all about? Katie looked about as nervous as a virgin on her wedding night. Not that Cole had any intention of sleeping with her. Oh, who the hell was he kidding? He wanted to fuck her so damn bad, it was all he could think about—but he wouldn't let his mind go there, even if his body was more than game.

Her pulse was ticking wildly in her throat, with that deer-in-the-headlights look settled on her beautiful face. She'd already shot him down once today. Wasn't that the definition of insanity?—doing the same thing over and over again, expecting to get a different result. Perhaps it was the thrill of the hunt that intrigued the alpha male in Cole so much—the challenge of whittling Katie into submission. She was so unlike any other woman he'd met.

Her hand felt fragile in his, so small and dainty. What was she so afraid of? Was it him or something bigger? Pound for pound, he dwarfed her, but she should be used to working with athletes, so it couldn't be his size that had her tensing beside him. He wasn't accustomed to women reacting to him like this. Usually, they were tearing at his clothes and throwing themselves at him. Unless . . .

"Do I frighten you, Katie?" Guilt flashed in her eyes when they briefly met before dropping to the floor. *Goddammit. Fucking De'Grasse* . . . Now that Hugh Hefner comment made a lot more sense, and it wasn't nearly so funny.

"You can't believe everything you read, Katie. I didn't hurt that woman. I was set up." A flash of anger tore through his veins. Why in the hell was he sitting here explaining himself to her? He let go of her hand and moved to get up. The cat let out a surprised, protesting mewy squawk, before hopping to the ground and darting away. Katie grabbed his bicep, her grip surprisingly strong. He turned his head and looked back at her. "What?"

"I don't know what you're talking about. This isn't about you, Cole. It's me. I'm . . . damaged."

The look in her eyes was so sad—so defeated. The invisible band around his chest squeezed until his heart ached. Cole swore if he ever saw the man again that had done this to her, he'd kill him. Already, he could feel Katie yanking up those walls. Before she could get them fully in place he sent a jab at her defenses. "Maybe you should talk about it, you know? The first step is letting someone in." Hell, was he really suggesting that someone be him? Guess so, because in the next breath he heard himself saying, "Sometimes it's easier to talk to someone you don't know very well." He told himself it was because of Marcus he cared so damn much. He owed it to the guy that saved his life to do what he could to help his niece.

"Sometimes it's easier not to open old wounds," she countered.

"Emotional wounds are like broken bones, Katie. If they're not set right, they'll heal wrong, and that bone will always be weak."

"Well, I've had more than my share of broken bones, and you're here so we can focus on yours, so how about we stick to that, huh?"

Katie pulled her hand out of his and the loss of contact was like a knife slashing through his gut. He liked the feeling of her touch—far too much, actually. For some inexplicable reason, she soothed him and stirred him at the same time. He silently watched her as she unfolded herself from the couch and headed for her bedroom.

"Good night, Cole."

As she walked away, he wondered if those broken bones had been literal or metaphorical. If he had to venture a guess, he'd say both.

CHAPTER

 13

Katie woke the next morning to the whirr of a blender and the scent of fresh-brewed coffee. She hadn't slept more than a few hours, and exhaustion rode her hard. Between the thoughts of Cole sleeping across the hall—naked, no doubt—and the phone call from Carter, she'd pretty much given up all hope of rest by the time three a.m. rolled by. Somewhere around four she might have dozed off, only to have her dreams filled with a certain MMA fighter who was proving to be far more of a distraction than she wanted.

She hadn't let a man touch her since Carter, and the dry spell must be getting to her. She'd woken in a sweat-drenched pant, her back arched, breasts reaching to connect with that solid wall of muscle that only moments ago had been pressing down on her as Cole's mouth claimed hers in a searing kiss. His hands gripped her hips, fingertips biting into her flesh as he anchored her to the mat, driving into her with reckless abandon—filling that void in her heart as well as between her parted thighs. He swiftly drove her to the pinnacle of release. His mouth was masterful, his flawless body ruthlessly demanding . . . Just as she'd reached her crescendo, the blender blasted to life, tearing her out of Cole's arms and back to reality.

She'd almost cried out at the injustice, and in a fit of temporary insanity, briefly considered walking into that kitchen to make her dream a reality. She knew Cole wanted her. She'd have had to be blind not to see the hunger burning in his eyes when he looked at her last night. But nocturnal trysts were far safer than the real thing. Even if she'd been brave enough to let down her guard long enough to give herself to Cole, she knew she would have chickened out before she even reached the living room.

Of all the blasted timing . . . How many months had gone by without her body craving the slightest hint of a man's touch? Months—too many to count. And now, seemingly overnight, Cole had managed to flip her switch, awakening her body to thoughts and desires she'd believed long dead and buried.

Katie wasn't sure whether to rejoice in the discovery that she wasn't entirely broken after all, or bellow in sorrow because of all the men her body could have chosen to awaken to, it'd picked the one man she could never have. For all the reasons Cole had admitted last night, he wasn't long-term material. This . . . whatever *this* was, was only temporary. Once she got him on his feet and fighting again, he'd leave her, going back to the MMA circuit, to his life in the fast lane, and to his—what did he call them? Oh, yeah, cage bangers. It was foolish to set her sights on a man who'd never even been in love—the women, the fame, the partying, the camps . . .

She was stupid to think there was even a chance he'd give it up if something between them were to develop. And why would he? The fame, the money, and all the tits and ass he could possibly want. What red-blooded male would ever want to leave that behind? And she refused to be a part of that lifestyle—not again—not ever. He was here because Marcus expected her to get him ready for the cage, not so that she could fall for the guy who'd never want more from her than a fling. If no woman had managed to steal Cole Easton's heart by now, it was doubtful one ever would, and she certainly wasn't going to be the one who tried.

119

But damn, that dream had been hot . . . Katie wasn't sure how she'd be able to face Cole this morning without remembering every lick, every touch, as the dream version of him explored and laid claim to her body. Just thinking about it now made her cheeks heat with embarrassment and unfulfilled desire. Her breasts felt heavy, nipples hardening to achy points. She shifted restlessly, attempting to relieve the gnawing emptiness centered deep between her thighs. What she wouldn't give right now to trade the damp cotton of her panties for Cole's tongue.

Katie closed her eyes, imagining it, easily calling her dreams back to mind as she let her fingers glide down her stomach to the cotton-covered juncture between her thighs. As she replayed the scene, she couldn't help wondering how close her imagination was to reality. Would his lips fit as perfectly against hers? Would his tongue be so bold? What would he taste like?—feel like as he ground his hard body against hers?

She'd never seen a man so cut, so chiseled to perfection. Her finger slipped beneath the lacy hem and her breath caught on a gasp as she made contact with her hot, silky flesh. She caught her bottom lip between her teeth to bite back the wanton groan. Oh, how she wished Cole would have been sunny side up when she'd walked in on him the other morning. That was one part where she wished her imagination didn't have to fill in the blanks.

She couldn't believe she was actually doing this—touching herself while fanaticizing it was Cole's hand instead of hers. This wasn't her. She didn't do things like this. Yet here she was, heart racing, breath catching, as she slipped her finger over the bead of her sex. "Mmm, Cole . . ." she exhaled, muscles tensing, her empty core contracting with the first tremors of her long-denied release. She was close . . . so close . . .

Bang, bang, bang!

Katie yelped, startled by the pounding on her door. And just like that, for the second time in as many hours, her orgasm had been stolen from her. "What!" she snarled, glaring daggers at the door.

"What do you mean, 'what'? You called me," he said through the door. "Do you need something?"

She felt her cheeks flush at the response that hovered so close to her lips. Did she need something? Did she ever . . . When had that blender stopped? Mortification burned through her as it dawned on her she must have been louder than she realized. Oh Lord, how utterly embarrassing. Cole had heard her calling his name.

"Are you all right?"

"I'm fine," she snapped. "I just . . . stubbed my toe."

Stubbed her toe, my ass. Cole had heard his name uttered on the lips of enough women in the throes of passion to know what that woman was doing in there—and he'd be damned if she was going to be doing it without his help.

By the snark in her voice, he'd gotten to her just in the nick of time. He smiled to himself, taking comfort in knowing he wasn't the only one suffering here. So, Cold Fish Katie might not be such a crappie after all. She might pretend to be unaffected by him, and she'd done a damn convincing job of it, too, but this was the proof he needed. She could deny she wanted him until her face turned as blue as his balls. He knew better, and this proved it. Cole smiled to himself, thinking of the ways he intended to make her suffer as badly as he was. Last night, when she'd just gotten up and went to bed, she'd left him so damn hard and miserable, he'd hit the weights for another two hours trying to work himself into exhaustion with the hopes of finally getting some sleep, but it still managed to elude him most the night. One thing was for certain: he had no intention of suffering alone. Misery loves company, so *game on, sweetheart* . . .

"You've gotta stop."

"Stop? Stop what? I wasn't doing anything," she squeaked from the other side of the door.

Yeah, right . . . He could hear her stomping around now, dresser drawers jerking open and slamming shut. "Stop at the grocery store. For orange juice. Remember? What were you talking about?" He bit the inside of his cheek, trying to keep from laughing as he imagined Katie scrambling to get dressed, cheeks flushed with either lust or embarrassment, a hot and bothered mess.

"Nothing! Just . . . go get ready to leave."

He chuckled as her footsteps marched closer and the door abruptly swung open. Katie stopped just short of running into him and craned her head back to meet his gaze. This was the first time she'd been this close to him while standing up straight and not hunched over like fucking Quasimodo. He filled her doorway, hands braced on both sides of the frame as he supported himself. His crutches were propped against the wall.

Katie took a measured step back, blushing a becoming shade of crimson, and then dropped her gaze to her feet, looking wholly guilty about something. "Wow. I . . . didn't realize you were so . . . tall."

He supposed using the crutches he'd used yesterday did shorten him a few inches. "I didn't realize you were so . . . little," he shot back, arching his brow in wry amusement, grinning down at her. Jeez, she was small. The top of her head barely cleared his nipple line. Her pale hair was a sexed-up mess his fingers itched to dive into. It looked as if he wasn't the only one who'd had a rough night of it. Damn, he couldn't remember the last time he wanted a woman this much.

"Excuse me," she said primly, unable to pass because he was blocking her entire doorway.

Cole shifted his weight and reached for his crutches that weren't where he'd left them. Fuck. He glanced down at the floor and found his gimp sticks lying there. Well, wasn't this a swell fucking predicament. He couldn't step out of her way because he needed the door frame for support. Perhaps she noticed his problem, because she stood there a moment watching him. Finally, he lifted his arm, sliding his hand up the door frame. Jumping at her chance for escape, she stepped forward and ducked her head beneath his bicep as she turned to the side and tried to squeeze between him and the door.

She slipped her arm around his side, open hand splayed in the center of his back, and her other hand palmed his chest as if to steady him as she slid by. Her breasts dragged against his ribs, pebbled nipples searing the muscled grooves of his flesh. A pained groan chortled deep in his throat as a startled breath caught in hers.

Okay, so this had been a bad fucking idea. She was lucky his hands were busy holding himself up or they'd be gripping her ass right now as he jerked her up against his rock-hard erection while his mouth plundered hers.

"Sorry . . . I'm sorry," she apologized for a second time as she wormed her way past him. "You're just so . . . big. I can't . . . get through."

He didn't speak, he couldn't fucking breathe. After another torturous moment of struggling past him, Katie managed to slide by. Standing behind him now, she'd yet to let go of him. Her breasts were pressed against his lats, her little body tucked tight against his. His head felt light, like he'd taken a left hook to the jaw. That was probably because the majority of his circulation was currently shunted to his other head.

"Here, let me get your crutches."

Aaaand just like that, she unmanned him. It wasn't her fault. But the feeling of weakness enraged him all the same. Her hands were still on him, but no longer did he feel the heat of her touch, or the sensuality of her full, soft breasts pressed against him. He felt like a fucking cripple who had a half-pint of a woman beneath him with the idiotic notion that she could somehow keep him from flattening her if he fell.

"Let go of me, Katie." At the cold briskness in his voice, she jerked back. He immediately wanted to kick himself in the ass for being such a prideful prick. He was here for her help, so why did he have such a damn difficult time accepting it?

She jerked away as if he'd burned her. Before he could apologize, she took another step back, bent to retrieve his crutches, and propped them against the wall, murmuring, "I . . . I'm sorry," before fleeing into the bathroom and slamming the door behind her.

Muttering a nasty self-damning curse, Cole shifted his grip on the doorway and reached for the crutches, propping one beneath each arm. He turned to enter his bedroom across the hall when a chirp sounded in the living room. He'd heard it periodically throughout the night, but hadn't cared enough to investigate. Seeking out the sound, Cole tracked it to the couch. Propping one crutch against the cushions, he balanced on the other and bent down, reaching between the cushions.

His hand connected with the small thin box and he pulled out Katie's phone. She must have dropped it when she'd been sitting on the couch last night. The iPhone chirped and vibrated in his hand. Cole glanced down at the screen and saw she had nine unopened messages—all from an unavailable number. The last one displayed across her home screen, sending a surge of possessive fury flooding through his veins: *You belong to me!*

The hell she did. The shower turned on down the hall, and after a moment of hesitation and a quick glance toward the bathroom, Cole swiped his thumb across the screen and opened Katie's other messages. They'd started shortly after midnight and continued throughout the night. Just like the call, the messages had started out coaxing. *I'm so sorry. I love you, baby. Don't do this to us. Please talk to me.* And when that didn't work, the messages grew more persistent. *Do you really think I can't find you? How long do you think you can hide from me?* To downright nasty. *I saw you with him tonight. I bet you're with him right now, you fucking cunt! You're nothing but a goddamn whore! I'll fucking kill you before I see you with someone else! You belong to me!*

Holy hell . . . this guy was fucking insane. Shit like this had a way of escalating—fast. Did Katie have any idea how much danger she was in? He wanted to talk to her about it, but after getting shot down enough times to ground a B-52 bomber, Cole wasn't hopeful he'd get the answers he needed from her. But he knew how else to get them. Pocketing Katie's cell, he grabbed his other crutch and headed for the kitchen and a cup of much-needed coffee.

Before taking a seat at the kitchen table, he set Katie's phone in the middle of it and grabbed his off the counter. He had no doubt she was going to be pissed when she learned he'd read her messages, and she'd be even more livid if she ever discovered what he was about to do, but he didn't fucking care. Her safety was at stake, and he wasn't taking any chances. Listening for the shower, he made sure it was still running before dialing.

The phone rang twice . . . three times . . . then, "Hey, kid, how's it going? You freezing your balls off yet?"

Despite himself, Cole's top lip tugged into a crooked grin at the sound of his old friend's voice. "Just about," he chuckled. "It's a damn dirty trick to put a guy on a plane and send him up here in nothin' but a hoodie."

Marcus busted out laughing, one of those belly laughs that ended in a coughing fit. The smile on Cole's face fell to a concerned scowl. "You get that cough looked at yet? No, of course not," he answered for the guy, already knowing the response. "I've been nagging you for months to get that damn thing checked. When I get home I'm hauling your ass to the doctor. No fucking argument."

"Oh, please. You sound like my wife, God rest her soul."

"Yeah, well, she must have been a smart woman," Cole grumbled.

"She was. The best. Too damn good for me. I was just lucky she never figured it out."

Cole smiled, his chest tightening with emotion at hearing the old man talk about his beloved wife—Katie's aunt, he realized, making the late connection. Marcus didn't speak of his wife often, and Cole suspected the wound was too raw—even after all these years. But in those rare instances when he did, Cole felt like he'd been given a rare glimpse into the life of the man he loved like a father.

"So, enough about me, kid. How are you getting along with my niece?"

Wow, that was a loaded question Cole wasn't touching with a ten-foot pole. "Fine," he answered ambiguously. "You were right. She's an excellent PT. She doesn't hesitate to bust my balls. Reminds me a lot of you, actually."

Marcus laughed. "You oughtta feel right at home, then. So what's the problem?"

"I didn't say there was one."

"You didn't have to. I know you, kid. I can hear it in your voice. Something's eating at you."

Cole let out a pent-up breath he didn't realize he'd been holding. "Tell me the truth, Marcus. You didn't just send me up here for rehab, did you?"

Condemning silence on the other line. It continued so long, Cole had almost given up all hope of getting an answer from the guy, when he exhaled a long troubled sigh. "How bad is it?"

"You knew?" Cole couldn't keep the accusation out of his voice any easier than he could stem his flare of temper at being blindsided. Goddamn manipulative bast—

"I suspected," Marcus confessed. "She's been home too long for him not to have found her. If he'd been looking, that is."

"He was, and he has."

Marcus cursed under his breath. "Listen, Cole, you're going to have to get her out of there."

What? "And go where?"

"Here. Come back to Vegas. Tell her that you've gotta do a CFA expo for Spike TV or something. I don't give a shit what you've gotta do or say, just get her the hell out of there before that bastard does something that can't be undone."

"You want me to lie to her?—because that's a great foundation for trust right there."

"It's not lying. Spike's been buggin' the hell outta me, trying to schedule a time to do a segment on your recovery ever since your accident. I've just been putting them off until you were in a better frame of mind to have a bunch of cameras in your face."

"And you think *now* is that time? Fucking A, Marcus, I'm a goddamn wreck! And even if I did agree to the interview, which I'm not, she wouldn't come with me. She's got no reason to follow me halfway across the United States—"

"Then give her one."

"Are you fucking shitting me? Are you hearing yourself? You're actually suggesting I seduce your niece? Jesus, Marcus, you of all people should know what a horrible idea that is. My track record with women is like oh-for . . . I can't even fucking count that high."

"Dammit, Cole! How many times do I have to tell you to watch your mouth? I'm asking you to protect her—whatever it takes."

Whatever it takes? Holy hell, nothing like having the man who'd effectively served as his conscience, the man he loved and respected more than anyone, pull out all the stops and give a green light to bang his niece. The only reason he'd shown this much restraint was out of respect for her uncle—his mentor—his friend. Talk about your broken moral compass. That Marcus would suggest something so far past the line was a red fucking flag if he'd ever seen one.

"How much danger is she really in here, Marcus? How serious is this guy?"

"Serious enough to have her hopping on a bus in the middle of the night with nothing but the clothes on her back and hardly a dollar to her name. Serious enough to disappear for two years where no one knew where she was."

"Fuck . . ." Cole growled, roughly dragging his hand through his hair.

"Don't you dare tell her I told you this, either. Katie doesn't like to talk about it. I'm the only one who knows—not her parents, not anyone. The only reason I'm telling you now is because I know she won't and I'm expecting you to keep her safe until you can get her to me."

"She's not going to up and leave her dad. He's the whole reason she's here in the first place."

"You can get her to do it, boy. I have faith in you."

The bathroom room opened and Cole muttered a ripe curse. "I gotta go. She's coming." He didn't wait for an answer before disconnecting the call. Steeling his nerve, Cole prepared to have a sit-down with Katie to discuss the situation with her ex, but taking a breath before inviting her to sit down was as far as he got. Cole's breath stalled in his lungs when she appeared in the hall, transformed from a hot mess to a fresh-faced angel. His heart momentarily stopped and all rational thought ceased.

Her form-fitting jade green scrubs matched her eyes. The light smattering of makeup she wore highlighted her flawless complexion. It was a drastic contrast from the face paint he was used to seeing on women, and he discovered he liked the natural look—a lot—or maybe he just liked Katie. Her still-damp hair was coiled in a twist and pinned up high on her head, giving her an innocent, sexy librarian look. The haphazard disarray at the ends hinted her hair was just as untamable as the woman. His chest tightened, suddenly making him aware of his heartbeat rioting inside his rib cage. *Utterly gorgeous* were the words that came to mind as she stood there wearing a mask of composure he almost bought.

CHAPTER

14

Katie was busy contemplating the need for a handheld shower head if she was going to survive living with Cole for the next few months, when she entered the living room and came to an abrupt stop. Speak of the devil . . . And he looked every bit the sinful beast, watching her from across the room. If anyone had perfected the art of impassivity, it was this man right here. Unwavering crystal-blue eyes, clear and vibrant as a cloudless day, bore into her with an intensity that sent a needle of apprehension prickling up her spine.

On a base level, the woman in her responded to him like a moth drawn to light. But the rational part of her knew she should be wary of him, of this attraction burning between them like a forest fire. Perhaps if she hadn't been so rudely interrupted this morning, she'd have a better handle on her hormones. But she had been, and she didn't, leaving Katie downright cranky. Her skin felt too tight for her body, her clothing irritated her flesh—brushing against overly sensitive areas and abrading others.

Drawing on her last reserve of control, Katie straightened her shoulders, stood every bit as tall as her five-foot-four frame would allow, and walked into the kitchen. "Have you eaten?" she asked primly, heading for the cupboard to grab a coffee cup and trying not to notice the heat of Cole's gaze searing her ass.

"I did. What about you? Would you like something?"

Was he actually offering to cook her breakfast? For a moment, she considered saying yes, curious to see how that would play out, but she was running late—and this time it was her fault. She shook her head. "I prefer to drink my breakfast." She raised her mug in the air in salute before taking a sip.

"When you're done, would you please come sit down? There's something I want to talk to you about."

The gravity in his voice told her this was a conversation she wasn't going to appreciate having. After the night she had, Katie was neither in the mood, nor of the patience, to have a sit-down with the sexy Cole Easton. "Can it wait?" she asked, moving toward the window over the kitchen sink to read the current outside temperature—minus fifteen. "I gotta stop at the store before I go to my parents this morning, remember? We should get going."

"It really can't, Katie."

Exhaling a sigh, she brought her coffee cup with her and slipped into the chair across from him. "Okay, what do you want to talk about?"

Cole's expression gave nothing away, nor did his voice when he reached into the center of the table and slid her phone toward her, then asked, "How long have you been getting these messages?"

Katie froze. In that moment, two emotions ripped through her. Rage competed with terror, and she latched onto the first and safest one of the two. "You read my messages?" she snapped in outrage, grabbing her phone. "What gives you the right to invade my privacy like that?"

"How long, Katie?" His deep voice was low and even—unrattled by her indignation. That piercing gaze of his never wavered.

"Just yesterday. Did you read them?" she demanded, scrambling to hang on to the anger quickly giving way to panic.

"Did you?"

No. And she wasn't sure she wanted to. Katie's hand was shaking so badly, she clutched the phone tighter, trying to steady the message displayed on the home screen so she could read it. *I'll fucking kill you before I see you with someone else! You belong to me!*

Katie's heart dropped into her stomach. Her gut clenched, threatening to give back the coffee she'd just drank. If Carter thought she was involved with Cole . . . he would kill her. And this text was proof he was just crazy enough to do it. How had he gotten her number? Only hours after seeing her with Cole at the bar, the calls and texts had started. It was only a matter of time before he discovered where she was staying. Maybe he already knew.

"Katie?"

She barely registered Cole was speaking; his voice a million miles away as her pulse hammered in her ears, drowning out everything but the panic threatening to consume her.

"Katie, talk to me. This guy's a fucking wackjob. I think you need to report this to the police. Get a restraining order or something."

She shook her head, unable to tear her gaze away from the death threat. "I've tried. Trust me, Cole, it'll only make things worse. If he knew I'd gone to the police, he'd come after me for sure."

"What makes you so sure he won't do that anyway?"

"What makes this any of your business?" she snapped defensively, knowing damn well he was right, but it was easier to shoot the messenger than face what Cole was suggesting. Setting her phone on the table, Katie shoved her chair back and walked over to the counter. Giving him her back, she braced her palms on the counter and leaned forward, shifting her weight off legs that suddenly felt weak in the knees. Dropping her head to her chest, she closed her eyes and took a series of slow, deep breaths, struggling to keep it together. Her mind raced in time with her heart as Cole's words began to take root.

She didn't hear him approach. Katie let out a startled yelp when Cole's hand circled her bicep and he gently turned her to face him. Casually, he leaned his hip against the counter for support, his free hand bracing against the granite counter to bear the brunt of his weight.

"This became my business when Marcus sent me here." Cole released his grip on her arm and slid his hand up to her shoulder, an innocent enough caress that she felt all the way to her toes. He gently squeezed, his thumb brushing over her collar bone. "I want to help you, Katie. I know it isn't going to be easy, but I'm asking you to trust me."

Help her what?—keep her safe?—for how long? In a few short months, Cole would be gone, and then where would that leave her? He wanted her to trust him, but he didn't realize what he was asking. How could she trust him when she couldn't even trust the feelings he was stirring inside her?—feelings she didn't want to have, not for him, not for anyone. They scared the crap out of her. *He* scared the crap out of her. In the short time she'd known him, Cole had gotten under her skin like no other man she'd ever known—awaking her in ways she'd rather pretend no longer existed.

"I'm sorry, Cole. I . . . just can't."

Something flashed in his cerulean eyes. If she didn't know better, she'd say it was disappointment. But the emotion was gone so fast she quickly convinced herself she'd been mistaken.

"I don't really know you. And trust doesn't come easily for me."

"You don't need to know me, Katie. Marcus knows me. He knows me better than anyone. Do you honestly think he'd send me here if he thought for one minute I would hurt you?"

Cole's hand moved to the side of her neck, his fingers wrapping around her nape. His thumb swept over the pulse pounding in her carotid—evidence of just how much his touch affected her. She closed her eyes and exhaled a shaky breath, forcing herself to remain still as fear warred with desire.

The last man to touch her nearly killed her—choking the life out of her as she struggled to breathe, clawing at the flesh-covered vice wrapped around her throat, squeezing . . . squeezing . . .

Tears burned her eyes as she tried to hold them back. Cole was not Carter, she reminded herself for the umpteenth time as she battled the memories and the rising panic gripping her throat. Katie tried to focus on steadying her breaths, concentrating on the masculine smell of earthy spice enveloping her as she pulled Cole's scent deep into her lungs.

Her lips parted, drawing him in, when Cole's mouth gently brushed against hers—light as a butterfly's kiss. She tensed to pull back, alarms sounding in her head, but then she heard Cole's voice breaking through her panic as he whispered against her lips, "Shh . . . you're all right."

She repeated his vow over and over in her head as his lips touched hers again, tentative and guarded, careful not to take more than she was willing to give. His kiss was gentle, nondemanding, and for a moment she felt the tide of desire rising up to break over the surf of her fear. Liquid heat suffused her body, melting into her muscles as she slowly began to relax against him. Katie's mouth yielded to his, and Cole immediately responded to her quarter, exhaling a growl of masculine approval.

She felt the rumble in his chest reverberate all the way to her toes as the angle of his mouth shifted to fit more fully over hers, the pressure of his lips growing firmer. Katie's pulse leapt as the tide swept back, revealing her shore of uncertainty. But Cole seemed to be completely tuned in to her and wholly in control of each measured touch. He immediately pulled back, teasing his lips over hers again, courting her mouth until another wave of desire rose up to take control of her again.

"That's it, Kat," he encouraged, his graveled voice an auditory caress that stoked the fire burning low in her stomach.

She thrilled at the pet name he whispered against her lips. It bespoke of familiarity, and the intimacy of it swiftly forged a connection to him that went beyond just physical desire. *This is dangerous*, her voice of reason warned. *You're getting in over your head.* She was a fool to open herself up to a man like him—a player who would see her as nothing more than another conquest. Yet all the common sense in the world couldn't seem to make her break away from the most amazing kiss she'd ever experienced.

"Open your mouth, sweetheart. Let me taste you," he coached softly.

His request was too tempting to resist, even when the little alarms sounding in her head warned her it was too soon. She wasn't ready for this. But Cole had been nothing but tempered with her, gentle and controlled. Surely, he was safe to explore a kiss with, she reasoned, letting him prove she could trust him.

Slowly, Katie parted her lips. As they met softly and exchanged breaths, the faintest hint of his cinnamon toothpaste tingled on her tongue. She shifted, moving a little closer, and his tongue swept over her top lip, sending a jolt of heat right into her core. Moisture quickly dampened the scrap of cotton between her legs and she uttered a soft mewl of approval when, this time, his tongue swept passed her lips and she tentatively met it with her own. They danced a moment and he retreated. A second later, he was back, teasing her wickedly, and then it was gone again.

They played like this for a while, his mouth seductively courting her to lower her defenses. Katie liked this game, thrilling at the feeling of power it gave her when another tortured groan echoed low in his throat. She grew bolder with her kiss. The next time when his tongue retreated, she followed, sweeping hers past his lips and entering his mouth. As she kissed him, Katie threaded her arms up around his neck, fingers slipping into the silky hair at his nape. Holy crap, he could kiss. No man had ever tasted so good. A soft moan escaped her on an exhale as she chased his tongue again, growing more daring—passion-drunk in the power of his kiss.

But then the game ended—abruptly and without warning. The growl that rumbled deep in Cole's chest became raw and untethered. His fingers gripping the back of her neck tightened, sparking a flare of warning she quickly tamped down as curiosity, and feminine longing temporarily overruled her common sense. But in the next moment, Katie quickly discovered that the dominance she thought she had over Cole had been only a mirage. The vestiges of Cole's control shattered like a stone thrown through untempered glass. His grip on her neck tightened—possessively—and before she could react, he pulled her up against his rock-hard body, shifted his head, and claimed her mouth in a searing kiss that stole every last bit of breath from her lungs. His tongue swept into her mouth, bold and dominating, conquering and possessive.

Katie froze as terror suddenly seized her heart. Instantly, she was ripped back into the past and it was no longer Cole's kiss she tasted, but the whiskey-soured kiss of Carter's mouth covering hers with punishing force. She tried to breathe past the choking grip he held on her throat, but could only draw small gasps of pungent air into her burning lungs.

"You ever try to leave me again and I'll fucking kill you, bitch!" he snarled the words against her mouth as he drove into her with brutal, rutting thrusts. Carter wasn't a small man, and he took delight in using his phallus as a weapon. Her sobs caught in her throat, choking off her

last gasps of air as his grip on her trachea tightened. Black spots blurred her vision, the pressure in her head was excruciating, second only to the pain between her legs. Katie prayed for death, knowing it was her only chance of ever escaping this monster. As the darkness came, she welcomed it, anything to free her from of this living hell.

It took Cole longer to realize something was wrong than he wanted to admit. Fuck, he was such an ass. He'd been doing so well, keeping the grip on his self-control tightly in check. It'd been so perfect, the way she'd slowly but surely opened up to him—so tentative and shy at first. But then Katie had grown bolder with her kisses, and operation "Gain Katie's Trust" had swiftly turned into a cluster-fuck of epic proportions.

She'd caught him off-guard with that toe-curling kiss that sent a blast of desire burning through his veins. The pressure coiling in the base of his cock strung him so tight, his balls began to ache. In the past, he'd been with more than his share of women, and none of them had ever snapped the leash of his restraint like Katrina Miller. He was always the one in control. Even when he let them believe they were in the driver's seat, he was always the one with his foot on the gas and brakes—until Katie got behind the wheel. She stomped on his accelerator and cut the damn brake line before he'd even known what hit him. Holy hell, how could this have gone so wrong so fast? One minute she was kissing him like he was her very breath, and the next she wasn't—breathing, that is.

Katie came awake on a startled gasp, and the terror he saw in those emerald orbs was like a roundhouse kick to the balls—which effectively deflated the cockstand he thought was going to take up permanent residence in his jeans. It was a good thing she was so damn small, or he would have had a hell of a time getting her to the sofa. After she'd passed out, Cole had tossed her over his shoulder, and using the one crutch he still had braced under his arm, carried Katie into the living room. He laid her on the sofa and sat down beside her. It was a tight fit, but he managed to squeeze in.

It took a moment for Katie's vision to clear. Slowly, her eyes focused on him, and his panic receded, as did the knot fisting in his gut.

"What happened?" she asked, looking around as if she were trying to figure out how she'd gotten to the couch.

"That's what I'd like to know." Cole reached down to brush a chunk of hair from her face. She flinched at his touch and he dropped his hand, exhaling a frustrated sigh. "What happened, Katie?"

"Nothing," she denied.

Which was a big fat lie. She tried to get up, and he planted his hand in the center of her chest, pressing her back down. He tried to ignore the way his palm molded between the deep valley of her breasts and the softness pillowed beneath his fingertips. "I'm not letting you up until you start being honest with me."

Katie scowled, pinning him with a testy glare. If he were a praying man, he'd be saying a Hail Mary for his balls right now, because this woman looked as if she was about to lay some serious ground and pound on his nut sac.

"Let me up, Cole."

Now this was the Katie he knew. The Kat the fighter in him admired—the woman who'd gotten under his skin. He much preferred her pissed off than frightened.

"What?" she snapped defensively. "What do you want me to say, Cole?"

"How about the truth?" he shot back, crossing his arms defiantly. If he had to bully her into telling him what the hell was going on, then so be it. It was for her own good. She shouldn't have to deal with this alone.

"You want to know all the wretched details of my past. Is that it?" She let out a harsh bark of laughter that held a lot of held a lot of pain, pain he was surprised to feel centered in his gut. "Where should I start?"

"You could start by telling me his name." *So I know who I'm going to kill.*

Exhaling a frustrated sigh of defeat, her deadpan gaze locked on his. "Carter Owens."

Cole's scowl twisted in confusion. "The football player?"

"Ex-football player. He was kicked out of the NFL a couple years ago for steroid and narcotic use."

"You're fucking kidding me." This was the guy who was harassing her? Holy hell . . . when he'd asked for a name, he hadn't actually thought he'd know of the guy. Cole reached up and scrubbed the back of his neck with his hand, trying to picture Katie with the athlete and not liking the images that conjured.

"Afraid not. I met Carter four years ago. He had a bad rotator cuff tear and was coming to me for PT. At first, he was kind and charming. We began dating. The first year was great. Things were going along fine and then he asked me to move in with him. Shortly after that, he began to change."

There it was—short, sweet, and to the point. She moved to get up, apparently having decided sharing time was over. He pressed her back down, and she exhaled a sassy huff. "What, Cole? What do you want to know? Do you want me to tell you about how he used to hit me? About how many times I was in the Emergency Room with bruised and broken bones, telling lies that no one questioned because God forbid an NFL star could possibly be beating the shit out of his girlfriend, right?"

He winced as if he'd just taken a kidney punch. Hell no, that wasn't what he *wanted* to hear. But he also knew she couldn't continue to carry the weight of this burden alone. He'd pushed her past her breaking point, and if he let her off the hook now, there was a good chance he'd never get her to open up like this again. Cole's jaw clenched as he locked his emotions down tight, refusing to give her the satisfaction of knowing how much hearing this was killing him. It'd only make her all the more justified in her struggle to hold on to her secrets and shut him out.

"Or maybe you'd rather hear about how I tried, time and time again, to get away, only to have him find me and drag me back home, and then punish me for trying to leave. Do you want to know about the sexual abuse he put me through? The degrading things he did to me?"

Of course not. He didn't want to hear any of this fucking shit. His gut clenched with rage, each admission worse than the last. Her words were like an insidious poison, wrapping around his heart, squeezing the life out of him as his mind quickly filled in the sordid details of her confession.

"Or should we talk about how I had to leave my career, my friends, and my family to hide halfway across the United States in bumfuck nowhere until he finally gave up his search for me? Only he's never really given up. He'll never give up. Not until I'm dead!"

"Katie, stop." Cole wasn't sure if he wanted it to end for his own benefit or hers. Already, he'd never wanted to kill another man more in his life. But she wasn't finished yet. He'd pushed her too far, and it was clear she intended to make sure he heard it all.

"Should I tell you about the fear that rips through my gut every time there's a knock on my door?—or the 'unavailable' call on my cell?" Her voice hitched with mounting hysteria. "Do you have any idea how many times I've changed my number and fled to a new city in the middle of the night because I was afraid he'd found me? Two years, Cole! I've been running for two years. I haven't let a man touch me since I escaped him, and I vowed I never would again."

He couldn't help but wince at the accusation in her voice.

"You want to know what happened in there?" She pointed to the kitchen, and he felt another stab of guilt. "You kissed me, and I freaked out! That's what happened. He's broken me, Cole. I'm ruined."

At her confession, he cupped her face in his hands, forcing her watery gaze to meet his stare. Tears slipped past her lids, running down her cheeks. He cursed softly, wiping away the wetness with his thumbs. "Kat, what happened in there was my fault. I lost control. I knew you were scared. I was arrogant and cocky. I thought I could handle you—but . . . goddamn, sweetheart, you just felt so good. And when you kissed me like that . . . I just lost it. " He couldn't believe he was telling her this. But then again, it was his fault things had gone down this way. He'd be damned if he sat here and let her take the blame for his fuckup.

"Please don't look at me like that," she whispered.

He frowned. "Like what?" Like she was the most beautiful woman he'd ever seen?—because she was. Like he wanted nothing more than to take her in his arms and erase every foul memory that bastard had imprinted in her mind?—because he did.

"Like you want to save me. It's no use, Cole. I'm a lost cause."

"You're far from that, Kat. It's going to be okay. You're going to be okay."

The faintest hint of a smile tugged at her kiss-swollen lips, making his heart kick in his chest. Tentatively, she reached up and placed her small hand on his cheek, her palm cupping the hard angle of his jaw.

"The way you say that, almost makes me believe it's true."

The sadness in her voice broke his heart. Katie deserved better than this, dammit—better than living every day of her life in fear, under the constant threat of her psycho ex finding her. Well, she wasn't alone anymore. Cole was here now, and he'd be damned if he was going to sit by while this piece of shit terrorized her.

"Carter isn't going to hurt you, Katie. Not again. I promise. But you have to let me help you, okay?"

Reluctantly, she nodded, forcing a smile that failed to convey she was totally convinced of his vow. But this time, when he reached for her she didn't flinch as he tucked that stray lock of hair behind her ear. It was a start, at least. "The last thing I want to do is frighten you," he said, letting the silk slide through his fingertips. "I don't want you to be nervous around me, or worry I'm going to keep coming on to you or something. I'm sorry that happened. I didn't realize . . ." And neither did her uncle, or Marcus never would have suggested what he had. "It won't happen again, Kat."

It was a promise Cole was determined to keep, even if it killed him—and it just might, he decided, shifting uncomfortably in his seat, trying to make room for his poor, aching dick.

CHAPTER

 15

Apparently, Cole intended to keep his promise. Much to Katie's chagrin, she couldn't stop thinking about that kiss. It haunted her dreams at night and preoccupied her thoughts during the day. The soft but firm feel of his lips . . . the delicious taste of his tongue as it teased hers . . . Thinking about that kiss swiftly resurrected an ache deep inside her—an emptiness she'd become all too familiar with over the last two weeks.

The days continued to pass with amiable politeness. They'd quickly settled into a routine that basically consisted of Cole accompanying her everywhere she went. He was taking this threat seriously, not that she wasn't. The mystery of how Carter had gotten her number had been solved easily enough when she'd gone to her parents' house the next morning and discovered he'd stopped by to "visit" them the night before, looking for Katie. Her number was in their address book by the phone. No doubt he'd gotten it from there when they hadn't been looking. She'd changed her number right away, which had immediately put an end to the harassing calls and threatening texts. But as much as she wished it otherwise, in her heart she knew the issue with Carter was far from finished.

Although Cole never seemed to be far physically—he took his self-appointed guardianship very seriously—the reserved distance at which he held himself since that kiss in the kitchen had become annoyingly inscrutable. Especially when Katie was finding herself making excuses to seek him out. Not that Cole wasn't easy to find. When they weren't doing his therapy twice a day—which she secretly looked forward to, welcoming the opportunity to touch him without consequence—Cole was most likely in the gym, whether at her work, or at home. He worked out incessantly, as if driven by an invisible demon he couldn't seem to escape. The fevered pitch of his training bordered on madness.

Before now, she'd never realized how much time and effort it took to keep a fighter's body honed and conditioned. But Cole was living proof of what one could attain through dedication and perseverance. He was making great strides in his recovery, moving around with much greater ease and fluidity. He'd abandoned one of his crutches altogether, and if it weren't for his tendency to favor that left leg, he wouldn't need to be using them at all. At the rate he was improving, no doubt it would hasten his return home—a thought that sat ill with her, and not just his absence would leave her vulnerable. The thought of Cole going home and returning to his old life, as if none of this ever mattered—as if *she* had never mattered—made Katie's heart ache.

She couldn't count the number of times in the past two weeks she'd been tempted to sneak across the hall. But in the end, her fears always won out. So instead, she contented herself with countless hours of what-if fantasies.

Even now, she was hard-pressed to focus on the task at hand. She'd been staring at Mr. Johanson's chart for the last five minutes in restless anticipation of Cole's two-o'clock therapy appointment. How much longer could she get away with *accidentally* touching his ass and brushing her breasts against his arm? How high up his thigh could her hands *accidently* ride before—

The knock on the door startled her from her musing—dream of the devil . . . "Hey there, I was just thinking about you." She smiled, glancing up from her computer to the doorway. The upturn of her lips immediately fell, her heart plummeting into her stomach. Her gut churned, immediately rejecting the fullness, threatening to throw it up. *Oh, my God!*

"Hello, Katrina."

Lesson number one: never make a promise you can't keep, and Cole was having one hell of a time sticking to his. He wanted Katie more than he'd ever wanted another woman in his life, and it was killing him—literally. In the last two weeks, Cole had worked his body into a continual state of self-preserving exhaustion. Even when he'd been in camps training for a fight, he'd never poured so many hours into such grueling exercise. But it was the only way he could stay focused and keep his head clear. Avoiding the temptation by removing himself from the source, while maintaining a close enough proximity to ensure Katie's safety, was proving to be a damn difficult task.

Each day that passed without incident, Cole could see her guard lowering, the tension in her shoulders easing. And damn if those bright, carefree smiles she'd occasionally cast his way didn't get him right in the heart. It pleased him to know his presence made her feel safe; her peace of mind was priceless—though it was coming at the high cost of his own. But it was worth it. Those rare moments when her carefully guarded walls slipped, he'd get a glimpse of the woman she used to be, the woman she still could become with the right encouragement—and damn if he didn't want to be that guy for her.

Unfortunately, Cole had a six-figure contract and a title that demanded otherwise. And he'd do well to remember that, a fact he was having more and more difficulty reconciling when he thought of leaving her and returning to his old life. He wasn't sure which suited him more: the anonymity and slower pace of life in a rural town, or sharing his days with a woman who was both gorgeous and intelligent. A rare combination of traits he'd yet to find in the circles he usually ran. Not that they couldn't be found, he supposed; Cole had just never been that lucky. He enjoyed Katie's company more than he ought to. The Marcus connection had provided a solid foundation in which something much stronger had begun to develop—something Cole purposefully ignored, though he feared if things kept continuing at this pace, he would eventually break. A man could only resist temptation for so long.

His twice-daily PT sessions were pure torture, delicious torture, but they killed him all the same. He swore to God if her breasts brushed against his arm, or those skillful delicate fingers accidentally rode up his thigh one more time . . .

Cole glanced up at the clock as he pulled down the bar attached to a weighted pulley—2:05. Katie was late. She was never late for his sessions. If anything, she was early—never missing an opportunity to inflict some torment.

Perhaps she'd lost track of time. When they'd had lunch in the cafeteria, she'd mentioned needing office time to catch up on her charts. Her twelve thirty had canceled, so she'd kept the afternoon open to get some paperwork done. It was only a few minutes. She'd be along soon.

When another five minutes came and went, an odd niggling of unease crept up Cole's spine. He released the bar, letting the weights clap back into place, and rose to go check on her. Tucking his single crutch beneath his left arm, he crossed the gym, using it mostly for backup in case his left leg fatigued. It wasn't quite as strong as the right yet, but it was coming along faster than he'd expected—a credit to Katie's amazing skill. Give it another week and he should be walking solo.

Cole had just stepped into the hall when he heard Katie's voice. "What are you doing here?"

The brittleness in her tone brought every protective instinct Cole possessed firing to life. He couldn't see inside her office from this angle, but the tension in her voice alerted him to danger.

"I'm here for therapy. It seems that's the only way I'm going to get you to talk to me."

The snark in that deep male voice conveyed aggression, which fueled Cole's: a healthy dose of his own testosterone flooded his veins. Stepping into the doorway, he moved up behind the guy hovering inside Katie's office. "Is there a problem here?"

He cast Katie a brief glance, noting the stark relief on her hauntingly pale face, before turning his full attention to the man filling her small office space. Cole recognized him from the bar. Now that he was getting an up close and personal look at the guy, his memory made the connection with the Packers. Carter fucking Owens . . .

The guy stood maybe a couple of inches shorter than Cole, but he was a solid twenty pounds heavier. He was big and bulky—steroid bulky. His muscles lacked definition and tone, but he was a bear of a man nonetheless.

"Who the hell are you?" he demanded, making a sweeping glower over Cole.

Cole wasn't intimidated, nor was he impressed by the badass scowl Carter leveled at him. He'd been in enough weigh-ins and had had enough guys staring him down that peacocking bullshit didn't faze him. In fact, he'd discovered over the years that the more they preened, the more they were posing. It was the silent, flat-affected ones you had to watch out for. Those guys would knock your head off if you weren't careful.

"Carter, this is Cole Easton—my patient," Katie offered, when Cole didn't.

Her patient? Oh really? So that's what this was?—good to know. Cole would have sworn they were more than that—unless maybe she felt up all her patients. Were it not for Katie's obvious discomfort, he might have taken offense at her swift dismissal of their— admittedly complicated—relationship. Cole shifted his weight, leaning his shoulder against the doorway, taking his weight off that damn aching left leg. When neither he nor Carter spoke, engaging in a weigh-in-worthy stare-down, Katie broke the mounting silence.

"Cole is an MMA fighter currently holding the CFA light-heavyweight title."

He detected the note of pride in her voice and knew it for the warning it was. Cole wanted nothing more than to sink his fist into this bastard's jaw, and it wouldn't take much provocation to make that happen.

The man crossed his arms over his beefy chest and cocked an arrogant brow. "Is that right?"

"That's right."

"Where do you come from?"

"Vegas." Cole kept his stance loose, which in no way meant his guard was down. He braced against her doorjamb, standing to his full height, while keeping his sole attention focused on the man in front of him—the man he wanted nothing more than to pound the shit out of. As tempted as he was to glance over and check on Katie, he wouldn't risk giving that prick the edge of a surprise attack, or chance him seeing Cole's concern for her.

"Awfully far from home, aren't ya?"

Cole shrugged. "I wanted the best. She's it."

Seconds ticked by with Carter just staring at him. "Are you fucking her?"

Katie gasped, her sharp intake of air sounding wholly offended.

Cole's jaw clenched. The release of adrenaline flooding his veins burned through his muscles, stringing the corded bands tight. He shoved away from the door frame with his shoulder and took a measured step forward. "If I was, it sure as hell wouldn't be any of your business." Before he could close the space, getting within striking distance, Katie shot around the desk, jumping between him and her ex.

"Cole, don't do it," she quietly implored, pressing herself up against his body. "That's what he wants. He wants you to hit him so he can have you arrested."

If it weren't for the fact he'd be leaving Katie alone and vulnerable, it might have been worth it—correction, it definitely would have been worth it. Cole slipped his arm around Katie's waist, tucking her into his good side. The protective gesture was more than enough to wipe that shit-eating grin off that fucker's face. His eyes hardened, narrowing with murderous rage. Cole met his glare full-on with one of equal censure and growled. "Careful, Owens, I hit a hell of a lot harder than a woman."

Carter's eyes flickered to Katie, the dig hitting home as the realization dawned on him that Cole knew the truth. As if seeking the reassurance of his strength, Katie slipped her arms around his waist, clinging tightly to his side, and implored, "Please, leave me alone, Carter. It's over."

He glared at her as if *she* had betrayed *him*—as if somehow this were her fault, which made Cole question this man's sanity. "I tried, Katie." He held his hands up in surrender and moved a step toward her. As Carter advanced, Cole pivoted, pulling Katie behind him. "I tried to make things right, but you just won't listen." He started to leave, then paused at the door, turning back to glower at her. "This is on you now. Because I promise, it is far from over."

Carter turned to leave. A low growl tore from Cole's throat as he lunged for the door. He didn't give a fuck if he got arrested or not. He'd get out of jail well before that bastard got out of the hospital. But Katie clung to Cole's waist, struggling to hold him back. Without the full use of his left leg, and dragging her across the floor, it slowed him down just enough for that piece of shit to make a hasty retreat. *Son of a bitch!* "You stay the fuck away from her, Owens!" Cole roared, his voice booming down the hall. "You hear me? You stay the fuck away from her!"

CHAPTER

16

Cole was vaguely aware of the petite body crushed up against him, clinging to his side. Her shaking finally caught his attention, her tears dampening his shirt, hot moisture searing his flesh. He looked down to find Katie's face buried into his chest, her shoulders wracked with sobs. She'd tried so hard to hold herself together. Now that Carter was gone, that strong façade crumbled, leaving in its wake the aftermath of her terror.

"Shh . . ." he crooned, wrapping his arms around her slender back, pulling her tight against him. She fit so damn perfectly, like she'd been made just for him. The invisible band around his chest squeezed, making it difficult to breathe. His heart ached from the pressure.

"You're all right. Everything's going to be fine." The vow tumbled from his lips with more assurance than he felt. Cole had known her asshole ex was crazy, and hearing stories was one thing, but to see it face-to-face was quite another. It was only a matter of time before that bastard snapped, and God help this woman if she was in his path.

Marcus was right in wanting to get her out of here—by whatever means necessary. But to what end? She couldn't keep running forever. At least here, she had him to keep her safe. Bottom line: as long as that bastard was sucking air, he would to be a threat to Katie. Which didn't leave Cole a whole hell of a lot of options.

Her sobs had quieted to the hitching-breath kind, the ones that accompanied sporadic hiccups. She looked so damn fragile, huddled in his arms, her own, wrapped tightly around him, clinging with a desperation that stole the breath from his lungs.

"Come on, sweetheart. Let's go home."

She nodded her consent into his chest, but made no attempt to move. He wanted to get her out of here—get her home. Home . . . the thought resonated with him as did the inexplicable desire to protect her. It wasn't out of any obligation to Marcus that he cared for her, though Lord knew, he owed the man that much. This . . . thing . . . growing between him and Katie was a different sort of beast altogether. The desire he felt for her was like a living, breathing force, something he was becoming hard-pressed to control.

The tenderness he felt toward her tugged at his heart. Since he'd never been in love, he had no reference to compare such emotions. But whatever it was he felt for Katie, the emotions were raw and visceral, and not entirely pleasant or welcomed. They made him feel vulnerable and exposed in ways he'd never experienced before—and he didn't like it. Yet there were those times when she'd give him a look from across the room, or curl up beside him on the couch during a rare moment when he wasn't killing himself in the gym, and he'd get a glimpse of what his life could have been like had he taken a different path and settled down.

Since meeting Katie, Cole was continually at odds with himself. He didn't want this complication, yet he wanted her—with an unquenchable need. He wanted to protect her, to take care of her, to love her . . . to make love to her and claim her for his own. And after witnessing her encounter with Carter, it brought all those emotions he'd been trying to bury bubbling up to the surface.

Cole's body stirred in response to her innocent touch. His blood heated, pooling in his groin. Despite his efforts to control his lust, he felt himself hardening against her. The light, lavender scent of her skin, the feel of her breasts crushed against his chest . . . God help him, he wanted this woman. If he didn't put some distance between them, she'd soon be feeling the evidence of his arousal digging into her hip.

Cole gently untangled himself from Katie's tentative grasp and took a step back. Framing her face in his hands, she met his stare as he dried her tear-stained cheeks with his thumbs. The urge to dip his head and taste her lips was nearly too great a temptation to resist. But he wouldn't take advantage of her like this. She was shaken and vulnerable, turning to him for comfort—not seduction—and considering what happened the last time he'd kissed Katie, Cole knew all too well how quickly he could lose control with her. The last thing he needed to do was frighten her more than she already was. He'd promised her he wouldn't touch her again— told her she could trust him to protect her. And he'd be damned if he was going to stand here and prove himself a liar.

"Do you want me to get your purse?"

She shook her head. "I'll get it." Katie took a step back, and it was hell to let her go. But then she paused, giving him a peculiar look. "Where's your crutch?"

Out of habit, he glanced to his left, just now realizing it wasn't there. "I don't know. I must have dropped it." He'd been running on adrenaline since he'd walked in here and found that bastard in Katie's office. Apparently his adrenal system worked just as well as that gimp stick. Right now, he couldn't even feel the ache in his leg. Though once the octane left his system, he was pretty sure he was going to be feeling it in more places than that. He'd jerked his back when he'd lunged for the door and already he could tell the muscles were tightening up.

"Oh, here it is," she said, pulling the crutch out from under her desk and handing it to Cole.

"Thanks." He propped it under his arm and reached for the light switch, waiting for her to walk by before hitting the lights. He followed her out, pausing to make sure the door was locked before he headed down the hall toward the elevators.

Neither of them spoke as they rode to the top. Though she was still visibly shaken, he couldn't help but admire her efforts to keep it together. Cole purposefully kept his mouth shut. That bastard had pushed his buttons, and he was having a hell of a time shedding the pent-up aggression bottled inside him. He needed about an hour with a heavy bag before even attempting to discuss the Carter issue with Katie.

When Cole thought about how close Carter had gotten to her, how easy it'd been to approach her—and what could have happened if he hadn't shown up when he did? His gut twisted with what-ifs. Right now, the bastard was still trying to win her back. How much worse would it get now that he knew it wasn't going to happen? Cole must have let his expressionless mask slip to the dark, broody scowl that mirrored his emotions, because Katie reached over and took his hand, giving it a little squeeze.

"I'm sorry I dragged you into this," she whispered. "How embarrassing and utterly unprofessional."

Unprofessional? Fuck unprofessional. They'd moved past that point about the time his tongue had been in her mouth. "You have nothing to apologize for, Katie. None of this is your fault. And you didn't drag me into anything. I offered."

"But you look so mad . . ."

That's because he *was* mad. He was bloody furious—but not at her. Maybe at himself, for letting that fucker get near her, but he could never be mad at her. Exhaling a sigh, he laced his fingers with hers and tugged her closer. "Come here." Katie took a step toward him and he pulled her into his arms, hugging her tight against his chest. "If anyone should be sorry, Katie, it's me. I never should have let him get that close to you."

"Don't blame yourself. You can't be with me every second of the day. I'm just grateful you came when you did."

He didn't respond, not trusting himself to say something he wouldn't regret. Instead, he held her as the elevator rose to the main level. When it bumped to a stop, a chime announced they'd reached their floor, and he let her go just as the doors slid open. They exited together, walking to the parking lot. Cole was about to suggest they swing by the house and get cleaned up and then head into the cities for supper, when they reached her RAV and the words died in his throat, replaced by a snarled oath.

Katie gasped and stumbled a step back, bumping into Cole. His hand immediately came around to steady her. "Oh, my God . . ." She couldn't believe what she was seeing. Keyed into the driver's door was the word *BITCH*. Her windshield was shattered, and two of her four tires were slashed.

Cole growled a ripe curse. "I know what you said before, Katie. But this has gone too far. We have to call the police."

Cole didn't give her a chance to protest. He dialed them himself, and fifteen minutes later, a squad car pulled up behind them. He remained silent throughout the interview, interjecting only when the officer specifically spoke to him. When he asked Cole the nature of their relationship, there was a moment of decided hesitation.

That was a really good question. What was the nature of their relationship? And would he be honest with the officer? The last time her mother asked him a similar question, she'd been painfully disappointed with the answer.

"Katie is my physical therapist. I'm staying with her during my recovery." When the officer's brows rose in suspicion Cole added, "I needed a place to stay that had certain accommodations for my injury. The house she's renting is handicap accessible, and her uncle is a close friend of mine."

It sounded so simple—so logical, she thought. So then why did it feel much more complicated than that? *Because you're falling for him, idiot*, her inner goddess was quick to answer. Katie didn't have time to deny it—which would have started an internal debate she stood no chance of winning—because the officer surprised her by asking, "That's it? You're not romantically involved then?"

"Would it matter if we were?" Cole challenged, his brilliant blue eyes hard and defensive.

"Well, apparently it does to someone." The officer pointed at her RAV. "Listen, I'm only asking because in my experience, these things have a way of getting out of hand. I'm not trying to pry into your personal lives, but in order to do a thorough risk assessment here, I'm going to need the whole story."

The officer turned to her expectantly. Katie reluctantly nodded, and recounting the past proved every bit as painful as she feared it would be—talking about things she'd rather not speak of, thinking about things she'd rather not remember.

When she got to some of the more sensitive details, Cole must have sensed how difficult it was for her, because he reached for her hand, giving it a supportive squeeze. She knew this wasn't easy for him to hear when she noticed the little muscle above his cheek twitching. Casting him a quick glance, she saw his jaw clenched in effort to restrain his anger.

What neither Cole nor the cop knew was that she'd given them a censored, abridged version of the story, telling him only what he needed to know for the report. The officer recommended she file a restraining order and helped her fill it out, which had required her to give more details than she'd wanted to. The officer was confident it'd go through, not that Katie had a lot of faith a restraining order would do any good. But at least having the decree would help exonerate Cole if things happened to get out of hand—and by the looks of her SUV, she'd say that ship had already sailed.

The tow truck arrived just as they were finishing the report, and the officer kindly offered to take them home. Once they got there, Cole headed straight into the gym. As the hours passed, he hardly spoke, withdrawing into a broody silence that set Katie's nerves on edge. By the sounds echoing from the room, he was wailing on that heavy bag with a fevered intensity.

She wanted to go to him, needing the comfort of his strength more than she wanted to admit. What happened with Carter had rattled her—badly. She didn't know what she would have done if Cole hadn't shown up when he had. She wanted to thank him, but she wasn't exactly sure what to say. The nervous energy thrumming through her veins made it nearly impossible to sit still.

Getting up from the couch, she paced a path from the kitchen to the gym door, hesitating every time she reached the solid oak panel, wanting to go to him, but afraid to take the first step. Turning around, she retreated to the kitchen and decided a glass of wine might help take the edge off her nerves. Perhaps then she'd have more courage to go talk to Cole. She pulled a bottle of Lambrusco out of the cupboard and was wrestling with the cork when she heard the door open. Before she could turn around, another shut, and a moment later the shower started up.

Well, alrighty then. That oughtta give her just enough time to down a glass of wine—maybe two if she was quick about it.

Cole tipped his face into the shower's spray, letting it beat against his flesh as the burn in his poor abused muscles slowly began to subside. Damn, his back hurt. He really must have jarred something. The muscles in his lower lumbar had tightened up like a board, which did zero to improve his pissy mood. The last thing he needed right now, on top of everything else, was the reminder of how far he still had to go if he had any hope of defending his title against De'Grasse.

Just as he'd suspected, as soon as the adrenaline had left his system, the aches and pains had set in. His legs ached, his hips were sore, but he hadn't let that stop him from beating the shit out of that heavy bag. The workout had helped to defuse some of his aggression, but had done zero to outlet another kind of aggression that had been building inside him for weeks now. Every man had his breaking point, and after today, Cole had just about reached his. The protectiveness he felt toward Katie only stoked his primal need to claim her for his own.

He'd never thought himself a male controlled by his baser instincts, which was ironic considering how he earned his living. It was that animalistic, testosterone-fueled drive that made him the great fighter he was. He'd just never found anything worth fighting for outside the cage—until Katie. Cole knew she was shaken by what happened today. And he wanted to be there for her. Problem was, he didn't think he was strong enough to do it. Not without breaking his promise to her and risking losing her trust.

It'd been hell to stand there, listening to her tell the officer about the suffering she'd endured at Carter's hands—the haunted look in her verdant eyes, the tremor in her voice when she'd spoken of the abuse. And as brutal and horrible as it had been, Cole couldn't shake the feeling there was a lot more she wasn't telling him.

Cole wasn't sure how long he stood there, letting the water beat into his tired muscles, but when the jet stream turned cold, it finally forced him to move his ass. Leaning heavily on his crutch, he used his other hand to grab a towel off the rack and did a quick dry job before wrapping it around his waist, tucking the loose end against his hip to hold it in place. Droplets of water fell from the ends of his hair, landing on his shoulders and sluicing down his chest and back.

He felt like a hunched-up old woman as he gimped his way from the bathroom, but at this point he just needed to find a tolerable position for his back, so granny style it was. Cole's progress from the bathroom to his bedroom was a painfully slow process. He purposefully didn't search out Katie's location, hoping to get into his room unnoticed. The thought of her seeing him like this was damn emasculating, and he knew the ass chewing he'd be in for if she discovered how much he'd potentially set back his therapy.

Stepping in tandem with his crutch, he gritted his teeth, biting back the groan of pain as he walked to his bedroom. He'd almost made it to the door when a glass bottle connected with the granite counter top and Katie demanded from across the kitchen and living room, "What's wrong with your back?"

Aww hell . . . This was the problem living with your damn PT. Nothing got past her. "I'm fine," he replied through gritted teeth.

"Bullshit. My grandma's got better posture than you. And she's dead."

He could hear her marching across the living room and quickened his pace, trying to escape to the do-not-enter zone of his bedroom before she caught up with him.

"I told you, you've been pushing yourself too hard, Cole."

Before he could pass through the doorway, Katie darted in front of him, planting her palm against his abs like a traffic cop. The moment she touched him, a hot jolt of lust shot right into his groin, making him instantly hard.

"Are you trying to get away from me?" she asked with a suspicious scowl.

Yes. "No."

"Liar."

Before he could respond, she slipped behind him, placing her hands on his back, deft fingertips tracing the line of his spine and fanning out to follow his muscles. She immediately found the sore spot in his back, but it was nothing compared to the throbbing pain in his cock. He bit back a groan, but it managed to escape him on exhale.

"That's it, isn't it? That's the spot."

It was so not the spot, but what-the-fuck-ever. Katie's hands were on him and it was blissful torture. She was in her bossy PT mode, which was so much better than how she'd been earlier. Perhaps she craved the distraction, needing something else to focus on besides her shitty afternoon, because Cole just about dropped to his knees when she said, "Why don't you go get dressed and I'll get the Biofreeze. We need to work these knots out."

Oh, for the love of God . . .

CHAPTER

17

Katie would have loved to blame her impulsive offer to rub Cole's back on the three glasses of wine she'd just consumed, but in truth, she was still stone cold sober and resorting to altruistic pretenses to get close to him. He was avoiding her—again, and after the day she had, she just wanted to be near him. Okay, that was lie. She was looking for an excuse, any excuse, to be near him, to touch him, without having to admit the truth of it—she wanted Cole Easton.

But she was scared—hell, terrified—to let him touch her again. She was afraid he would lose control again, like when he'd kissed her. The moment had been amazing, his touch consuming and intoxicating, but Cole was a powerful man, a passionate man— more man than she was prepared to handle. In theory, she wanted him to make love to her, to blot out any remaining memories of Carter that still haunted her dreams. But in reality, she was a sad, broken woman using pathetic excuses to be near the man she desired but was too big a coward to go after.

At the thought of rubbing Cole's back, her pulse leapt with anticipation. The bottom dropped out of her stomach as she grabbed the tube of Biofreeze off the shelf and headed for the couch. Minutes felt like an eternity as she sat there waiting for him to come out. When Cole didn't appear, she started to wonder if he changed his mind about taking her up on her *selfless* offer. The thought that he might have disappointed her more than she wanted to admit. Had hearing the details of her horror with Carter scared him away? Had he finally realized what she'd been trying to tell him all along?—that she was just too ruined? Rallying her nerve, Katie rose from the couch and approached his room.

The door was ajar. She could see Cole between the crack, standing at his dresser. His back was to her, and he was clad in nothing but a pair of red low-riding gym shorts with the word *Tapout* printed across the ass in white. Katie's breath halted in her lungs. She took a moment to appreciate his exquisite form—broad shoulders tapered to a trim, narrow waist—before making her presence known. Cole's muscles rolled and flexed as he leaned on his crutch, maneuvering to apply deodorant beneath one arm and then the other.

He truly was a thing of beauty. It was amazing to watch the rate at which he was recovering. She just hoped the damage he'd done today didn't set him back. Katie had never worked with an athlete more driven, more focused, or more dedicated than Cole. It was incredible to watch how he pushed his body, day after day, to limits that would break any other man. Cole had the heart of a survivor, the heart of a champion, and the more time she spent with him, the more she grew to admire him. But right now, she was mostly admiring his ass.

If he knew she was standing there, ogling him from the doorway, he gave no indication of it. Taking a deep breath and steeling her nerves, Katie knocked softly on the door frame. Cole looked over his shoulder, not seeming surprised to find her standing there. She held up the tube of Biofreeze, reminding him why she was hovering in his doorway.

"Are you ready?"

"You sure this is such a good idea?"

His tone was soft and husky, like a caress she felt all the way to her toes. If she didn't know better, she'd have sworn she heard a hint of warning in his question. Perhaps she should take heed.

"Of course," she replied, using her best professional voice. "Why wouldn't it be?" He looked as if he was about to say something, but then thought better of it. "I'm your therapist, Cole, and you're hurting. It's my job to help you." She wasn't sure who she was trying to convince more of this charade, him or herself.

But apparently he wasn't buying it, because his brow arched in question, silently challenging her motives.

"Can I come in?" she asked a bit testily.

As if decided on something, Cole gave her a smile that warmed all the way to her toes. Seriously, it wasn't fair for a man to be this sexy. Although her nerves were still rioting, a part of her relaxed at his charming grin.

"Do you need an invite?" He capped the deodorant and set it of the dresser. "What are you, a vampire? You're not gonna sneak in here in the middle of night and attack me if I let you in, are you?" He shot her a teasing grin over his muscled shoulder.

She laughed, but the tension thrumming through her veins made her sound a bit hysterical.

"Besides," he continued, moving gingerly toward the bed, "that was your rule, not mine."

Cole set his crutch against the nightstand before easing himself down on the edge of the mattress. His handsome face tensed in the slightest wince. If she didn't already know him so well, she would have missed it. He was hurting more than he let on, which helped renew her determination to help him.

Leaning back against the pillows, he stretched out in a lazy sprawl. The woman in her couldn't help but appreciate his masculine grace. Her therapist's eye couldn't help but notice he was favoring his left side. Cole took up a good amount of the queen-size bed that now looked more like a twin. Lacing his hands behind his head as if he hadn't a care in the world, he gave a crooked grin. "You've always been welcome in my bedroom, Kat."

Her heart slammed inside her chest as the meaning behind those words sucked the air from her lungs. He'd used that intimately playful nickname again. He hadn't called her Kat since the day he'd kissed her in the kitchen. Was he thinking about kissing her again? By the way he watched her beneath his heavy-lidded gaze, the way his unnaturally blue eyes raked over her, lingering on her breasts that suddenly felt heavy and tingly, she'd guess he was thinking of more than kissing.

Her throat felt ash dry. "Don't you, umm . . . think we should do this out there?" Suddenly the thought of climbing into bed with Cole didn't seem like the greatest idea. After weeks of avoiding her, limiting their interaction to passably polite, he seemed to have suddenly flipped a switch, assaulting her with the full weight of his seductive charm. Gripping the tube of cold therapy gel like it was her lifeline, she told herself to stop being such a wuss. *You can do this, Katie. He needs your help, and he won't break his promise.*

Cole shrugged. "There's more room in here. This way I can stretch out."

Well, she couldn't really argue with that logic, now could she? Tentatively, she moved closer to his bed. He wouldn't hurt her. She was safe under the guise of wanting to help him. As she sat on the very edge of his bed, she couldn't help but remember the last time she was in his room—staring at a very naked, bare-assed Cole.

His brow arched in a look of wry amusement and something a lot less playful. "Are you planning to use your bionic arm to rub my back?"

"What?" Oh, seriously, her palms were actually sweating.

"Having second thoughts?"

"No," she denied a bit too quickly. "I'm waiting for you." Maybe if he'd stop looking at her like that, she could catch her breath. "Quit being such a smartass and roll over."

The bed bounced beneath her bottom as he rolled onto his stomach. His husky chuckle was muted as he wrapped his arms around the pillow and propped his chin against the fluffy down. Katie scooted farther up the bed. When she reached his hips, she popped the lid on the bottle and squirted a bright blue strip down the center of his spine. He flinched as the cold gel hit him, and she let out a little malicious giggle.

"Think that's funny, do ya?" His muffled voice playfully growled into the pillow.

"Maybe just a little." She began rubbing the gel in with slow, small little circles, starting at his shoulder blades and then working her way down his spine. He exhaled a moan that sounded part pleasure, part pain. Lord help her, he felt incredible. It was like touching flesh-covered steel—hot, flesh-covered steel. "You have pretty bad knots."

"Before my injury I'd go in weekly for deep-tissue massages. It helped to keep me loose and maintain my flexibility. It's been a while since—oh, yeah, right there."

She couldn't get at the knot beneath his shoulder blade from this angle. Focused now on loosening up his back, which was imperative for his healing, she crawled over him and straddled his hips so she could center her weight and get more pressure on the knot.

He tensed, his whole body going rigid beneath her bottom. Burying his face into the pillow, he groaned, the muffled complaint a tortured-sounding exhalation.

"I'm sorry. I know this hurts, but we have to get these out."

He didn't respond, but she knew he was suffering through it. His breathing had become irregular. After several more minutes of silence, Cole finally said into the pillow, "Katie, how long are you going to keep doing this?"

Oh God, was it that bad? "I don't know. I'm almost done. You have a few more tight areas in your sacrum—"

He lifted his head so she could hear him more clearly. "That's not what I'm talking about."

Her hands stilled on his low back, her pulse jumping. She resumed her task, the heat of the Biofreeze tingling against her palms, heating her touch as she used her thumbs to follow the mapping of muscles across his flanks. She tried not to think about *his* heat radiating through those neoprene shorts, warming the insides of her thighs and the sensitive juncture between them.

"Then what are *you* talking about?"

Without warning, he rolled beneath her. Before she could catch her breath, Cole was staring up at her. The solid length of his erection was wedged firmly beneath her ass. The tip of him was pressed tight against the bead of her sex, and it took every last bit of her willpower not to shift her hips.

A muscle ticked in his jaw as he ground his molars together in what she feared was flagging restraint. When he spoke again, his rough, husky voice was audible foreplay. "Pretending you don't want me just as badly as I want you."

He shifted beneath her as if to make his point, rubbing the blunt head of his cock against her clit. She gasped in surprise as electrical shock waves shot up into her core, making the muscles involuntarily clench.

"Are you trying to see how far you can push me before I break? I promised I wouldn't touch you again, but goddamn, you're killing me, Kat."

She didn't know what to say. Her body was literally weeping for his touch. Could he feel the hot moisture of her desire gathering between the thin barriers separating her sex from his? Her pulse was clamoring in her veins, screaming at her to let go, but she just couldn't bring herself to take that step. "I'm . . . I'm sorry. I do want you, Cole. I'm just so scared."

He reached up to cup her cheek in his battle-scarred hand and whispered, "I know you are, sweetheart, but eventually you're going to have to trust someone again. You can't keep going on like this. And if not me, then who? I'm not going to hurt you, Kat. I want to help you get past this."

"But what if you lose control again? You're so big . . . the sight of you thrills me and terrifies me at the same time. You could hurt me without realizing it."

His top lip quirked up in a flirtatious grin. "You think I'm some clumsy youth that doesn't know how to handle a woman? I promise you, Kat, one night with me and you'll retire that shower head you've gotten so friendly with."

She gasped in outrage, her cheeks burning with embarrassment. Before she could muster up a convincing denial, he said, "I have an idea. My jujitsu belt is in my gym bag. Go grab it, will ya?"

Well, that wasn't what she was expecting to hear him say. More than a little curious as to where he was going with this, Katie climbed off the bed. She could feel the heat of Cole's gaze watching her as she crossed the room and unzipped the CFA bag. She dug through it, pulled out a black cloth belt, and held it up to make sure it was what he wanted. Cole nodded. She brought it over, but he didn't take it from her.

"Now come back up here." Curiously aroused, she climbed onto the bed. When she got closer, he reached for her, his hands circling her waist as he effortlessly lifted her the rest of the way up, depositing her back over his hips. The intimate position sent her already clamoring pulse kicking into a serious case of tachycardia. As she stared down at Cole, she became acutely aware of her false position of power. She was sitting on top of two hundred pounds of rock-hard muscle and primal strength that could strike at any moment, and she'd find herself on her back, completely at Cole's mercy. At the thought, her traitorous core clenched with longing but the adrenaline flooding her veins sent her fight-or-flight instincts into overdrive.

She felt a little like the unsuspecting fly suddenly caught in the spider's web, helplessly stuck, waiting for the superior species to descend and devour her. She couldn't do this. Her grip on his belt tightened as she struggled to rein in her panic. Perhaps he sensed her spike in fear because he took that moment to present his wrists to her—held together as if they were already bound.

"I tell you what, we'll do this slow, okay? I'll give you this one night of total control, Kat. You can bind my hands. That should take away your fear of me losing my restraint with you. You can have full access to my body—learn it, discover it, use it for your pleasure."

Holy. Shit! Was he actually serious? "Why . . ." She swallowed past the lump in her throat. "Why would you do this?"

"Because . . . I want you, Kat. I want you so damn bad it's killing me. And this is the only thing I can think of that might get you to let your guard down long enough to realize I'm worth the risk. But I'm telling you right now, this is a now-or-never offer I can't even believe I'm making, because I never submit—not in the cage and not in bed."

She couldn't believe she was actually considering this. He was offering her the one thing that threatened to break through her fear and shatter her resistance—total control. She'd be a fool not to take it. To have Cole at her disposal, to do whatever she wanted with . . . just the thought of it sent a jolt of longing flooding every cell in her body. Her core wept at the prospect of being filled by this gorgeous man.

As Katie unfolded his belt and began to wrap the black cloth around his wrists, her gaze anxiously flickered to Cole's for reassurance. It surprised her to see the melee of emotion swirling in his stormy eyes—passion, triumph, anticipation . . . and perhaps a small measure of uncertainty. Like he'd said, Cole wasn't the kind of guy that gave up control—ever. And that he was desperate enough to suggest this told her just how much he wanted her, how desperate he was to help her. In that moment, another layer of the ice she'd built around her heart melted. She was almost finished binding his wrists when he spoke and she froze midtie.

"I only have one rule, Kat."

Of course he would. She should have known it was too good to be true. Her anxiety was gearing up to make a swift and devastating return when he said, "No sex."

What?!

"You heard me."

Oh hell, did she just say that out loud?

"No sex," he reconfirmed.

Just in case she wasn't clear? Oh, she was crystal. She just couldn't believe what she was hearing. What kind of a game was he playing?

"If you can't agree, then the deals off."

He was really serious. Well, this confirmed it, Cole had officially lost his ever-loving mind. She couldn't believe it. *He* was actually telling *her* no sex? And then it suddenly hit her. Cole wasn't out of his mind at all, he was flipping brilliant. By taking sex off the table, he was retaining some of his precious control, while at the same time axing a chunk of her fear. He was dividing it into more palatable chunks for her to conquer. All the while, baiting her human nature to want the one thing she couldn't fully have—him.

She didn't think it was possible, but in the span of a few seconds, Cole had just managed to up the ante by substantial proportions. *No sex, huh?* She'd make him regret that stipulation and was thrilled at the idea of seeing him eat those words. The challenge he posed certainly helped to quell her last lingering doubts and fears. With a jerk of her wrists, she cinched the knot of his belt tight and said, "No sex, huh?"

He shook his head, looking as determined as ever. "No sex. When we're together for the first time, you're going to know you've been well and thoroughly loved."

CHAPTER

 18

The bonds were as much for Cole's benefit as Katie's. Truth?—he wasn't sure he could trust himself to keep his hands off her without them. Desperate times called for desperate measures, and he was nothing if not that. He couldn't very well renege on his vow and then expect her to trust him, nor did he completely trust himself not to break it if she didn't get off him. She'd straddled his low back to work out his knots, but was only succeeding in tightening the knot in his groin.

Unable to bear the torture another minute, he'd finally confronted her. Frustrated with her response, he'd rolled beneath her and immediately realized his mistake. Her cush little ass and searing heat of her core was centered directly over his cock. The damn thing bucked in response to her pressure. She must have felt it, because she gasped at the intimate contact and tensed, looking like a deer caught in the headlights.

He'd tried to shift his weight beneath her, which only succeeded in grinding her more tightly against his straining member. Biting back a growl of frustration that would wholly succeed in frightening her away, his mind raced with options, desperate to keep her here and force her to finally confront the attraction they'd both been fighting like hell to deny.

Enough was enough. He'd had all he could stand of pretending this elephant didn't exist. It was time to take the bastard out—with a fucking bazooka, if necessary. But then perhaps a gentler approach would yield better results.

It'd been an epiphany of genius in a moment of flagging desperation. He'd taken one hell of a gamble and only time would tell if it was going to pay off. With any luck, Katie would take advantage of his body and get herself worked up past the point of her fear. It was a great plan—if it worked.

Right now, tied to the bed and at Katie's mercy, Cole was rapidly rethinking the wisdom of his less-than-well-thought-out strategy. He'd told her no sex, determined to hold on to at least some semblance of control. Perhaps she would be more confident if she didn't have the added pressure of worrying he might have expectations about where this was going to lead. But now, Cole was starting to wonder if she wasn't going to use his clause against him.

His arms were stretched above his head, his wrists fastened together by the length of his belt and secured to one of the thick rungs on the headboard. It was by sheer will he remained at her mercy. Though she'd bound him tightly, he was plenty strong enough to break free if he'd had a mind to escape, but in doing so, he'd also be breaking Katie's trust and forfeiting any chance of being with her.

At first her touches were shy—timid—as the soft pads of her fingertips trailed the path of his triceps to his chest. But from the very beginning, her gaze devoured him, searing every place she intended to touch, ratcheting his anticipation for what was to come. It didn't take long for her feather-light caresses to grow firmer, bolder. She traced his collar bones with her thumbs, her hands moving over his chest as she took in every muscled dip and curve of his flesh. She missed nothing. It was erotic as hell . . . Never in his life had a woman studied him so intently, so thoroughly. As she touched his pecs, her pressure increased, and when the blunt tips of her nails dragged over the flat discs of his nipples, he knew he was in trouble.

A jolt of white-hot pleasure seared through his veins, he couldn't bite back the groan of delicious pain arrowing into the twin weights throbbing between his thighs—pressure building, making his shaft swell with the demand of release.

Her eyes nervously darted to his, but at seeing what felt like an inferno blazing inside them, her lush lips parted into a bold, sassy grin that ended with her catching her bottom lip between her teeth. She looked starved to taste him and the offer for her to do so hovered so close to the tip of his tongue he bit the inside of his lips to keep silent.

He wouldn't interfere—and as much as he wanted to give her bold, ear-blistering directions on where to place her hands and mouth next, he had to let her do this at her own pace. He had to allow her to work through her insecurities and discover the woman she'd buried deep beneath those hurts and fears—the woman she didn't believe existed anymore, but Cole knew was fighting for a chance to be set free.

As if Katie had read his mind—or perhaps she just wanted to drive him crazy—she dipped her head to his chest and slowly dragged her tongue over the nipple she'd just abraded. He hissed in a sharp breath through clenched teeth. His muscles drew tight, his back bowing off the mattress. The headboard creaked as he pulled against the tethered cord, his belt stopping him from lowering his arms and fisting his hands into Katie's pale, silky hair, desperate to guide her head down to his throbbing cock.

The thought of those lush lips, that hot, wet mouth tasting his cock, brought a bead of anticipation rising to the tip. Mercy, she was killing him—slowly and torturously killing him. Cole wasn't sure how much longer he could withstand this erotic agony without shaming himself by coming like some inexperienced adolescent.

The protesting headboard sent Katie's gaze darting to his bonds. She was checking to make sure they were still holding firm. Seeming satisfied that she'd adequately secured him, she gave him a seductive grin and dipped her head, tracing the trail blazed by her hands with her tongue. She mapped his abs, tracing the muscular ridges. It didn't take her long to discover he got off on the feeling of her teeth grazing his flesh, mixed with the softness of her sucking kisses. Each nip tore a tortured groan from his throat that seemed to fuel her fire, emboldening her exploring caresses.

"You have the most amazing body I've ever seen," she whispered against his stomach as her hands dragged over his hips, skimming the waistband of his gym shorts.

He would have responded, said something like *Thank you*. Coming from this woman it was a hell of a compliment, considering she'd spent a good portion of her career around athletes. But Cole couldn't seem to form a coherent thought in his head, let alone put one to voice. Her fingertips followed the line of his waistband, her thumbs teasing the indents of flesh at his hips. His breath stalled in his lungs as he waited to see if she'd have the nerve to do it— would she take them down?

Seconds felt like minutes. Eventually he had to take a breath, and the gasp of air ripping into his lungs broke the tortured silence in the room. The headboard creaked once again as Cole wrapped his hands around the belt, already stretched to its limit, and pulled tighter still. His back arched up just enough to lift his hips off the mattress, silently begging Katie to do it.

She hesitated another moment, before he felt her fingers slip beneath his waistband and the satiny neoprene slide down his thighs. His breaths were coming in quickened pants, as if he'd just finished a ten-mile run in the blazing heat of the Nevada sun. He was ready to explode, and she hadn't even touched it. No woman had ever affected him like this, and in truth, his reaction to her unsettled him. Desperate to rein in the last scraps of his control, Cole closed his eyes, forcing his breaths to slow as he began to recite grappling techniques in his head—anything to delay the inevitable release bearing down on him.

The cool air kissed the moist tip of his throbbing head, the bead of precum making it more sensitive. The pearlescent fluid escaping his restraint proved just how fine an edge Katie had so swiftly and effortlessly brought him to. As he talked himself off the ledge, the coiling pressure knotting in his groin eased enough to allow him to take full breaths again.

Realizing Katie was no longer touching him, nor was she speaking, Cole lifted his head and looked at the woman knelt between his parted thighs—her gaze fixed solidly on his cock. He'd expected to see that mischievous light in her emerald eyes, perhaps a smile of wicked intent as she imagined the torture she'd put him through. What he didn't expect to see, however, was the doubt and fear edging into her stare and the concerned frown wrinkling her delicately arched brows.

He wanted to reach out and pull her into his arms, to kiss her softly and ask her what in the hell had caused such a sudden shift in passion. But of course he couldn't move his fucking arms. For not the first time, he cursed his rash idea and vowed never again to do something so stupid and desperate.

"Kat . . . ?"

She didn't respond. Her eyes were locked on his straining erection, but that unfocused stare told him she wasn't seeing him.

"Katie, look at me." He spoke louder, his own haze of passion quickly fading in the wake of her renewed anxiety, his mind sharpening. When she still didn't move, he knew a moment of alarm and briefly considered freeing himself, but he wasn't ready to take the risk of frightening her further. *Goddammit!*

"Katrina! Look at me!"

She blinked a couple times, her gaze slowly coming back online as she hesitantly dragged her eyes up his body. By the time her eyes met his, hers were clear and focused. A bright blush was starting to stain her cheeks. "I'm . . . sorry," she quickly apologized.

"Kat, let me go." He purposefully used her pet name, hoping it would help anchor her to the present and clear away the remnants of the past that were clearly fighting to gain a foothold and drag her under.

Her eyes darted to the belt and she shook her head in refusal— because she feared him, or wasn't ready for this to end, he couldn't know. Of course she wouldn't make this easy.

"You mind telling me what's wrong, then?"

She blushed full-on crimson now, and he had no doubt that given the choice, she'd rather swallow her own tongue than admit the truth. Were he at all uncomfortable in his skin, Cole might have felt awkward as hell having this conversation with his dick hanging in the breeze. But at the moment, he was more worried about Katie's discomfort than his own. He refused to release her stare, waiting with growing impatience for her to speak.

After what felt like an eternity, she released her bottom lip from between her teeth and said, "I just wasn't expecting . . ."

"Expecting what?" he prompted, when she didn't finish her thought.

Looking wholly embarrassed now, she exhaled sharply and said, "I wasn't expecting you to be . . . so . . . big."

Cole covered his surprised laugh with an awkward cough and tried like hell not to grin like the Cheshire cat. "Sweetheart, I gotta tell you, that's usually a selling point."

She scowled at him and snarked, "I think we've already established I'm not like other girls."

Ouch. Okay, so that'd been a little insensitive. Cole instinctively reached for her, and was abruptly stopped by the tether of his belt. He frowned, glowering up at the bonds. He wanted to pull her into his arms and soothe her ruffled feelings. He wanted to tell her that it was part of her charm—that she wasn't like other women—and he didn't want her to be, either. But he couldn't move his fucking arms, and Katie wasn't making any move to rectify that.

"I'm sorry, Kat. I shouldn't have said that. It was insensitive. Maybe you're right. You're just not ready yet. Let me go."

"I don't want to."

Her refusal earned her the full glower of his wrath. "It wasn't a request."

"You were right, Cole. If I'm not ready now, I never will be. I'm more attracted to you than I ever have been to any other guy—ever. So if I can't do this now, with you, what makes me think I could ever do it with someone else?"

Okay, well first of all, the idea of her doing *this* with anyone but him made Cole want to kill someone. Katie was his, and he was done trying to fight it. Second of all, she had a valid point about now or never. She would never *be* ready. This was one of those things where she was just going to have to jump in and go for it—all in or all out. That she refused to release him told Cole she hadn't entirely decided.

"Can we, umm . . . just keep going a little bit?"

His dick must have thought she was asking *him* because he was saying *Hell yeah!* before Cole could answer her either way. In truth, he wanted out of these damn bonds and wasn't sure he had the patience for any more discovery time. But Katie's gaze dropped to the rising flesh between his legs and her smile roundhouse kicked him right in the chest. She still looked nervous, but at least the panic was gone.

Katie must have taken his body's swift response as all the answer she needed, because she crawled back over him and lowered her face to the side of his neck. As she licked and nipped a path to his collarbone, the brief thought crossed his mind that she'd yet to kiss him. He was about to ponder that thought some more, when she reached between them and palmed his rock-hard length. The tight grip of Katie's little hand circling his throbbing flesh obliterated any remaining thoughts in Cole's mind.

He exhaled a throaty moan as she nipped his pec, dangerously close to his nipple. She was getting brave—perhaps a little too brave. By the time Katie re-explored her way down his body, she'd gotten herself sufficiently worked up. The way she touched him, moved and rubbed her lush body against his . . . He'd lost count of how many times she'd nearly made him come just by grinding against him. He wondered how many marks he'd find on his neck, chest, and stomach by the time she was finished with him. And it was killing him not to be able to touch her back. He wasn't exactly sure what had flipped Katie's switch, but the longer she touched him, exploring his body, the deeper she seemed to bury her insecurities. A healthy dose of lust was a good balm for just about any ailment. It numbed the mind. Heightened the senses . . .

"I could climb on top of you right now, take you inside me, and there's nothing you could do to stop me," she taunted, seeming to enjoy his state of immobility far more than he was.

Holy. Fuck. It was probably a good thing he was bound right now, because this woman had worked him into such a lather, he was near out of his mind with the need to roll her beneath him and bury himself balls deep inside her hot, wet cunny.

"You won't do that," Cole warned through gritted teeth, praying she wouldn't do it.

"How do you know?"

Katie's breathy challenge tickled his ear, her teeth pressing into his lobe, riding that fine line of pain and pleasure like a pro. She'd spent the last torturous hour learning his body—discovering his erotic hot spots. She was still a little shy around his cock, but that was probably for the best. Any more attention down there and he'd be coming with the force of a fucking geyser, and this was not about him or his pleasure. It was about Katie and her needs—both physical and emotional.

"Because you gave me your word," he growled through clenched teeth.

"You want this," she pressed. "I can see it in your eyes. I can feel it in the way your cock pulses between my thighs, begging to be inside me."

Fucking A . . . what kind of a monster had he unleashed? She was getting too brave. Feeling too confident in the power she held over him. This would be hot as hell if he wasn't hog-tied to the goddamn bed while she tempted him mercilessly. He knew what she was doing. She wanted him to give in and let her find her release within the safety of his bonds—not a fucking chance.

"You're right, I do want this, but I want your trust more. And as good as it would be, feeling your tight little glove around me, it'll never be good enough for either of us if you can't completely trust me, Kat."

Katie froze. She lifted her head and scowled down at him. Fuck . . . it looked like he'd just gambled and lost. It surprised him when that disappointment took hold of his heart and squeezed painfully. He'd expected to feel that gripping pain deeper south.

But then Katie leaned forward, reaching above his head, and tugged the slipknot free. Exhaling a shaky sigh, she said with a soft voice that bore the painful edge of defeat, "All right, Cole, you win. We'll do this your way."

Thank God. It's about fucking time . . .

CHAPTER

19

The moment his wrists were free, Cole took her face in his hands and kissed her. "You have no idea how bad I've wanted to do this," he growled against her lips before claiming her mouth in a soul-searing kiss. Katie could feel the veritable passion thrumming through his veins. The power, the need, coiled inside him—desire she'd courted. It was a heady feeling to know she could affect this man so strongly, and she'd taken great pleasure in toying with him. But now was a completely different story. He was no longer bound and unable to do anything about it. The silver-tongued devil had convinced her to let him loose.

Katie instinctively tensed against the initial flare of fear struggling to break the surface. If Cole noticed the flicker of trepidation, he gave no indication. Slipping one hand up to cradle the back of her head and the other around her side, pressing flat against the center of her back, he pulled her closer, deepening their kiss. A satisfied growl of pure masculine pleasure rumbled in his chest. The vibration teased her nipples, sending currents of pleasure right into her core. Lord, he felt good . . .

After a few minutes of oral courtship, Katie began to relax, melting in his arms. Tension eased from her muscles as her lips yielded to the pressure of Cole's demanding mouth, his tongue stroking hers with breathtaking skill. She let out a startled gasp when her world suddenly tilted. A split second later, she was on her back, pinned to the mattress by Cole's solid weight. He moved so fast, so fluidly, the rapid change in position left her grappling for her bearings for a moment.

Cole is not Carter, she reminded herself again when those old memories tried to resurface. No, nothing about these men was the same. Not the build of Cole's definably cut body, molding against every inch of hers, or the ardent touch of his hands that nearly trembled with the power of his flagging restraint. Hands that earned a living giving pain offered her only pleasure if she could just let down her guard and accept it. She wanted it. She wanted Cole—wanted to know what it was like to be loved by a man like this.

"Stay with me, Kat."

Had he sensed her slipping? Cole's low, husky voice whispered next to her ear. Hearing the name only he called her ripped Katie back into the present. And it was that moment, she was sure Cole had stolen her heart. He was more in tuned to her needs than she'd given him credit for, allowing her time to battle her demons. But when he'd sensed she might be losing the fight, he swept in to save her—his voice a beacon of light to guide the way back, his touch an anchor, pulling her out of the quagmire of suffering and pain, pulling her back to him—back to the promise of pleasure.

"I'm here," she whispered, sliding her hands up his back to grip his shoulders, needing him closer.

Cole lifted his head from the trail of kisses he'd laid down her throat, his vibrant azure gaze locking on hers. In that breathless moment, something indescribable passed between them. It was spiritual and kinetic—lustful, yet loving—passionate, but gentle. Without exchanging words, she knew what he was asking of her, knew where this was headed, and to the depths he wanted to take her.

Did she trust him enough to let go and surrender to him? Because the fire in his eyes promised it was going to be one hell of a ride.

Yes. She did. She wanted this—more than anything. With her heart clamoring inside her chest and the stir of butterflies rioting in her stomach, she nodded, answering Cole's unspoken question.

Passion flared in his eyes. He tensed, his hard body turning to stone above her. For a breathless moment, he appeared to be warring for control and the strain in his voice confirmed it when he said, "Say it, Kat. It's not for me. You need to hear yourself say the words. Say that you want me—that you want this. That you trust me."

He didn't know what he was asking—then again, maybe he did. Perhaps she wasn't giving him enough credit. Cole was a man who demanded total control—in every aspect of his life—so why would she think he'd be any different in the bedroom?

"Say it now or this stops," he warned. "I won't be with you until I know for sure you will have no regrets."

She had no doubt that as much as it would kill him to do so, if she didn't meet his demands, Cole would indeed get up and leave her there. And the knowledge that even when he seemed out of control, drunk with lust and mindless with passion, he was still ultimately in control, gave her the last bit of courage she needed to push past her fears and hand Cole 100 percent of her trust.

Meeting his stare, she laid her palm against his stubble-roughened cheek and said, "I want this, Cole. I do trust you."

Something flashed in his eyes, but she was too afraid to name the emotion for fear she was wrong. He wasn't offering her love, he was promising her passion, a chance to heal, and she'd do well to remember that.

"I'm going to take good care of you, baby. I promise," he vowed before capturing her mouth in a plundering kiss as he slipped the thin straps of her tank top off her shoulders. Katie let go of Cole long enough to pull her arms free of the elastic straps and then dove her hands into his hair. He growled his approval when her nails scored his scalp. The cloth abraded her nipples as he dragged her top down, her breasts coming free of the confining cotton. Heavy and tingling, they ached for his touch—the heat of his mouth, the slick softness of his tongue, and the sensual bite of his teeth.

How many times had she fanaticized about this moment, imagining what it would feel like to be at the mercy of this man's touch? Cole didn't disappoint. Shifting his weight, moving down her body, he grasped her breast and squeezed with just the perfect amount of pressure as his thumb teased her nipple to a turgid peak. Katie moaned, her back arching into his touch. Her grip on his still-damp hair tightened, and he chuckled wickedly as his mouth descended on her breast. He sucked hard on the sensitive tip, sending a jolt of erotic electricity right into her core. She gasped as her muscles contracted against the emptiness, the ache in her womb tightening as her body wept to be filled.

Katie's breaths quickened, and she squirmed beneath his solid weight, trying to find some relief from this growing restlessness. Cole took his time torturing her, trapping her nipple between his tongue and teeth, toying with her as he learned her body, just as she had his. Only now she was the helpless one, writhing beneath him as he kissed and nipped a trail down her stomach.

When he gripped her bunched-up tank top and the hem of her pajama pants, she eagerly raised her hips to help him slide them down. He chuckled at her haste, a satisfied masculine rumble that suddenly cut off, morphing into a furious growl.

Katie's hands instantly shot to cover her inner thighs, a cold slap of reality making her heart clench, the fire burning inside her core rising to her cheeks. Ashamed and self-conscious, she made a grab for the covers, but Cole was faster and caught her wrist before she could reach them. How could she have forgotten? She never forgot . . .

Fighting back tears, Katie struggled to banish the emotion in her voice as she met Cole's eyes, now blazing with something other than passion. "Let go," she told him, struggling to close her legs, but he was kneeling between them. She could feel her control slipping, the panic edging in. She tugged harder to be free of his steel-tight grip. "Let me go!"

How could she have let this happen? She was always so careful . . . but Cole had swept her into such a mindless bliss, she'd forgotten to make him turn the lights off. And now he knew—knew the shame she lived with every day of her life, the scars she could never fully heal from—marks that ruined her for any other man, because no one could ever touch her again without thinking of that monster.

You're mine and now everyone will know it . . . If I can't have you, Katrina, no one will . . .

It didn't matter that Cole wouldn't be to able read the scarred letters that were now just a bunch of crude disfiguring slashes on the insides of her thighs. She knew what they said. Katie flailed to get her leg around Cole, to get free before she broke down in front of him and humiliated herself even further. Her panic escalated, hysteria shrilling her voice. "Goddammit, Cole, let me go!"

But instead of loosening his grip, it tightened. And the look of determination that settled on his face told her he had zero intention of releasing her. Katie snapped; her only thought, freedom. Tears blurred her vision, distorting Cole's face as she balled up her fist and punched him. Pain exploded in her hand as she connected with his jaw. Cole muttered a foul curse and before she could get in another swing, he was on her. It didn't matter how much she fought, how much she flailed, she was battling against an MMA fighter. In a matter of seconds, he had her subdued—pinned to the mattress, and she was pretty sure it only took him that long because he was trying not to hurt her.

She couldn't move. Cole's legs were locked around hers, his chest pressed against hers, trapping her between a wall of muscle and the mattress. He held her arms stretched above her head, hands locked tight around her wrists. They were both breathing heavily— she from exertion and Cole no doubt from the effort to control his temper. Shit, she'd just decked the CFA light-heavyweight champion of the world. What in the hell was she thinking?

"You want me to tap?" she snapped, bucking beneath him in a futile attempt to dislodge him. Not her best idea. They were both naked, and grinding against him wasn't going to help the situation. "Fine! I tap! Now let me go! I'm done!"

She rallied her anger, using it to keep herself together as she clung to her last scraps of self-preservation. If she started crying now, she was pretty sure she'd never stop. She couldn't believe how quickly a perfect moment could go so terribly wrong. And the heartbreaking thing was, she'd almost believed Cole could get her through this. For the first time she could remember, she'd finally felt safe . . . cherished. And God forbid . . . loved.

And then just like that, in the blink of an eye, it'd all been ripped away. Cole would never want her like this, damaged and scarred with the name of another man carved into her flesh. Every time Cole crawled between her legs, the scars would haunt him just as they haunted her. How could she ever expect him to get past this? She couldn't, she didn't. It was over . . . Her one chance at happiness—ruined.

Cole didn't say anything as he stared down at her with that inscrutable glower, all emotions locked down tight. The only hint at his anger was the muscle twitching in his tightly clenched jaw. The stubbled skin on the left side of his jaw was a little red, the only sign he'd weathered the storm of her wrath.

"That's not what I want, Katie. This isn't a competition. You're not my opponent, dammit."

Then what was she to him? She wasn't his girlfriend, and after tonight she certainly wouldn't be his lover.

"If it isn't a game, Cole, then why do I feel like we've both lost?"

He winced, a fracture in his steely resolve, a show of pain he hadn't even yielded when she'd decked him.

"I saw the look on your face when you saw my scars, Cole. Don't lie to yourself, or to me, by trying to pretend this is something you can get past."

"You're not being fair by assuming I can't. And to tell you the truth, it pisses me off that you won't even give me the chance. How in the hell was I supposed to react? I'm furious that bastard's done this to you, and knowing he's gotten away with it just makes it all the worse. I could kill that piece of shit for what he's put you through."

"That's just it, Cole. Don't you get it? I don't want my past becoming your future. I can't stand the idea of you thinking of that monster every time you look at me—" Her voice broke off and she swallowed back the well of tears rising up her throat.

"What were you planning to do, Katie? Just never tell me he'd done this to you? Did you intend to hide yourself from me forever?"

Her silence was just as good as a response.

Cole swore a vile curse, dragging a hand through his hair, his other still trapping both her wrists. "You were, weren't you?" he accused. "Dammit, Katie, why do I always feel like I'm flying blind with you? Maybe if you'd talked to me, I'd have been better prepared—"

"What was I supposed to say, Cole? My fucking psycho ex found out I was leaving him and he beat the shit out of me? For crissake, he held me down and carved his name in my legs with a hunting knife! That's not exactly the kind of thing you tell the guy you're falling for." Cole winced. But she wasn't done yet. Not by a long shot. "When he finished cutting me, he raped me—over and over again. There was so much blood . . . I thought I was going to die. I prayed I would so I could finally escape his torture. That was the last time a man has ever touched me and I swore to God it would be the last time one ever would. But then I met you . . ."

The horror of that night tumbled from her lips and with it an unexpected burden lifted. No one knew the suffering she'd endured, not even Uncle Marcus. She felt a sadistic stab of *See, I told you so* when she saw the shock in Cole's eyes as her nightmares became his reality. The damage was done. She'd already lost him, so she might as well tell him the truth—the whole truth. "I didn't want to be attracted to you, and I've been fighting it since the moment I met you. But then the more time I spent with you, the more I could see you were nothing like him. I found myself wanting to be near you, and then I'd become afraid when you'd get too close. I guess for a moment I thought—I'd hoped—I could have a shot at being normal again." A tear slipped from the corner of her eye and she turned her head to wipe it away with her shoulder. "But I know now that's not ever going to happen. I'm sorry, Cole. I should have told you. You're right, it wasn't fair to you. Now, please . . . will you just let me go?"

Something had cracked in his steely expression. She wasn't sure exactly what it was, or when it had happened, because she hadn't been able to face him any longer. But God help her if that was pity in his cerulean eyes. She'd endured enough humiliation for one night. Katie bumped her hip against his, nudging him to let her up. They'd both said all there was to say, and she just wanted to go to her room and have a good, long cry. When he didn't move, she pinned him with an *I'm serious, let me up right now* glare. What she wasn't expecting was for him to actually respond.

"You have a fighter's heart, Katie. You're stronger than you realize, and I admire your spirit. It's what draws me to you. Well, that and you're smokin' hot."

A choking laugh caught in her throat. It sounded about as pathetic as she felt.

"Your right hook has some promise, too. I think we could work on that. Give me a little time, and I think I could turn you into one hell of fighter."

Was he for serious? Cole let go of her wrists and shifted his hold, slipping his hands beneath her shoulder blades and untangling their legs to slide between hers, leaving her torso the only part of her still pinned against him. Bracing his weight on his elbows, he stared down at her, raw emotion etched on his gorgeous face.

"I don't want to let you go, Kat. And if you're honest with yourself, I don't think you want me to, either."

He shifted again, bringing his erection into contact with her parted thighs. There was no pressure, no prodding, just the delicious heat of him resting against her opening. The temptation to part her legs wider and grant him access to her aching core was nearly too much to resist. The proof that he still wanted her was undeniable, and just as surprising as her own resurgence of longing. Already, she could feel herself growing wet for him, the coil of desire tightening around her womb. Despite her misgivings and flat-out fear at the size of him, her body still craved Cole's touch. But how could he still want her after seeing her shame and knowing her secrets? How could he still be looking at her with such hunger and raw, honest yearning?

A part of her was afraid to trust it. As much as she wanted this to be about physical healing, and as much as she'd convinced herself she didn't need more from him, deep down she knew it was a lie. If she gave herself to Cole, she'd be giving him her heart and soul. And she was scared to death that when this was all over, he was going to go back home—back to Vegas—and he'd take her broken heart with him.

His granite flesh bucked against her slippery folds, asking for permission, begging for entrance as he held himself statue-still above her. "I want you, baby. But if you say no, I'll understand. If I'd only known, I wouldn't have pushed you so hard. I feel like a selfish bastard for wanting you still. If I let you go without telling you, I'm afraid you'd get the wrong idea. I want nothing more than to make you mine. But this is your decision—no pressure."

He didn't have to give her any pressure. The pressure building inside her was already nearly unbearable. Everything that made her a woman, every nerve ending, every desire, every instinct, all clamored for Cole's touch. She wanted him to fill the emptiness inside her—she needed to experience what it meant to be a woman again.

"I want you to make love to me, Cole." Would he know what she was asking? Did he realize this was about more than just sex to her and was he capable of giving her more than that? He'd told her before he'd never been in love. Perhaps he just wasn't equipped for such emotion. Sadly, some men weren't, and she was taking a big gamble on him now.

He dipped his head to kiss her, but she turned her head to the side and stopped him by planting her palm on his chest. "Do you think you could . . . umm . . . turn off the lights first?"

His brows tightened to a disappointed scowl and he shook his head, refusing her request. "Not a chance, Kat. I don't want you hidden from me. You are so gorgeous . . . this body is every man's wet dream. Trust me, you have nothing to be ashamed of." He pulled her hand away from his chest and bent down to kiss the tip of her nose—her cheek—her jaw—her neck . . . "Besides," he whispered next to her ear, "I want to see your beautiful face when you come apart for me."

She gasped at his bold, erotic words, and he chuckled—a wicked, seductive chortle that warmed all her achy places. She'd never thought dirty talk could be so . . . hot. Then again, Katie had the feeling Cole was going to show her a lot of things she'd never known before.

"I'm going to try to go slow, but I want you so damn bad. If I move too fast or you start to get scared, you have to tell me, okay?"

She nodded.

"Promise?"

She nodded again.

He nipped the sensitive spot on the side of her neck and then licked away the sting, sucking and kissing a trail down her throat. "I can't hear you," he teased, slipping his hand from beneath her back and cupping the side of her ribs. He swept his thumb against the underswell of her breast and then over the sensitive tip—back and forth he played, waiting for her to answer.

"Yes . . ." she whispered. "I promise."

"All right then." He inched down and slowly dragged his tongue over the tip of her breast and then lifted his head to meet her gaze, his eyes a mesmerizing brilliant blue. "I'm not going to handle you with kid gloves, Kat. That's not my style and I don't think it'd be doing either of us any favors. I can't get you past this if we're dancing around it, you know?"

She nodded. His brow arched in question. "Y-yes." She hardly recognized her own voice. It sounded so husky, so breathless, so . . . needy.

"Good. Then just sit back and enjoy the ride, sweetheart."

CHAPTER

Was it possible to come without actually being touched down there? Katie was sure she was about to find out. Her breaths sawed from her lungs, her kiss-swollen lips parted, and she panted as she writhed beneath Cole's wicked mouth and skillful hands. Every nerve ending was on fire. Her nipples burned from his attention—overly sensitive and throbbing to the slightest touch, and at the same time aching for more.

Cole hadn't shaved tonight and he put the stubble to good use, abrading her flesh and heightening her pleasure in the most erotic and creative ways. All the while he'd yet to touch her where she ached to feel him most. His hands had been everywhere else. And his mouth . . . oh mercy, she'd known he was an excellent kisser, but that tongue of his was a multitalented tool, whispering the most erotic promises she'd ever heard.

Katie wiggled up the bed, trying to inch Cole's mouth closer to her clit. He chuckled sadistically and grasped her hips, dragging her right back down the mattress to where he wanted her. A startled gasp broke from her throat as his tongue dipped into her navel. His hands returned to her thighs, teasing, stroking, sweeping ever so close, but not close enough to give her the relief she was ready to start begging for.

At first, when he'd touched her thighs—her scars—she'd tensed, a moment of alarm clouding her thoughts. Anxiety swelled in her chest and she'd almost protested, telling him to stop. But then she'd recognized the intention of his touch, and trapped her bottom lip between her teeth in order to keep silent.

Little by little, Cole was imprinting her with his touch, desensitizing her while training her body to recognize and respond to him—and only him. It was working. In this moment, nothing else mattered, not her past, not her hurts, not her fears or insecurities—nothing—only the feel of his strong, calloused hands, the softness of his lips, and the warm wetness of his tongue as he took masterful command of her body. A body that was so tuned in to his, the only thing she could think of was finding that elusive release she longed for.

"Please, Cole, I can't stand it anymore. Touch me," she begged. "Let me come."

He lifted his head and the smile he gave her was so triumphant, so primal, Katie nearly found that release right then and there.

Dipping his head, he placed a chaste kiss on her mons and said, "Sweetheart, all you had to do was ask."

Her gasp of mock outrage turned to a moan of pure bliss when he slipped his hands beneath her bottom and lifted her just enough to tip her hips. His thumbs slid along the juncture of her thighs, parting the folds of her flesh to receive his kiss. Upon contact, a jolt of pleasure shot into her core so hard, she instinctively recoiled, pulling back. But Cole had a firm hold on her bottom, and his grip tightened possessively, strong fingers curling into her soft flesh, preventing her from going anywhere but to the moon.

She knew the moment Cole was done toying with her, and his sole purpose became her ultimate pleasure. Each caress of his tongue was so masterfully played, Katie found herself fighting against the rising waves she'd been desperate to dive into only moments ago. She didn't want it to end, and yet she was helpless to stop it. The pressure coiling inside her was too great, building higher and higher until . . .

Katie shattered with a hoarse cry of release, her back arched off the bed, hands fisting into the sheets, grasping to hang on. Cole skillfully pulled every last tremor from her quaking body, leaving her wrung out, her body exhausted from the delicious torture. He took his time kissing his way up her body, and by the time he reached her lips, she was writhing beneath him again, desperate to be filled by him.

"Holy hell, Kat, you're so hot," he growled against her mouth. "Your body's so responsive, so needy. You're going to make me come before I even have a chance to get inside you."

"Then what are you waiting for?" she pleaded, clasping the sides of his face and boldly returning his kiss. She shivered with erotic pleasure at the intimacy of tasting herself on his tongue. Inhaling his moan of flagging restraint, she refused to let her mind think. Instead, she focused on feeling—the weight of Cole's hard body grounding her, the feel of his hand slipping between her thighs, his finger sweeping between her wet folds and then entering her . . .

Katie gasped at the sudden invasion, the first niggling of doubt seeding into her mind. Cole stilled. He lifted his head, staring down at her, concern infiltrating the lust-filled haze in his startling blue eyes.

"You all right?"

She nodded. He didn't look convinced. In fact, he looked a little . . . worried. "Are you?" she asked him.

"Uh-huh."

"What is it? Tell me what's wrong."

"Nothing," he denied. "You're just . . ."

Oh God, just what? What is wrong with me?

"You're just . . . really tight. I can feel you're scared and I don't want to hurt you. Baby, you're going to have to relax or this isn't going to work."

Easier said than done. But she wanted this—she wanted it with Cole. She hadn't come this far only to have her fears rise up and conquer her now. "What do you want me to do?"

The smile he gave her was so tender, so . . . loving, her heart swelled with the emotion.

"Just let me touch you and try to relax."

"Okay." She took a deep breath and let out a long, shaky exhale.

Cole leaned down and kissed her, a sweet coaxing of his mouth against hers, courting her body to yield to him. His touch deepened—in and out, his thumb mercilessly teasing the bundle of nerves at the top of her sex. As he toyed with her, his kiss grew more ardent, more demanding, as he boldly claimed her mouth. The taste of her mixed with his fresh cinnamon-laced flavor, creating an erotic combination that sent her senses spinning. Her heart was pounding, the persistent sound banging in her ears . . .

Wait, pounding? Was that outside? "Cole," Katie panted, struggling to climb through the haze of passion and clear her mind so she could focus. "Do you hear that? I think someone is pounding on the door."

Cole tensed above her—listening. He must have heard it, too, because a moment later he muttered a nasty curse and rolled off her with startling speed. Snagging his gym shorts off the end of the bed, Katie glanced at the clock as he yanked them on. Her pulse quickened. "Cole, it's after midnight. Who could that possibly be?"

Their gazes momentarily locked, neither of them voicing the thoughts running through their heads, though they must have reached the same conclusion, because Cole's handsome face hardened into that merciless mask he donned in the cage—one of no fear and only pure, primal male aggression.

"Stay here."

He shot the command over his shoulder as he left the room, adrenaline apparently substituting for his crutch. Outside, an engine revved and squealing tires echoed down the street. The *snick* of the deadbolt sounded before the front door was yanked open, followed by an abrupt slam and a snarled curse. Katie's stomach dropped.

When Cole didn't come back, the knot of dread fisting in her gut tightened. Digging through the covers, she found her pajama pants and tank top tangled in the blankets at the foot of his bed, and rushed to get them on. With each passing moment, mounting fear quickened her pulse until her heart rioted inside her chest. As Katie stepped into the living room, Cole was coming back inside. The door slammed shut behind him.

"Who was it?" Katie stopped by the couch, unsure if she should proceed or sit down. Her head felt light, her legs unsteady.

"I don't know." His tone was as tense as his stance, the hardening of his muscles turning his already cut body to stone.

"Did you see anyone?"

"No. The car was taking off before I got to the door. But I can damn well guess who it was."

She gripped the arm of the couch and lowered herself to the cushion before her legs gave out. Her vision lost focus as she stared straight ahead. "Oh, God . . ." *Please don't let it be him.* But Katie knew her prayers would go unanswered. Despite her efforts to be so careful, telling no one where she was staying, using her parents' address for mail delivery, he'd still found her. "He's been following me," she voiced the realization out loud. That was how he knew what vehicle was hers. How long? How long had he been watching her? Had he been watching her tonight? The thought turned her stomach, and was followed by an even more alarming one.

Jumping up on wobbly legs, Katie ran back to the bedroom and abruptly stopped in the doorway, grasping the frame to steady herself. Just as she feared, the curtains hung open. A wave of revulsion swept over her and she pressed her hand to her stomach, fighting back the urge to vomit. Turning, she fled to the front door and wrenched it open. Unmindful of the bitter cold, she ran out the door, ignoring Cole as he shouted after her.

She barely felt winter's bite as she ran into the yard, her bare feet sinking into the snow past her ankles. The house lights provided just enough glow for her to see the trail of footprints leading around the house. Her heart rioted in her chest, her throat tightening with dread, making it nearly impossible to draw the frigid air into her lungs. Forcing one frozen foot in front of the other, she followed the tracks, already knowing where they would lead.

"Katie!" Cole's voice echoed into the night.

As she rounded the corner of the house, she stopped, and so did the footprints—directly below Cole's bedroom window.

"Katie, get back inside the house!"

Oh God, she was going to be sick! Turning back, she ran toward the house and burst through the front door where Cole stood, looking both worried and pissed as hell. Reaching out, he caught her in the doorway, grabbing her shoulders and forcing her to stop.

"What the hell was that about?" he demanded.

"He saw us!" she wheezed, her lungs burning from the frozen air. "The curtains are cracked and there are footprints leading around the side of the house that stop below your window!"

Cole snarled a curse that would have blistered her ears if she wasn't busy trying not to throw up on his feet. The feeling of violation mixed with frostbite made her skin crawl with the burn of a thousand fire ants. Her stomach rebelled—really, this time—and she shoved past him, tearing out of his grasp as she ran for the bathroom. Slamming the door behind her, she dropped to her knees before the porcelain throne.

Who knew it was possible to cry and puke at the same time? A wholly unpleasant experience, that. Thankfully, Cole gave her a few minutes to pull herself together before knocking on the bathroom door, though she'd need a hell of a lot longer than that.

"Hey, Kat, can I come in?"

Self-preservation had taken a strong hold of her now, the urge to shut down and draw into herself was instinctive. She knew she was pushing Cole away, but it didn't matter. This was never going to work, anyway. As much as she wanted to get over her past, it would forever haunt her.

"Kat, you're scaring me. Talk to me, sweetheart."

"I . . . can't . . . do . . . this," she hiccupped between sobs. "Please, Cole . . . just leave . . . me alone."

A soft thud echoed from the other side of the door. The sound one made when resting his forehead against it. A deep sigh resonated through the barrier and settled heavy on her heart. "Don't do this. Don't shut me out, Kat. I want to help you. We're going to get through this."

She wanted to believe him. She really did. But he had no idea what they were up against. Carter was toying with her, and he wasn't going to stop until she was dead.

CHAPTER
21

Cole wasn't sure how long he sat outside that bathroom door, but it felt like fucking forever. He'd never been one to cater to a woman's histrionic behavior, but something told him if he moved away from this door, he'd lose Katie forever. She was pushing him away. He could feel her withdrawing, shutting down, and in truth, it scared the hell out of him. They'd come so far, so close to breaking through her barriers and getting past her fears, and with the knock of a door, it'd all been undone.

He swore to God the next time he saw Carter Owens, he'd fucking kill him. The thought that he'd watched them through the bedroom window, seen Cole and Katie together, didn't bother him nearly as much as it did her. One man to another, it was the ultimate *fuck you*. He hoped that son of a bitch got a good long look at what he'd never have again—hoped the scream of her release would echo in that bastard's ears until Cole put him out of Katie's misery.

Damn, she'd been hot—so sweet—so responsive to his touch. The tentative trust she'd given him was a humbling gift Cole had been honored to receive. Never had a woman felt so good, tasted so amazing . . . never before had he experienced the soul-deep connection he felt when Katie was in his arms. Which made her rejection now sting that much sharper.

His ass was numb, having taken post on the floor some time ago. His legs ached, which was nothing new. He'd been abusing his body and pushing it past its limit for weeks—of course it was going to bitch at him, but he refused to move from this spot and seek the comfort of the couch. He needed her to know she could depend on him, that he wasn't going to let her push him away. He meant it when he said she could trust him, and not with just her body, though he wanted that, too. He cared for her, more than he was willing to consider at present, because that would just open up a whole other mess of problems.

How much longer could she stay in that shower? He posed the question in his mind for the tenth time when the water finally shut off. His imagination filled in the blanks as he heard the glass door rasp open. The cupboard door opened and shut. She'd be retrieving a towel to turban her wet hair, then grabbing a larger one from the bottom shelf to dry her body before wrapping it beneath her arms and tucking the corner near her breast. The soft pad of her bare feet against the tile drew closer. She was finally coming out. Thank God.

Cole went to rise, but before he could get to his feet, the door swung open and Katie nearly tripped over him. She let out a startled yelp and stepped one leg over his waist, quickly regaining her balance. He looked up at her, but was having a hard time meeting her surprised stare. She'd grabbed the short towel. It barely covered her ass, and from this position, he got a spread eagle view of those gorgeous thighs he'd been buried between just a few short hours ago, and that hot little cunny he'd been moments from sinking his co—

"What are you doing down there?" Katie demanded, reaching between her legs and grasping the ends of her towel closed.

Cole cocked his brow. "A little late for modesty, don't you think, Kat? You might try covering up some place my face hasn't been." He knew he was baiting her, but he didn't give a shit. He did it to remind her it wasn't going to be so easy to shut him out, and given the choice, he'd rather deal with a temperamental Katie than a tearful one—those tears just shredded him—so he'd court her temper if that's what it took to buck her up.

By the pinch of her brows, he knew it was working. He gave her a lopsided grin that was sure to melt some of the ice she'd no doubt been walling around her heart for the last two hours. She exhaled a disgusted sigh and let go of her towel to brace her hand against the doorframe, and held out her other to help him up.

"Come on, get up."

"If you're going to keep standing here, I'd rather stay on the floor." He slipped his hands behind her legs, sliding them up the back of her thighs, and tugged her closer.

"Cole, what are you doing?"

"Waiting for you."

"Why?" Her tone was soft with exaggerated patience.

He met and held her emerald stare. "Because you're worth the wait."

Tears gathered in her eyes, pooling on her lower lashes. One broke loose and landed on his arm. The hot moisture made his chest constrict, his heart ached with an emotion he dare not name.

"You're wasting your time, Cole."

"I'll be the judge of that. I know what you're doing, Kat, and I'm not going to let you." His grip on her legs tightened, his thumb skimming the inside of her thigh.

Her breath hitched. "I don't know what you're talking about," she denied. "Let me do what?"

"Push me away. Pretend that *this* isn't happening."

"That's because it isn't."

"Oh, it's happening." He slid his hands up beneath her towel to cup the firm globes of her ass. She gasped in surprise and locked the arm braced above his head, preventing him from pulling her closer. He wouldn't muscle her to get his way, though he could easily enough pull her to him, nor would he sit here and let her pretend she didn't want him just as badly as he wanted her. "For weeks I've been avoiding it—avoiding you. Pretending this isn't real, that I can control it. Well I'm done fighting, Kat. I can't do it anymore, not knowing how amazing you feel in my arms, how delicious you taste on my tongue—"

"It can't happen." She shook her head in denial. Was she trying to convince him or herself? "I can't. I was stupid to think it would change anything."

Okay, now he was getting pissed. Letting go of her, he shoved himself to his feet and glared down at her. "What are you talking about? What happened in there"—he pointed to his bedroom—"it changes everything. You're not a victim anymore, Kat. You need to stop seeing yourself as one, and I refuse to treat you like one." She flinched as if he'd struck her, which landed a solid blow to his gut. He didn't want to hurt her, but dammit, sometimes you had to reopen a wound to give it a chance to heal properly. He should know—been there, done that. "Carter has no control over you. Sure, he's being a pain in the ass and is doing his damn best to scare you, but I won't let him hurt you. This can't last forever."

"That's where you're wrong, Cole. It's not going to stop. *He's* not going to stop!"

"Oh, he's going to stop. I promise you that."

"The police can't do any more than they're already doing. We have no proof it was even him who came here tonight, though we both know it was. I know how this works. I've been through it before."

Cole reached up, taking her face in his hands, forcing her to meet his gaze. Locking his eyes with hers, he vowed, "Kat, you're

safe with me. I promise Carter will never hurt you again. One way
or another, this will end."

She wanted to believe him, but he didn't know Carter like she did.
It'd do no good to stand here and try to argue that point with him,
so she acquiesced, nodding her head in abject agreement. "It's late
and I'm getting cold. I'd like to get dressed and go to bed."

He seemed reluctant to let her go, though he could hardly
refuse her request. Tipping her head closer, Cole bent down and
pressed a chaste kiss to her forehead and whispered, "Good night,
Kat. It's going to be okay, I promise."

Stepping out of his embrace, Katie headed for her bedroom,
stopping at the doorway and turning to cast Cole a regretful glance.
This wasn't how she'd envisioned the night ending. Carter's inter-
ruption had effectively killed any hopes she had of putting her past
behind her. As much as she hated to admit it, it was probably better
this way. Better that Cole not get any more involved than he already
was with her fucked-up life.

He watched her from the hall, remaining silent, though she
sensed it was eating at him to do so. Cole was a fighter through and
through, and when he found something he wanted, he wasn't apt to
just let it go. She could see the determination shining in his vibrant
stare.

She'd crossed the line with him tonight, changed the dynamics
of their relationship the moment she'd submitted her body to this
awe-inspiring man. It was just semantics that he hadn't fully
claimed it. The intention was there all the same. She'd thought she
could do it—convinced herself that somehow giving herself to Cole
would right the wrongs done to her—heal her brokenness, but she

was wrong. She could see that now. It wasn't fair to put that kind of responsibility on him. Unable to hold his stare another moment for fear of breaking down, Katie looked away and entered her room, murmuring, "Good night, Cole."

Katie startled awake at the god-awful grinding sound coming from the kitchen. So much for *I'm not much of a morning person*. Who ran a blender at six a.m. on a Saturday morning? Stuffing a pillow over her face, she tried to drown out the noise. Big surprise, she hadn't slept for shit last night. When she wasn't jumping at every little noise, she was running a mental replay of being in Cole's bed. Either way, it equaled one sleepless night and one cranky Katie. In the still, early morning hours, she'd allowed her imagination to finish where Cole had left off—when they'd been so rudely interrupted. It didn't matter that she'd drawn a new boundary with him. In the privacy of her own mind, where anything goes, he'd taken her to Heaven.

Just thinking about it now made her pulse beat a little harder, throbbing in all the sensitive places Cole had explored. Her breaths quickened. She couldn't breathe with this pillow over her face. Snatching it off her head, she hurled it across the room. It landed against the wall with a soft thud, sending a poof of feathers puffing into the air.

Great. She'd just ripped a hole in her grandmother's feather pillow. Exhaling a sigh, Katie tossed back her covers and stomped around her bedroom as she got dressed, because, yeah, that was certainly going to help things. She would have preferred to stay in her pajamas, but after last night, she decided it wouldn't be very appropriate.

After pulling on a pair of black flare-leg yoga pants, she grabbed one of her stretched-out, ratty college sweaters and put it on over her tank top. Katie paused at the mirror above her dresser to get a quick look before heading out to face Cole, and was glad she did when she caught a glimpse of her hair. Good Lord, she looked like she'd been rode hard and put away wet—and no, the irony wasn't lost on her. She'd gone to bed with damp hair, and it had dried in an absolute mess. Snatching her brush off the counter, she raked it through her knotted tresses and then pulled her hair back in a severe, messy bun knotted on top of her head. It wasn't much of an improvement, but at least now she looked like controlled chaos.

She turned her head to the side for a quick back view and gasped. Stepping closer to the mirror, she leaned forward and pulled the skin on her neck taut for a better inspection. Oh Lord, there were two bright reddish-purple hickeys on her neck. Her cheeks instantly heated at the sight of them, whether from embarrassment, because the last time she had a hickey she was sixteen years old, or from the memory of getting them, she didn't know—probably both. But seeing Cole's mark on her flesh felt strangely intimate and arousingly possessive. For a moment she wondered where else she might have similar marks upon her body, but refrained from searching out the answer. She was better off not knowing, she decided, tearing her gaze away from the mirror.

The blender finally stopped. Katie opened her bedroom door and walked into the living room, intending to give Cole a piece of her mind. She made it as far as the couch when her feet suddenly refused to move, her ass-chewing lodging in her throat. Cole was standing at the kitchen sink, chugging what appeared to be a yellow smoothie. Apparently, he hadn't given as much thought to his state of dress—or undress—as she had, because he was standing there in nothing but a white skin-tight pair of Under Armour gym shorts. The wide black waistband sat low on his waist, the stretchy neoprene hugging every inch of those solid, muscular thighs. They left no detail untouched. Even at rest Cole was a man of impressive length. The outline of his sizable asset arched to the left and pointed down his thigh.

She might have made a noise, a gasp, or a startled squeak, she couldn't tell over the pounding of her pulse in her ears. Cole lowered his glass and turned his head as if just now realizing she was there. The seconds it took her to drag her eyes from his crotch were precious moments lost. By the time she dragged them past his abs and chest to reach his face, he was wearing a crooked grin that hovered between boyishly handsome and cocky male arrogance. Either way, the woman in her responded to him. The moisture dampening her black lace panties made her feel like Pavlov's dog, which did absolutely zero to improve her mood.

"Hey, Kat, you're up." He sounded surprised.

"Of course I'm up," she crabbed, forcing one foot in front of the other to enter the kitchen. "Who can sleep with that blender roaring away out here?"

He gave her a sheepish grin.

"And where's your crutch?"

"Not using it," he replied, sounding a bit like a defiant child. Turning back toward the sink, he rinsed out the remnants of his smoothie. "I'm sick of gimping around on it. The only way my leg is going to get stronger is with use."

Spoken like a true pig-headed athlete.

"I made you a smoothie." He grabbed the yellow drink off the counter, and turned to fully face her.

Katie gasped at the up-close sight of him, more specifically at the smattering of red marks on his neck. There was one on his pec, and Lord help her, even one in that sexy indent of flesh near his hip, just above his waistband. He'd been angled away from her at the sink, but now as he faced her full-on, she was forced to acknowledge, if only to herself, what she'd done to this magnificent body standing before her.

He said nothing about it, but she noticed his gaze briefly travel over her own neck as he handed her the glass.

"What's in it?" she asked, taking the glass from him, eyeing it skeptically.

"Butternut squash, mango, protein powder." He shrugged. "Lots of good stuff."

Katie lifted the glass to her nose and sniffed. "You know I don't eat breakfast."

Cole gave her a roguish grin. "Well, today you do. Go on, taste it."

She hesitantly took a sip.

"You're going to need your energy for what I've got planned for you."

Katie gasped at his comment and immediately started coughing, choking on her smoothie. Cole patted her back, chuckling. The deep timbre rumbling in his chest was like sex to her ears. "Cole, I don't think—"

"Relax, Kat. It's not what you think."

She was definitely going to ignore that twinge of disappointment.

"Finish your smoothie. I'm going to go get dressed."

CHAPTER

22

A gain."

Seriously? Katie stared up at the ceiling, trying to catch her breath, her heart galloping inside her chest. A fine sheen of sweat covered her body. The hair at her temples pulled loose from her messy bun, sticking to her face. They'd been going at it for the last two hours, and Cole had yet to break a sweat.

"I can't do it anymore," she panted. "I need a break."

"You'll get a break when you take me down. Come on, up."

He reached down and waited expectantly for her to grasp his hand. This guy was seriously a machine. When Katie locked palms with him, he hoisted her up from the mat as if she were weightless, which drove home the very obvious fact that she was not taking Cole anywhere he did not want to go—up, down, or sideways.

"Cole, this is impossible. Look at you. You're expecting me to mat the CFA light-heavyweight champion. Do you know how crazy that sounds?"

"It can be done. Trust me. No one is immune to hapkido. Just do what I showed you."

He looked at her as if he had all the faith in her ability to take him. The mixture of hard-ass stubbornness and a playful, mocking challenge stoked the fire of her determination. He was thoroughly enjoying this, the bugger. Then again, though she'd never admit it to him, she kinda was, too. "Getting dressed" had consisted of trading skintight gym shorts for a looser pair. Both ensembles left her with the torturous pleasure of viewing Cole's hard body as he faced off with her—legs bent, muscles tense, crouched and ready to pounce.

When Cole had proposed Katie start training with him, she'd been more than a little hesitant. Violence, in any form, just wasn't her thing, and a part of her was suspicious of his motives, wondering if he wasn't borrowing a page from her own playbook and taking advantage of an opportunity to get close to her, to touch her. But to her surprise, and somewhat disappointment, Cole had been nothing but professional. He took his training seriously—and apparently hers, as well.

For the last two hours, Cole patiently had taken her through a sequence of self-defense techniques. He taught her all the weak points to strike and how to get free from almost any hold. With each conquered move, her confidence grew, along with her competitive streak.

Damn, she wanted to beat Cole at his own game. Not only to prove to herself she could do it, but to show him she was paying attention. Cole was a great fighter, wickedly talented, and an amazing teacher. She couldn't believe how much she'd learned in just one afternoon. If she trained with him daily, she'd be well on her way to becoming a bona fide badass in no time. It was a pity he didn't own a gym. People would come from all around for the chance to train with Cole Easton.

"Come on, Kat, you got this."

She understood why he was so insistent she get him on the mat. Pound for pound, he was a close match to Carter. If she could master the techniques to take down a titled MMA fighter, she'd have the confidence and skill set necessary to take down anyone.

"Remember what I told you," he coached. "Use your size to your advantage. You're small and you're quick. Don't try to meet me head-on, you'll lose every time. You can't overpower me—you have to outpace me."

He shifted his right leg behind him, holding the majority of his weight, and turned his hips, angling his torso, arms up, fists clenched. "See how much this fighting stance reduces your target space?"

She mirrored his position and nodded.

"Good. Now where does your weight go?"

"Seventy on the back, thirty on the front," she recited.

"That's right. Now when I come at you, use my weight against me. Don't hesitate this time or you'll lose your momentum. Solid follow through. K?"

Katie nodded. She could tell when Cole was ready to pounce. All playfulness left his vibrant blue eyes, and he pinned her with one of those looks he gave his opponents in the cage. Each and every time he did it, a ripple of fear shivered up her spine, and she had to remind herself he was just playing. Cole would never hurt her, but good Lord, Heaven help whoever got on the opposing end of him in the cage.

It was his only tell that he was about to strike—that locked-down, emotionless glare. His gaze never wavered from hers, never strayed to the place he intended to target. All those clues he taught her to look for—the restlessness, the mounting tension, the shifting eyes—he had none of them. There was no harbinger of his attack. One moment he was facing her, the next he was just there.

With the speed of a striking viper, Cole lunged for her. Reflexively, she jumped back and pivoted, narrowly escaping his reach. His fingers grazed her throat, and Katie grabbed his outstretched hand with both of hers. She twisted hard to the right and bent down, sending him over her back.

Just like he'd told her, she used Cole's momentum against him and he hit the mat—hard. The satisfying sound of two hundred pounds of solid muscle caving to her will was an exhilarating feeling she'd never forget.

"I did it!" she cried, leaping into the air and cheering. "I took you down! Wow, that felt amazing!" Cole watched her from the mat, smiling up at her as she happy-danced circles around him. The moment that grin turned mischievous, she should have realized it wasn't over, but she was too far into her gloating to see it coming. It was a hard lesson to learn, but a mistake she'd never make again. As she rounded Cole's feet, he swept her leg and grabbed her wrist. She let out a startled squawk and flailed, landing on top of him. His arms immediately locked around her, pinning her against his chest.

"You didn't finish me," he said, his husky voice a low, whispered growl. Although it carried a warning message, the undertone sparked a jump in her pulse that heated the blood coursing through her veins. Her breasts were crushed against his chest. She could feel his heart beating a rapid staccato to match her own. "Never turn your back on an opponent."

Despite his best efforts to keep their training professional, he wasn't unaffected by her after all. His erection was wedged tight between her parted thighs. Her triumph made her reckless, getting physical with him for the last two hours made her hotter than she wanted to admit. After the way they'd parted last night, he hadn't pushed her today, keeping their contact platonic, which by the evidence of his arousal, had obviously come at great cost to his person.

The thought occurred in a flash. She didn't take the time to consider the wisdom of it, which was probably her first mistake. She only knew she didn't want Cole to steal her win. Smiling down at the cocky fighter, she gave him a sexy grin and purred, "Do you want me to finish you?"

His pupils dilated with surprise, his cerulean stare darkening with desire. She was cruel for playing such a dangerous game, but her adrenaline high clouded her better judgment. Katie knew she'd found her edge when his breath stalled in his lungs. Slowly, she slipped her hand between them and over the waistband of his gym shorts. His breath hissed through clenched teeth when her fingers skittered over his steel-hard length. "Is that a yes?" she teased sweetly, answering for him when he didn't speak. "I think you want me to."

His gruff, grunted consent turned into a sharp inhale when she slid her hand lower and gripped the twin weights hanging heavy between his parted thighs. She squeezed hard enough to get his attention.

"Tap," she commanded.

Something flared in Cole's lusty indigo stare that gave her pause. It wasn't the surprising approval at her boldness, or appreciation for her cleverness. No, it was anger banked in those icy blue depths, because when you had a guy by the balls, it was a surefire way to piss him off. But she hadn't appreciated him stealing her thunder for a well-fought take-down. He wanted her to finish it? She'd finish it all right—her way.

"Tap out," she demanded again. He winced when she applied a little more pressure and she smiled triumphantly. But Cole didn't tap. She knew it'd eat at him to do it, even if this was just training, and she did have him in an illegal hold.

"Let. Go," he warned her, his voice a low, gravelly rasp she felt all the way to her toes.

"Not until you tap."

"Dammit, Kat—"

"What?" she asked innocently. "I'm just doing what you told me to. I'm finishing it. Perhaps you should take your own advice and never underestimate your opponent."

"Let go," he warned again through tightly clenched teeth.

"Tap."

Moments went by in stalemate, neither one willing to concede to the other. Cole might be committed to helping her, to training her, but to his very core he was a fighter, and quit was just not in him. Perhaps she'd underestimated the depth of his stubborn male pride. He'd grossly underestimated her need for this win—by whatever means necessary. Tightening her grip another degree, she purred, "Tap. Out."

A frustrated growl rumbled deep in his chest as his hand shot out and slammed down on the mat. *Bam!* The echoing boom reverberating off the walls was deafening. No sooner had the thought *I won!* crossed her mind and she released her grip on his sac, than her world suddenly flipped upside down. The next time she blinked, she was on her back, staring up into the glower of one pissed-off MMA fighter.

The feral look in his eyes sent a shiver of fear racing up her spine and a rush of longing right into her core. She was sure the only thing saving her from both was the fact they were at her work. The gym here was bigger than the one at home, and they'd needed room to grapple. The place was nearly empty, but not vacant enough for Cole to act on whatever thoughts were running through his mind right now—or so she thought.

Cole closed his eyes. When he opened them again, the strain of self-control was etched in his face. *She's crossed the line—again—only this time, there was no going back.* It was incredibly sexy to watch a powerful man like him grapple for control, and know she'd been the one who stole it. It made her want to forget all her protests last night, and push him over the edge.

"That was dirty, Kat. And clever. You may have won round one, but there's no way in hell you're winning this fight."

His mouth descended on hers with the finesse of a freight train, kissing her with a passion that stole the air from her lungs. Abruptly, he broke away, as if just now realizing where they were—a fact lost on her as much as her breath.

"Damn, you're so fucking hot," he groaned against her mouth, diving his tongue past her lips to taste her again. Apparently round two was to be an oral assault—the victor undecided, because a moment later, the lights went out.

Katie knew a moment of true panic, the blackness immediately reminding her why she had no business fooling around with Cole. He must have felt her tense beneath him, because his hard body shifted over hers protectively, covering her more fully. "Shh . . ." he whispered, lowering his head beside her ear. "Stay here."

His soft command spurred a jolt of terror racing through her veins. What? He was leaving her? Cole moved above her, silently rising to his feet. It didn't matter that it was the middle of the day. They were in the bowels of the hospital, without any windows, and it was black as pitch in here. She wanted to hang on to him and beg him not to go, but it was too late. He was already moving to the door. How he navigated the gym, in the dark, she'd never know. She knew he'd reached the exit when she heard the door's squeaky hinge.

A moment later, she heard a crash in the hall and a loud thud of a body being slammed against the wall. Katie jumped, startled by the emasculating cry for help that rang out. Oh no, she knew that voice! Katie scrambled to her feet and made a blind run for the door, praying she wouldn't trip. "Cole, stop!"

Just as she reached the hall, the backup generator lights flickered on, providing a dim glow in the hall. "Cole!" Her exclamation was cut off at the sight of Cole pinning Walley, the head of maintenance, to the wall, his hand clamped tightly around the terrified man's neck.

Cole must have realized his error, because he immediately released the poor guy who promptly bent over, hands braced on his thighs, as he flew into a coughing fit.

"Walley! Are you all right?"

The man nodded. Katie rushed to his side and laid her hand on his back. She rubbed small apologetic circles between his shoulder blades as he fought to catch his breath. "We didn't know it was you," she tried to explain. "When the lights went out, I thought . . ." At a loss to explain *what* she thought, she reverted back to apologizing. "I'm so sorry!"

"It's all right," Walley replied, his voice a little hoarse. "I didn't realize anyone was down here or I would have warned you. We're checking the generator's delay."

"Walley, this is Cole, my—" At a loss to explain *what* Cole was, she let the failed explanation hang in the air.

But he didn't miss a beat. Stepping forward and extending his hand, Cole supplied, "Boyfriend. I'm Katie's boyfriend."

Walley gave him a funny look—funny surprised, not funny ha-ha—but it was nowhere near as stunned as the one she gave Cole. Her boyfriend? Was that really how he saw himself, or was this just a show for Walley? As much as she fought it, determined to keep Cole on the edge of her chaos, it seemed he just kept forcing his way in. But her boyfriend? Really . . . ?

Walley appeared apprehensive to take the offered hand—not that she could blame him—but Cole waited patiently for the man to come around. Hesitantly, as if reaching out to touch a feral cat, Walley connected palms with Cole, whose fingers wrapped around the man's hand as he firmly shook it and offered his own apology, which was graciously accepted.

"I thought you were someone else," Cole told him.

Walley scrubbed the back of his neck with his hand. "Well, I sure would hate to be that someone else. Can't say I enjoyed that brief experience at all."

Cole chuckled at the joke, a crooked smile tugging at his lips, lessening the severity of his handsome face.

And then Walley asked the question she was dreading, while praying all the while he wouldn't. "Who'd ya think I was?"

CHAPTER

Katie looked like she was about to be ill, more so than when Cole declared himself her boyfriend. Then again, he'd surprised himself, too. He hadn't meant for it to come out like that, but now that he'd said it, the word tasted better on his tongue than he'd expected.

As she stood there hesitating to respond, Cole gave Walley's hand a distracting squeeze. "What size generator does it take to keep a place like this running?"

At the question, Walley's eyes lit up like the Fourth of July, and Cole knew he had him. "Oh, it's not just *a* generator. It takes five of those bad boys to keep the hospital functional."

"Seriously?" Cole feigned amazement. "I'd love to see them. Don't suppose we could go check them out?"

"Heck yeah, let's go."

As Cole turned to follow the maintenance man down the hall, he winked at Katie. She silently mouthed *Thank you*, and it was worth the sacrifice right there, seeing the look of relief on her face. In truth, he couldn't give two shits about electricity and generators, but if that was what it took to distract the old man, then he'd take one for the team. Besides, he kinda owed him after nearly scaring the poor guy to death. No harm in letting him revel in his glory a bit.

Unfortunately, that glory took forty-five minutes of hard-core explaining. Cole was anxious to get back to Katie, not only because the idea of leaving her alone for so long made him uneasy, but he just flat-out wanted to be with her. This was one of the first days she'd had off since he'd come here, and he'd be damned if he was going to spend it with Walley when he could be with Katie. Cole had spent far too much time avoiding her—avoiding the inevitable—to waste another day.

He knew where she'd be and wasted no time thanking Walley for his time and very informative talk on generators. Stopping at her office, Cole leaned against the doorway and silently stood there a few minutes, watching her work. The way her computer sat on the desk angled her away from the door. The entrance must have been just shy of her peripherals. Her pale blond hair was pulled up in a messy disarray he found utterly charming. Rogue strands had fallen loose during their training, reminding him of how they'd spent the morning rolling around on the mat together. Cole had had many sparring partners in the past, but none had ever been this much fun to take to the mat.

Katie had done exceptionally well for her first day of training, and he couldn't wait to do it again. Not only was she learning to defend herself, but she was gaining confidence she couldn't acquire any other way. Not to mention the added bonus of all that physical contact. Torture, that was what it was—pure, blissful torture.

Cole allowed his gaze to travel along the delicate arch of her neck. A stir of possessive, masculine pride stoked him at the sight of his marks on her neck. It was Neanderthal-ish of him, but what-the-fuck-ever. Since meeting Katie, Cole was discovering the roots of his gene pool.

Her attention was solely fixed on the screen in front of her—so much for her day off. He stood there another minute or two con-templating backing away and letting her work. But the decision was out if his hands when she swiveled to the right to grab a piece of paper and saw him standing there. Her startled gasp instantly dissolved to a relieved smile that hit him in the solar plexus.

"There you are. I was wondering when you were coming back." Katie looked up at him over the rims of her black-framed librarian glasses.

"I didn't know you wore glasses." The observation tumbled out of his mouth. *Fucking. Hot.* At least he kept that part to himself.

Seeming embarrassed, she quickly pulled them off and tossed them to the desk. "I don't. Not really. They're cheaters."

They're sexy is what they are.

"So," she finished, swiveling her chair to fully face him. "How'd it go with Walley?" The little twitch in her top lip told him she was doing her damndest to hold back a teasing grin.

"Great. I now know more about generators than I ever hoped to."

"That's good," she said, keeping up her ruse. "You never know if that'll come in handy."

He arched a *seriously?* brow, and she started laughing. The melodic sound made his chest tighten, more specifically in the region of his heart. Damn, he was getting in over his head with this woman—correction, *was* in over his head. Funny thing though, the idea didn't bother him nearly as much now as it had a few weeks ago. Fuck him . . . he was falling for his PT.

"Think that's funny, do you?" he growled with mock anger as he shouldered himself off the door frame and ambled into her office. He stopped long enough to close the door. Katie's playful grin faltered at the decisive snick of the lock. Her gaze darted over his shoulder to her only escape, suddenly looking nervous.

"Cole . . . what are you doing?"

He came around the front of her desk and planted his palms on top of her mass of papers and leaned forward, locking his gaze with hers. "There's something I've wanted to do with you since the moment I first met you. And I was thinking today might be the perfect day for it."

He bit back a grin as Katie exhaled an exasperated sigh and closed her eyes. Bending her head down, she pinched the bridge of her nose as if searching for patience. "I already told you Cole, this isn't a good idea—"

"Why not? You haven't even asked me what it was yet." He gave her a crooked grin, knowing damn well what she was thinking and enjoying like hell watching her squirm. After what happened last night, Cole quickly figured out that the harder he pushed, the faster she ran. Getting close to her was going to take an entirely different approach than what he was used to when dealing with women. If Cole wanted her, he was going to have to work for it—woo her—which was something he knew absolutely nothing about. But he knew how to tease, how to cajole and entice. As long as he kept himself just out of her reach, he was willing to bet she'd eventually lower her guard and come after him.

That lip-lock this morning had been a mistake—a crack in his resolve to keep his hands and mouth off her. It was a mistake he vowed not to make again. The next time they kissed, it would be her doing.

"All right. I'll bite. What do you want to do with me?"

Katie's eyes dropped to his mouth as he wet his lips with the tip of his tongue and leaned a little closer, silently cursing the three feet of Formica separating them. Reaching up, he tucked a fallen lock of pale hair behind her ear. As if drawn by an invisible thread, she leaned into his touch as he dipped his head close. Her lids fluttered closed, lips parting in anticipation of his kiss. At the last moment, he dipped his head to the side, whispering near her ear, "Go ice fishing with me, Kat."

WTF? Katie's eyes flew open to find a smirking Cole starting back at her. "Ice fishing? Seriously? *That's* what you've wanted to do since you met me?" *Ice fishing, my ass.* Cole was up to something. He looked about as into ice fishing as she was into macramé. Not that she'd tell him that. Although she wholly doubted sticking a baited line into an ice hole and staring at a bobber for endless hours was his end game here, she was curious enough to play along. Besides, it'd been years since she'd been ice fishing. In fact, the last time she could remember going had been a competition Uncle Marcus had taken her to on Mille Lacs Lake when she was eight.

"Yeah, ice fishing. Is that so surprising?" he asked, arching his dark brow innocently. "Why, what did you think I was going to say?"

Not going to touch that bait with a ten-foot pole. "I think ice fishing sounds great!" *Ice fishing with you is a horrible idea.* It was bad enough rolling around with Cole on the mat for the last two hours. Now he wanted to stick the two of them in a little fish house together? Was he trying to break her? Yes, he was, the thought hit her with sudden clarity. Well, it wasn't going to work. She wasn't one of his simpering cage bangers, helpless to resist the charms of the mighty Cole Easton. "There's a great place a few hours from here Uncle Marcus used to take me to. They have a house and poles we can rent. I'll call and make sure something is available." She glanced up at the clock on the wall and then back at him. "I'm assuming since we're getting such a late start, you'll want to be spending the night, right?"

Katie wasn't sure what possessed her to up the ante like that. Perhaps she'd taken the bluff too far. If she was expecting Cole to tip his hand, she was sorely mistaken. Butterflies erupted in her stomach at the wicked grin that spread across his handsome face. *Steady, girl,* she coached her goddess.

"Absolutely," he answered without a moment's hesitation, his voice a dark, velvety rasp that sent a shiver of goose bumps prickling up her arms.

"Do you prefer to be on the top or bottom?"

"Excuse me?" Katie's head whipped up as she stepped into the fish house, smacking it on the doorway. Her winter hat softened the blow but it still stung like a bad word.

Cole winced, giving her a *that's gotta hurt* grimace. "The bunk beds. Do you like the top or the bottom?"

She wished he'd quit with the insinuating remarks already. Well, two could play at that game. "I'm good with either one, but it's going to be a tight fit for you." *Boom. Roasted.*

Cole's smug, shit-eating grin momentarily froze and was immediately replaced by something darker—something much more primal. He muttered a curse under his breath and snatched the winter cap off his head, tossing it on the bottom bunk. He scrubbed his hands through his hair as if the cap was itching him. When he turned back toward her, his dark hair looked as wild and untamed as the man himself. "Don't worry about me, sweetheart. I'm a master of small places." Unzipping his coat, he shed that, too, leaving it on the bed.

"Then you don't mind being on the bottom?" she asked innocently.

His brow arched, a flirtatious grin tugging at his top lip. "Not as long as you don't mind getting on top."

Her cheeks warmed and Katie turned away, before he could see the telltale color of her discomfort. It was useless, bantering with this man. He had no shame. Walking over to the table, she set down her duffel bag packed with overnight essentials, and placed the rented fishing poles on top of it. She took a quick survey of the fish house. Wow, it was lot smaller than she remembered. Then again, she wasn't eight, and the man she'd shared it with wasn't a mammoth. She'd rented the largest one they had available. There hadn't been much to choose from on such short notice. A heater was mounted to the far left wall and a small stove sat near the right. The bunk beds lined the far back wall, and a table with chairs filled the center of the shack. Four trap doors were positioned near the four corners of the fish house. She remembered that beneath those hinged doors would be the predrilled ice holes.

Stepping up behind her, Cole lifted one of the miniature poles and looked at it skeptically. "So how exactly does this work?"

Katie laughed mockingly. "Don't tell me *you* need instructions on how to handle your pole."

Cole took another step closer, trapping her between the table and a wall of solid muscle. She swore she felt the rumble of his throaty chuckle against her back as he pressed in tighter. "What if I did? Could you help me out?" His breath brushed the lobe of her ear not covered by her stocking cap, skating a heated trail down her neck. She shivered at the contrast of warmth against her chilled flesh.

"I'm pretty sure you'd be disappointed. It's been a long time since I've touched a pole." *Last night excluded.* Suddenly, this game didn't seem so much fun anymore.

"Mehh . . ." He shrugged behind her, his big body brushing against her shoulder blades. "It's like riding a bike, right?"

Katie couldn't help but laugh. "Is that so? I'm not sure what bikes you've been riding—"

"Tandem, mostly. Not as fond of solo."

Another bubble of laughter rose up inside her. "Stop it." She shoved her shoulder back, playfully bumping it into his chest. "We're here to fish."

"Isn't that what we were talking about? Fishing?"

She rolled her eyes and stepped to the side, escaping the furnace behind her. Who needed a heater with Cole in here? "Yeah, for crappie, not trouser trout."

"Good to know."

He laughed. The deep masculine rumble was infectious, and before she knew it, she was laughing with him. Who would have thought the Beast of the East was such a cajoling rogue. If she wasn't careful, this champion fighter would lay some serious ground and pound to her defenses. Getting away with Cole, holed up in this little cabin on the lake, she found pushing Carter out of her mind was easier than she thought. She was safe here. No one knew where they were, and it wasn't until that burden of fear fully lifted that she realized just how much it'd been weighing on her.

Cole turned on the heater and the little unit rumbled to life. Not that they needed it, she was already overheated. Pulling off her winter cap, she tugged the hair binder off her wrist and held it in her teeth as she twisted up her hair. Feeling Cole's eyes on her, she turned toward him. "What?" she asked, the word muffled as she spoke through clenched teeth.

"Nothing," Cole answered innocently, though the sexy grin on his handsome face said anything but.

He busied himself unpacking the grocery bags, but the damage was already done. The butterflies had woken again, their fluttering warming her core. Though he hadn't mentioned it, more than once today, she'd caught his gaze straying to her neck. She knew he was thinking about last night. What had happened, and would have happened if Carter wouldn't have—

"So, Marcus loves ice fishing, huh? I gotta tell you, I'm looking forward to discovering the appeal."

"You might really enjoy it. Many people find it cathartic."

She shed her winter coat, shoved the hat into the sleeve along with her matching mittens, and crossed the small floor, tossing it onto the bed above Cole's. "It forces a person to slow down—to unwind and relax."

Cole pulled a bottle of brandy out of a paper sack and saluted her with a wink. "Sounds good to me."

CHAPTER

24

eriously? What are you, the freaking fish whisperer?" Katie shook her head as Cole pulled up his tenth crappie in an hour.

He laughed, grabbed hold of the flailing, slimy thing, and unhooked it like a pro. If she didn't know better, she'd swear he'd been fishing his whole life. Was there anything this guy wasn't great at?

"You laugh now. We'll see who's laughing when you're cleaning all those things." She made a disgusted face, and he chuckled again.

He tossed the fish into a large water-filled bucket and then grabbed the towel draped over the handle. "It's just beginner's luck," he said, drying his hands. "If you want to come closer, I'll let you hold my pole." His brow arched in invitation.

Come closer? If she sat any closer, she'd be in his lap. Hold his pole indeed . . . Cole Easton was an incorrigible flirt. Katie scoffed, "I can catch my own fish, thank you very much."

"Well, you better hurry up," he teased, "cuz we're like ten and oh."

"Since when is this a competition?" she feigned indignantly. "I don't remember agreeing to that. Besides, we haven't even made a wager."

He thought about it for a minute, seeming contemplative as he boldly let his gaze travel over her. Like he needed to think about it. She'd bet her ass she knew damn well what he was going to say—

"If I win, you have to clean these fish."

—and that was *not* it. She must have made a face, because he busted out laughing.

"I'm not taking that bet!" she said. "You're already ten fish ahead of me. I say the winner has to make me supper while I sit back and drink his brandy."

"Oh, you think so, do you?"

"As a matter of fact, I do. You deserve the whole ice fishing experience. I wouldn't want to cheat you out of a single moment of fun." And it had been fun—spending the afternoon out here with him. It was exactly what she needed, getting away from the stress and anxiety of the world, where her biggest worry was who could catch the most fish.

"I'm not so sure you're going to think it's such a bargain when you have to eat it."

Lord, his smile made her weak in the knees. The man was irresistible. Worse, he knew it. Setting his pole aside, Cole got up and went to the cooler sitting beside the table. Grabbing a red solo cup, he scooped some ice from the bag and pulled out a can of vanilla Coke. After setting it on the table, he broke the seal on the brandy and filled it part of the way before topping it off with the Coke.

His arresting eyes locked on her as he swirled the glass, mixing the drink, and then tipped it to his lips. He tasted it, then took another long pull from the glass before adding the rest of the Coke to dilute it. "Here you go."

"Thanks," she said, accepting the glass. "My royal taste tester," she teased.

"I'm not used to making drinks for someone half my size. Too many of those and you'll be completely shit-faced."

Katie laughed, "Good to know you're not trying to take advantage of me." She lifted the glass to her lips. The carbonation kissed her tongue as the buttery vanilla flavor teased her taste buds. It wasn't too strong, just enough to warm a path to her stomach.

"Oh, I never said that," he teased, giving her a lopsided grin. "But when I take advantage of you, I want you to be able to remember it."

She swallowed wrong and started to cough. Cole's amused smile told her that was exactly the reaction he'd been expecting. Without another word, he fixed himself a drink and began setting up to clean the fish and cook supper. The ice house was minimally stocked with a cabinet that contained the bare essentials for cooking a modest fish fry—a pan, a cutting board, knives, a bowl—just the basics.

Cole had gotten the food at the store while she'd stayed home to make reservations and pack a bag. Apparently he planned well, because after taking a sip of his own drink, he set it on the table and pulled out a box of Shore Lunch from the grocery sack, two large baking potatoes, and an onion. Seriously? She'd been teasing him, having no idea he'd planned on making supper.

"You're really going to cook for me," she said, astonished.

Cole glanced up at her from the table, knife in hand, and potato on the cutting board. "Correction. I'm attempting to cook for you. I make no promises."

"What would you have done if we hadn't caught anything?"

He shrugged. "Taken you out to supper. Though you'll probably be wishing I had soon enough."

Katie's chest tightened at the swelling emotion, and her smile faltered at the realization of *what* that feeling was. *I'm falling for Cole Easton* . . .

"Hey, you don't have to look so terrified. It may not be great, but I'm not going to poison you."

The lightness in his voice didn't match the concern in his eyes. He was far too perceptive of her. "It's not that," she said.

He set the knife down and came around the table, crouching down in front of her. "Then what is it?"

She couldn't very well tell him, so she modified the truth. "It's just . . . no one has ever cooked for me before. I know it sounds stupid, but—"

He silenced her by placing a chaste kiss on her forehead. Leaning back just enough to pin her with his vibrant blue stare that never failed to heat the blood in her veins, he whispered, "I'm glad. That means I get to be your first."

Shocked speechless, Katie just stared at him as he stood and made his way back to the cutting board.

"Oh my gosh! This is the best fish I've had in . . . I seriously can't remember."

Cole smiled at her. "You probably can't remember because you drank three brandy Cokes, and one of them was mine," he teased. "I told you that you should let me mix them for you. That shit'll sneak up and bite you in the ass."

"But you were busy with the fish," she tried to explain. Okay, maybe she should have paced herself a little better, but she'd been so rattled by her revelation, and that feeling in her chest wouldn't go away. She'd thought perhaps a few drinks might chase the unwanted emotion back to wherever it'd come from. No such luck. She wasn't drunk yet, but if she wasn't careful, she'd find herself well on her way to Lushville. Cole was still nursing his first glass, well his second, because she'd drunk his first one.

He watched her with an amused smirk.

"What?"

"Nothing. I was just thinking I probably should have bought a bottle of ibuprofen because I have a feeling you're going to need it in the morning."

"Stop it. I'm just fine."

"All right." He held up his hands in surrender. "If you say so."

"Why did you buy this, anyway? I thought you didn't drink hard liquor anymore."

"I don't—in public. I've gotten myself into too much trouble thinking I was 'just fine.'" He mocked her with air quotes.

She snorted, planting her elbows on the table and leaning forward with rapt interest. "Ooo . . . a genuine MMA bad boy—ice fishing and cooking me supper. I don't buy it," she declared, folding her arms over her chest and kicking back in her chair. "You're far too disciplined and controlled . . ."

Cole laughed. "If you're goading me to tell you my secrets, it's not going to work. I'm not that drunk, Kat."

"If I can guess, will you tell me? Oh, I know! Let's play Never Have I Ever. My friends and I used to play it in college, though I'm pretty sure the guys were just trying to get us wasted so they could take advantage of us."

Katie's hand flew up to cover her mouth as Cole's brow arched questioningly. Crap, did she just say that out loud? Perhaps Cole was right, and those brandy Cokes were catching up with her. His top lip twitched, as if he was struggling to hold back a smile, while amusement danced in those brilliant blue eyes.

Losing the battle, he broke into a full-on, panty-dropping grin and spread his arms wide. Mother Mary, he had a long reach. No wonder his opponents had trouble getting within striking distance.

"Hey, if you're trying to take advantage of me, sweetheart, you don't need to get me drunk first."

"Ha-ha." She rolled her eyes. "So have you ever played or not?"

"I can't say that I have."

"Okay then, here's how it works. I'm going to say something I've never done. If you haven't either, it's your turn. But if you have, you drink a shot of brandy. If you refuse to answer, you have to drink twice. Get it?"

"I got it."

"Good. I'll go first."

"Why do you get to go first?"

"My game. My rules. That's why."

He chuckled, looking wholly amused. He crossed his arms over his chest and stretched into a lazy sprawl, those tree trunks he called legs slipping between her feet. "All right, Kat, shoot."

Katie looked fucking adorable sitting there across from him, cheeks flushed by her buzz, trying to think of what to say. She thoughtfully tapped her finger against her lips, drawing his gaze to the full, lush softness of that amazing mouth. He couldn't believe he'd let her talk him into this. Cole didn't play games, nor did he talk about himself. So what the hell was he doing?

"Oh, I know! Never have I ever . . . passed a swimming test."

"Seriously?" Cole grabbed the bottle of brandy and lifted it in salute, tipping it back. The undiluted liquor burned a trail into his gut.

"Nope. Can't swim a lick. Being on the water pretty much terrifies me. That's why never have I ever been on a cruise."

He took another swig.

"You have? Where did you go?"

"Belize. It was a CFA-sponsored cruise. A bunch of the fighters and the octagon girls traveled to some ports. It was a big publicity thing."

Katie looked like she just bit into a lemon. "You travel with the octagon girls? Do you guys have to do that kind of thing often?"

Cole shrugged. "It depends on how high profile the fighter is, and how much publicity he's pulling before a fight."

"Are *you* high profile?"

How cute. She's jealous . . . Cole nodded. "All title fighters are big money."

She looked like she wanted to say something more, but then paused, thinking a moment. "Never have I ever slept with one of my co-workers."

Aww . . . fuck me. Cole lifted the bottle once—twice.

"You did! I can't believe you slept with an octagon girl!"

It wasn't just one. "Hey, you don't know that. I drank twice!" But he couldn't hold back his guilty grin.

"Everyone knows that's the same as admitting it!" She tried to feign offense, but couldn't quite pull it off.

"So I slammed a second shot for nothing? This game sucks, Kat."

"Well, maybe if *someone* didn't have to drink every time, he'd get a turn, too!"

"I have a better idea. Instead of playing I Never, let's play I Want. Same concept. I tell you something I want. If you don't agree, it's your turn. But if you want it, too, you drink. If you don't want to answer, you drink twice. Ready? Go! I want a million dollars."

Katie rolled her eyes and reached across the table, grabbing the bottle, and took a swig. She gasped at the burn, eyes watering. "Uhh . . . this stuff tastes terrible!" Cole handed her a Coke to chase it down.

"I want a beach house in Kauai."

She took another swig. "Come on, Cole. These are too obvious. You're gonna get me drunk."

"Do you want me to be more specific?" he asked innocently.

She nodded. He smiled when a hiccup escaped her parted lips and she giggled.

"I want to kiss you."

Her gaze shot to his, holding Cole's stare as he waited for her response. Slowly now, she lifted the bottle to her lips and tipped it back. She'd almost returned it to the table when he added, "Between your legs."

Something flashed in her verdant eyes. It was so raw, so needy, it took every last bit of his self-control not to leap over the table and take her right then and there. She said nothing as she lifted the bottle to her lips and tipped her head back. Lust flooded his veins as he watched Katie's delicate throat working the swallow. Holy hell, this woman was his own personal brand of octane.

"I want to finish what we started last night," he added before she could put the bottle down.

She drank. She drank again.

"I knew it!"

Katie leaned forward and set the bottle on the table. "I drank twice, Cole."

"But everyone knows it's the same as admitting it," he teased, throwing her taunting words back at her.

"You know what I want?" It wasn't her turn to go, but he was too curious to point that out.

He grabbed the bottle and began lifting it to his lips in anticipation as she started to speak. "I want a man who will put me above everything else, and will be in it for the long haul." Cole's arm froze midway to his mouth and he sat there, motionless, staring at her, caught completely off guard, as she continued. "I want someone who isn't afraid of commitment or afraid to love. Someone who will be there today, tomorrow, and forty years from now."

Fuck. Slowly, Cole lowered the bottle, setting it on the table. As much as he wanted to agree with her—as much as he wanted to be that guy—he couldn't. He wouldn't lie to her and pretend otherwise. He had to go back. It wasn't a matter of wanting to.

"I didn't think you'd agree," she said softly, and rose to stand.

The emptiness in her eyes nearly broke him. Exhaling a sigh, Cole stood and caught her arm before she could walk away. "Listen, Kat, it's not like that. Even if I wanted to stay, I can't. I'm under contract for at least one more fight, and if I successfully defend my title, that contract extends until I'm defeated. I owe Tapout and Under Armour two more years. We're talking hundreds of thousands of dollars in lawsuits. Not to mention what it would do to my reputation."

She kept her head turned away. Dammit, he wished he could see her face.

"I get it, Cole. You don't owe me any explanations."

Maybe not, but dammit, he wanted to give them to her. "Kat, look at me." When she didn't move, he reached up and gently took hold of her chin, turning her head and forcing her eyes to meet his. The vulnerability he saw reflecting back at him was like taking a sucker punch to the gut. "I care about you." More than he wanted to admit. But what would be the point in telling her that?

"I know you do," she said softly. "Just not enough to make you stay."

He knew she was tipsy, because there was no way in hell the Kat he knew would open herself up enough to be this raw and honest with him. Though he was hardly one to talk. When he'd shot out of his chair, his equilibrium tilted and he'd nearly taken a header into the wall. Even standing here now, he was having a little trouble keeping it vertical. If he had any doubt as to the level of his intoxication, there was zero left when he heard himself say, "You could come back with me, Kat." Perhaps that was something he should have consulted sober Cole on before offering, though he was pretty sure that guy was on board, too.

Now Katie, on the other hand, not so much. "How long do you think that would last, Cole? You said it yourself, your life is not conducive to having a relationship." She let out a bitter laugh. "What the hell am I even saying . . . *my* life isn't conducive to having a relationship. Besides, I can't leave my dad—he needs me."

She looked like she was about to cry, which twisted his gut into knots. The pain took his breath away, and the urge to make it stop swept over him with wild desperation—anything to ease her pain—anything to quell the agony in his heart.

"You're smart to stay away, Cole. You don't want to get any more involved in this mess."

Did she honestly think that was holding him back? "Kat . . ." He slid his hand up to cup her cheek, his thumb brushing against her plump bottom lip. Lord help him, he wanted to kiss her, to taste the sweet ambrosia on her tongue. "Kat, look at me. What's going on in your life has nothing to do with us. If anything, it only makes me want you more. I want to fix this for you. I want to keep you safe. When you smile, I want the satisfaction of knowing I'm the man who put it there. You deserve so much—so much more than I can give you. As much as I wish it were otherwise, what I can offer comes with an expiration date. I want you so much it's killing me, but I refuse to lie to you. I won't make you promises I know I can't keep. But goddamn . . . knowing how this story is going to end only makes me want to cherish every day with you all the more."

It hadn't been his intention to pour his heart out to her like this. Damn brandy. Nor had it been his intention to woo her into submission, but he could hardly resist when Katie stood on her tip toes and whispered, "Then let's just make sure we make every day count from here on out then." When her lips touched his, it was electric, like a current of live energy raced under his skin to lightning bolt straight into his cock. A hungry growl filled the small ice house, and it took him a second to register that the sound was coming from him. He slipped his arms around Katie's narrow waist and tugged her up against him as he took control of the kiss. Untethered lust tore through his veins, the governor on his control gone with his last shot of brandy. Fuck, she tasted amazing, the honey sweetness of her kiss mixed with the darker, rich, liquored-vanilla flavor.

He wasn't drunk enough to impair his decision making. He'd wanted her long before he'd ever put a drop of alcohol to his lips, but Katie on the other hand, he wasn't so sure. She'd done a one-eighty on him, and he'd have hated like hell for her to wake up in the morning and regret this. Perhaps she, too, was tired of fighting this attraction. She'd been ready to give herself to him last night, before that bastard had shown up and ruined an amazing moment, and she'd been stone-cold sober then.

Her hands slipped up his shirt, nails raking against his back as she wiggled herself closer, grinding her flat stomach against his painfully hard arousal. She consumed his tortured groan, her tongue tangling with his, her kiss growing more uninhibited, more frantic with each passing moment. He broke his mouth away, struggling to catch his breath and clear his mind as doubt hedged in. The last thing he wanted to do was take advantage of her—he'd never forgive himself if he hurt her like that.

But holy hell, she was a wildcat in his arms. Her breath came against his throat, fast and hot as she sucked and nipped her way down his neck. Her hands slipped to his waistband, fumbling with the button. Okay, those needed to stay on or he was done for. Bending forward to remove the temptation from her reach, he caught her hands and dragged them back up his chest. Katie whimpered her protest and then bit his neck when he refused to release her wrists.

The sting hovered just shy of painful, and courted the male in Cole to retaliate.

Bending Katie's arms behind her back, he held them firmly in one hand, while his other slipped into her hair, gripping her knotted twist. The tie slipped loose, releasing bounds of pale silk into his hand as he pulled her head away from his neck. Their eyes met and briefly held. Katie's gaze was heavy-lidded, from alcohol or lust he couldn't know, and he wouldn't take the chance of presuming. Before he could think too hard on it, Cole dipped his head, burying his face in her lush cleavage generously on display by the deep vee of her cable-knit sweater.

His name escaped her lips on a sigh as he slipped his tongue between the valley of her breasts and latched on to the generous swell of flesh, nipping and sucking, marking her as his own, even if only for a little while. He wouldn't have sex with her, not like this, but that didn't mean they couldn't enjoy each other a little. Everything they'd done together sober was fair game as far as his conscience was concerned.

He walked her back a few steps to the bed and released his hold on her wrists as he eased her down, blanketing her with his body. With her hands now free, she dove them into his hair as she greedily sought his mouth. Gone was the shy, timid woman he'd had to tease and seduce, courting her to lower her guard and let him in. She'd made him work for it. The only thing he was working for now was the restraint to hold her back.

Katie's hands slipped between them, again going for his waist, only this time her hand went lower, stroking him through his jeans. He tensed above her, grappling for control as the pressure built in the base of his cock, his balls aching with the need to come. A pained groan rumbled deep in his throat. Her hand stilled its torturous play.

"What's wrong, Cole?"

Perhaps Katie wasn't as wasted as he thought. That she was this aware of him and in tune with his response spoke volumes to her lucidity. Before he could answer her with some lame-ass excuse, she contrived her own answer, and damn if it wasn't spot fucking on.

"You need to come. Last night when we . . . You didn't . . . Wow, Cole, I'm so sorry."

Seriously? She was apologizing to him for that? Sure, he'd hurt like hell, for hours, but it wasn't her fault. He didn't blame her. What he had blamed her for, however, was pushing him away, shutting him out when he knew she needed him—if for nothing more than to hold her, to keep the nightmares at bay.

Cole shifted his weight over her so he could see directly into her eyes. "Kat, are you drunk?"

She gave him a funny look. "No. Are you?"

"Not drunk enough to not care if you are."

She laughed. "I'm not drunk, Cole. That's not to say I should be driving a car right now, but I know what I'm doing. I want this."

"That's what drunk people always say. Count to forty-nine by sevens."

Katie laughed. "Are you actually giving me a sobriety test before you'll have sex with me? I gotta say, this is a first. I can't decide if it's either the sweetest or most offensive thing you've done."

"Considering how much it's killing me not to be inside you right now, let's go with the sweetest."

"Considering how much it's killing me not to have you inside me right now, let's go with sober—definitely sober."

She didn't have to tell him twice. Cole reached behind his back and yanked his shirt over his head. He leaned back, giving Katie room to wiggle out of her sweater, and banged the back of his head on the mattress springs above him. He muttered a curse and Katie giggled.

"You think that's funny, do you?" he growled.

"I told you it was going to be a tight fit. These twin beds weren't made with a six-foot-four, two-hundred-pound cage fighter in mind."

When she tugged her sweater over her head, all teasing stopped—along with his heart—at the sight of her gorgeous breasts bound in a red lace bra. She reached behind her back to unclasp the hook and he stopped her. "Uh-uh . . . unwrapping the package is my job."

Sliding out of the bed, Cole rose to his full height and unbuttoned his jeans. He could feel Katie's eyes on him as he jerked down his zipper. Her surprised gasp stoked his male pride a couple good hard tugs and had his erection straining for the chance to wring more gasps just like that from her kiss-swollen lips.

"You don't wear any underwear."

She sounded shocked and completely scandalized by her discovery. He shrugged, giving her a roguish grin. "Not always," he replied, stepping out of his jeans. "You should try it sometime."

Her mischievous grin hit him below the belt, knocking the air from his lungs. Without a doubt, he'd never wanted a woman more than he wanted this woman right here—right now.

"Maybe I will."

Damn, she was hot. "Take your pants off, Kat. I want to see if you're wearing a matching set."

Her knowing smile was pure temptation. "You know I am . . ."

No sooner had she slipped out of her jeans and Cole laid eyes on those candy-apple-red lace panties, than he was on her.

CHAPTER

25

Katie's laughter quickly turned into a soft moan as Cole's hungry mouth found hers. His hand gripped her breast, teasing her nipple through the thin lace barrier as she arched against him. He took the hint and slipped his hand beneath her back, deftly unclasping her bra. The lace came loose and he wasted no time tearing it away to reveal the bountiful feast before him. "Damn, sweetheart, you're the most beautiful woman I've ever seen." And he meant it. She was thin, but curvy. Her breasts were naturally full, and so achingly soft with raspberry nipples that made his mouth water. Slowly, he dragged his hands down her waist, spanning the narrowest part with both of them. She was so small, so fragile, but the feminine flare of her hips and shapely breasts kept her from looking too willowy.

She frowned at his words as if she didn't believe him. Subconsciously, her gaze flickered to where he knelt between her thighs, but he refused to follow her stare, hating like hell the uncertainty, the self-consciousness he saw reflected in her emerald eyes. This woman was stunning, with or without scars. Hell, they all had them. He certainly had more than his share. Hers just happened to be more visible than others, that's all.

"You don't have to lie to me, Cole. You already got me in bed."

Her admonishment was meant to be teasing, but he could hear the inflection of truth behind her softly spoken words. "Hey," he whispered, taking hold of her chin and gently turning her gaze back to his. "I wouldn't lie to you, Kat. I'm telling you, without a doubt, hands down, you are the most beautiful woman I've ever seen."

Her smile stole his breath, and he dipped his head, kissing her before he did something crazy like tell her he loved her. The thought suddenly hit him with the force of a roundhouse kick to the gut, nearly knocking the wind out of him. *Holy hell . . . I'm in love with Katrina Miller.* The realization was enough to bring this CFA champion fighter to his knees—which was exactly where he wanted to be right now, kneeling between Katie's sweet, delectable thighs . . .

Sliding his hands over her legs, she reflexively tensed. He didn't expect her to miraculously get over her apprehension of being touched there overnight, but Cole silently vowed she eventually would. Placing his hands on her knees, he parted her legs further and slowly grazed his palms up her thighs. This time, her tension wasn't quite as apparent. He brushed his thumb over the thin strip of red lace covering the best package of all. A tortured groan rumbled in his throat at finding them damp for him.

He meant to take this slow, but his restraint was quickly slipping. "Watch your head," he warned, slipping his hands beneath her bottom and boosting her to the top of the narrow mattress. The damn bed was so small Cole was hard-pressed to get up again. A dilemma he quickly solved. His top lip curled in a wicked grin as he hooked the thin elastic straps stretching over her hips and tore her panties free with a sharp tug.

Katie's surprised gasp melted into moans when his fingers swept over the petals of her moist flesh. As self-consciousness gave way to passion, she eased her legs wider, opening herself to him like a slow blossoming flower. Unable to resist, he slipped a finger inside her. Her half-lidded gaze widened in surprise, locking on his, a bit apprehensive and a whole lot curious. "You are utterly captivating," he crooned, mesmerized by her beauty. Adding a finger, he pushed in further, stretching her tight little glove and seating his palm firmly against her clit.

She gasped, a brief pinch of discomfort crossing her face, but the pressure of his palm quickly drown out the pain. The last thing he wanted was to hurt her, but he had to do it. If she couldn't take his touch, she'd never be able to handle his cock. "Shit, Kat, I could come just touching you."

His thumb found the bundle of nerves at the hood of her sex. After a few circular swipes and coaxing strokes of his fingers, Katie began to melt. The muscles in her core relaxed and she began to rock her hips against his rhythm. Her pupils dilated, her lids growing heavy with pleasure. *Holy hell, she's going to come . . .*

He'd barely touched her and already the early tremors of her impending release were beginning to grip his fingers. Cole couldn't remember the last time he'd been with a woman so . . . responsive, so . . . fucking hot! He was tempted to palm his throbbing flesh and take his own release while he wrung Katie's from her lithe little body. Better yet, he'd love to feel her tiny fist milking him as she chased after her orgasm. Tension began to build in the base of his spine, warning him he was running out of time, but Cole wasn't ready for this to end.

"Do not come," he warned her through gritted teeth.

"Then . . . you'd . . . better stop . . . touching me," she panted. "Make love to me, Cole."

Her pleading request unraveled him. It took his last bit of control to pull his hand away and her moan of protest nearly sent him over the edge. "Hang on, sweetheart." By the time he seated himself against her hot, wet core, Cole was out of his fucking mind with want. Protection was a trailing afterthought. If it weren't a habit ingrained in him since adolescence, he probably wouldn't have said anything at all, but his conscience told him to warn her before things got any further out of hand. It was the responsible thing to do, and he respected the hell out of this woman. He didn't want her having any regrets.

"Hurry . . ." she pleaded, wiggling beneath him, inching herself closer.

"Kat, wait," he whispered against her lips, grabbing her hips to keep her still before he said fuck it and dove right into her hot little cunny—consequences be damned. "I don't have a condom." Fuck, this was embarrassing, of all the things to forget to pack.

"It's okay," she said between kisses. "I'm covered."

There was no chance of her being at risk. He never—ever—had unprotected sex. In fact, this would be the first time he'd ever been skin on skin with a woman, and the thought of it being with Katie, sharing that level of intimacy with her, was a huge fucking step for him.

She fisted her hands into his hair and pulled him close. Her scorching kiss shot straight into the base of his cock. The impatient member bucked against her satiny flesh, pulling a tortured groan from his throat. She responded with a wanton moan that lit up every one of his nerve endings. Shimmying beneath him, she pressed him past her outer folds and against her tight little opening. Katie's mouth was on his neck. Kissing. Sucking. Biting, as she whispered, "I know you wouldn't, Cole. It's all right. I trust you."

Her confidence in him sent a pang of doubt needling his conscience. Damn, he didn't want to fuck this up. Was that why he hesitated to push forward? Was he actually . . . nervous?—a completely foreign and unwelcome sensation, that. But something she'd said a few minutes ago kept replaying in his mind on an endless loop. *Make love to me . . .* Was that what she was expecting? Gentle touches? Ardent kisses? That wasn't him. At least it never had been . . . What if he wasn't what she'd been expecting? What if he disappointed her?

Fuck, he didn't know the first thing about making love to a woman, and if that was Katie's expectation . . . Now, if she'd said *Fuck me blind*, he was her guy. But knowing her past, and the courage it took for her to give herself to him . . . Damn, he didn't want to mess this up—or scare her. He'd told her he wouldn't handle her with kid gloves, but that was exactly what he was doing now. And since when did he have performance anxiety?—never, that's when. But Kat was different. She meant something to him. She wasn't some horny cage banger, and he highly doubted she'd appreciate being rutted like one.

Katie's mouth stalled on his neck, her exhaled breath hot against skin left damp from her teasing tongue. She tensed beneath him. "Is something wrong?" she asked, uncertainty hedging in her voice. Before he could deny it, she said, "If you're having second thoughts . . ."

What? Oh, hell no . . . Pushing aside his sudden attack of conscience, Cole gave her a wicked grin and bent his head, growling against her kiss-swollen lips, "Not a chance, sweetheart."

Cole crushed his mouth to her parted lips, his tongue sweeping possessively against hers as he pushed his hips forward, stretching her to accommodate his unyielding girth. The mixture of pain and pleasure made her gasp, drawing his breath into her lungs, the exotic entanglement dragging her deeper under his spell. Power and strength radiated from this man like a current of energy, crackling over her flesh everywhere their bodies touched, all centering at their point of intimate connection.

Inch by inch, he consumed her, each thrust bringing him closer to that aching point of contact deep inside her. Cole's jaw clenched tight, a fine sheen of sweat dampening his back, conveying his restraint as he eased into her. The heady sensation of being filled by this powerful man was intoxicating.

She'd been preparing herself for that trapped, panicked feeling to rise up inside her as memories struggled to invade her conscious. What she hadn't been prepared for was the jolt of awareness, the connectivity that pierced her heart when Cole's burning gaze locked and held hers. Time may have stopped, her heart certainly did, when he rasped in a voice raw with emotion she feared to name, "How ya doing, sweetheart? You with me?"

Oh, she was with him all right. She hadn't thought it possible, pinned beneath two hundred pounds of rock-hard muscle, but the fight-or-flight instinct she'd been expecting to battle didn't come. Somehow, Cole had managed to wholly consume her, banishing all thought, all memories, from her mind. Unable to force words past her emotion-clogged throat, she held his gaze and nodded. He smiled down at her, a grin of pure male satisfaction that sent a tremor of need rioting through that elusive spot deep inside her—the spot he drew achingly close to, but seemed for some reason hesitant to hit.

Cole was an impressively large man—everywhere—so she knew the lack of contact was deliberate as he withdrew and pushed forward with aching, frustrating restraint. She wanted him deeper—harder. What was he waiting for?

And then the answer suddenly occurred to her as she watched him grapple for control. He was struggling to rein in his passion—for her. He was fighting against his base instinct to fully claim her. Katie wasn't sure whether to be touched by his efforts or scream in frustration because he was doing the one thing he'd vowed not to do—treat her like she was broken.

She wanted Cole, the real Cole, untethered and 100 percent in-it-to-win-it. It was how he lived his life, and she had no doubt it was how he took his pleasure—raw and undone. Perhaps it was time she earned her nickname, and put the limit of Cole's restraint to the test. The thought that she, a woman almost half his size, might break this rock of a man was too great a temptation to resist.

Slowly, she dragged her nails down Cole's back, following the narrowing taper to the muscular curve of his ass. Holding him firm, nails biting into his flesh, she arched into him, taking him deeper. She grasped at the stretch that was now more pleasure than pain. His brow arched in question, in silent warning that she was pushing her luck and might be getting in over her head. To this point he'd held her tenderly, cradled in his powerful arms. His kisses were languorous and gentle, his movements purposeful and controlled. He felt amazing—but this wasn't him.

He dipped his head and kissed the sensitive spot below her ear. When she arched into his measured thrust, claiming ground he'd refused to cede to her, he bit her neck. She gasped in surprise, finding she enjoyed the teasing sting that shot darts of pleasure between her legs.

"Tell me what you want, Kat."

She was pretty sure he knew exactly what she wanted. But for some reason he wanted to hear her say it. By now she had no shame. Cole had worked her into a frenzied mess. If he wanted her to beg, she'd beg. "I want you . . . deeper," she panted, the wicked confession burning on her lips. She'd never spoken so boldly.

"Like this?" Gripping her shoulders and anchoring her to him, he plunged deep inside her, burying himself to the hilt.

She almost came right then and there when he connected with her core. The fullness was excruciating bliss that tore a raptured cry from her throat.

"Fuuuck," Cole groaned a tortured growl, pulling back far enough to surge into her again.

His muscles strained beneath her fingertips and she knew he was fighting the same losing battle that she was. As much as she'd have loved for this to last all night, the tension coiling inside her was threatening to shatter. "Yes," she panted when he hit that secret spot again . . . and again . . . and again.

Just as she'd thought, Cole was as much a force to be reckoned with in bed as he was in the ring. He'd taken time to study his opponent—he knew all her weaknesses and used them to his advantage, exposing her for the shameless wanton she secretly was. He knew right where to touch her, how to exact the maximum amount of pleasure from a body that no longer belonged to her but to the fighter masterfully controlling her every desire. It seemed ironic that a man who specialized in giving so much pain could deliver such pleasure with the same seamless efficiency. Cole knew her body better than she did—what she wanted—what she needed—and he seemed to love making her beg for it.

But with her final plea, something inside him snapped. Playtime was over. His tempo increased, working them both into a fevered frenzy. The pressure was incredible . . . building until she didn't think she could stand another moment of the erotic torture of his hands, his mouth, his cock driving inside her . . .

And then she shattered—a strangled cry tearing from her throat as euphoric waves crashed over her, dragging her under. Her channel spasmed against him as he drove into her one final time. With a primal growl of release, heat pulsed against her core, prolonging the blissful shockwaves ripping through her body.

As the last tremors ebbed, Cole collapsed on top of her, giving her the brunt of his weight. She could feel his heart hammering against her breast, the rapid sawing of his breaths tickling the sweat-dampened flesh of her neck. All too soon, her mind started to clear and reality began vying for its place in her thoughts. What did this mean for them now? How would this affect their working relationship?—their friendship? But the biggest question weighing on her mind right now was what did this mean to Cole?—the guy who'd had countless one-night stands, and professed he'd never been in love.

She'd been a fool to think she could compartmentalize sex with this man. She'd never been a "friends with benefits" kind of woman, so what in the hell had made her think she could start now? Cole had not only touched the deepest places inside her, he'd touched her very soul, and the tenderness she felt for him, the gratitude, was an unexpected and wholly unwelcomed complication. Her heart stuttered and skipped a beat as the realization suddenly hit her full force. *God help me, I'm in love with Cole Easton . . .*

CHAPTER

26

Katie woke to the worst foot cramp—ever! Hissing in a sharp breath, she tried to bolt upright, grabbing for her foot, but couldn't move. Cole's arm was wrapped around her chest, his leg draped over her as he held her tight against his body. "Ow! Ow! Ow!" she chanted, struggling to get out from under him.

Cole startled awake and flew upright, connecting with the bunk above him. "Son of a bitch!" he growled.

She would have laughed if her foot didn't hurt so damn bad. "Ow! Ow! Ow!" She reached for her foot but couldn't get to it beneath the tangle of covers.

"What's wrong?" Cole demanded, his eyes dragging over her—searching for injury.

"It's my foot! I have a horrible cramp!"

"Which one?" he asked, yanking the bottom of their covers loose.

"My left!"

He grabbed her foot.

"My other left!" she cried, not realizing her legs were crossed.

Cole pulled her leg onto his lap, grabbed her toes and pointed them toward her shin, stretching out her tendons. After a few more seconds and a lot more whimpering, the sharp cramping pain began to ease. Taking a deep breath, she flopped back on her pillow, completely uncaring she left the covers pooled at her waist. "Oh . . ." she sighed dramatically. "That's better." Cole released her toes and put the pads of his thumbs into the bottom of her foot, gently stretching and stripping her arch. It felt amazing. His touch had the skill and feel of an athlete who'd been-there-done-that and knew his anatomy well. He quickly loosened the muscles in her foot before working up her calf.

"You're dehydrated. You didn't drink enough water yesterday and drank too much brandy last night," he scolded. Which was definitely not helping right now.

A wicked thought came over her and she impulsively acted on it. "Oh, my head is killing me." No lie, it really was. Lifting her head she looked down at her naked breasts, then over at Cole, and then back at her chest. "Did we?" He tensed. His hands froze on her leg, his grip tightening ever so slightly as his expression took a note of alarm. "You know. Did we umm . . . ?"

"You don't remember?" he growled. "I fucking knew it!" Cole jacked his hand through his hair, looking like he was about to be sick.

Unable to carry out the ruse, she busted out laughing. Knowing he'd been had, Cole gave her a mock glare and growled, "Think it's funny, huh?" With the speed that made him such a formable striker, Cole dove on top of her, pinned her to the mattress, and began tickling her. "Stop it!" she cried, laughing harder. She'd never seen this side of Cole—so carefree and playful—she loved it!

"Not until you tap."

"That's cruel! Tickling a girl who has to pee!" she squealed between fits of laughter, fighting to get out from under him, and making no progress.

"So is pretending you don't remember the best sex of this guy's life."

"So is giving a girl a sobriety test before sleeping with her!" Wait. What did he just say? Best sex of his life? Seriously?

Cole stopped tickling her and turned serious, shifting his weight so he could see her better. "Hey, there've been a few times I wish someone would have given me a sobriety test. Would have saved me a lot of trouble and a whole hell of a lot of regret."

"You thought I would regret this?"

"I hoped not. But you've worked pretty hard at pushing me away. Not that I haven't done my share of avoiding you these past few weeks myself."

"What changed?"

He shrugged. "I guess I finally hit my breaking point. What changed for you? And if you say the brandy, be warned the tickling will wholeheartedly resume."

"Well, that would be to your own detriment, because I wasn't kidding when I said I had to pee." Seriously, could she stall anymore? What could she say? *I realized that I love you?* Yeah, not going to happen. She was not going to drop the L-bomb on a guy who (a) probably had panty-dropping cage bangers throwing that word at him all the time, and (b) professed just a few short weeks ago never to have been in love. Besides, he had the perfect opportunity to tell her if that had changed, and "I guess I finally hit my breaking point" just didn't cut it.

"Umm . . . can we talk about this when I get back from the johnny? I really gotta go." So yep, she was a big fricking coward. A hint of disappointment wrinkled his brows, but after another brief moment, he relented, rolling to the side and allowing her to escape. Katie slipped out from underneath him and scrambled to get dressed under the weight of Cole's bold, unapologetic stare. Snagging her bra off the floor, Katie wrestled it on, shoving her arms through the straps and stuffing her boobs inside the fragile lace cups.

Feeling the heat of Cole's eyes boring into her, she cast him a quick glance and felt her heart skip at his pure, masculine beauty. Sprawled on his back across a bed about two sizes too small, Cole watched her, enjoying the show with his arms up, hands laced behind his head, and a cocky grin spread across his handsome face.

"Enjoying the show?"

"Immensely . . ."

She didn't need to ask. By the size of his manhood proudly on display, he was having a grand ol' time of it. Pulling her sweater on, she stood there a moment, turning around to search. "Where's my underwear?" He cocked his brow and gave her a shit-eating grin. And then she remembered. "Oh, yeah, that's right. You owe me a new pair of panties, mister. That was my favorite set."

"They were mine, too," he teased. "I'll take you shopping when we get back. Probably ought to get a few backup pairs while you're at it."

"Why?" she asked, stepping into her pants commando style and wiggling them over her hips. "You plan on tearing them off again?"

"Absolutely."

That cagey grin began to stir all her achy places with blossoming heat. Her deliciously sore nipples hardened against their flimsy barrier, and the tender, well-loved place between her legs hurt just enough to remind her of the incredible night she and Cole had shared. She'd done it! With Cole's help, she'd faced her fears, and the freedom she'd found in his touch had been so liberating, so unlike anything she'd ever experienced before. If she thought too hard on it, she might just cry, which would be a total mood killer. Talk about your mixed signals.

Turning away from him, she busied herself bundling up in her coat, boots, mittens, hat . . . "Well, I gotta tell you." She shifted her weight on her legs, then wiggled her hips back and forth. "I don't get the appeal to this commando stuff. It just feels weird."

Cole laughed as she made her way to the door, promising, "You will," as she marched out the door and trudged into the freezing cold.

"So I'm sitting beside Marcus, laughing my ass off because this voice comes through the speaker saying, 'Apple pie, I get you one.' Marcus tells the woman, 'No, I don't want an apple pie. I want a Coke. Just give me a Coke.' The voice says again, 'Apple pie, I get you one.' Marcus looks at me, you know that look he gets when he's trying not lose his temper, but that shit's about to blow."

Katie nodded, laughing too hard to talk.

"This goes on a little bit longer, the same back and forth. 'Apple pie, I get you one.' And finally Marcus gets so pissed he pulls up to the drive-through and tells the woman when she opens the window, 'I want a Coke, lady, just a Coke.' And the woman looks at him like he's a complete idiot and speaks real slow and loudly, like he belongs on the short bus or something, 'A dollar five. Window one.'"

Katie went into another fit of laughter, grabbing her aching sides. Lord, it felt so good to laugh. She couldn't remember the last time she'd laughed so much, or so hard. "And you knew the whole time!"

Cole smiled, chuckling as he nodded.

"Why didn't you tell him?"

"Are you kidding me? That was funnier than shit! Besides, I'd been hounding him for months to get some damn hearing aids and he wouldn't do it. It only took about a week of me saying 'Apple pie, I get you one' before he finally went in and got some."

"That sounds just like Uncle Marcus," she laughed. The whole ride home, they'd been laughing and sharing stories about her uncle. As if she needed one more reason to love this man sitting beside her. Listening to Cole's stories, seeing the admiration in his eyes when he spoke of her uncle, only deepened her connection to him. This morning, Cole had shown her another side of himself she hadn't known existed. It was as if he'd finally lowered his walls, allowing her a glimpse of the man he truly was—the man hidden behind the injury, the paparazzi, the fame . . . Buried somewhere deep beneath that tough exterior and that serious, stoic mask, Cole had a wonderful sense of humor. He was fun, flirtatious, and charming. Katie suspected she was seeing a side to the rough fighter few others got to experience, and it made her feel . . . special— loved—which was a dangerous thought, because if she wasn't care- ful, this man could very well break her heart.

She glanced at the clock on the dash and frowned. It was already early evening. Where had the day gone? They'd gotten a late start in heading home. When she'd returned to the fish house this morning, Cole was already up and making her breakfast. She'd been disappointed to find him out of bed and dressed so fast. Despite being a little sore, she would have liked to spend a little more time with him horizontal, pretending the rest of the world didn't exist. How easily being in his arms made her forget . . .

After breakfast, she'd finished packing up while Cole went over to the fish house next door to donate their catch. When nearly an hour came and went, and there was still no sign of him, Katie bun- dled back up and headed over to see what the delay was. She'd knocked on the door and pulled it open on the command "Come in!" and found Cole standing there with a beer in hand, and another guy standing beside him, also holding a beer, as both men smiled for the camera. As soon as the stranger snapped the pic with his phone, he declared, "My turn" and switched places with his buddy. Neither guy had yet to glance her way. They were both too starstruck to be sharing a beer with the Beast of the East. But Cole noticed her. His gorgeous glam-cam smile melted into the softer, more carefree grin he seemed to save just for her. When the the flash went off, she couldn't help the insane flare of jealousy that surged up inside her at the thought that *her* smile had been caught on camera.

It was ridiculous to think that she owned a smile, but any grin that could have that strong of an effect on her, making her heart patter like it did, her knees go weak, and the place between her thighs grow wet, owned her enough that she felt she had the right to reciprocate.

"Hey, Kat."

When Cole greeted her, both guys whipped around. One muttered "Holy shit" under his breath, but in the small fish house, sound traveled and suddenly Cole's smile wasn't quite so amiable anymore. "Sorry I kept you waiting, babe." Without missing a beat, he moved forward and slipped his arm around her waist, tucking her into his side and clearly staking his claim. "Guys, this is Katrina, my girlfriend. Kat, this is Matt and Drew. They're fans."

Katie hadn't heard anything after *girlfriend*, and she went through the motions of introductions and numbly accepted a beer when it was shoved into her hand, all the while trying not to read too much into what he'd just said. Did Cole really consider her his girlfriend, or had it been a glib term spoken to stake his claim? Whatever the intention, it'd worked, because the men's appreciative stares had been quickly diverted, and their full attention returned to Cole.

He'd finished his beer with the guys, answering questions and talking about the likelihood of a rematch between him and De'Grasse. Hearing him speak of the future only further drove home the temporary state of their situation, and along with it, solidified her conviction to make the most of the time she had left with him. When the guys had gotten up, heading to the cooler for another beer, Katie leaned over and whispered an offer into Cole's ear he couldn't refuse.

She just about laughed when he all but jumped up and grabbed her hand, telling the guys it was great meeting them and that he had to go. The rest of their time before checkout had been spent between the sheets, and she knew she'd never look at a bunk bed the same again.

CHAPTER

27

A re you hungry? Do you want to stop and eat before we go home?"
"I could eat. We burned a lot of calories this morning," she
teased, casting him a flirtatious, sideways glance.

Cole chuckled and slipped his hand around the back of Katie's
neck, pulling her close to plant a quick, hard kiss on her lips before
turning his focus back to the road. It felt good being with him like
this, so natural. For a little while, she could almost pretend they
were a normal couple—and that was exactly what Katie did.

All through that morning when Cole had brought her back to
the fish house and made love to her, taking her to heights she'd
never been before, and all through the afternoon where they talked
and laughed, sharing some stories and touching on others that
weren't so easy to talk about. For almost a whole day, Katie pretended that her life wasn't a complete fucking nightmare. And she'd
almost convinced herself of it, too, until they'd pulled into the
driveway.

Dusk had fallen, leaving enough remnants of the sun behind to
see without the aid of a light. She was busy chatting away about
something unimportant as she dug through her purse, looking for
the house keys, when Cole abruptly slammed on the brakes. The
rental came to a jarring halt, and Katie's hand flew up to the dash,
bracing herself as her head snapped up to see what was wrong.

"That motherfucker!" Cole snarled.

Katie followed his stare, her breath catching in her throat on a strangled gasp, her hand flying up to cover her mouth. "Oh, my God! Is that . . . blood?" Katie's nails bit into the dash as she stared at the snow-covered yard. The pristine white pallet, stained crimson with the words *Fucking Whore* on display for all to see. "OhmyGod ohmyGod ohmyGod," she chanted. Her stomach knotted, sending a surge of bile rising up the back of her throat, choking off her air. "Is it blood?" she cried shrilly when Cole didn't answer her.

"I don't know. I can't tell from here. Don't move." He jumped out of the rental SUV, slamming the door behind him, and entered the house through the garage. Minutes passed and he still hadn't returned, ratcheting Katie's fear to a whole new level. Panic gripped her throat like an invisible hand, squeezing . . . squeezing . . . She couldn't breathe! She had to get out of here! Just as her hand dropped to the handle, the front door of the house opened and Cole came out carrying a blanket. He charged over to the crimson-stained snow and after taking a closer look at the words, covered them with the cream-colored fleece.

When instead of turning back, he kept his gaze fixed on the ground, Katie's heart sank with dread. Helplessly, she watched as Cole followed a trail across the yard and into the bushes. Bending down, he pushed the bushes aside, as if searching for something— but what? And then the thought hit her, with the striking force of an anvil.

A broken sob escaped her throat as she threw open the car door. "Scarlet! Oh no, Cole, it's Scarlet, isn't it!" she cried, charging into the snow. But before she could reach the bushes and confirm her fears, Cole caught her around the waist and pulled her into his arms. His large hand cupped the back of her head, forcing her face against the side of his neck as he turned them away from the bushes and began walking them toward the house.

His silence should have been all the confirmation she needed, but for some reason, she had to hear the spoken truth. "Tell me!" she demanded, wrapping her arms around his neck, holding on with a death grip as she sobbed into his shoulder. "I have to know!"

"It's Scarlet."

She barely recognized his voice, the low growl of rage mixed with the tight strain of grief. "I knew it!" Frozen in horror, her legs refused to cooperate and Cole lifted her into his arms. "He killed their cat!"

"I'm so sorry, sweetheart . . ."

The heat of his breath warmed the top of her head. She shivered but was incognizant of the cold, the shock of it all seeping into her bones with an insidious chill that she feared she'd never rewarm from. Cole hugged her tighter, stopping just inside the garage. What was he waiting for? Why weren't they going inside? Impending doom swept over her, taking with it the last vestiges of her self-control. Any second now, she was going to lose it. Pulling back far enough to see Cole's face, she could tell he was busy fighting his own battle, though she was sure if he snapped it would be a far different result. She'd never thought a man looked more capable of murder than this man did right now. For one insane moment, she almost wished Carter was here. Without a doubt, Cole would end this. Despite the rage he was struggling to control, Katie could tell there was more—something he wasn't telling her.

"What is it, Cole?"

He shook his head. "Come on, Kat. Let's just wait in the car until the police get here."

"You already called them?"

He nodded, turning to usher her back toward the rental when she put the brakes on. "Wait, Cole. Why do we have to wait in the car? What aren't you telling me?"

His next words were the final blow, and if Cole hadn't been holding onto her, she would have hit the ground.

"He's been in the house, Kat. It's completely trashed."

"I want to go in," Katie insisted, her little nails biting into his biceps as she clung to him. "I need to see it before anyone else gets here—alone—with you."

Despite Cole's gut instinct telling him how horseshit an idea this was, he acquiesced. If she truly wanted to go in, it wasn't his place to stop her. Upon entering the first time, he'd made a thorough sweep of the house, just to make sure the bastard wasn't lying in wait somewhere. The place was empty—trashed, but empty. Fuck him, Katie wasn't exaggerating when she'd said Carter was crazy. The shit he pulled with the cat . . . that was just fucked up.

Taking a deep breath, he pushed back the anger—the rage—boiling inside him. He wasn't going to do Katie any good if he lost his shit. She needed him to remain cool, calm, and collected. She needed his strength if she was going to get through this without losing it herself—a fine line she seemed to be walking at the moment.

Wrapping his arm around her waist for support, Cole walked her into the house through the kitchen entrance. "Watch your feet," he warned when they stepped inside and glass crunched beneath their shoes. Katie gasped. Her shaky hand flew up to cover her mouth as tears filled her emerald eyes. He kept his own expression locked down as he watched her absorb the carnage in the kitchen.

The cupboard doors hung open, the ones still attached, anyway. Broken dishes littered the counter and the floor.

He watched as her gaze strayed to the living room, seeing it again, except now through her horror-filled eyes. The couch was overturned, its cushions slashed. White mounds of stuffing covered the floor in large, fluffy tufts. The end table was missing a leg, no doubt becoming a makeshift bat for Carter's carnage. The lamp lay broken on the floor, the TV knocked off its stand.

"Oh, my God . . ."

It was all she'd been able to say. Rage boiled up inside him anew, and Cole wrapped his arms around her, pulling her against his chest, but holding her was like trying to console a block of wood. She stood stiffly, staring numbly past his shoulder, seemingly unable to tear her eyes away from the destruction.

"It's just stuff, Kat. I'll have a cleaning crew come in here and it'll be set to rights in no time. I'll replace what's broken and damaged. It's going to be all right." But as the words tumbled from his lips, even he had a hard time believing them.

Nothing was left untouched, which made the white, square box with a large red ribbon sitting in the center of the table look even more out of place amongst the chaos. He knew the moment she saw it. Felt it in the tension shuddering through her.

"What's that?" She pointed to the package.

"It was here when I came in the first time."

"Did you open it?"

He shook his head. "Do you want me to?"

She looked from him to the box and then back to him, her verdant eyes wide and terrified. A single tear rolled down her cheek and she quickly swiped it away. His jaw clenched against the pang in his heart at seeing her like this. Damn, she was a fighter, standing there, struggling to keep it together—and he respected the hell out of her for it. But one wrong move from him and he knew she'd crack.

After another moment, she nodded.

Reluctantly, he let her go and walked over to the table. Standing before the box, he hesitated, glancing over at her. "Are you sure about this?"

"Do it."

Damn, he loved this woman. His brave little Kat . . . If he could bear this for her, he'd do it in a heartbeat. He'd bear it and more—anything to spare her the pain and mental agony this bastard seemed intent to inflict upon her.

Pulling an end of the bow, the silk ribbon let loose. He grasped the side of the lid and looked at her once more, just to be sure she hadn't changed her mind. When she nodded, giving him the go ahead, Cole lifted the lid. At the sight of Katie's black lace panties nestled on top of the white cloud of tissue paper, a feral growl rumbled in this throat. But it was the white, crusted stains defacing the lace that tore the curse from his lips. "Motherfucker!" Grabbing the envelope out of the box, he slammed the lid back down.

"What is it?"

Ignoring her question, he slipped his finger beneath the seal of the envelope and ripped it open. Cole pulled out the card. The front of it was generically patterned with colorful daisies—Katie's favorite flower. How in the hell he remembered such a trivial fact was beyond him. It wasn't the kind of thing he ever would have paid attention to in the past, but with Katie, things were different—*he* was different. Apparently, he actually listened to the things she had to say. She'd mentioned it in a passing comment, even, while complaining about how long the winters were here.

For some insane reason, seeing those bright, colorful flowers collaged across the card pissed him off even more. He didn't believe for a minute it was a coincidence. He just didn't realize how significant those flowers were until he opened the card, allowing her to see the cover.

A picture fell out, landing facedown on the table. Katie's startled gasp was barely heard over the wild pounding of his heart thundering in his ears as he read the scribbled words: *Until death do us part.*

That bastard was about to get his fucking wish. Cole snatched the picture off the table and turned it over. Smiling up at him was a pic of Katie and Carter. He stood close to her, his beefy arm slung possessively over her shoulder, which was like poking Cole's green-eyed monster with a big fucking stick.

They were at some sort of a barbecue. Smoke was rolling out of the grill they were standing by. Adults lounged and children played in the background. Katie looked surprised, as if she hadn't been prepared for the pic, or the man to come up and throw his arm around her. A Bud Light Lime hung loosely in his grasp, resting against Katie's arm.

He stuffed the pic back inside the card and shoved them inside the envelope. When he glanced back at her, Katie looked like she was about to tip over. Every ounce of color was drained from her beautiful face as she stared at the card on the table beside the box.

"The card, what does it say?"

No fucking way was he telling her that. "It doesn't matter. It isn't true."

"You don't understand. That card is from my stationery."

Well, that explained the flowers, but Cole failed to see the significance here. They'd already established he'd been in the house. "What am I missing here, Kat? We know he was here."

"Not this house! The stationery is at my parents' house, Cole!"

Oh fuck . . .

"It's in the bottom desk drawer in my bedroom. He's been in

their house! Digging through my room! What does the card say?" she demanded, her voice hitching toward hysterics.

As much as he didn't want to tell her, he couldn't keep it from her. Broken glass crunched beneath his feet as he walked over to her. How she was still on her feet, he didn't know, but he wasn't about to give her the final shove without at least hanging on to her. Taking care to keep all emotion from his voice, he stated matter-of-factly, "It says . . . 'Until death do us part.'"

Her knees buckled and he pulled her into his arms, holding her tight as she buried her face into his chest and began to sob. "You have to call my parents. Make sure they're all right. I can't . . . I can't talk to them like this."

"All right," he soothed, bending down to place a kiss on top of her head. Tightening his grip on her with one arm, he let go with the other and dug his cell out of his pocket. "What's their number?"

Katie recited the number between hitching breaths. The phone rang a couple of times and just before someone picked up, she whispered, "Don't tell them what happened. My dad can't handle the stress. Just make sure they're okay."

"Hello?"

At the sound of her mother's voice echoing through the phone, Katie sagged against him in relief and whispered, "Oh, thank God." He tightened his grip, holding her up against him.

"Hi, Carol, umm . . . This is Cole. Katie asked me to give you call to uhh . . . check and see if you need her to bring you any orange juice in the morning before she stops over."

"Oh, let me check." There was a moment of silence before she asked, "Where's Katie?"

He hated lying in general, and he particularly hated lying to Katie's mother, but she hadn't given him much of a choice. She needed to come clean with her parents about the nightmare she'd been living these past two years, but it wasn't his place to out her, as much as he wanted to. In trying to protect them, Katie was making them vulnerable to a very dangerous man. Hopefully after tonight, she'd see that and finally tell them the truth.

"We're at the store. She's, umm . . . shopping. Her phone is dead so she asked me to call and see if you were good before we left."

The lie seemed to satisfy her mother because the note of surprised hesitation was gone from her voice when she said, "Oh, well thank you for checking. That's very thoughtful. Looks like we're good on orange juice."

"You need anything else? Everything good there?"

"Nope, not that I can think of. We're all good."

"All right. We'll see you in the morning, then."

"Sounds good. Thank you for calling, Cole."

As he hung up with Carol, a knock sounded on the kitchen door and Katie startled in his arms.

Before he could move to answer it, a voice called from the other side, "This is Officer Wyatt with the Somerset Police Department."

CHAPTER

28

The next two hours were a blur. Thankfully, the officer who responded was the same one who'd taken her report the other day, so she was spared having to repeat the backstory. Cole did most of the talking now, answering the officer's questions as they walked through the house, surveying the damage. The place was completely flipped, and of all the rooms, hers was the worst. Her mattress was slashed. The feather pillows she'd gotten from her grandmother's house before she died were destroyed. A layer of small, fluffy feathers coated the room like dust. Her clothes were strewn around, many of them torn and ruined. It was all just too much to take in.

She nodded appropriately when spoken to directly, but couldn't seem to find her voice past the lump of dread lodged in her throat. Once she'd discovered her parents were all right, self-preserving numbness had spread through her limbs, dulling her senses, clogging her mind from processing it all. The only thing keeping her grounded right now was the man standing beside her. His towering height sheltered her, his powerful strength protected her, his hand never broke contact, as if in silent avowal he would not leave her. Whether pressed comfortingly against the small of her back, or slipped around her waist as his arm held her tucked against his side, Cole kept in constant connection with her. It was as if he knew the moment the comforting touch left her, she would be lost.

Had she really thought to push him away? That she could do this alone? She needed his calming strength like her lungs needed oxygen. In the span of a few short hours, Cole had become her lifeline—her thread to sanity. The horror of her past had finally caught her in its riptide, and it was threatening to drag her under.

Katie watched, only half-processing what was happening around her as Officer Wyatt lifted the lid on the box and looked inside. The momentary surprise on his face was quickly replaced by a scowl. What was in that box? Cole wouldn't tell her, so it must be bad. A part of her didn't want to know. He took out the card and slipped it from the envelope. After quickly looking at it, he shoved it back inside the box. The look he exchanged with Cole didn't need words. It ratcheted the terror pumping through her veins all the same. When he spoke, the sound was muffled by the chaotic beating of her heart and she had to focus, straining to hear what exactly the officer was telling her.

"I've seen enough. I'll need to take this box in and mark it for evidence. We'll photograph the rest and I'll have animal control come out and take care of the cat. There will be a warrant issued for Carter Owen's arrest. But the problem may be finding him. I don't usually speak so frankly, Ms. Miller, but in this case I feel it's warranted. Do you own a gun?"

What? She shook her head.

"I would get one. We will do everything in our power to protect you and to get Mr. Owens into custody as quickly as possible. And we're only a phone call away. But I'm also a realist, Ms. Miller, and a lot can happen in a very short time." His gaze shot to Cole. "If I were you, I'd take her some place this asshole can't find her. At least until we get him picked up."

"I'm planning on it."

"I have your number, Ms. Miller. We'll contact you as soon as it's safe for you to return. I should get yours as well, Mr. Easton."

Cole and Officer Wyatt exchanged information, then, with the box tucked under his arm, the officer left.

The next several hours were another blur. If Katie hadn't been in shock, she might have put up more of a fight, but she was too busy battling her internal demons to wage war against Cole—not that it would have done much good. He was one of the most stubborn, single-mindedly determined men she'd ever met. A force to be reckoned with, and right now, she just didn't have it in her to resist him.

That was how, in a whirlwind of a few short hours, Katie found herself first in front of her parents, telling them the truth, her bags minimally packed, and currently on a plane bound for Vegas with Cole sitting beside her. His hand held hers tightly, as if he feared she'd bolt the moment he let go. And she might have, if she'd had anywhere to go other than plummeting to her death.

He spoke very little during the three-and-a-half-hour flight. Perhaps giving her the time and space she needed to process it all—which she'd been doing for the last two hours. Digesting what had happened bit by palatable bit.

Although deep down she knew it was the right thing to do, and she'd really had no choice, a part of her resented him for forcing her hand. In the brief time it took her to gather what few belongings Carter hadn't destroyed, Cole had contacted a locksmith to change out her parents' locks, and hired a security company to install a system in their home.

He'd arranged to leave his rental car at the airport, booked her and himself one-way tickets to Vegas, and called Marcus to tell him they were coming in on a late-night flight. Marcus had insisted on picking them up at the airport, even though Cole had suggested several times they take a cab. Their flight wouldn't even be landing until three a.m. But Uncle Marcus was stubborn, and once he set his mind to something, there wasn't anything anyone could do to change it.

Katie wanted to see her uncle—really she did. She'd missed him like crazy, though she could have visited him under better circumstances, and she would have preferred a day to rally her nerve and get her head back on straight before seeing him. So many thoughts were racing through her mind right now—the unknowns and what-ifs were overwhelming.

"I didn't want to tell my parents, Cole. Not like this."

"I know you didn't," he answered, his tone devoid of emotion. "But they needed to understand you're in danger, why you're leaving. Besides, it'd look awfully suspicious when both the locksmith and ADT show up on their doorstep tomorrow if they didn't know what was going on. They love you, Kat. They want to be there for you. Let them."

"I shouldn't have left them like that. My father needs me—"

"Your father needs you to stay safe, Kat. I'll hire someone to go to the house and keep up with his PT while you're away. Of course, they won't be as great as you."

She couldn't help but smile when he bumped her arm with his shoulder.

"But I'll make sure they're good. I promise."

"I can't let you do that, Cole. It's too expensive. You're already doing so much. The bills—"

"—are none of your concern," he cut in firmly. "Trust me, Kat, I can afford it."

Cole's generosity was just one more layer on her confusion cake. What did this mean? Was he just being nice or was there more to it? Maybe he just felt sorry for her? Where did this leave them?

He'd yet to profess his feelings for her. For all she knew, this was nothing but a fling to pass the time while he was in rehab. He'd told her the previous night this had an expiration date. And yet, like an impulsive fool, she'd given herself to him, anyway. If that didn't scream *mixed signals*, then she didn't know what did. As much as it pained her to think that Cole might not return the same level of affection she felt for him, she couldn't bring herself to regret what they'd done. Even if he couldn't love her, Cole had done more to help her, more to heal her, than she'd ever hoped or imagined. It felt good to be taken care of for a change, even if it was out of some misplaced obligation he might feel after a night of mind-blowing sex. She just didn't think she had it in her to deal with Carter again. She'd already run once. That she was doing it again was enough to crumble the shell she'd worked so hard these past years to rebuild.

"That's not the point, Cole. You shouldn't have to do this. I'm so sorry you were dragged into it. I tried . . . I tried to keep you out of it—"

"Kat, stop. Don't you dare apologize to me. You didn't do anything wrong." He squeezed her hand. "I'm just glad Marcus sent me here when he did. Besides, do you have any idea how much *you* have helped *me*? I'm on my feet again because of you. Every day you're making me stronger. Hell, you've saved my career. It's the least I could do for you."

And there she had it—the truth—the motivation behind Cole's actions. It wasn't love that drove him, it was gratitude. Ouch . . . Well that hurt more than she cared to admit. Tears burned behind her eyes. She held her breath, fighting back the inevitable well blurring her vision. She wouldn't cry, dammit, not here—not in front of Cole—not over this. But her emotions were too raw. She was exhausted and emotional, and trapped here on this fucking plane with a man she was hopelessly in love with who didn't love her back, while being carted halfway across the United States.

"Excuse me," she mumbled, shooting to her feet and trying to push past him into the aisle. Even sitting in first class, Cole took up all the extra room and some of hers, making it a scramble of unhelpful arms and tangled legs to get past him before she broke down right here in front of the entire first-class audience.

"Kat, are you all right?"

Cole looked a cross between surprised and concerned as he tried to help her across his lap. She stumbled into the aisle and nearly fell on top of the couple across from them. They, too, looked alarmed, though for an entirely different reason. Thankfully, she didn't have far to go until she reached the first-class bathroom. Wrenching the door open, she rushed inside, and slammed it shut behind her. The lighted *Occupied* sign blurred behind a well of tears as she gave herself over to her heartache.

What in the hell was keeping her? Cole glanced behind his shoulder for about the tenth time. Since Katie had bolted for the bathroom, he'd downed one of those little travel-size vodkas in a glass of orange juice, needing to calm his own jacked-up nerves. What a horrible fucking day. He knew Katie had hit her emotional limit, but he couldn't help but think he'd said something to set her off. What, he had no damn clue. He'd spent the last half hour replaying their conversation in his mind and coming up blank.

"Would you like another screwdriver?" the overly attentive stewardess asked with a *meet me behind the first-class curtain* smile.

"No, thank you." Cole held up his hand, stopping her before she broke the seal on the vodka.

"Well, let me know if you change your mind." Seriously? Did the woman not see Katie sitting here with him? Speaking of which, he was done waiting for her. As the stewardess passed him, Cole slipped out behind her, heading the opposite direction, and took the six steps that put him in front of the bathroom. He knocked. No answer. He knocked again. "Kat, open up. It's me."

Hearing the obligatory flush, which he knew was total bullshit, he stood at the door, fingers tapping restlessly against the metal frame as he waited for her to open it. A moment later the door cracked open, but before she could step out, he slipped in, locking it behind him. Damn, it was a tight fit. If they hadn't been in first class, squeezing in here would have been impossible. As it was, Cole was quickly rethinking the wisdom of his plan with Katie's body crushed tightly up against his. Holy hell, he hadn't come in here for anything other than to talk to her, knowing there was no way in hell she would open up to him out there, surrounded by a bunch of strangers. But now that he had her pinned up against him, trapped between his hard body, growing harder by the second, and the small vanity sink, he was having a damn difficult time remembering what he'd wanted to say.

"Cole, what are you doing in here?"

She didn't sound very happy about it. But the way her body softened against him, nipples hardening to little beaded pearls against his chest, was telling him another story. He could tell by the luminous intensity of her dark green eyes and her flushed blotchy cheeks that she'd been crying. And the knowledge kicked him right in the balls, knocking the wind out of him.

Framing her face with his hands to keep her from looking away, he said, "What's the matter, Kat?" Wow, was that a stupid fucking question, considering the hell she'd been through today. "How can I make it better, baby?" Bending down, he placed a chaste kiss on her forehead. "Just tell me," he coaxed, kissing one of her cheeks. "I want to help you." He brushed his mouth over her other cheek, and then her lips. His heart ached at the taste of her briny kiss. He wanted to make it go away. He wanted to wipe away all her tears, take away all her fear, to bear her burden of grief—if she would just let him in. But he didn't know what to do, what to say, to get her to take that leap of faith—to make her trust him with her heart.

He wanted to tell her he loved her, but couldn't risk scaring her away with such a proclamation, especially on the heels of her ex's latest mindfuck. It wouldn't be fair to lay that one on her. It was too much for her to handle—too soon.

But what he couldn't say with words, he could sure as hell say with his body. He could ease her pain, even if only physically—at least it was something. Slipping his hands down her throat, he gently traced her delicate collarbones with his thumbs, moving his hands over her body as if he were the one sculpting her miraculous form. His mouth moved to her jaw and then to that sensitive spot just below her ear. "Tell me, Kat," he coaxed, his whispered voice growing coarse with his own need.

She closed her eyes, and a pent-up breath he didn't realize she'd been holding shuddered from her lungs. Her hands slipped into his hair, fingers curling, tightening in his overgrown locks he usually wore shorter, but now swore he'd always wear this long if it meant feeling the erotic tug of her little fingers as they twisted into his rebellious waves. Her head tipped to the side, granting him full access to the graceful arch of her neck.

"Tell me, Kat," he pleaded on a groan of flagging restraint, his hands covering her breasts, squeezing the soft, ripe flesh as those nipples he ached to savor pebbled into his palms. "Tell me what you need, baby. Let me help you."

"I want to forget."

Her whispered plea shredded him.

"Can you do that, Cole? Can you make me forget?"

Katie wasn't the only one who wanted to forget. Cole's temper had been a hair's trigger from going off the moment he'd pulled into that driveway. And then when he'd opened that box . . . the sick, twisted fuck. It'd taken self-control he hadn't even known he possessed to keep it together. But it wouldn't have done Katie any good to see him lose his shit. His gut twisted every time he thought of what that bastard had done to her, what he was still putting her through.

Cole lifted his head and hooked his knuckle under her chin, tipping her face up to meet his unwavering stare and growled, "Sweetheart, I can make you forget your own name." Dipping his head, he took her mouth in a searing, possessive kiss. He licked and nipped the salt of her tears from her lips, erasing the evidence of her grief and taking it into himself. The urge to protect her, to soothe away her fears—her hurts—rode him nearly as hard as his desire. He'd never wanted a woman more than *his* Kat, and it showed in his hurried, uncoordinated efforts to pull off her sweater. But his frenzy only seemed to excite her. She grabbed at his shirt, her nails dragging up his lats as she pulled it up. The sharp sting arrowing into his groin, the pressure of his much-needed release making his balls ache. The moment she tore it off, those hands were back in his hair, guiding his mouth back to hers. He could taste the urgency in her kiss as she sucked at his tongue, nipping his bottom lip between desperate kisses. Her hands dropped to his waistband, and with the flick of a button and tug of his zipper, his hard, aching flesh sprung into her eager hand. He exhaled on a strangled moan when her small, slender fingers wrapped around his length, gripping him tight, just how he liked it.

His hips surged forward, pumping into her hand, and he growled into her mouth, deepening their kiss as he unfastened her jeans and shoved them past her hips. She still bore the faintest hint of his masculine scent on her skin, and it made him fucking wild. Stepping on the crotch of her jeans, he shoved them past her knees, hobbling her ankles, as his hands circled her tiny waist and he boosted her onto the vanity. Katie guided him forward, seeming as desperate to be filled by him as he was to oblige. He grabbed her hips, his fingers biting into the soft flesh of her ass. The moment she brought him into contact with her hot, wet folds, and felt the opening of her tight cunny greedily swallowing his throbbing cockhead, he surged forward, burying himself balls deep in her silky glove. Her mouth broke free of his, head tipping back in glorious surrender as her lustful cry blended with the roaring sound of the jet engine.

Mine . . . The claim echoed in his head, over and over, until it became a desperate mantra he pumped his hips to—drawing back and surging forward, again, and again, and again. *Mine . . . mine . . . mine . . .*

CHAPTER

 29

"Katie Bug!"

She heard her uncle's booming voice before she saw the man standing by the conveyer belt of the luggage pickup. At the sight of him waving to get her attention, a rush of joy squeezed her heart until her eyes burned with tears. Honestly, she wasn't a crier, but these last twenty-four hours had wrung just about every emotion out of her until the surplus of tears she'd stored up over the last two years hovered ever ready at her lids, prepared and waiting to burst forth at the drop of a hat.

"Uncle Marcus!" She returned his smile and waved. Quickening her pace, she stepped away from Cole's hand resting against her lower back, and rushed forward to throw her arms around her burly uncle. He squeezed her tightly and lifted her off the ground, just like he used to when she was a little girl. The feeling of her legs dangling in the air immediately brought her back to another time. Suddenly she was eight years old again, without a care in the world, basking in the love of her adoring uncle.

Aaaand the waterworks started again, except this time she was helpless to stop them. She cried tears of joy at seeing her beloved uncle, tears of sorrow at the circumstances that brought them together again, and tears of frustration at the total loss of where things stood between her and Cole.

He'd rocked her world in that cramped little bathroom, making her an official member of the mile-high club. Hell, she might as well face it, he'd rocked her world since the moment she'd met him. And now they were on his turf. In the land of My-lifestyle-isn't-exactly-conducive-to-having-a-relationship, not that he'd even said he wanted to have a relationship with her. And FYI, she reminded herself, calling her his girlfriend out of the blue in front of a group of guys did not equal relationship consent.

If Cole wanted this to be more, was interested in this being more, then he was going to have to talk to her about it. The uncertain ground they stood on, combined with all the other uncertainties in her life right now made her feel like she was skydiving without a parachute. She needed something to hold on to, something that was certain and true, and right now Uncle Marcus seemed to be the only one volunteering to be that anchor. Perhaps sensing her need, he squeezed her tighter. She had no idea how far above the ground her feet dangled. It might as well have been a hundred feet, considering how lost she felt.

"Now, Katie Bug, everything is going to be just fine. You're here now. Uncle Marcus is going to take care of you."

It was a vow she wished had come from Cole's lips. But she was grateful to hear it, nonetheless. Perhaps she was being unreasonable to expect a man like Cole to jump in with both feet so soon. Some guys had difficulty expressing their emotions. Maybe he just needed more time. She could give him that, she decided. Right now, with her life on hold, she had nothing but time.

Wrangling in her escaped emotions, she kissed her uncle on the cheek when he set her back down. "Thanks, Unkie." He chuckled at the nickname she'd given him when she'd been too young to say his name properly. Unfortunately for him, the nickname had stuck and most people in the family still called Marcus "Unkie" to this day.

She hastily dried her cheeks before turning back to face Cole, and she found his eyes locked on her. She felt the heat of his gaze watching her closely, but he wore no expression on his drop-dead gorgeous face. What she wouldn't give to know what he was thinking right now. Since their bathroom tryst, he'd been contemplatively silent. But she noticed he'd made a point to touch her at all times—as if he couldn't stand the loss of contact. Whether holding her hand, or pressing his palm to the small of her back as he escorted her off the plane, his hand was always touching her somewhere. Surely, this wasn't just gratitude with a healthy dose of lust, was it? Honestly, the man was impossible to read.

"Cole, my boy!" Uncle Marcus bellowed, demanding the draw of Cole's attention as he stepped up and clapped Cole soundly on the back in a manly half hug. "Good to have you home, son! Damn, I missed your cranky ass."

At the ribbing, Cole smiled, the affection he felt for her uncle clearly displayed on his face—a rare moment, that. To glimpse the unguarded emotion warmed her heart. He clearly loved the man as much as she did, which made her love Cole all the more as she watched them together.

"Hey, old man." Cole clasped him back in an equally powerful back-slapping hug. "Well, see if you're still sayin' that in a week. You'll probably be tryin' to ship my ass to Siberia next. It's about just as fucking cold."

Marcus threw back his head and laughed that deep, hearty belly laugh Katie loved—the one that could silence a room. But she didn't think the jest was funny at all. The thought of Cole going anywhere, the idea of being separated from him, even hypothetically, made her want to throw up. But then she remembered the other reason she was here. The reason that had nothing to do with the fact she was in love with this cage fighter and couldn't wait to get back to his place so she could jump him in a real bed where they both had plenty of room to move. She was his PT, which meant *she* was the one in charge of his training—not dear old Unkie.

Instead of focusing on Carter, who deserved zero percent of her time and worry, she put her attention on something she could control—Cole's rehab. She was safe here. No one knew where she was. Not even her parents. She'd trust the police to do their job, and soon Carter would be behind bars.

In that moment, Katie made the decision that she would not walk out of this airport a victim. She was here to help Cole complete his rehab, and she was single-mindedly focused on achieving that goal. She would monitor his training at the gym to make sure he didn't push himself too hard or too fast. She'd dedicate herself to getting him back into cage condition, and she would *not* allow herself to think about Carter or the true reason she was here.

Grabbing her bag off the conveyer belt, she slung it over her shoulder and said, "Well then, I guess it's a good thing for you that I'm in charge of your training right now." She almost laughed as both men whipped their heads around to stare at her with varying degrees of shock. "I for one am sick to death of the cold, and can't wait to get in some bikini time, so we are *not* going to Siberia. We will, however, be in your gym bright and early to continue your therapy and training, so I suggest we get a move on, boys."

Katie didn't look back as she turned and marched toward the door—having no fucking clue where she was headed. But she couldn't resist the smile that tugged at her lips when Uncle Marcus's deep, throaty chuckle rang out behind her. "That's my girl!" he laughed. "Holy hell, Cole, I feel sorry for you. And you thought *I* was a ball breaker . . ." Another back-slapping clap rang out, and she could have sworn she heard Cole mumble under his breath, "Oh, fuck me . . ."

Had Cole honestly thought this was going to break her? That he'd entertained the idea, for even a moment, told him just how much he still needed to learn about this amazingly resilient woman conked out in the backseat of Marcus's Tahoe. Sure, she'd been rattled. Who the fuck wouldn't be after having a psycho stalker trash your house and kill your cat. He was just thankful she hadn't insisted on looking inside the box. She did not need the image of her cum-stained panties seared into her brain. It was bad enough he couldn't get the fucking picture out of his head.

He'd been watching her since they got off the plane. Fuck, who was he kidding—he hadn't been able to take his eyes off her since they left that bathroom. He swore he'd never be able to step into another airplane lavatory without thinking of her and remembering some of the best sex of his life. He'd known the moment she made the decision she would not let this break her. It seemed as if she'd made a decision, and just like that, flipped a switch, blocking out that painful part in her life.

He could relate. He'd certainly had plenty of experience blocking out painful shit. Problem was, he also knew that shit had a way of unearthing itself. It wouldn't stay buried forever. Eventually it would rise up and demand to be dealt with. He just hoped when it happened to her, she'd let him in enough to help her pick up the pieces. Katie was a strong woman—stronger than she even realized—and a master at shutting people out. The fighter in him connected to her on that level, the hidden plane where broken souls went to heal. She could pretend she was fine for only so long. But until then, he'd play along, watching for the signs he'd seen in himself, knowing it was only a matter of time before she cracked. Hopefully by then, he'd earn her love and trust enough that they could get through it together.

"I can't thank you enough for bringing her back here, Cole."

Marcus glanced at him from the driver's seat, and Cole exhaled a pent-up sigh, dragging his hand through his hair. He didn't respond.

"Looks like you're about due for a trim," Marcus commented offhandedly. "Never known you to wear your hair so long."

Cole shrugged. "That's because it's too hot to fight in, makes me sweat. Hasn't really been an issue of late."

"Well, that's about to change, son. You look amazing. I can't tell you how good it is to see you up and on your feet again."

"Not as good as it feels."

Marcus chuckled. "We'll set up some light-contact sparring this week, see how you flow. Maybe put you in the ring with Kruze."

"Sure. Whatever you think," he responded halfheartedly, his thoughts too wrapped up in Katie right now to give any serious thought to getting back in the cage.

Perhaps sensing the direction of Cole's mind, Marcus cleared his throat a bit awkwardly and said, "I, uh . . . owe you an apology."

Cole glanced into the backseat, checking on Katie, needing to see her and wishing he would have climbed into the back like he'd planned. But Marcus had asked Cole to ride up front with him so they could they could catch up and Katie could sleep. Cole had wanted to tell him Katie could rest in his arms just fine, but out of respect for his manager, he sat up front instead.

Finding her slumped against the rear driver's-side door, eyes closed, head resting against her arm, Cole tore his gaze away from the woman his arms ached to hold, and glanced over at Marcus.

"Yeah, why's that?"

"I shouldn't have said what I did the last time I talked to you—when I asked you to get Katie here. Giving you permission to seduce her was wrong of me."

"Giving me permission? You say that like it was *my* idea. You *asked* me to do it, Marcus."

Realizing how bad that sounded, Cole shot a quick glance at Katie to make sure she was still asleep. Fuck, he must be tired to let something like that come flying out of his mouth. Wishing like hell he could redact the last thirty seconds, he shot Marcus a dark scowl. "What's done is done. I don't want to talk about it anymore."

Was this Marcus's way of asking him if he was sleeping with his niece? (a) It was none of his damn business. Both he and Katie were adults, and what they did behind closed doors was between them. (b) If this was a real apology, then it was bad fucking timing.

"I'm just saying, I let my fear for her safety cloud my judgment. I shouldn't have suggested it."

"Fine. Apology accepted. Now, will you please drop it?"

"God damn, Cole, did I honestly say I missed your prickish ass?"

"No, you said you missed my 'cranky ass,' and considering the day I've had, you'll probably like me a whole hell of a lot more if I just don't speak."

Katie lay there, forcing her breath to maintain the even, rhythmic cadence of slumber. All the while her heart rioted inside her chest, breaking a little more each time it slammed against her ribs. She wouldn't have believed it if she hadn't heard it herself. And to think she owed the truth to a pothole. Betrayal lashed at her, the cords of truth tearing into her flesh, serrating the fragile bond of trust that had formed between her and Cole.

How could he do this?—pretending to care about her when all along it'd been nothing but a lie to get her here to Vegas and under her uncle's wing. Now his offer that night in the fish house made much more sense. He'd suggested she come back with him, planting the seed, and growing the hope that there was something special between them. Had she really been that stupid as to think she could snag and hold the interest of a man like Cole Easton—a man who claimed he'd never been in love—seriously? Did she think she possessed some magical vag that after one night of hot sex, and voilà, Cole Easton would suddenly be in love with her? *Give me a fucking break!*

Now that she knew the truth, everything else clicked into place. Cole's end game?—get her to Vegas by any means necessary. Oh, and while he was at it, help himself to some free PT and pussy—big fucking hardship there. But the most pathetic thing was, it probably had been. His reaction to her scars had proved that much, though he'd provided a smooth enough cover-up. Give that guy an Oscar. Really . . . he deserved it—he was a better fucking actor than Matthew McConaughey. Guys like Cole were probably used to giving out a pity fuck or two. And he did owe Uncle Marcus. He'd said as much himself—the guy had saved his life.

Afraid that if Cole looked back he'd see the silent tears streaming down her face, Katie shifted in her seat, facing away from Cole and Uncle Marcus. With any luck, they'd think she'd rolled over in her sleep to get more comfortable. How much longer was this fucking car ride going to last?

Her answer came a few minutes later when the Tahoe came to a stop.

"Bet this place is a sight for sore eyes, huh, kid? You got your key?"

A door opened, sending a balmy breeze brushing past her. "Don't need one. I've got the house passcoded."

She felt Cole's eyes on her and forced herself not to tense. Never once had it occurred that she might not be staying here with him. And the knowledge he was leaving her was just a little more salt in her hemorrhaging wound. The door remained open for an unusually long time. Forcing herself to lay still under his stare, pretending to be asleep, was torturous. Marcus said something to him she didn't catch.

"I'll be by in the morning to pick her up."

He must be tired. The low, rough timbre of his voice made him sound like he was in pain. He probably was. With everything that happened, she hadn't gotten a chance to stretch him today. The thought that he might be hurting bothered her, which only added further insult to injury. She was busy berating herself for being such a gullible fool when the door finally closed and the SUV began backing away.

CHAPTER

30

Cole was lucky if he'd gotten two hours of sleep. He should have listened to his gut and never let Marcus take Katie home with him. He wanted her with him, in his bed, wrapped safely in his arms. Considering he'd never let a woman he was sleeping with past his front door, that was saying a whole hell of a lot. The fact that he couldn't unwind without her and give his body some much-needed rest told him he had it really fucking bad for this woman, and he'd be lying if he said that didn't scare the ever-loving hell out of him.

Perhaps being separated from her when they'd spent the last several weeks sharing a house together, knowing she was only a hallway away, was the cause of this disquieting ache in his chest. But he couldn't shake the feeling that something was wrong. Then again, his nerves were on high alert and frayed like old rope after the last couple days, so he was probably just being edgy.

Anxious to see Katie, Cole rolled out of bed and glanced at the alarm clock on the nightstand as he trudged into the bathroom—seven a.m. Yep, two fucking hours, and this was the first day in over six months he was setting foot back in the gym. That thought alone had his nerves doing cartwheels. Was he ready for this? He sure as hell didn't feel ready. The thought of seeing his friends again, and the questioning looks on their faces . . . He knew what they'd all be thinking, even if they didn't have the balls to say it—the same damn thing he was thinking. *Will Cole Easton fight again? Will he ever be 100 percent, or is he nothing but a washed-up has-been who can't admit that his fucking career is over?*

Cole stood beneath the shower's hot spray, letting the water beat into his sore, tired muscles as he battled his own inner demons. His back ached, his neck was stiff. Overnight, he felt like he'd aged ten fucking years. After a quick scrub, he quit the shower and stepped onto the bath mat. The silence in his house was deafening; the solitude he'd once craved above all else now left him feeling alone and vacant. It'd been only a handful of hours, and already he missed Katie. He wanted her with him, *needed* her beside him, when he stepped into that gym today. Katie filled a void inside his heart he hadn't even realized was there.

Dammit, he never should have let Marcus leave with her last night. What would she think when she woke this morning and found herself at her uncle's house instead of his? Fuck. Cole wrapped a towel around his waist and headed back to the bedroom. Wanting to hear her voice, he grabbed his cell and called her. He felt like a pussy for being so needy. This wasn't like him. In fact, Cole had made a point of needing as few people in his life as possible. Yet somehow, in the matter of a few short weeks, this woman had climbed to the top of the list.

Cole exhaled a frustrated sigh and dragged his hand through his wet hair as he stood there, waiting for her to pick up. She was probably still asleep. When the call rolled over to voice mail, he disconnected and shot her a quick text instead.

Hey.

It surprised him when his phone buzzed a return text before he could toss it on the bed and get dressed.

What?

"What?" Really? The little niggling in his gut that told him something was wrong stepped up and hit him tenfold. This wasn't like her. He shot off another text.

You awake?

Yes. What do you want?

What did he want? He wanted to fucking see her, that's what he wanted. Why in the hell was she acting like this? *Because she's pissed that you left without her last night, asshole.* He typed a quick response, testing the waters of her anger a little more.

I want to see you. Have breakfast with me.

You know I don't eat breakfast.

Still want to see you.

Will see you at the gym.

Okay, wow, she was really pissed. All Cole could think of was crash and burn, and he did *not* want to be the match that lit her fuse. The last thing she needed was him pushing her and making things worse. He knew from experience how someone reacted, or overreacted, was a direct result of emotional stressors, and Katie had more than her share going on right now.

Common sense told him to back off, let her cool down, and they'd discuss what was bothering her later. He'd explain that Marcus had insisted on bringing her home with him last night, and that the old guy didn't know how close they'd become. Cole hadn't told him because he wasn't sure it'd been his place to do so. Uncle trumped coach, and Cole wasn't sure how much Katie wanted Marcus to know about their relationship.

But head knowledge was not heart knowledge, and Cole was a fighter. He didn't play games, dance around issues, or walk on eggshells with anyone—and he sure as hell wasn't about to start now. Although he knew it was probably relationship suicide, a part of him wanted to go over there right now and confront this head-on. Before he could respond and send her a text that he was coming over, his phone vibrated again.

I'll be at the gym in one hour.

Let me come get you.

Getting a ride with Uncle Marcus.

Shit. She was super-fucking-pissed. Okay, it was only one hour. He could wait that long to see her. Maybe by then she'd cool off a little.

"What the fuck, Kat?"

She looked down at him with innocent doe eyes he didn't believe for a minute and purred with saccharin sweetness, "What's the matter, Cole? Too rough? I thought that's how you liked it."

Unfortunately, his cock was deaf to sarcasm, because it was standing tall, screaming, *Bring it on!* Only this soldier wouldn't want any of what Katie was throwing down right now. When he'd gotten to the gym, she was already there waiting for him. He'd tried to talk to her then, but she was busy stretching, and coolly informed him they didn't have time for anything other than training and therapy. Apparently, Marcus had dropped her off before heading to a meeting with the CFA commissioner, and told her he'd be back as soon as he could to get Cole sparring.

"Holy fuck!" Kruze yelled from the other room. "Easton just got matted by a chick!"

Aaaand that was why he'd insisted they work on Katie's self-defense sparring *before* his PT. Unfortunately, the guys had shown up earlier than usual to begin training for the day. He'd forgotten Kruze had a big fight coming up, so of course he'd be going at it from dawn till dusk. And although Kruze and his team were excited as hell to see him, Cole wasn't arrogant enough to think for one minute he was the cause for all the stir in the gym this morning.

If Katie noticed she had a half-dozen CFA fighters dragging their tongues across the mat, she gave no indication of it. From the moment she stepped onto the mat, she'd been solely focused on her self-defense training—and kicking his ass. It'd been a cheap-ass shot, and she knew it. There was zero play in this woman's eyes as she stepped down harder on the base of his cock, digging her toes painfully into his sac.

This was not the Katie he knew. This woman was completely shut down and seriously pissed off at him. All right, he'd fucked up last night, and he was the first to admit it, but Katie better get her damn foot off his dick and balls—right fucking now—or they were going to have some serious words.

Cole turned his head to look behind him and growled, "Shut that fucking door, Kruze, or you're next!"

He glared up at the cocky bastard leaning against the doorway, arms crossed over his unclothed chest, enjoying the show with a shit-eating grin on his face.

"Hey, if that means I get to go a round with her, then I'm in."

"It means you're going to go five with me," Cole snarled.

Katie gave him a disgusted snort and lifted her foot, swinging it over his head in a graceful arch, before walking toward the table in the corner and grabbing her water bottle. Tearing his gaze from her, he glanced back at Kruze to find his eerie, dark amber eyes fixed unabashedly on her ass. A low, warning growl rumbled in his chest as he rolled to his feet and stomped across the mat. Kruze dropped his cocky grin mighty damn fast. Laughing, he held up his hands, warding Cole off as he stepped back from the doorway.

"Hey man, I'm just kidding. No need to get so testy."

Aiden Kruze was one of his best friends, and he knew the bastard was just yanking his chain. He'd been fighting one weight class below Cole since he'd been accepted into the CFA a year ago. Kruze had a title fight on the horizon, but he had to make it through Mallenger first. It was going to be a tough fight, but not impossible. Before Cole had been injured, he'd been working with the guy pretty hard-core, getting him ready for the fight that was now . . . Shit, was already next week?

Meeting Kruze in the doorway, he growled under his breath, "FYI, that woman you're eye-fucking is Marcus Miller's niece. She's my PT and my girlfriend. That give you enough reasons to stay hands-off? Or do you need five more?"

Cole curled his fingers into a fist, and his friend took another cautious step back and laughed. "Seriously, bro? That's fucking awesome! About time you met a chick that could give you a run for your money."

Kruze had no fucking idea.

"I was just givin' ya shit, bro. Hey, a bunch of us guys are going out after the Mallenger fight next week. You in?"

Cole shot a glance over his shoulder and found Katie still turned away. He hesitated a moment before answering, then said, "You kidding me? Of course I'm going to be there. Who's cornering you?"

"Marcus, of course."

Over the years, Marcus coached a lot of fighters. Now that he was getting closer to retirement, he still hung on to a handful of his favorites, and Kruze happened to be one of them.

"I was kinda hoping, I mean, if you're not too busy, that is, that you'd corner me, too?"

"Absolutely. It'd be a fucking honor."

"Thanks, man. Listen, if you free up at all this weekend, let me know. I'd like you to watch me knock around, let me know if you can spot any holes."

"Sounds good, just let me know when you're coming in." Cole turned to head back into the wrestling room.

"Great. Oh, and Cole?"

He stopped and turned back toward his friend.

"Glad to have you back, man."

"Thanks." Cole shut the door behind him and turned to find Katie watching him. Aside from a small section of the room cornered off for a few tables and a vending machine stocked with Powerade and protein bars, the room was empty, except for the mats covering the floor. Katie looked so freaking hot standing there in her black ass-hugging, flare-legged yoga pants with the hot pink waistband. Her bare feet and French-tipped painted toes peeked out from beneath the floor-brushing hem. Her matching pink spandex tank top outlined her narrow waist. The scoop neck showed off more mouth-watering cleavage than he'd have liked, considering where they were.

"Why did you do that?" Katie demanded, walking into the center of the mat, looking more than ready to put the hurt on him again.

"Do what?" He sauntered into the center of the mat, ready to take her on. If she was going to keep throwing cheap shots, though, he was going to have to put a cup on.

"Tell that fighter I was your girlfriend."

Cole tensed, sensing a trap. This wasn't the first time he'd introduced her as such, but it was the first time she looked pissed off about it. Exhaling a sigh, he dragged his hand through his sweat-dampened hair. "I told Kruze you were my girlfriend because you're going to be spending a lot of time here and I don't want to have to worry about the guys hassling you. This is a fighter's gym, Katie. It's not fucking Snap. There's a lot of testosterone that gets flowing in here and I don't want you on the receiving end of it. Kruze is a great guy, one of my best friends, actually, but he's got his own issues—one of which happens to be his inability to keep his dick in his pants."

"Oh, so he's like you?"

Where the fuck did that come from?

"Oh, that's right," she said, slapping her hand to her forehead. "I forgot, you were doing my uncle a favor, so that doesn't really count."

Oh fuck . . . this is not happening.

"Well, mission accomplished, asshole! You got me here—signed, sealed, and delivered." Katie spun away and marched over to the table, snagging her purse and jerking the strap over her shoulder. "You'll be relieved to know you can quit with the pity fucks, Cole. You've whored yourself out for my uncle enough."

As Katie stormed past him, Cole grabbed her arm, jerking her to a stop. "God, Kat, it's not like that. I swear—"

"Did my uncle ask you to bring me to Vegas?"

"Yes, but—"

"Did he or did he not suggest you seduce me to get me here?"

Oh shit . . . this was bad. Every second that ticked by, he could feel her slipping further and further from his grasp. He knew after what she'd been through, she didn't trust easily, and she'd taken a huge risk on him. He also knew how bad this looked. Of course she would think he'd played her. That was exactly how it fucking looked!

"Kat, listen to me. That's not how this is. I can explain—"

"Cole, let go of me."

He should have listened to the warning in her deadpan voice, but all he could hear was the thundering of his heartbeat echoing in his ears, and the little voice inside his head screaming, *You're going to lose her, asshole! Do something!* She jerked her arm to get free, and his grip instinctively tightened. He didn't mean to hurt her, but the only thought racing through his head was, *If you let her go now, you've lost her for good.* But Katie didn't give him a chance to respond. The moment his fingers bit into her bicep, she reached across her arm with her free hand, grabbed Cole's wrist, and twisted it clockwise, just like he'd taught her.

Cole barked a foul curse and dropped to his knees, yielding to the pressure that would snap the bones in his wrist if Katie applied much more pressure. He could get out of the hold, but not without hurting her. A part of him was glad to see she'd been such an adept learner. Another part of him wondered if he hadn't created a little monster. Perhaps he'd taught her a little too well, especially if she was going to be turning his knowledge around on him.

Glaring at Katie, the air fled his lungs when he saw the tears rimming her eyes and the heartbreak on her beautiful face—heartbreak he had put there. Not Carter—him. Unable to bear seeing her pain, he closed his eyes, dropped his head, and whispered, "God, Katie, I never meant to hurt you. This isn't how it looks."

"And yet it's exactly that. Good-bye, Cole." Katie turned and walked away—shoulders back, spine straight, her steps stiff and hurried.

"Goddammit, Katie! Don't you dare walk out that door!"

Her hand froze on the doorknob, but she didn't turn back around. "Why not, Cole? What could you possibly say at this point that could make me want to stay?"

"I love you." The words rolled from his lips before he could bite them back. After everything she'd been through, words were not going to be what it would take to make this better. If anything, they were only going to make it worse. All Katie had heard from Carter was that he loved her. In her mind, those three words were probably the most damning thing he could have said. Actions were every-thing to a woman like her, and they were the only thing that was going to make this right. And her next words proved it, though it didn't make hearing them hurt any less.

Slowly, she turned, tears rolling down her cheeks. "I really wish that I could believe that. But coming from the guy who professes never to have been in love, and who has lied to me from pretty much the moment I met him, I don't think you even know what love is."

One good thing about Vegas, there were taxis everywhere. As Katie burst out the door, walking at a determined clip, she hailed the cab getting ready to pull away from the curb. When the brake lights flashed, she quickened her pace, jogging to catch up with the car. She definitely wasn't running away from Cole.

Liar . . .

Just as she reached the cab door, the gym doors crashed open behind her.

"Dammit, Kat, don't do this!"

Her heart twisted in her chest at the note of desperation in Cole's voice, but it was the note of warning seeding his undertone that made the fine hairs on the back of her neck stand at attention.

"When your uncle asked me to bring you here, I'd just met you. Is it so impossible for you to conceive that I could have fallen in love with you since then?"

Perhaps it was. And maybe that was why it had been so easy to latch on to the deception spawned by her uncle.

"If you run from me, Kat, if you run from *this*, you're going to regret it. You want to know what I think?"

No, she really didn't.

"I think you're scared. You're scared of what this is between us, and instead of working through it, you're choosing to run the first chance you get. Well, I have news for you, Kat. I'm not going to chase you. And eventually you're going to have to stop running, and when you do, you're going to find yourself very alone."

God, that hurt. Was that what she was doing? Was she looking for an excuse to push him away? No. She wouldn't let him turn this around on her. He lied to her, conspired with Uncle Marcus to manipulate her. Steeling her nerve, Katie climbed into the backseat and slammed the door. "Drive," she commanded the driver, her voice cracking with unshed tears.

The cabbie glanced at her from the rearview mirror, a worried frown wrinkling his black, bushy brows. "Where to, lady?"

"I don't know, anywhere but here. Just drive."

The man behind the wheel looked at her like she was crazy, and maybe she was, just a little bit. Who else would walk away from a man like Cole Easton? Answer: A woman who had trust issues and hated being lied to.

"If you don't mind me sayin' so, you look like you could use a drink."

Katie frowned, grabbing her phone to check the time. "It's nine a.m."

"That don't matter. This is Vegas, sweetheart."

"Well, thank you . . ." She waited for the man to supply his name.

"Habib," the fifty-something Middle Eastern man offered with a big rearview-mirror grin.

"Thank you, Habib. But I think I'll pass," she replied distractedly, seeing she had a missed call from an unknown number. Dialing her voice mail, she entered her passcode and held the phone to her ear.

"Hi, this message is for Katie Miller. It's Officer Wyatt, I'm contacting you to let you know that Carter Owens was arrested and booked

today. I can't give you the specific details of the arrest over the phone,
but I do need to go over some paperwork with you, and get your signa-
ture on a few statements before this case goes in front of the judge. No
date has been set yet, so I'm not sure if the judge will need to speak with
you. Please contact me or stop in at your earliest convenience."

"Habib, please take me to the airport."

She made a quick call to her uncle and told a very unhappy
Marcus she was heading back to Wisconsin. She decided not to tell
him that she knew about his deception or the breakup with Cole.
Instead, she kept it short and sweet, sticking to facts he couldn't
argue with. Carter was arrested and behind bars, so it was safe for
her to return. Her father needed her. The arresting officer needed
her to sign paperwork and possibly testify when this went to court.
She finally had to face this, and in Cole's ill-quoted words, she
couldn't keep running forever. When Uncle Marcus asked her
about the fighter, pointing out that Cole needed her, too, Katie's
composure nearly cracked.

Despite her anger and disappointment that Marcus would be
so manipulative, she still loved her uncle, and that was the only
thing saving him from the royal ass chewing he deserved. She told
him Cole's therapy had gone fabulously well, and in the condition
he was in right now, another good PT could take over and turn him
out with the same result. She promised to contact the best physical
therapist in Vegas, one who had experience working with fighters.
She would forward Cole's records when she contacted her uncle
with the information.

When he tried to ask her more questions about Cole on a more
personal level, she quickly shut him down, telling him she had to go
and that her flight was leaving soon. She didn't have enough time to
stop by the house and grab her bag, so would he please ship it to her.

Not that she had a lot in it, anyway. Most everything she had was ruined, but then again she was a pro at having nothing but the clothes on her back and starting over, right? At least this time she was going home, and she knew she would be safe. Besides, who cared about a half-filled duffel bag when she was leaving her heart behind?

CHAPTER

31

"All right, it's been over a week, dude. You've gotta snap the fuck out of it."

Cole shot a murderous glare at Kruze as he slid into the empty seat beside him, most recently vacated by the third woman attempting to get him into the private VIP room in the back for a quick fuck in the last hour. Damn, this shit was old—the parties, the cage bangers, the countless opportunities for casual, meaningless sex. Had this really been his life once? Had he actually found it fulfilling? Cole tipped back his brandy and Coke, draining the glass. He was fully aware he was breaking his own rule about drinking hard liquor in public, but he wasn't sure he could take another minute of this shit sober. If it weren't Kruze's postwin party, he never would have come, but the fighter had worked his ass off for this, fought his heart out for this win, and he deserved to have his friends here supporting him.

Working with Kruze this last week and fixing the holes in his game had been the only thing keeping Cole sane. He thought of Katie constantly, missed her like crazy, and worried about her incessantly . . . His only peace of mind was in knowing that bastard, Carter, was behind bars, so at least she was safe. Marcus had been beside himself with guilt and regret when Cole had told him what happened at the gym. Cole had shown up at the old guy's place looking for her and just lost his shit when he'd discovered she'd hopped on a plane and flown back to Wisconsin.

Fuck, he still couldn't believe she'd just left like that, though he probably shouldn't be surprised. A part of him understood why she'd done it. She'd warned him more than once she was damaged, and he knew she had trust issues—big trust issues. He'd just never thought she'd run from him. And *that* was what pissed him off. Her anger, he could handle. They could work through that. But how in the hell could he have a relationship with a woman who took off every time she got upset? He never claimed to be Dr. Phil, but even a fucking moron could see this for what it was. She had feelings for him, and it scared her. She didn't know how to deal with them. So when she'd thought he'd lied to her, instead of talking to him about it like any other rational adult in a healthy relationship, she'd chosen to believe the worst about him and bailed.

Of course she was hurt. Who wouldn't be if that had actually been the truth, but it was the furthest thing from it. He loved her, and in telling her so, just as he feared, he only succeeded in driving her away. She wouldn't trust love, and she obviously didn't trust him, which really fucking hurt. And that pain was the anchor he clung to, keeping him rooted right here instead of chasing her halfway across the United States to make an even bigger ass of himself.

No way would he pull a Carter on her. Not only would chasing after Katie freak her out, but believe or not, he actually did have some semblance of pride left—what she hadn't shredded before getting on that fucking plane and flying home without looking back. It wasn't like she didn't know where he was. She had his number, and yet she hadn't even done him the fucking courtesy of telling him she was home and safe. Nor did she tell him she was transferring his care to another PT. Yeah, that little nugget he'd learned from Marcus when his medical records had arrived at his doorstep courtesy of Fed-fucking-Ex.

A camera flashed to his left and Cole muttered a curse under his breath, shooting a glare at the photographer who snapped another pic as if to say, *Fuck you. Just wait until you see the headlines for this one.* The paparazzi had been on him like damn lice since he'd been back, which did absolutely zero to improve his surly mood. The brave ones who had a death wish asked him about his relationship with Katie, because, yeah, some asshole sold that pic of him and her in the airport together. But mostly, the press wanted to know about him and De'Grasse. Did Cole think he would ever fight again? Was he nervous to get back in the cage with the man that nearly ruined his career? Yes, he'd fight again. No, he wasn't scared. Finally, he'd caved and told Marcus to set up a CFA-sponsored interview to get all this shit out in the open. Perhaps then, the vultures would finally leave him the hell alone.

The whole damn thing was just so fucking daunting, he found himself longing for the simplicity and slower pace of small-town living. He'd never considered it before, always thought Vegas was where he'd live. MMA was his life—until he'd met a certain fair-haired slip of a woman who'd rocked his world and turned his life inside out. He was a fighter, dammit. It was what he'd been made for.

But after meeting Katie, he'd begun to wonder if there wasn't more. Was he missing out on a whole other life? Who the fuck knew . . . Before he'd gotten a chance to wrap his head around the idea, she'd bolted on him, leaving a huge, gaping hole in his heart. In the last week he'd been coaching Kruze, and after cornering him tonight, Cole was finding he enjoyed developing the talent of other fighters as much as he enjoyed being in the cage. And that he could do anywhere. The only problem was, where he wanted to be, the person he wanted to be with, didn't feel the same way.

"I wasn't going to say anything, bro, but you're obviously too fucking stubborn for your own good—and a total killjoy, in case you didn't know. This is supposed to be a party! I still can't believe it. I KO'd Mallenger forty-seven seconds into the second round with that hook kick you taught me. Man, this is as much your win as it is mine. I couldn't have done it without you." Kruze slapped him on the back and yanked him in for a hug. "Next stop is the middle-weight title, baby!"

"And you'll take it, too." Cole waved the bartender over and bought his friend a drink. "You looked great out there tonight, and I'm proud of you. You fought hard and prepared well for this. You deserve all the credit. "

"Thanks, man."

They toasted and tipped back their glasses. Cole drained his in one chugging gulp. When he set his glass on the table, he noticed Kruze watching him. He recognized that look, had seen it more than his fair share of times when they'd been out partying in the past. It was that same amber-eyed warning Kruze gave him whenever he was concerned Cole was about to do something stupid or wild—the *I disapprove of what you're doing, but I'm trying like hell to keep my mouth shut* look—which only proved you can take the guy out of the law office but you can't take the lawyer out of the guy. Kruze was a walking, talking, breathing contradiction. If anyone was a fucking mess, it was this guy. Though admittedly, most of his problems weren't of his own doing. But when your father was a US senator, and you'd been groomed your whole life to be a lawyer and take over the family business, the fam doesn't smile too kindly when you walk away from it all and join the CFA.

"What?" Cole challenged, returning his scowl, the booze numbing him just enough to lower his brain-mouth filter, but not enough to help numb the constant pain in his chest.

"You're fucked up."

"I'm not fucked up. You're fucked up. Who the hell walks away from Daddy Warbucks to climb in a cage and get his ass kicked?"

Kruze's scowl darkened. It was a low blow, and Cole felt like a royal bastard for dealing it.

"First of all, *my* ass isn't the one getting kicked. And now I *know* you're drunk, because sober Easton doesn't shoot below the belt. But now that you've pissed me off, I'm going to say what I've been wanting to tell you for the last week, and I'm not even going to feel bad about it. You're a moronic asshole if you let that woman walk out of your life without fighting for her. I met her all of two seconds, and I could tell she was worth every bit of the fucking hassle it's going to be to get her back. You were miserable before you met her, and now *I* even want to start on Prozac just from being around you. If you love her, fight for her. If not, then go get with one of these cage bangers that have been throwing themselves at you all night, and fuck that woman out of your system, because, bro, you can't keep going on like this."

Cole exhaled a frustrated sigh and dragged his hand through his hair. "You don't understand. It's not that easy. *She's* not that easy."

Kruze chuckled and downed his drink, then held the iced glass against his bruised cheek. "No woman worth her salt is, and if they were, you wouldn't want them anyway."

"Point made, counselor," Cole grumbled. Arguing with a lawyer was fucking pointless.

"Thank you. Now you know why I've never lost a case. So why don't you get out of here, and go get your woman?"

With a slap on the back, Kruze got up and headed straight for a gorgeous redhead sitting at the bar. The seat wasn't open ten seconds before a leggy blonde with dark brown eyes and red painted lips sat down beside Cole. The heavy scent of smoke and perfume assaulted his nostrils. Doing his damn best to ignore her, he waved the bartender over for one last drink while he mulled over Kruze's advice.

As the man behind the counter slid another drink in front of him, the heel of a stiletto slowly dragged up his calf. Unable to avoid it, Cole slowly turned his head to look at the woman. She smiled at him. The stir stick she'd been chewing on was trapped between her teeth. Her ravenous gaze boldly dragged over him, making him feel like a big, juicy steak. The woman's too-large, too-round boobs nearly spilled from the top of her peacock-blue, curve-hugging dress.

"Hi-ya," she purred when Cole didn't speak.

He made no effort to disguise his disinterest, not that the buxom blonde seemed to notice. She was a typical cage banger, looking for a good, hard fuck—nothing more. The woman couldn't be more the opposite of Katie if she'd tried. Thinking of Katie, comparing her to every woman who'd approached him tonight, only drove home his need to see her, to talk to her, and try to fix this misunderstanding between them.

"You're Cole Easton, right?"

She'd known damn well who he was before she ever slid her curvy ass into the empty seat beside him. In no mood to play her coy games, he removed his leg from the heel of her shoe and pushed his chair back before standing. "Yes, I am. And I'll tell you the same thing I told the last nine women who approached me tonight, I'm not interested. I'm seeing someone."

Maybe. Hopefully. If she'll have me. But he kept that part to himself. Digging into his pocket, he tossed a hundred-dollar bill onto the bar and told the man behind the counter, "This'll cover my tab and whatever she's having." Turning away from the shocked woman who couldn't seem to conceive that he was turning her down, Cole took his friend's advice and cut out of there. He hailed a cab because, truth, he was in no fucking condition to be driving at this point. Once he was headed toward the airport, he pulled out his cell and dialed Katie's number before to could sober up and convince himself this was a bad idea.

Her phone immediately rolled over to voice mail, so it was either off or dead. At least she wasn't answering because she was screening his calls. He checked the clock on the driver's dash. It was getting late, almost too late to call her parents' house, but what the hell, he was committed now. The phone rang—no answer. Marcus had told him Katie was staying with her parents. The cleaning crew he'd hired to put her place back to rights had just sent him the bill, so he knew the house was put back together. Maybe she'd gone back there?

He was about to call there when his cell rang. Swiping his thumb across the screen, he answered the unavailable number. "Hello?"

"Mr. Easton?"

"Yeah."

"This is Officer Wyatt. I've been trying to get ahold of Katrina Miller. You wouldn't happen to know how I could reach her, would you?"

A knot of dread fisted in Cole's gut. "No. I haven't been able to reach her myself. What's going on? Why are you trying to get ahold of her?"

"I wanted to notify her that Carter Owens's bail was set today. He posted it and was released about an hour ago."

Cole swore under his breath.

"Yeah, my thought exactly. I'm on patrol tonight, so I'm going to swing by her parents' house and her place and check things out. She has an active restraining order against him, and he knows if he comes within five hundred feet of her, he'll be back behind bars with no bail."

"You really think that's going to stop him from going after her?"

The officer hesitated before answering. "Truth? Not a chance. That's why I've been trying to get ahold of her."

Hearing the officer confirming Cole's fears sent his pulse racing. The adrenaline flooding his veins burned through his buzz, leaving him stone-cold sober. Feeling violent and helpless, he shot an impatient glance out the window and told the cab driver to step on it. Here he was, stuck three and a half hours away from the woman he loved—the woman who could right now be in serious danger, and there wasn't a damn thing he could do about it.

"I'm in Vegas now, and I'm heading to the airport. Please let me know if you get ahold of her, and I'll keep trying from my end."

CHAPTER

32

Without a doubt, this had been the most miserable week of Katie's life—and she'd had a lot of shitty ones to compare it to, so that was really saying something. She sat beside her father's hospital bed, holding his limp hand while thinking about how much she missed Cole. She wished he were here with her right now, lending her that ever-present strength and a broad shoulder to cry on.

When he told her he wouldn't chase after her, a part of her hadn't believed him. But then the days passed, and he'd been true to his word. He hadn't even tried to call—not once. In the last week, when she wasn't filling out statements or down at the court-house meeting with a judge, she'd done little else but reflect on that day she'd walked out on him. The things he'd said haunted her, and the way she'd reacted shamed her.

With the heat of the moment faded, and her hurt feeling some-what soothed by the balm of time, she could see that he'd been right. Sure, she was hurt to discover Uncle Marcus and Cole had conspired to deceive her, but that being said, the bottom line remained unchanged. She was scared—scared of her feelings for Cole and how vulnerable they made her feel.

These past weeks she'd spent with him had been a whirlwind. He'd made her feel things both physically and emotionally that she didn't think she'd ever feel again. Then add the stress of Carter to the mix and she'd finally cracked and was utterly shattered emotionally. And in the process, she'd lost the best thing in her life: a chance for happiness with Cole.

The monitor beside her dad's bed began to sound, the display flashing 88 percent. "Hey, Dad," she whispered softly, "take a deep breath." Reaching up, she readjusted his nasal cannula to make sure the oxygen was getting up his nose properly. His eyes fluttered open and she smiled, holding her breath to fight against the tears stinging the back of her eyes. He was so weak, so tired . . . She could hardly wrap her mind around it—another stroke. They'd been so careful with his Coumadin, so diligent in monitoring his INR. How could this happen again?

She'd been upstairs in the shower when he'd collapsed yesterday morning. After hastily dressing and racing to her father's side, the ambulance had arrived and rushed her father to the hospital. She and her mother had followed behind them, and in the chaos, she'd forgotten her phone on the bedroom dresser. Katie hadn't left her father's side since then, and neither had her mother. The nurses had brought a small cot into the room for her mother to sleep on. She was resting now, emotionally and physically exhausted.

Her poor mother wasn't the only one. Katie had been up for the last thirty-six hours, and as much as she didn't want to leave her father's side, she was going to have to head home and get some rest. "Hey, Daddy, I'm going to go home for a little bit, all right? Mom is here. She's resting on the cot. But I'll be back really soon, okay?"

He nodded. A good sign that he understood her. He hadn't been able to speak since the stroke. Doctors were optimistic the impairment was temporary, but Katie feared the worst. Setting his hand on the call light, she brushed his finger over the button.

"You feel that? Press this button if you need anything."

He nodded.

"I love you, Daddy." Katie stood and bent over him, kissing his forehead. "Everything's going to be all right," she said with more certainty than she felt.

He nodded.

Straightening, she turned away before he could see the tears of truth clouding her eyes. Wiping her cheeks, she dried the evidence and forced a reassuring smile as she glanced back over her shoulder. "See you in a little bit."

Katie was numb. Exhaustion seeped into her bones, leaving her physically and emotionally drained. She drove home on autopilot, going through the motions without really seeing, unable to think about anything beyond the soft down of her pillow and the cushion of her pillow-top mattress that would soon be cradling her weary body.

She could have gone to the other house. It was closer, and the cleaning crew Cole had hired contacted her the other day and informed her it was finished. But the thought of being there without him made her heart ache more than it already did. It would only stir memories she couldn't deal with right now.

Pulling into the driveway, Katie parked her RAV in the turn-around. She had just gottent her SUV back and hadn't switched the spare garage door opener back over yet. She'd have to remember to do that. It was a pain in the ass getting out of a warm car and trudging across the snowy driveway and up the porch steps. Fumbling with the keys through her bulky mittens, she unlocked the door and kicked it shut with the heel of her boot.

She shed her winter layers, leaving them in a pile on the entry-way floor, along with her purse and car keys. Her thoughts didn't go beyond getting into the shower and chasing away the chill before collapsing into bed. As she passed the end table next to the stairs, the red flashing light of the answering machine caught her attention. She paused a moment, briefly considering listening to the messages, then continued on, having no energy or ambition to deal with it right now.

Leaning heavily on the railing, Katie methodically placed one foot in front of the other, trudging up the stairs. Once she entered the bathroom, she took one look at the tub and decided a hot soak sounded more relaxing than a shower. She turned the faucet on, tossed in a scoop of lavender and rosemary bath salts, and made another pile of clothing on the floor next to the tub before stepping in.

The hot water enveloped her like a lover's caress—Cole's caress . . . The thought of his hands on her skin made Katie's pulse quicken, her lips parting to draw in shallow breaths, and the pang in her twisted sharply. Lord help her, she missed him. She missed the way he made her feel when they were together—safe and protected. She missed the husky, seductive rasp of his voice whispering against her ear, and the skilled touch of his battle-scarred hands giving her pleasure she'd never imagined. She missed everything about him— his smile, his sense of humor, his protectiveness. For the first time in her life she'd truly felt alive, and now without him, she felt like she was dying on the vine.

Leaning against the back of the tub, she took a deep breath, inhaling the steamy scent of her water and exhaling a soft, tortured sigh. What she wouldn't give to have him with her here right now, kneeling beside the tub with a soapy sponge in hand. He'd bathe her bone-weary body and tell her everything was going to be all right. It didn't matter if it wasn't true. She knew the chances of her dad recovering from this were not good, but she needed to hear Cole's voice, needed that quiet confidence that seemed to naturally exude from him. She wanted to be wrapped in the shelter of his arms, where nothing and no one could get to her, where time seemed to stop—even if for only a little while.

Unable to fight the battle with her eyelids any longer, Katie let them fall shut and focused on the feeling of the hot water lapping at her breasts. The cool air kissed her nipples, teasing them to puckered points that ached for something more . . . Hell, who was she kidding?—her whole being ached for something more. It longed for the fighter who'd commanded her body and stolen her heart.

Katie was hovering in the realm between consciousness and sleep, when the distinct creak of the floorboard in the downstairs hall shattered the silence in the house. She bolted upright, water splashing over the sides of the tub, soaking her clothes. Her heart stuttered, plummeting into her stomach, where it suddenly began beating erratically. Adrenaline flooded her veins as a burst of panic seized her. She strained to hear past the thundering of her heart— silence. Maybe she'd imagined it—dreamed it?

She was safe, she reminded herself. Carter was in jail, and the house was wired with a state-of-the-art security system—a security system that never went off when she'd walked in tonight, she suddenly realized. They'd been so upset and panicked when they left the house yesterday, her mother must have forgotten to reset the alarm.

You're all right, she told herself, trying to calm her rioting heart. If Carter had gotten out of jail, someone from the police department would have called her. Then again, she'd left her phone on the bedroom dresser, so how would she have known if anyone had tried to reach her? Remembering the flashing message light on the answering machine she'd bypassed on the way to the bathroom, an eerie jolt of *oh, fuck* sent her feet scrambling beneath her. Rising on shaky legs, Katie stood, grabbed a towel off the rack, and quickly dried herself.

Grabbing the night shirt she'd left on the floor from the morning before, she quickly pulled it on and left a soggy trail from the bathroom into the hallway. She'd just stepped toward her bedroom to check her cell when the house phone rang, shattering the silence. Katie let out a startled yelp, her hand flying up to her cover her mouth. It took until the second ring for her heart to start beating again and her feet to begin moving. She ran downstairs to catch the phone before the answering machine picked it up. It was late—too late for whoever was calling to be doing so with good news. What if something had happened to her dad? She'd never forgive herself for leaving him.

Katie reached the bottom of the stairs and rounded the corner to find the phone missing from the docking station. Shit! Where was it? Her mom had last used it to call 911 . . . She followed the ring into the living room and abruptly stumbled to a halt. A startled gasp ripped from her throat. Sitting on the couch with the phone in one hand, and a gun in the other, was Carter.

"Looking for this?" he asked innocently, holding up the cordless and waving it in the air as the answering machine picked up.

"Hi, you've reached the Millers. Sorry we're not available right now. Please leave a message and we'll call you back."

Beep . . .

"Hey, Kat, it's me. Baby, if you're there, please pick up. I've been trying to reach you for hours, so have the police. Carter has been released. Listen, I know you're upset with me, and fuck, I'm so sorry . . . Just please call me back and let me know you're okay."

The line went dead and a broken sob threatened to tear from her throat. At the panic in his voice, the pleading for forgiveness, regret like she'd never known slammed into her with the force of an anvil. And now, it was too late. She was going to die without ever getting the chance to tell Cole how she felt about him. Katie knew it as certain as the very breath she dragged into her air-starved lungs.

The soul-deep knowledge of his love both comforted and devastated her. She was oddly solaced in the knowledge she'd die possessing the undeserved love of an amazing man, and utterly broken, because in the next few minutes, Carter was going to pull that trigger and take away any chance she had of having a happily-ever-after with the man she loved more than anything in this world.

"Trouble in paradise?" Carter sneered. "You know, that's the problem with you, Katrina." He tossed the phone aside and scolded her with the gun. She stared helplessly as the muzzle waved up and down, traveling between her stomach and her chest. "You've got commitment issues."

How pathetically ironic was it that her insane ex was psycho-analyzing her and he was spot-fucking-on? Refusing to take the bait, she asked as calmly as she could manage, "What are you doing here, Carter?"

He scowled. "Isn't it obvious? I've come to take you home. You'll see, Katrina, things will be different this time." And then as an afterthought he added, "Of course, I will have to punish you for running away from me, and for being such a fucking whore."

He cocked the gun, and Katie's heart plummeted to her feet. Her hands flew up reflexively, because that's just what you did when someone was going to shoot you. "Carter, please don't do this," she pleaded, not that she expected it to make any difference. She'd seen that wild look in his eyes enough times to know there would be no reasoning with him. He was skating on the fine line of insanity and in the blink of an eye, he could snap and it would all be over. He looked like shit, unshaven and all twitchy, like he was strung out on something—no doubt he was. His clothes were dirty and wrinkled. She could smell the sour scent of whisky across the room—always his drink of choice.

If she could get to her phone, she might be able to call for help. Or if she could reach the security panel on the wall, she could trip the silent alarm. But both were upstairs in her bedroom. One place she didn't particularly want to lure Carter, but at the moment, she wasn't seeing much alternative. If he would just put that fucking gun away . . .

Taking a deep breath to calm her nerves, she tried to focus on what Cole had taught her, replaying the self-defense techniques over and over in her mind as she ran through scenarios and tried to formulate a plan to get away. Unfortunately, she and Cole hadn't spent much time focusing on unarming someone—that, she'd have to try to get Carter to do voluntarily.

Forcing her foot forward, she took a step toward him. In the past, her fear only seemed to empower and provoke him, perhaps if she were bolder . . . "I'm sorry, Carter. I'm sorry that I hurt you. Please, put the gun down. You're making me nervous. You said you wanted to take me home, right? Well, I want that, too . . ."

She'd always been a good liar when it came to that man, and he was just insane enough to believe her. How many times had she been forced to pretend she welcomed his touch?—wanted to be with him? Her confession seemed to catch him off guard and momentarily de-escalated his rage. The gun wavered and he dropped his wrist, letting the barrel point at the floor.

"Do you think it would it be okay if I went upstairs and packed a bag before we go? I promise I won't take long." She had little hope he'd let her go alone.

"All right," Carter stood and tucked the gun in the waistband of his jeans behind his back. "You've got five minutes, Katrina, and then we're leaving." She tried not to flinch when he grabbed her arm and guided her toward the stairs.

Five minutes—it wasn't very long to figure out how she was going to get away, because if she left this house with Carter, she was as good as dead.

CHAPTER

Cole drove like a bat out of hell to Katie's parents' house, the rental car's tires slipping and sliding on the snow and ice. The high-pitched beeping and flashing skid marks on the dash confirmed once again the traction control had stepped in to take over as he rounded the corner to her parents' street. With a muttered curse, he hung up his phone. He'd called her cell so many times her mailbox wouldn't allow him to leave any more messages. Where in the hell was she? Officer Wyatt had done a few drive-bys this evening and told him her SUV hadn't been in the driveway. Technically, his hands were tied until she'd been missing for twenty-four hours, if she even was missing—which apparently she was not, because her RAV was sitting in the fucking driveway right now!

Wherever she'd been, she was back now. But that didn't explain why she wasn't returning any of his calls. He knew she was pissed at him, but she would at least return his call to tell him she was alive, right? Cole slowly drove past the house, looking for anything out of the ordinary. It was late, and the last thing he wanted to do was start ringing the doorbell and wake the whole house. He was almost past the light blue, two-story home, when he noticed the light in Katie's bedroom was on. Her window was on the side of the house, so Cole cut the light and pulled into her neighbor's driveway where he could get a better view.

Her curtains hung open, providing him an unobstructed view of the back half of the room. Warring against his instinct to barrel in there, Cole forced himself to take a moment and scout things out. He'd look like an epic asshole if he busted into Katie's parents' house and scared the hell out of them, only to find that everything was fine. For all he knew, she could have changed her number and he was stalker-messaging some random person. On the flip side, if there was something going on and Katie was in danger, he wouldn't be doing her any favors if he went in half-cocked and got her killed, either.

All of Cole's questions were answered a few minutes later when Katie arrived in the bedroom window. She stood at the dresser, her gaze fixed down. She appeared to be packing. What the hell? Had she gotten his message about Carter being released? Was she preparing to run again? Not without talking to him first, she wasn't.

Cole's hand dropped to the handle of the door and he was about to get out, when he saw her lips move. She was talking to someone. Who? Then she tensed as that someone stepped up behind her, and into Cole's line of sight.

"Motherfucker . . ."

Cole grabbed his cell and returned his last received call.

"Wyatt, here."

"I found Katie. She's at her parents' house and that bastard's got her."

"Shit. Cole, stay right where you are. I'm on my way."

"Sorry, that's not going to happen. I told you I'd let you know when I found her, and I did that." Cole disconnected the call and shoved his cell into his pocket as he climbed out of the car, his steely glare locked right on that fucking window. Rage exploded inside him when that fucker moved closer, sweeping Katie's hair back over her shoulder, and kissed her neck.

"Time's up, Katrina." Carter stepped up behind her, pinning her between the dresser and his solid, bulky body. Her hands flew out to balance herself on the top of the dresser, bile surging up her throat as he pulled her hair aside. She flinched as his whisky-soured breath ghosted over her throat. The fine hairs on the back of her neck prickled with revulsion as his mouth touched her flesh.

Dear God, she couldn't do this. Perhaps she didn't want to live so badly after all. But then she thought of Cole. The thought of never seeing his gorgeous face again, never getting the chance to make things right between them, never telling him she loved him—never feeling his incredibly hard body against her, inside her . . . and that was just too many nevers. Steeling her nerve, Katie forced her body to relax, to accept Carter's kiss. She'd have only one shot at this, and she knew she had better make it count.

Carter inhaled deeply, drawing her scent deep into his lungs. "Fuck, Katrina, you smell so damn good. I'm not sure I can wait to get you home and show you just how much I fucking want you. It's all I've been able to think about." He reached around her and squeezed her breast—hard. His meaty fingers biting into her flesh with a punishing grip. Katie bit her bottom lip to hold back her pained whimper, his touch triggering a barrage of other painful memories. The knowledge of what was to come released a surge of panic ripping through her veins. Her throat tightened as terror took its insidious hold on her.

If she wanted to survive this, she had no choice but to use Carter's desire against him. It was the most powerful weapon she had. With a feral growl, he thrust his erection against her backside, knocking her forward and slamming her thighs into the dresser with enough force to topple her jewelry stand. God help her, if he took her like this, she'd be helpless to stop him. Forcing her mind to shut down before she threw up, Katie reached behind her and slid her hand up his thigh to palm his engorged penis.

"Miss that, did ya?" He thrust himself against her hand, and this time she did retch. Thank God she was still turned away from him. "You fucking whore. Nobody gives it to you like I do."

When she didn't say anything, he twisted his fist into her hair and yanked her head back. She couldn't hold back the pained cry that broke from her throat.

"Say it!" he demanded. "Nobody fucks you as good as me!"

His control was slipping. She could see in the wildness of his eyes, he was about to lose it. "It's true!" she cried, tears blurring her eyes. "Nobody!" The pain in her scalp was sharp and biting, making her knees buckle. "Only you know how I like it," she choked out the words past the bile burning the back of her throat. It was now or never . . . "Let me turn around and I'll show you just how much I want you."

With dizzying speed, he jerked her around and crushed his mouth to hers. She forced her lips to part and accept his tongue, the sour taste of alcohol assaulting her senses. Tentatively, she slipped her arms around his neck as she kissed him back, vowing if she survived this she'd have to drink Listerine to purge the taste of this man from her mouth.

He growled with satisfaction, and gripped her breast again, fingers biting through the thin cotton of her nightshirt. Holding back her whimper, Katie interlocked her fingers behind Carter's for leverage, and drove her knee up into his groin, exactly how Cole had shown her.

Air exploded from his lungs on a sharp cry. When he bent over, she was ready for him, and sent a hard palm strike right into his nose. The sickening crunch of cartilage broke beneath her hand, and following Cole's instruction exactly how she'd practiced it, Katie spun out of his grip and slipped beneath his arm, bolting for the door.

The roar of pain and outrage exploded behind her. "You fucking cunt! I'll kill you!"

Katie didn't waste the time to look behind her as she tore down the hall and hit the stairs like a herd of elephants. Once her feet touched the landing, she was full-tilt racing for the front door. She could hear the footsteps crashing on the floor above her, Carter's bellow echoing behind her as he blasted down the stairs.

Without hesitating to even put on shoes, Katie threw open the front door and barreled outside, crashing right into Cole, who was charging up the porch steps. It was like running into a flesh-covered brick wall. His arms instantly banded around her, pulling her into the shelter of his embrace, and she nearly crumbled, right then and there. For that brief moment, time seemed to stop.

"Cole!" she cried, wrapping her arms around him and holding on as if her life depended on it—and it sure did, for the man inside that house had every intention of killing her. "You're here! How?"

The crash inside the house cut her off. "Katrina! You fucking bitch! I'll kill you for this!"

Then time seemed to move in fast-forward and she was helpless to stop it. A snarled growl tore from Cole's throat along with the command, "Stay here." Before she could respond, Cole set her aside and charged into the house.

Fury licked through his veins, lighting him up like a man possessed. The calm, centered focus that always descended on him before a fight failed him now. All he could think of was getting his hands on that bastard and making him pay for everything he'd done to Katie.

As Cole cleared the hall, Carter hit the landing, his movements pained and slow with the bent-over hunch of a man who'd just taken a hit to the balls. His nose was bleeding. Seeing the damage his girl had inflicted on this piece of shit made Cole's heart swell with pride.

"Katrina!" Carter roared, not yet seeing Cole approaching from behind.

"She's not here." Cole held out his arms as he walked into the living room, an unspoken invitation to bring it on. "Why don't you try taking on someone your own size? Or do you only beat on women?"

That was all the bait that bastard needed. With a roar, he spun around and charged Cole like a linebacker—probably because he was a linebacker. Cole sidestepped the dive and drove his fist into Carter's side. The satisfying crunch of his ribs only heightened Cole's need for blood. Carter crashed into the wall, but turned around faster than he expected, taking a wild swing Cole barely dodged. He countered with a sharp uppercut that caught Carter in the jaw. His head snapped back, he stumbled, but the bastard didn't go down.

Cole shot in for a takedown, driving his shoulder into the bastard's bulky chest, and that took him down—hard. But Cole knew he wasn't going to stay that way. With an enraged snarl, he swung his elbow up and nailed Cole in the jaw. The guy was a hard hitter. There was no finesse. Raw power and brute strength was all he had going for him, and it wouldn't be enough to beat Cole. His fist slammed into Carter's face, stunning him enough for Cole to pass his guard as he proceeded to pound the shit out of him.

The fighter in him took over—the rage tunneled his vision and he couldn't stop. Even when the fucker quit fighting back, Cole drove his fist into his face. Again. Again. Again. His knuckles broke open with the force of the impact. He welcomed the burn, the pain lancing up his arm with each punishing blow. He might not have quit if he hadn't heard Katie's tearful plea, felt her pulling on the arm that held Carter pinned to the ground, his hand wrapped tightly around that bastard's thick throat—squeezing . . .

"Cole, stop! Please!" she cried, pulling him off the lifeless piece of shit. "Please, stop! I need you . . ."

Hearing her desperate cry snapped his mind back into focus. Rallying his self-control, Cole relented from his assault and rose to his feet. Tears stained her beautiful face and it absolutely shredded him. He took a step toward her and Katie threw herself into his arms. Her knees buckled and she collapsed against him, dissolving into a fit of choking, gut-wrenching sobs.

"Shh . . ." he soothed, cupping the back of her head and holding her against his chest as he moved them a few steps farther away from Carter's motionless body. He wasn't sure if the bastard was KO'd or dead. Given the choice, Cole would prefer the latter. "Shh . . . It's over now. You're going to be all right, Kat."

"I can't . . . believe . . . you're . . . here," she sobbed between hitching breaths.

Emotion clogged his throat, he couldn't speak. It just felt so damn good to hold his girl in his arms again, to know she was safe. Officer Wyatt would be here soon, and finally this nightmare would be over for her. He smoothed his hand up and down her back, his gut clenching with each shuddering sob that wracked her small frame. He wasn't certain how much time passed while he stood there, holding her. But as her breaths began to slow and her body softened against him, he sensed she'd weathered the worst of it for now. They needed to talk. There was so much left to say, but he'd be damned if he could bring himself to utter the words hovering on the tip of his tongue—not again—not after the last time.

Seeming to rally her strength, Katie stepped back, and it took everything in him to let her go. Looking up at him with those heart-stopping emerald eyes she said, "Cole, I—"

But he never got to hear what she was about to say. Her confession died on her lips, cut short by a startled gasp as her gaze darted past his shoulder, her luminous eyes growing impossibly large. Before he could turn around, Cole heard the distinct *snick* of a cocking gun and froze, icy dread crystalizing the blood in his veins. *Fuck*, he silently cursed himself for not killing that bastard when he had the chance. This guy was a damn tank. He should have known that asshole would be packing. Slowly, Cole turned, placing himself between Katie and that gun. Her fingers curled around his wrist, nails biting into his flesh.

"Get away from her," Carter snarled, leveling the muzzle at Cole's chest as he staggered to his feet. Carter was too far away. There was a good chance he'd get a shot off before Cole could tackle him again. His vision had to be impaired, which brought Cole no measure of comfort. The only thing worse than a crazy man with a gun was a blind crazy man with a gun. One of Carter's eyes was completely swollen shut; the other was sporting a shiner with a cut above his eyebrow that was still bleeding. Blood was smeared across his face; his nose, swollen and deformed.

In the distance, Cole heard the whir of a police siren growing closer by the second. He cursed under his breath. That might be all it'd take to light the fuse on this loose cannon.

"I'm not going to tell you again," he warned. "Get the fuck away from Katrina."

Her grip on Cole tightened—her panic as tactile as a living, breathing entity. It shredded him to see her like this. He could practically feel her terror coursing through his veins. Slowly, he pried her hands off of his. "It's all right," he assured her with more conviction than he felt. Cole stepped away from her and experienced a measured amount of relief when the gun followed him instead of remaining pointed in Katie's direction. The siren was close now, so close it couldn't be more than a few blocks away.

"It didn't have to end like this," Carter told her. "You ruined everything."

Her hands covered her face as she struggled to hold herself together. "Carter, don't do this," she pleaded, shaking her head as if she couldn't quite fathom the sudden turn of events. "Just let Cole go and I'll leave with you."

The fuck she would. Over his dead body was this woman going anywhere with this psychotic asshole. Sadly, that might become a reality in pretty short order. With that gun trained on his chest, he wasn't seeing this playing out in his favor.

"It's not too late," she insisted, pleading with Carter.

The siren roared closer, the police lights flashing a strobe of red and blue through the living room. A car door slammed outside, and footsteps pounded up the porch steps.

"Yes, it is."

Carter looked at her and the decided, deadpan stare in his eyes struck Cole numb with terror. Holy fuck, he was going to do it! As Carter swung his arm to the left, training his gun on Katie, Cole dove for her. The front door crashed open, and Officer Wyatt charged into the living room, shouting, "Freeze, police!"

A gun went off with an ear-ringing pop and something slammed into the back of Cole's shoulder, tearing through his chest. The force of the blow knocked him off his feet and he hit the ground—hard. He couldn't breathe. Hot, burning pain lanced down his arm. Katie screamed. Another shot rang out, this one a deeper, louder bark.

Crack! Crack!

Katie's screams were muffled by the gunfire. Cole tried to get up, but a pair of hands pushed him back down. He opened his eyes, forcing them to focus. His vision momentarily cleared. Katie knelt, hovering over him. "Don't move!" she cried, tears raining down her cheeks, landing on his chest. "You've been shot!"

He was well aware, though Cole doubted she'd appreciate him pointing that out. His shoulder and chest burned like holy fire; even moving his fingers sent jolts of white lightning racing up his arm and into his shoulder. The pain made him dizzy. It was difficult to keep his gaze focused on her, so he closed his eyes. In the distance he heard Officer Wyatt on his radio, calling for an ambulance. Katie was sobbing now. He winced, stifling a groan when she flopped over him, clinging to him with desperation.

"Don't die, Cole!"

The floor was wet beneath him; a bone-deep chill was setting in, making him shiver, which sent another blast of pain rocketing through him. Dizziness swept over him in waves and the room began to spin. *I'm not going to die, Kat.* He tried to tell her, but wasn't certain if the reassurance reached his lips before the darkness finally dragged him under, numbing the pain with blessed relief.

CHAPTER

ole had lost an alarming amount of blood. The doctor said the bullet had shattered his shoulder blade, nicked his subclavian artery, and exited the front of his chest. They'd rushed him into surgery, where he'd been for the last two hours. Katie had spent the first hour giving Officer Wyatt her statement. He'd then left to file the paperwork and begin whatever it was cops did when they shot someone in the line of duty. She was thankful to him for everything he'd done. If he hadn't gotten there when he did, there was a good chance neither she nor Cole would have survived.

Now alone, Katie paced the small waiting room, the white walls providing none of the serenity they were intended for. The coffee at the nourishment station was cold and black as tar. Not that she needed the caffeine. Right now, she was running on pure adrenaline, and she guessed it would be that way for some time. Reaching the wall, she turned around and retraced her steps until she met its counterpart, then turned around and started all over again, rehearsing all the things she wanted to tell Cole if he made it out of surgery—when he made it out.

Nothing forced clarity and straightened out one's priorities like staring death in the eye. And that was a sight she was certain would haunt her the rest of her days. Carter was dead, and she felt no guilt over the relief that brought her. Her nightmare was finally over. No more living in fear, looking over her shoulder—no more running. Finally, she could bury the past and move on with her life—a life she hoped to share with Cole, if he still wanted her. But after the way she'd reacted, the way she'd pushed him away, perhaps it was too late for them. For crissake, she'd nearly gotten him killed.

He'd saved her life tonight, diving in front of a bullet meant for her, but at what cost?—his own life?—his career? His shoulder was shattered. Was this the clincher to end this fighter's career? Would she be the ruin of Cole Easton, the CFA light-heavyweight champion, aka the Beast of the East? How ironic that her uncle had sent him here so she could save his career, only to have him lose it in the end because of her.

Thinking of . . . she really needed to call her uncle and tell him what happened and that Cole was in surgery. As far as she knew, he was the closest thing Cole had to family, and it didn't seem right not to call someone on his behalf. She also needed to tell him about her father's stroke. It was a call she didn't relish making. She was still angry with him for what he'd done, but she couldn't put it off any longer.

A dull, throbbing pain in Cole's right side pulled him from unconsciousness. The soft, steady beep tracking his pulse and the cuff on his arm, inflating as the machine began to hum, confirmed he was in the hospital. The worst case of cotton mouth ever, and a whopping anesthesia hangover, told him he was definitely narked up.

Slender fingers slipped between his and squeezed gently. "Cole . . . ?"

If that sweet, angelic voice didn't make him want to open his eyes and join the living, nothing would.

"I think he's waking up," she whispered.

"Well, it's about damn time."

And if that grouching voice didn't make him want to give up his ghost, then it looked like he was here to stay. Who would have thought taking a quarter-inch piece of lead would make a guy feel like he'd been hit by a Mack truck?

"Hey, Sleeping Beauty, unless you want me to kiss you and prove I'm your true love instead of this gorgeous little chica here, I suggest you open your eyes."

What the hell . . . ? What was Kruze doing here? Cole forced open his eyes to find the trio sitting vigil at his bedside. A haggard-looking Marcus was on his left, and beside him was the ever-cocky, God bless him, Aiden Kruze. Which only left . . . Cole tipped his head to the right and his heart stuttered at the sight of Katie's beautiful, worried face. His monitor announced the palpitation along with his quickening pulse. She glanced up at the screen, her worried frown deepening as she looked back at him anxiously.

He gave her a sedated grin. "Don't worry . . . It happens every time I see you." Damn, his voice sounded like he'd been eating glass. And if someone could just remove this hot poker from his lung, that would be real swell.

Tears filled Katie's eyes and she let out what might have been a poor attempt to laugh, but sounded more like a choking sob of relief. Marcus muttered a curse under his breath and scrubbed his hand over his head, a nervous gesture Cole had seen him do from the cage more than once. Kruze outright laughed, never losing that unshakable smirk.

"Leave it to Easton to put on the moves from his deathbed."

Katie gasped in alarm, clearly not appreciating it was a joke. He scowled at Kruze and croaked, "I'm not dying, asshole. Quit scaring her, will ya?"

"Sorry . . ." Kruze's halfhearted apology earned him another scowl.

"What are you doing here?"

Kruze gave him a negligent shrug. "I was with the old man when Katie Bug called him."

Katie Bug? Why in the hell was Kruze "Katie Bugging" his woman?

"Hey, who are you calling old?" Marcus piped up. "I ain't too old to kick your scrawny ass."

At the threat, Kruze laughed again. "Anyway, when she told Marcus what happened, and that you caught a bullet, I figured you might need to lawyer up, so . . ." Kruze spread his arms as if to say, *Isn't it obvious? Here I am to save the day.*

Katie coughed, sounding like she was covering a surprised laugh. "Aiden is a lawyer?"

"That's right, sweetheart. Board-certified and everything." He winked, giving her one of those infamous panty-dropping grins that had gotten him laid more times than Cole could count. Normally, he found it amusing, but turned on his girl?—not so much.

"Wink at her again and I'm going to punch you in the fucking eye," Cole growled.

"Take it easy, tough guy," Kruze laughed, holding his hands up in surrender. "I'd hate for you to bust a stitch or something."

"Ha-ha." He glanced at Katie, noting some of her fear seemed to have eased at listening to him banter with Kruze. She looked like she could use the distraction, though things were going to get serious in pretty short order. They needed to talk. There were things between them that needed to be said—things that couldn't wait any longer. "I hate to seem unappreciative of having you all here. It's damn good to see you, but I could use a little privacy."

Katie's face fell. Worry replaced the little upturn of those lush, delectable lips he longed to kiss. Fuck, she looked exhausted. If he had his way, he'd lift these covers and tuck her in beside him, but (a) he was pretty sure that was against some hospital policy, and (b) no matter how much he wanted to, Cole refused to allow himself to touch her again, not without knowing where things stood between them.

"Say no more," Kruze said, scooting back his chair and rising. Marcus was right behind him. When Katie released his hand, looking like her favorite dog had just died, and moved to stand, he caught her wrist, stopping her.

"Not you. You stay," he told her. The brief moment of relief that crossed her face was quickly replaced with anxiety. Did she think he was upset with her? After everything he'd done for her, how could she still doubt him like this? The knowledge came like a stinging blow and had him scowling in response. Her gaze darted to the two men, and for a moment it looked like she might bolt with them. If Marcus or Kruze noticed the shifting tide of tension, neither of them said anything.

"Well, kid, I'm glad as hell you're not dead." Marcus reached over and ruffled his hair like a parent might tease their two-year-old.

Despite himself, Cole smiled, shaking his head. "I love you, too, old man."

At the gushy confession, Marcus grunted and turned away, but not before Cole noticed his eyes watering. He made his way to the door, and Kruze wasn't far behind him.

"I think I'll head down to the station and see what's doin'. I'll catch ya later, yeah?"

"Sounds good."

"See ya, Katie Bug."

"Will you quit calling her that?" Cole growled.

The fighter laughed, sending her a parting flirtatious wink as he passed by.

He was nearly out the door when Cole called, "Hey, Kruze." The fighter stopped and looked back, that classic Kruze crooked grin splayed on his too-handsome-for-his-own-good face. Not that Cole was a good judge of such things, but if his popularity with the women was any indication . . . "Thanks for being here, man."

"My pleasure."

Kruze pulled the door closed behind him, leaving him and Katie alone for the first time since things had ended so badly. Her gaze was fixed on an interesting knot of thread on his bedspread. She nervously picked at it, rolling the strand between her fingers. Silence stretched between them as he waited for her to say something. When it became evident that wasn't going to happen, he patted the empty space beside him. She glanced up, looking a little surprised and a whole lot hesitant.

Rising from her chair, she sat facing him. The firm mattress barely caved to her slight added weight. Her slender legs were crossed as they bent over the side of his bed, half committed to her new seat, like she might up and bolt at any moment. Damn, this was more difficult than he'd thought it would be. His mind raced with things he wanted to say, shifting and sorting the important from the things that could wait until later.

He wasn't sure where to start. It was hard to concentrate with her sitting this close to him, her light lavender scent teasing his senses, heightening his awareness of her. He attributed the slight wave of dizziness to the shunting of blood heading south. The way she affected him, so swift and guttural, even just being near him, had Cole second-guessing his suggestion she move closer.

It was hard enough to think clearly with whatever it was they were pumping into his veins. He was having a hell of a time focusing when all he wanted to do was pull her into his arms and hold her. He'd nearly lost her last night, and when he thought of how close he'd come to never seeing this beautiful face again, never touching this incredible body, never hearing that angelic laugh . . . It clogged his throat with so much emotion, he probably couldn't speak right now if he tried.

Moments passed as he lay there watching her, struggling to rein it in. Finally, when he thought he might be able to speak without choking up, he laid his hand over the one picking nervously at the thread. "Kat, look at me."

Her emerald eyes shot to his. The uncertainty and regret reflecting back at him sent his pulse spiking with anxiety. His monitor began beeping at a whole new level, and he shot an impatient glower at the damn thing. When he looked back, it was to find Katie watching him with tears in her eyes. His chest tightened. The pain from his gunshot wound paled in comparison to the heartache he'd been living with for the last week. The pain made infinitely worse by seeing that same suffering reflected back at him now.

What the hell was the matter with him? He was a fighter, dammit, so why was it so fucking hard to fight for her? Taking a deep breath and steeling his resolve, he went for it. And to his surprise, so did she.

"I'm sorry," they said in unison, and then responded at the same time, "It wasn't your fault."

They both smiled at the cheesiness of it and her little bubble of laughter helped break the mounting tension. "Why don't you go first," he offered. When her nervousness seemed to creep back in, he took her hand, holding it between his, and waited patiently for her to speak.

"I don't know where to start, Cole," she confessed softly. "You were right. I was scared and I overreacted in Vegas. Trust doesn't come easy for me, and when I felt you'd broken mine, I freaked out.

It just made too much sense, why a guy like you would pretend to be interested in someone like me."

He scowled. "What do you mean, 'a guy like me'?"

"Look at you, Cole. You're famous, you're gorgeous, and you're really a great guy. And I'm . . . I'm a mess. I can't compete with the beautiful women you have throwing themselves at you day in and day out."

"It was never a competition, Kat. And even if it was, you'd have won, hands down, every time. I told you, I love you—"

"I know." A tear ran down her cheek and she swiped it away.

"I've never said those words to another woman in my life. I've never had unprotected sex with another woman, I've never chased halfway across the country for another woman. I don't know what more I can do to convince you of how I feel."

"Nothing. There's nothing you could have done. God, Cole, I'm so sorry. I was hurt, I was scared, so I ran—just like I always do. You were too good to be true. I guess deep down, I was looking for a reason to prove this wasn't real, that when it came right down to it, you couldn't be trusted—"

He'd suspected as much, but hearing her admit it was no fucking picnic. It only showed him how far he had to go to win her heart—to prove to her that she *could* trust him. It was a challenge he was up for, because the alternative was inconceivable. Anything worth having was worth fighting for, right? He'd been so damn miserable this last week he honestly didn't think he could live without her.

"—But I was wrong, Cole. You came back for me. You saved my life." Her voice broke and a fresh wave of tears filled her eyes. "I'm so sorry I doubted your love, and now . . . I'm scared it's too late."

When those big heart-wrenching tears spilled over her lids and rolled down her cheeks, it broke him. *Fuck* . . . Reaching for her with his good arm, he pulled Katie against him, slipped his hand into her silky hair, and held her as the last of her walls finally crumbled and she broke down. For the longest time he lay there holding her, letting her cry it out.

"Shh . . ." he soothed, gently rubbing his hand up and down her back. "It's not too late. Baby, I was coming back for you before I even knew Carter had been released."

She lifted her head and peered up at him with watery, red-rimmed eyes, and dried her blotchy, tear-stained cheeks with her palms. "You were?" she asked, sounding so fragile and hopeful, his heart clenched with the need to hold her tighter.

"Yeah, I was. I couldn't stand being apart from you. I missed you so damn much, Kat. I was coming back to convince you to give us a chance—to prove to you that I love you, and what happened between us had nothing to do with your uncle. I didn't find out about the Carter thing until I was almost at the airport. Then I raced here as fast as I could when I couldn't reach you, praying I wouldn't be too late."

"And then you got shot!"

The tears started anew, and Cole suspected they wouldn't be able to talk about last night without those waterworks for quite some time.

"It's my fault you were shot. That bullet was meant for me!"

"Hey, it isn't your fault. You didn't pull that trigger, and you cannot keep letting that bastard come between us. I don't blame you, Kat, and you can't blame yourself, either."

"We'll see if you're still saying that six months from now. Cole, your shoulder was shattered. The doctor said you may never fight again. Your career could be over because of me."

"Hey," he slipped his knuckle beneath her chin, tipping her head and holding her verdant stare. "I've been through this before, Kat, doctors telling me I might not fight again. But you know what? Even if they're right and I don't get back in the cage, it's all right, because I finally found something I love more than my career. As long as I have you, sweetheart, I can be happy no matter what I'm doing. Besides, I'm not going to hang up my gloves yet. I know a great PT."

Twelve Months Later

"Well, folks, we have a sold-out house in the MGM tonight! It's the grudge match you've all been waiting for, as the Beast of the East prepares to defend his title against Crazy Dan De'Grasse!"

The crowd cheered, the lights went down, and the strobes began to flicker. Katie couldn't hear what the announcer said next over the pumped-up fans and booming bass of "Bodies" by Drowning Pool blasting from the speakers. It was Cole's song. Butterflies battered her insides as she peered down the aisle from her front-row seat, waiting for her fighter to appear.

"Don't worry, kid. He's got this." Uncle Marcus winked, nudging her with his elbow.

It wasn't that she doubted he did. Cole was an amazing fighter, the best she'd ever seen, but he was about to get into the ring with a guy that didn't fight by the rules. And she'd just spent the last year pouring herself into her fighter, into his body, his heart, and his soul. It wasn't just Cole stepping into that cage tonight. She would feel every blow he took, every kick he weathered. He might win this fight, but at what cost?

This last year had undoubtedly been the best of her life. With the past finally behind her, she'd been able to embrace the future and, with Cole's help, had begun to truly heal. He'd healed her emotionally, and she'd done her best to heal him physically. Tonight would be the test to see if she'd done her job well enough.

"I've already picked out the perfect spot at the gym to hang his belt," Uncle Marcus told her, shouting above the noise.

"Right next to the first one?" she asked, grinning sarcastically.

"Nope, below it."

She knew what he was doing, and it was working—trying to distract her, talking as if the win was already a done deal. Cole and Uncle Marcus had opened a CFA-sponsored gym nine months ago in St. Paul, Minnesota, a manageable commute from Somerset. Her father had partially recovered from his stroke, but not enough that Katie felt comfortable moving away, so Cole had bought her a beautiful house on the Apple River, complete with a white picket fence and a chocolate Labrador, but he'd told her he was drawing the line at a minivan. She'd laughed, wondering where that had come from, because she'd never once suggested they get one.

Cole's contracts still required him to travel some, but she went with him whenever possible. The gym was an overnight success. Cole was busy coaching and training other fighters and CFA hopefuls, while Uncle Marcus focused on the management end of things. He was always scouting out new talent. Right now he had his eye on Tommy Thorson, who according to Cole, had a ton of heart and was showing a lot of promise, despite his knee injury.

Cole claimed a large portion of the gym's success was due in part to her coming to work for him. There weren't many gyms that also provided PT. Katie had her own portion of the gym specifically designed for rehab. Her client list was huge; her schedule was booked out months in advance. It'd been a great opportunity and career move, even if she was sleeping with her boss. But ultimately, the gym's success was all Cole. Who wouldn't want to train under the soon to be two-time CFA light-heavyweight champion?

Just as the crowd went wild, Kruze put a hand on her shoulder and leaned in close. "Here comes our boy!" He pointed down the aisle, and she followed Kruze's arm, but Cole was hard to miss. The spotlight shone on him, flooding his path to the octagon. Katie watched as he walked down the stretch of carpet at a steady, determined clip. He did none of that hopping up and down, pump-yourself-up showboating. She knew that steely, determined look, and for a brief moment, she almost felt sorry for De'Grasse—almost.

Cole didn't seem to notice the hands slapping his back, or the women pawing at him as he walked by. His determined stare was fixed solidly on that cage. As he approached, Katie's pulse quickened. Lord, he was gorgeous—beautifully masculine and powerful . . . Everything feminine in her came alive at the sight of him, responding to him in the basest way. Damn, she was going to fuck his brains out when they got back to the hotel tonight.

Cole stopped beside them and his corner rushed in to "atta-boy" him, crowding in front of her. She took a step back to keep from getting knocked into, her hand protectively covering her stomach. Cole briefly acknowledged the guys, his icy-blue gaze searching . . . searching . . . and then locking on her. Moving forward, he stepped through the crowd and reached for her, slipping his hand around the back of her neck. He pulled her forward and crushed his mouth to hers in a quick, hard, possessive kiss, before pulling away to rest his forehead against hers. "I love you, Kat."

"I love you, too."

Lord, did she ever. She loved him so much it scared her, and now . . . for weeks she'd been keeping her secret, not wanting to do or say anything that would take his focus off this fight. Maybe tonight, when it was all over, and they were both sated and sweaty, she'd tell him. A part of her was nervous about doing it. She wasn't entirely sure how he'd react. She hoped he'd be as thrilled as she was, but in truth, she wasn't even sure Cole wanted children.

They'd been so careful, except for that one weekend two months ago when he'd picked her up after work and, instead of taking her home, he'd driven them straight up to Bayfield, where they'd spent the weekend tucked away in a little cabin on Lake Superior. He'd packed her clothes, but not her birth control pills. Oops . . .

In the background she heard one of the announcers exclaim, "Did you see that? It looks like Easton's woman is in the crowd tonight, folks. I didn't know he was seeing anyone, did you, Payton?"

"I think that's his physical therapist," the other announcer responded.

Cole stepped back and reached behind his head, tugging off his T-shirt emblazoned with Tapout, Under Armour, and the names of several other sponsors she wasn't familiar with. He tossed it to Uncle Marcus, along with his baggy satin shorts, revealing a pair of form-fitting spandex. A small man stepped up to Cole and began spreading something greasy on his forehead and cheeks. She couldn't hear what he said, but Cole nodded in response several times. Then, with one final glance her way, he turned and headed for the octagon.

Wham! Cole hit De'Grasse with an upper cut that sent him stumbling back into the cage. He could take the bastard down and finish it right now, but Cole wasn't ready for this fight to end. They were in the second round and he'd barely broken a sweat. De'Grasse had tried to stand up and pound with him, but three minutes into the first round, it was obvious Cole was the superior boxer.

He'd trained hard for this, harder than he'd ever trained for a fight in his life, and he'd be damned if all that work, all the time he'd spent in the gym and away from Katie, was going to be blown in seven minutes. "Get up!" he yelled past his mouth guard, arms thrown wide in taunting frustration. The crowd went wild, but it wasn't about them this time. He wasn't here to give them a show. This was about Cole. This was about six months of misery he'd spent wondering if he'd ever fucking walk again. This was about proving, once and for all, who deserved to hold this fucking title.

Cole stepped back so that asshole would have no choice but to get up and fight, or be labeled the coward he truly was. De'Grasse pushed himself to his feet and shoved away from the cage. His gait was unsteady as he approached. Cole dropped his guard, begging the bastard to hit him. De'Grasse swung. Cole ducked and drove his fist into his side, swift satisfaction washing over him at the feeling of ribs cracking beneath his knuckles.

Ooohmf . . .

The whoosh of air leaving De'Grasse's lungs was auditory coke, fueling Cole's high and pumping the adrenaline through his veins.

De'Grasse stumbled.

"Finish him!" Marcus demanded, slamming his fist onto the mat.

Cole's eyes searched past his coach and locked on Katie. In that brief moment, something inside him shifted. It was like a moment of pure fucking clarity. That woman sitting over there was his life— a life he never would have had if not for De'Grasse. Had Cole not been injured, he never would have met her and she would probably be dead. And with that change in perspective, all the pent-up emotion he'd been fighting with suddenly leached from his body—the anger, the hatred. The force relentlessly driving him for the last year and a half simply vanished with one look at her beautiful face.

It was a look he indulged in a moment too long, because he never saw that fist swinging for his head until it was too late. The blow came hard and solid, snapping his head to the side. An explosion of pain erupted in his jaw, and it took a moment for the cage to stop spinning.

But when it did, De'Grasse was shooting for his hips to take him down. Apparently, the guy was done trying to stand up and bang with him, which was fine with Cole, because he was ready to end this now.

More than Cole wanted revenge and to punish De'Grasse, he wanted Katie. He wanted to skip the after-fight party, take his woman back to their hotel, and have a private celebration with her between the sheets. The fact that he was thinking about making love to Katie when he should be focusing on winning this fight told him two things: (a) he was completely pussy-whipped, and (b) he was so head over heels in love with this woman, it wasn't even funny.

Over the last few weeks, she'd been acting a little strange. He hadn't been around very much, practically living at the gym while either coaching or preparing for this fight, but he'd noticed something was different about her. She was acting funny. He sensed she wanted to tell him something, but she denied it every time he'd tried to ask her about it. Even though she wouldn't admit it, he knew she was keeping something from him. What, he had no idea, but he'd get to the bottom of it tonight. He had ways of making her talk . . .

De'Grasse's shoulder connected with Cole's stomach, sending him back. He let De'Grasse take him to the mat and they landed with his torso between Cole's legs and De'Gresse gave him a triumphant *I got you now, fucker* grin as he began raining fists and elbows down on Cole's face. Cole did some of his best fighting on his back, and was more than prepared to weather the blows. He was doing a damn good job of it, too, when one elbow slipped by him and connected with Cole's eyebrow, splitting it open. It didn't hurt as much as it was annoying, because now he had to worry about getting blood in his eye, and the ref splitting them up for medical to look at it. He needed to end this quickly.

Grabbing De'Grasse's right arm, Cole shoved it toward his right shoulder, controlling his center of gravity. Using the leverage on his arm, he shoved De'Grasse farther down, while Cole pushed his body up. Cole hooked his leg over De'Grasse's shoulder and around his neck while lifting his other leg, and locking his ankle around his knee, trapping De'Grasse's head against his own outstretched arm.

De'Grasse kicked and flailed as Cole squeezed, struggling to get out of the triangle choke, but Cole held tight, waiting for the tap, the KO, or the ref to jump in and call the fight. A few seconds later, Cole felt the tap against his side, and the ref dove in pulling them apart. The crowd went wild, the cacophony of cheers nearly drowning out Payton's proclamation, "Easton's done it again! The still-reigning CFA Light-Heavyweight Champion, the Beast of the East, Cole Easton!"

His arm was raised, and someone wrapped a heavy belt around his waist as more cheering erupted from the stands. It all seemed a bit surreal. An eerie sense of déjà vu washed over him as he searched the crowd for Katie, only half-listening to Payton. She was so small, she'd easily get lost in the sea of fighters—mostly his camp—flooding the octagon and joining the celebration. He worried about her getting hurt in the chaos.

A couple of refs flanked De'Grasse, making sure there would not be a repeat of the last fight. He was still pretty rocked and moving slow. Someone from his corner helped him to stand, ushering him out of the cage. Taking another sweep of the encroaching crowd, he searched for Katie. *Fuck!* He was turning to grab Marcus and ask him to help find her, when someone slammed into him, arms wrapping tightly around his waist. Before he could look down, her scent hit him—lavender and rosemary . . . and instantly, all became right in his world. Everything pulled into sharp focus as he wrapped his arms around her.

"You did it!" she cheered. "Oh, Cole, you were amazing!" Seeing the pride in her eyes, the love shining up at him nearly brought him to his knees. Right here on live TV, wearing the title belt, he'd hit the mat and tap out for her in a heartbeat. If she had any idea what she did to him, what she meant to him . . .

"Cole, you have made one of the greatest comebacks of all time in CFA history. Tell us how you did it." Payton shoved a mic in his face, and the noise in the crowd dimmed to hear him speak.

"Well, I didn't do it alone. It was a tough road and I wouldn't be here today if it wasn't for this amazing woman beside me."

Katie looked up at him, a surprised look gracing her beautiful face. But she shouldn't be. Didn't she realize what she'd done for him?

"And who exactly is this woman? We've all been wondering."

"Her name is Katrina Miller. She's been my PT, my cheerleader, my best friend, and I hope, if she'll have me, my wife."

The crowd fell silent—pin-drop silent. Katie gasped and took a stunned step back, completely shocked. He was taking a huge risk proposing to her on live TV in front of millions of people. What if she said no? But, no guts no glory, right?

A couple of seconds passed and then, Payton, grinning from ear to ear, said, "Well, what do you say?" and shoved the mic in her face. She looked like a deer in the headlights, and for a moment he wondered if he should have thought this through a little more carefully, but nothing said *I love you* like laying your heart out there for millions of people to see it get stomped on.

They hadn't spoken of marriage before, not that he didn't want to marry her. God knew he wanted to spend every day of his life making this woman happy, but after everything she'd been through, he wasn't sure if she was ready to take that step yet, or if she ever would be. She'd done a lot of healing in the last year, but it hadn't been easy, and she still had obstacles to overcome. He had no doubt she'd get there, though. They'd get there together—hopefully—if she'd just say yes.

He was starting to get a little nervous, when a brilliant smile broke across her beautiful face. Keeping her captivating eyes locked on his, she leaned a little closer to the mic and said, "Yes. A thousand times yes, I'll marry you, Cole."

The crowd erupted into cheers again, louder than before. Cole hugged her tight and spun her around. Undoubtedly, this was the best night of his life. He'd reached the pinnacle of joy. Nothing could make this moment more perfect—or so he thought—until she whispered in his ear, "I'm pregnant."

ACKNOWLEDGMENTS

First and foremost, I want to thank God for blessing me with the opportunity to pursue my passion. Many thanks to my wonderful editor, Hai-Yen Mura, and the amazing staff at Montlake for your dedication and commitment to Cole and Katie's story. To my agent, Nalini Akolekar, you've literally made my dreams come true overnight. I can never thank my fabulous critique group enough for all your hard work. Sally, Mikayla, Linda, John, and Lyanne, you make my stories shine, and I love you dearly! Last but certainly not least, I want to thank my wonderful family for your patience and continual support, for all the times you've heard "In a minute" or "Just a second" and patiently waited for me, knowing it was going to be another hour. I love you with all my heart!

PASSING HIS GUARD

MELYNDA PRICE

Montlake
Romance

In Fall 2015, it's Aiden's turn to meet his match . . .

M s. Andrews?"

"Yes?" Her grip tightened on the receiver at the sound of that all-too-familiar voice, dread taking up residence where her heart used to be, which was now beating wildly in her throat.

"Twenty days, Ms. Andrews."

"I'm well aware of how much time I have left," she snapped. "And like I said before, you'll get your damn money."

"All seventy-five thousand of it."

Okay, so that could be a problem. "I, umm . . . might be a little short."

"How short?"

"Ten thousand."

He chuckled, that insidious rumble chilling the blood in her veins.

"You're going to have to suck a lot of cock for ten grand, sweetheart."

Revulsion sent a surge of bile burning up her throat. God, she hated this man—this faceless stranger who'd played a starring role in her nightmares for the past month. The day after her father died the calls had begun, and not a day had gone by since that she wasn't reminded that time was running out.

"You're being unreasonable. This isn't even my debt."

"Sins of the father, Ms. Andrews. It's unfortunate the life insurance policy wasn't large enough to cover what he owed."

What in the hell was that supposed to mean?

"We've been more than patient with you."

That was debatable. If by patient he meant hounding her day after day and threatening her bodily harm if she didn't pay, then yes, he'd been patient. The line went dead and she exhaled a defeated sigh, willing her clamoring heart to calm so she could think. Ten thousand dollars . . . How in God's name was she going to come up with that kind of cash? It might as well be a million. There was no way she could earn ten grand in two weeks—not even if she did take that prick up on his less than helpful suggestion, which she'd rather die than do.

Between her father's life insurance, and exhausting her credit with the bank, she was still short. The only thing she had left was her father's business, Andrews Private Investigation Services, and now even that was slipping through her fingers. The house, the business—all of it, mortgaged to support her father's secret gambling addiction.

How had things gotten so out of control? She'd known her dad had a penchant for cards, but he'd hidden his vice well—too well. She had no idea he'd squandered it all, or that he owed Vincent Moralli seventy-five thousand dollars. Not until a man approached her at her father's funeral last month with a pile of debt notes, all bearing her father's undisputable signature.

She knew the hit-and-run accident that claimed her father's life was no accident. Moralli's enforcer all but admitted as much, but proving it was another matter entirely and the police certainly weren't trying very hard. She'd spent the day at the precinct—again—trying to light a fire under someone's ass and running into roadblock after roadblock.

After an exhausting eight hours of senseless paperwork and being shuffled from one detective to another, it was obvious that Moralli's reach extended deep into the pockets of the Manhattan police department. Her suspicions were confirmed when an officer pulled her aside as she was leaving and told her, in no uncertain terms, that unless she wanted to end up like her father, to let it go.

The thought of giving up, of letting her father's killer get away, went against every fiber of her being. But after today, it was glaringly evident that no one was going to help her. At this point she saw little alternative than to keep her mouth shut and just pay the debt. Which brought her around full circle to the blatantly obvious problem—she didn't have enough money. What was she going to do? Desperation clawed up her throat, choking off her air as she fought to stave off the threat of tears pricking her eyes.

"Excuse me."

She startled at the unexpected voice, letting out a surprised yelp. Her head snapped up to meet the impatient scowl of a woman standing in the doorway of her office. Before she could greet the fifty-something brunette dressed in a calf-length fur coat and black leather boots, the woman snapped, "I'm looking for Private Detective Ryan Andrews. Is he here?"

Her dangling diamond earrings weighed heavily on her lobes, stretching the skin unnaturally taut. A matching necklace, easily worth the remainder of Ryann's debt, encased the woman's long, slender neck, drawing her gaze to the fine lines and wrinkles apparently no amount of money could erase.

"I'm Ryann," she replied, silently cursing her father for giving her a boy's name. How many times did mistakes like this happen?— every damn day, it seemed. It might have been cute when she was younger, but now that she was an adult it wasn't funny anymore.

Well, that wasn't exactly true, because the look on this woman's face right now was pretty freaking hilarious.

"There must be some mistake."

Disdain oozed from the woman, as potent as her heavy floral perfume.

"I assure you, ma'am, there is no mistake. I am Ryann Andrews—two *n*'s," she added with mirroring crispness.

The woman's disapproving scowl deepened, putting all that Botox to the test.

"What can I do for you?" Ryann asked, forcing a smile and sweetening her tone as she grappled for patience. The office had been closed for well over an hour. Since she'd lost the day getting the runaround at the police station, she'd come in after hours to work on a few cases. She must have forgotten to lock the door behind her. Her assistant usually took care of those things, but since Ryann discovered Andrews Private Investigation Services was nearly bankrupt, she'd unfortunately had no choice but to let Joyce go, and she was now running a solo operation here—and apparently not very well.

She held the woman's bold stare as she waited for the aged diva to state her name and business. Something about her pricked Ryann's memory, giving her the distinct feeling she should know who this woman was—or at the very least *she* thought Ryann should. The woman was obviously of importance, if the two Men in Black flanking her was any indication. She stepped into Ryann's office like she owned the place, which immediately tap-danced on her last nerve, considering how close she was to losing it.

"I was told Ryan Andrews specializes in missing persons cases."

The woman spoke her name as if she were still unwilling to accept that said "Ryan" had a vagina and was sitting across from her right now.

"Oh, Ryann does," she replied, referring to herself in the third person. "In fact, Ryann is very good at what *she* does. What can I do for you, Ms. . . . ?" She waited for the woman to supply her name; in lieu of answering Ryann, she glanced back at her heavy, as if undecided whether or not to proceed. Agent J nodded his approval.

"But she's a woman," she hissed under her breath.

"Then perhaps she'll have better luck than the last man you hired," Agent J replied, a mumbled response meant only for the woman's ears. "It's unlikely he'll put this one in the hospital."

And *that* was definitely not for her ears. *Seriously? In the hospital? Oh, hell no!*

"Very well." Exhaling an exasperated sigh, she turned back toward Ryann, opened the snap of her Louis Vuitton clutch purse and pulled out a photo. "I need you to find my son." She set the photo on Ryann's desk and with one perfectly manicured nail, slid the picture toward her.

She plucked up the photo and studied the glossy pic. The man appeared to be in his late twenties, maybe early thirties. Dressed in a dark blue suit that easily cost two grand, his tawny hair was tamed by product that would ensure every strand remained perfectly in place. His square jaw drew her eyes to the grim set of his mouth that appeared to be the masculine version of the pursed one frowning at her right now.

The man was breath-catchingly gorgeous. Even from the picture, Ryann could see he exuded discipline and rigidity. He appeared tempered and in control—except for the eyes. They didn't fit, and damn if that wasn't the most stunning thing about him. Dark amber with flecks of brown and gold, the closest color she could compare it to would be a tigereye stone. How utterly fitting, because the eyes staring back at her held an undercurrent of untamed wildness and caged discontent.

Gauging the man's size compared to the park bench he stood beside, she'd put him at a few inches over six feet and just shy of two hundred pounds—not exactly the kind of missing-person case she was expecting.

"If you don't mind me saying"—Ryann handed back the photo—"in my experience, a grown man that looks like this isn't *missing*. If you don't know where he is, it's because he doesn't want to be found. There's a difference."

"Hardly," the woman scoffed with enough disdain to officially put her on Ryann's bitch list.

"How long has he been *missing*?"

"Officially? Fourteen months. But it's been going on long before that, disappearing for days, missing important meetings—"

"It sounds like he's on drugs," Ryann interjected. *There, mystery solved, you can go now.*

"It's not drugs," the woman snapped.

She seemed awfully sure of that, giving Ryann the distinct impression there was a hell of a lot more to this story than Ms. Stick-Up-Her-Ass was telling her. Considering what she'd overheard, Ryann wasn't the first person this fierce threesome standing in front of her had hired to track that guy down, and by the sound of it, he didn't want to be found.

"Listen, Ms.—" Again Ryann waited for the woman to supply her name.

"Madeline Kruze," she said with all the haughtiness of a woman dressed to the nines with two body guards trailing behind her.

Shit. Now the face connected with the name. This woman was Senator Kruze's wife. And she was every bit the hell on wheels in person she appeared to be on camera. So the senator's son was missing, huh? Interesting . . . And she wanted to hire Ryann to find him. Well, this day just kept getting better and better.

"So do you want the case or not?"

No. She most certainly did not. But before Ryann could tell her as much, the woman continued. "Finding him won't be the problem. Now getting him home will be quite another story."

"Wait, so let me get this straight. You actually know where he is?"

"Marginally. I'll pay double your fee, plus a five-thousand-dollar bonus if you can find him and deliver him to me within two weeks."

Wait. What? "Deliver" him? She wasn't the freaking UPS. Her job was locating missing persons, not returning them home like little lost pets, which was the distinct impression Ryann got that this woman expected. There were missing children, runaways, desperate parents that needed her help. *This* was definitely not one of those cases, and it would no doubt turn out to be a big waste of time.

But the woman was offering Ryann a lot on money to find her son—enough money to pay off the remainder of her father's debt and get her out from under the Morallis' strong arm. Coming to grips with the fact that she was going to have to take this case, Ryann exhaled a sigh and leaned back in her chair. She pulled her cheaters off and dropped them on the desk. Closing her eyes, she pressed her fingers back into her throbbing temples.

After a moment, she lifted her head and met the woman's determined stare. "Two weeks, you said?" That was a short amount of time to track down someone who obviously didn't want to be found and bring him home—short of kidnapping, that is. And this guy didn't exactly look like the abductable type. "Why the hurry? He's been gone for over fourteen months. What's happening in two weeks?"

"His wedding."

"Get up!"

The rasp of curtains ripping open sent a blast of bright Nevada sun beaming onto Aiden's face. He squinted against the unwelcomed light and lifted his arm, shielding his eyes from the blinding assault.

"What the fuck, Coach?"

"Don't you 'what the fuck' me, boy. Easton's at the gym waiting for you and he's pissed as hell."

"Aww shit . . ." he muttered under his breath and lifted his head, squinting to see the alarm clock on the nightstand—5:50. Trapped beneath a tangle of arms and legs, Aiden tried to wrest himself free without waking the women on either side of him.

Marcus, his surly coach, wasn't so considerate. "Come on, ladies," he announced, kicking the foot of Aiden's bed. "Up and at 'em." As he made his way across the bedroom, Marcus swiped up the litter of clothing off the floor and tossed it at the women. When it began raining bras, panties, shirts, and miniskirts, they stirred. Stretching lazily beside Aiden, their bare breasts rubbed against his ribs, their long legs dragging over his as they reluctantly untangled amid moans of protest.

They didn't seem to care they were no longer alone. Modesty was a foreign concept to these women. Aiden, on the other hand, would have preferred not having a cranky Marcus glowering at him while the woman on his right crawled between his legs to suck his—

"Uh-uh," Marcus barked, kicking the foot of his bed again when the blonde tried to slip beneath the covers. "This disco-stick is done dancing, sweetheart. Get dressed and get out—now."

Damn . . . Coach must really be pissed. It wasn't like him to be so rude. The man had the patience of Job, which was something Aiden always admired about the guy—so opposite his own father. The girls booed and whined about getting tossed, but they were smart enough not to push the old guy, who looked like he was about to lose his shit. They began exchanging bras and sorting out whose clothing belonged to whom as they dressed, making no attempt to cover their nakedness from Marcus's scowling view.

"It's not even six a.m. yet," Aiden complained, scrubbing his hands over his face, trying to wake up.

"Cole's been at the gym since five."

"He still bitchy?"

"As ever. He's the jackass and you're the jack-off. I swear between the two of you, you're gonna force me into early retirement."

Once dressed, the blonde on his right turned and kissed his cheek. "See you later, Disco."

"Call me," the brunette added, planting a lip-lock on his mouth before crawling off the bed. They took another moment to search the floor for their shoes. The girls held on to each other for balance as they slipped into their stilettos and wobbled precariously toward the door. Marcus stood by the entrance, ushering them out. Whether their instability was from sleep deprivation or intoxication, Aiden wasn't sure. He tipped his head, his gaze following the girls as they walked out, appreciating the way the black miniskirt hugged the blonde's barely-covered ass.

Once out of view, he glanced at Marcus, who was glaring at him, arms crossed over his burly chest, shaking his head in disgust.

"What?" Aiden grouched. "Don't judge me." He threw back the covers, oblivious to his own nakedness. "You're not my father." Swinging his legs over the side of the bed, he stood and then promptly grabbed hold of the nightstand to steady himself against the spins. Fuck, he was still drunk.

"Son of a bitch . . ." Marcus muttered under his breath, dragging his hand over his hairless head.

Once the topsy-turvys slowed down, Aiden made his way to the foot of the bed and snagged his own clothes off the hotel floor.

"You're right," Marcus snapped. "I'm not your dad—thank God. But I am your coach, which means you do *what* I say *when* I say, and right now I'm telling you to get your ass in that shower. Wash those women off and be ready to leave in fifteen minutes. You've got a fight in two days. What the hell are you thinking? I can't believe you're out until God knows how late, getting shit-faced and whoring it up."

With his clothes wadded in his hands, he had the decency to hold them over his groin as he shuffled toward Marcus, the self-appointed doorkeeper. The old man was tough as nails and hard on his fighters, but that was nothing compared to the bear he'd become since his niece, Katie Miller, had made a rather abrupt and unexpected departure to return back home. Not that Aiden let that stop him from kicking the hornet's nest as he passed the guy, even though he knew damn well he was going to pay for it once they hit the gym.

"Whoring implies there was payment for services rendered. That right there was for free. YOLO . . ."

ABOUT THE AUTHOR

Melynda Price is a multipublished author of contemporary and paranormal romance. What Price enjoys most about writing is the chance to make her readers fall in love, over and over again. She cites the greatest challenge of writing is making the unbelievable believable, while taking her characters to the limit with stories full of passion and unique twists and turns. Salting stories with undertones of history whenever possible, Price adds immeasurable depth to amazingly well-crafted books. She currently lives in Northern Minnesota with her husband and two children where she has plenty of snow-filled days to curl up in front of the fireplace with her Chihuahua and a hot cup of coffee to write.